BUCK'S COUNTRY

BUCK'S
COUNTRY

A Novel of the Modern West

JOEL H. BERNSTEIN

SUNSTONE
PRESS

SANTA FE

Sunstone books may be purchased for educational, business, or sales promotional use.
For information please write: Special Markets Department, Sunstone Press,
P.O. Box 2321, Santa Fe, New Mexico 87504-2321.

Book and cover design › Vicki Ahl
Body typeface › Cambria
Printed on acid-free paper
∞
eBook 978-1-61139-327-9

———————————————

Library of Congress Cataloging-in-Publication Data

Bernstein, Joel H.
  Buck's country : a novel of the modern West / by Joel H. Bernstein.
    pages ; cm
  ISBN 978-1-63293-029-3 (softcover : acid-free paper)
  1. Cowboys--Fiction. 2. Ranching--Fiction. I. Title.
  PS3602.E76284B83 2015
  813'.6--dc23

                    2014038430

———————————————

WWW.SUNSTONEPRESS.COM
SUNSTONE PRESS / POST OFFICE BOX 2321 / SANTA FE, NM 87504-2321 /USA
(505) 988-4418 / ORDERS ONLY (800) 243-5644 / FAX (505) 988-1025

To the memory of my parents who encouraged me to follow my dream and head out West and to my wife Gail who has shared this dream with me for many years.

PART 1

MONTANA

Buck Cooper was a confused and uncertain cowboy.

After more than a dozen years of fighting the long winters, the droughts, and the emptiness of Montana, he was at long last headed back to his beloved New Mexico, hoping it would finally be the culmination of a dream he had been nurturing for years. All he wanted to do was see the sun for the whole year and never again have to endure winter for eight long months. Was he making the right move? Time would tell.

He had talked about the Land of Enchantment for so long that most of his friends in Montana usually laughed and just humored him in the most condescending way. No one really thought he'd actually head back south. It seems no one ever left Montana. Maybe it was the isolation or maybe it was the beauty of the landscape or maybe... No, it was the isolation that kept people under the Big Sky. Most of the Montanans who wanted to leave just didn't seem to know how or even where to go. Real isolation can do that to a person. But for whatever reason no one ever seemed to leave. Sure they bitched about the yuppies and the traffic in Missoula, or the multitude of coffee houses, subdivisions and all the wealthy newcomers that had settled in Bozeman, but they didn't leave. Everyone agreed that Great Falls had little or no cultural life and the wind never stopped blowing, but they didn't leave there either.

So today Buck Cooper was leaving and was headed out over Lost Trail Pass, the same route that had brought Lewis and Clark into the Bitterroot Valley nearly two hundred years before. Hopefully he was leaving for the last time from the ranch he had lived on for a good part of his more than twelve years in Montana. Unfortunately, he was also leaving with some unresolved problems and he knew they would have to be solved before life was going to be what he wanted it to be in New Mexico. He knew he'd miss the Bitterroot Mountains, with their jagged peaks serving as sentinels over the valley and the easy access to the wilderness just above his ranch's west fence line. He loved saddling up and taking the trails and old logging roads through the ponderosa pine and larch forest that led to the pristine lakes that were sheltered way up at the top of Kootenai Canyon under towering St. Mary's peak. He was just hoping he hadn't gotten himself into some kind of mess just because he had talked about leaving for so damn long. As he stood leaning against his U-Haul truck with the silver Subaru Forester in tow, he stopped just long enough to look back down the Bitterroot, north to Missoula and think about the past and his own plans for his future. All the while he realized that this might be the last time he would ever see the spectacular Bitterroot Valley.

■■■

Buck had come to Montana more than a dozen years ago as a professor at the University of Montana in Missoula. By the time he was ready to leave, he had been in the West for more than twenty years and except for a three years teaching stint at the Women's College of the University of Virginia in Fredericksburg, he had lived at one time or another in Wyoming, Montana or New Mexico, studying as a graduate student, teaching or ranching. But even while teaching in Virginia he had kept in touch with ranch life, such as it was, by taking a job as the manager of small horse farm—a term he hated. Why, he often wondered, weren't these horse ranches? You farmed vegetables and hay, not horses. Just the term ran against the westerner in him and made it more and more imperative that he get back West. "Horse farm!" Somehow, in Buck's way of thinking, the whole concept conjured up rich women, fancy, over priced European horses and all the gentility only Virginians think they can muster up. It was that dressage crowd of weighty, pompous divas who drank their bottled water carted around in holsters on their fanny pack and who were constantly yelled out by foreign instructors. It was the world of woman who loved their horses but seemed to be scared to death of them. What he could never understand was that since these women and their horses never seemed to leave their arena, where were these expensive, massive horses from Europe, going to run off to? Coming from Wyoming to Virginia was a big enough leap, but to be in a "horse farm" environment wasn't something he saw in his long term plans. He wanted to get back to the West, the place of his boyhood dreams.

■■■

After three years in Virginia where he enjoyed the teaching, being around horses, and the cultural life of nearby Washington, DC, but little else, he had an opportunity to go back to New Mexico to finish his graduate studies. He leaped at the chance without thinking very much about the implications of his decision. Nor did he have to. Buck was offered a full fellowship to go back to graduate school, something he wanted to do. He knew it was the right move and it felt as comfortable to him as putting on an old pair of boots and a ten year old Resistol hat.

When he returned to the University of New Mexico in Albuquerque to finish his PhD, he arrived with a bride of two years and hopes they would eventually settle permanently in New Mexico. The former Holly Townsend was an elementary school teacher when she met Buck at a meeting at the college. She was smart and attractive, with long, sandy colored hair and bright green eyes. Holly had traveled quite a bit and when they met and started to date, Buck had made it as clear as was possible for him that their life was to be in the West—not the East, not the South, but the West—somewhere between the Canadian and the Mexican borders and way west of the Mississippi River. There wasn't any wiggle room in his decision and there was no negotiating. To Buck this was an absolute and Holy seemed okay with that. She was a good horsewoman and although she had no ranch experience she seemed willing to give it a try. But New Mexico and the desert are not easy places to live and she had never been there, not even as a tourist. For nearly everyone who comes to the desert, it seems to be an environment you either love or hate. There doesn't appear to be any middle ground. Holly's father had been with the State Department and the family had lived in Spain where Holly had gone to high school. Buck assumed that because she was fluent in Spanish and familiar with Hispanic culture and because of that this was all going to work out just fine. He was absolutely certain New Mexico would be a good fit for his new bride.

Well, it wasn't. Holly just flat out didn't like New Mexico or the desert and Buck wasn't sure how to handle his disappointment and the abrupt changes it was going to cause for him. This was all going to have a big impact on his future. He knew, or at least he thought, that he just couldn't walk out on his marriage but he also knew he couldn't stay under those conditions, that's how committed he was to living in the southwest and particularly New Mexico. In his own mind he had become something of a "desert rat," and he had spent so much time thinking about the desert and the southwest that he had convinced himself that that's where he wanted to live and that the desert was the one and only place that would make him happy. What he didn't know was how to solve his new found conundrum.

After a year at the University of New Mexico, where he completed his graduate studies, there was a job opening at the University of Montana and Buck was offered a position in the American Studies program. He decided that despite the salary that was an embarrassment, he would rather go there than take another job that paid three times the amount offered by Montana at one of the Midwestern schools he had been encouraged by his faculty advisor to apply to as backups. Although he had been unable to find a job in the southwest, there was no question about him staying somewhere in the West. He had heard from a variety of colleagues around the country that the University of Montana was a pretty good school with several strong departments although it was badly under funded by the Montana legislature. The reputation of some of the faculty was well known throughout the region and even throughout the country. Buck was actually anxious to head north, explore Montana and continue his promising career as a university professor. He was certainly going to give "The Big Sky" every chance to be his new home although he didn't have a clue about how he was going to get the desert out of his system.

So Buck and Holly headed for the "Big Sky Country" after a year in the desert and Holly's resolve never to return. Well, what the hell, maybe Montana would be all the romantics said it was and that you actually could get used to the winters. Winters with their long, dark nights, often dreary days and snow so deep that it reached the eaves of your house and you had trouble just getting out your front door. What the hell was right! Montana was one of those places the romantics, particularly the wealthy romantics, love, mostly because they usually don't have to live there, at least not during the everlasting, bone rattling winters. Celebrities, most often from show business and high finance, buy ranches, hire some local kid at the minimum wage, put him up in a house trailer, tell him he is a ranch foreman and occasionally let him hang out with a celebrity. The local kid thinks he's died and gone to some sort of Hollywood heaven and the owner/celebrity appears for a few weeks a year. This arrangement wasn't a bad deal for the owners, except it didn't do very much for their new ranch foreman. For him it was, for all intents and purposes, a dead end job.

■■■

When Holly married Buck she thought she was marrying a young college professor with a bright academic future—maybe a deanship or even a university presidency. For a long time Buck thought the same thing except always lingering in the back of his mind was an idea that what he really wanted was a full time life as a cowboy or a rancher. It had been a dream of his since he was in grade school back east. But it was his middle class upbringing always suggested rancher because rancher implied ownership and he figured you could only get so far away from your roots. Buck wanted to own his own spread and be his own boss.

At first life in western Montana wasn't too bad. The Coopers were settled in on a beautiful, old ranch in Arlee on the Flathead Indian Reservation, home to the Salish and Kootenai tribes, just a thirty minute drive north of Missoula. Buck couldn't face the reality of living in Missoula. There were just too many people and too much traffic there and it was getting worse each year. Buck and Holly were able to rent the ranch, 310 acres or a little less than half a section, for far less than it would have cost to rent a house or even an apartment in Missoula. The ranch was owned by an elderly, widowed white woman who lived in Billings and she wanted someone to live on the place. She didn't want it to sit there empty and since Buck had no intention of living in the city they each solved the others predicament. The ranch had abundant grass spread over several pastures, plenty of water, good neighbors and the main house was close enough to the highway so that in the winter the snow didn't become an obstacle keeping him from getting to his job at the university. The wide open valley guarded by the Mission Mountains to the east was a perfect backdrop for the Cooper's initial years in Montana.

Living on the reservation was an exciting prospect because Buck wasn't sure how he would be treated or if he could get along in a culture that wasn't remotely close to his own or anything he had ever experienced. But Buck had no trouble fitting in with his tribal neighbors. He made some good friends and bought a couple of horses so he could work cattle and ride the country around the ranch. He even leased one 200 acre pasture, more than half the ranch, to a neighbor who was a tribal member. Bobby Whitehorse wanted to run about 85 pairs, mother cows with their calves, on the land for several months each year. Buck liked having the cattle around and helped Bobby with the cattle whenever he could. All the while he was learning what ranching and cowboying in Montana were all about. Bobby, whose family had ranched for several generations, turned out to be a good teacher.

Most of Holly's friends were from around the university and were either professionals or married to professionals—doctors, folks from the forest service, people in business and investments, real estate and teaching, and most of them, like Holly, relative newcomers to Montana. None of them were people from ranching or rural backgrounds.

But as their lives progressed, almost on parallel tracks, Buck knew things weren't going to work out in his marriage. He wanted to get away from the town folks and the new comers who were flooding into Missoula and the surrounding areas and he didn't want to go to their pot luck dinners every weekend and listen to the same conversation about the same things and watch them drink themselves into thinking they were having a good time.

His friends were the cowboys and the Indians, his neighbors, and he was happiest at the local general store, the only store in town, talking about horses, cattle, trucks, dogs and the weather. In his own way he loved Holly but their lives were going in such different directions. She was becoming part of an intellectual enclave in town and he was staying as far away from town as he could, even from his colleagues on the faculty at the university.

About the only person from the university who Buck saw on a regular basis was Neil Lafromboise, a Blackfeet graduate student in the history department. Neil often stopped by the ranch on his way north, to his home in Browning, often staying over with Buck and Holly. Neil and Buck could talk far into the night about American history, Indian history, and both their cultures and Buck enjoyed his time with Neil because Neil was so real and anxious to engage in a true exchange of ideas. For Neil the future meant getting his degree and then returning to the reservation and helping his tribe in whatever way he could. Buck was sure he had a major contribution to make for his own people.

But in Buck's personal life, a life that was not going as well as he wanted, maybe the real raw edge was that Holly was beginning to talk more and more about having children and Buck was damn sure he didn't want to be a father. He had finally worked out in his head after many long sleepless nights, that he would eventually leave his job and career at the university and be free to move around, work on a variety of ranches, learn as much as he could about cattle and horses, and then own his own place, and still with every expectation it would be in New Mexico. Buck loved the thought of raising good cow horses and having his own herd of cattle. It wasn't the kind of life he felt was a good life for a son or daughter, at least not the early years that would mean too much moving around, some financial sacrifices and a lot of struggle. There was going to be too little stability and a much smaller income than he was even making at the university. But what Buck wanted most was the freedom he would have if he didn't have children. This is what Buck thought—it was all about freedom.

All the rest was merely a way of justifying what he wanted to do. Buck's sister, when he told her about not wanting to have children, accused him of being selfish but Buck couldn't understand that. He thought he was being realistic and even a bit altruistic. He just didn't think he could do right by any offspring and still live the way he wanted to. He never did fully understand why everybody thought it was some societal obligation to have children. To his way of thinking there were already too many people all around him.

After more than almost four years on the Flathead Indian Reservation, Buck gathered up every penny he could muster without going into significant debt and he and Holly bought an old ranch in the Bitterroot Valley, near Stevensville, a little over half an hour south of the university. Stevensville was the oldest white settlement in Montana and the town and the surrounding area had generations of Montana history. Fortunately for them it was still a few years before the big real estate boom in the Bitterroot caused prices to escalate beyond anything reasonable. It was the time before the celebrities discovered the lush valley and bought it up like trinkets they would find rummaging through a second hand store in Beverley Hills. It was a time before Californians built million dollar second homes they rarely used. It was probably the last of the "good old days."

Together Buck and Holly enjoyed putting the new place back together, rebuilding and restoring a ranch that was a little rundown. Holly concentrated on the house and Buck took care of the land and the stock. Buck leased about 215 more acres he could use to augment the 425 acres he had bought. Although the leased pieces weren't all connected, he took great pride in moving the small herd of Red Angus cattle, all with his Rafter BC brand, and the quarter horses, and keeping the pastures healthy and never overgrazed. Even his neighbors, some of them real old-timers, began to appreciate that this new guy, this cowboy from up in the Flathead Country, was a pretty good hand. They began to call on him for day work or whenever they needed help and he was able to count on them when he needed their assistance and advice. Over the years he was learning to ranch from some pretty damn good cowboys. Buck really did enjoying working with the young horses and was more and more convinced the decisions he was in the process of making about his long term future were the right ones.

Things were going along well at the ranch and at the university as he hoped they would. It was his personal life he couldn't get a handle on. By now Buck's time in Missoula was only a Monday, Wednesday, Friday teaching schedule and except for some departmental and committee meetings, he rarely went to Missoula on the other days. He found great comfort at the ranch, working with the horses, checking his own small herd of cattle, keeping his fences in good repair, riding the high country, helping his neighbors, and the free time gave him a chance to catch up on reading that had nothing to do with his classes in American Studies. And he was doing more and more writing, mostly about the contemporary West. He published several articles in popular journals and enjoyed the research and the additional money that all went back into the ranch. The extra time also gave him plenty of opportunities to begin to seriously think about and make plans for the future. He was still young at 40 and a young and healthy 40 at that. Buck didn't want the years to get away from him.

■■■

One early spring night, Buck and Holly were sitting in the living room. Buck had just come in from feeding the horses and checking on the herd of Red Angus cattle they had been putting together and was still invigorated by the crisp spring air. Holly, who was an exceptional cook, had dinner on the stove and the wonderful aroma took over every corner of the house. She had baked some bread earlier in the day and rich smell just overpowered Buck. It just seemed to be such a normal, quiet evening on the ranch.

"Holly, there's something I need to say. We both know things aren't working out the way they should. We don't agree much about the future and I think we need to think about getting a divorce. Our lives are going in such different directions and what we want for the future is just too damn different to reconcile. You must realize by now that I'm not anxious to have kids. There's no middle ground for that. I just don't think we can resolve all of this." When it came out of his mouth, Buck was shocked by how awkward and slightly stupid he sounded. Holly didn't say a word. She looked at him in total silence and Buck could almost hear her trying to clear her thoughts—did she really just hear Buck ask for a divorce?

"What in God's name are you talking about? What the hell's going on? Why do you want a divorce? What's wrong? Do you want to talk about something or is there something I've missed all these years? Is there someone else in your life? Are you seeing some graduate student?"

Buck didn't say a word and just stood there, looking out the full length window over to the small horse pasture just south of the house. His back was to Holly. He hadn't the slightest idea of where this conversation should go or how to take the next step. He realized he did love Holly in his own way but probably not the way she wanted to be loved. He still liked her so much but he had just fallen out of the romantic love needed to keep a marriage alive and vital. And more than anything else he didn't want to hurt her, but down deep he also knew he was doing the right thing. Two lives can't keep together if they don't share the same dreams for the future. And if everything else was equal, the conflict over having children was just too much for them to overcome. In fact, it was impossible for them to overcome.

Holly was very bright and had a good job in Missoula as a book editor, and Buck was certain her life would go forward—she was just turning thirty-two—and she could meet someone who wanted to live her lifestyle and have children with her. Buck thought all of that because it made him feel less guilty and let him off the hook. But there was no turning back now.

Well, the discussion, such as it was, drew on for several days...Holly doing some crying and Buck staying out of the house as much as possible. He just couldn't face up to the long term hurt that was going to be part of their separation, and it was going to be a permanent separation. Buck knew that. But Holly had other ideas. She still loved Buck and wanted them to stay together. Unfortunately she had no better idea of how to fix all of this than Buck did. She wasn't even sure what there was broken or what there was to fix because she wasn't sure what was really was behind Buck's decision making and Buck sure wasn't the most communicative cowboy in Montana.

She was sure though, she did want to have children.

A few days after Buck announced his intentions, Holly asked him to go see a marriage counselor with her.

"I don't know if it will do any good but maybe we can sort out whatever is bothering you. You mean enough to me I want to try."

Buck agreed because he thought he had to but he knew it was just a formality because it was always his understanding that a marriage counselor only worked if you wanted to save your marriage—and he didn't. He agreed to go to a few sessions but he never agreed to pay much attention to whatever was going to happen behind closed doors with someone he didn't know and probably wouldn't want to know. It's probably fair to say that Buck had a rotten attitude, even an arrogant one, before he even started but he was fascinated by the idea of there being such an "expert" on marital problems in isolated Missoula, Montana.

■■■

Buck was right about the direction this was all going to take. After about three or four sessions, the counselor, Holly and Buck, all agreed it was best to have a trial separation. Buck went along with this because it was the first step toward ending his marriage and a big step for both of them. For him the results of the trial separation were already determined and although it might take some time, in his mind this was all a done deal.

Holly rented a very comfortable apartment in Missoula, to be closer to her job, and Buck stayed on the ranch where he wanted to be and where he felt the most at ease. Holly came down to the ranch one weekend when Buck was gone, as they had agreed, and she took some of the furniture and other odds and ends. Over the years they had collected some fine antiques and Buck wanted Holly to take whatever she wanted. It was a small attempt to ease his growing guilty conscience. Financially Buck knew he would do whatever was necessary to make sure he didn't have to sell the ranch in some fire sale to settle a divorce. For the time being he wanted to hold on to the ranch but if the ranch was going to be sold it was going to be on his terms.

■■■

After a couple of weeks of a very unsettling experience, of living alone and really being alone for the first time in quite a few years, Buck was surprised at how comfortable he was and at peace with himself. His marriage had hung over him for the last couple of years, sort of like a cloak he just couldn't shed. Finally he felt free. This was the same feeling he had when he was younger and on the rodeo circuit riding bareback horses. He just enjoyed his newly regained freedom. He liked getting up whenever he wanted to, he liked not making his bed and he even got used to cooking for himself. But most of all he just enjoyed doing what he wanted, when he wanted and with anybody he wanted. In fact, he enjoyed doing nothing when the urge got to him. The one thing he wasn't sure about was his love life...was there even going to be any?

Buck didn't want to be without a female in his life for that special kind of companionship, at least not all the time. In fact, he didn't want to be without female companionship even most of the time. But where were these new women and how do you meet them? That's how unsure Buck was of himself and what the future would hold. The idea of dating again scared the hell out of him. And since Buck didn't frequent the bar scene and was not a joiner—he didn't belong to a church or any civic group and never did really socialize with his colleagues on the university faculty—he realized his options were probably limited.

Buck should have known right from the start that what Holly had asked about as a throw in thought—was he involved with a graduate student—wasn't a bad direction to investigate. As he looked around at his colleagues at the university he was surprised when he realized how many of them were involved with their graduate assistants and the number who were actually married to their former students. Well, that was sure going to be a possibility to look into. But because American Studies didn't have a graduate program he might have to cast his rope a little further than some other professors but his loop was big. He just didn't have any of his own graduate assistants.

With his new independence Buck actually dated here and there but nothing that was very serious. He met women at the university and in Stevensville, and even around Missoula. Friends were eager to fix him up with a visiting cousin, sister, or some friend of a friend. But nothing really seemed to click for him.

Sometime later, in the late fall, a few months after Buck's divorce had been finalized and classes where in full session, it didn't take long for the cowboy from the Bitterroot Valley to get together with a young professor in the history department. She was about 5'6", blonde, with the most penetrating blue eyes—a real knockout, all Norwegian, and a look Buck found very appealing. To top that off, she was from the West. For several generations her family had ranched in South Dakota and it was a pretty big move for her to go to college and then get her PhD at the University of Minnesota. To make things even more interesting, her field was contemporary American history, not a very big leap from American Studies. Buck was sure that sooner or later they would be working together professionally at the university.

Buck and Jennifer Olson were introduced at lunch in the university cafeteria one day by a professor in the history department who was just a casual friend of Buck's.

"Buck, I'd like you like you to meet Jennifer Olson, a coming star in the history department. I told her about your ranch and she said she'd like to meet you. You're a very lucky guy."

It didn't take very long or much conversation for Buck to ask her out—even before the lunch was over and the dishes were cleared. She accepted, never missing a beat, and they agreed to have dinner. Jennifer then really stepped it up and invited Buck over to her place for a home cooked meal.

"Jennifer, I'd really enjoy that. You have no idea how lousy some "home cooked" meals can be, especially if I'm cooking at my home. Just tell me when and where you live and I assure you I'll be there."

"I sort of figured that. I know how you bachelor cowboys eat. And since you are a rancher and a cowboy, I'll even show you some photographs I have of my family's ranch in South Dakota. It will probably be new country for you. What would you like for dinner?"

As the arrangements were being made, Buck was surprised at how excited he was by her reception. He had only wanted some female company but this seemed to be going in a more significant direction. Buck had been out of the serious dating scene for so long he was sure everything would be a surprise for him—and it was.

■■■

When Buck arrived at Jennifer's apartment, within walking distance of the university and the Clark Fork River, he was greeted warmly. When she opened the door she was dressed in tight fitting jeans, a very form fitting fireman's red shirt and she was wearing a pair of ropers and very little makeup. Her hair was down and loose. Jennifer the professor had morphed into Jennifer the cow girl. Her blond, shoulder length hair seemed to reflect all the light in the apartment.

"You look really good," he sort of mumbled.

"Well, I wanted you to feel comfortable and I know how tired you are of all the stiffness and formality our colleagues bring to everything. You made that pretty clear at lunch. You can't know how much I like to get out of my stockings and heels. Come on in."

Buck thought for a moment that the reason he did virtually no entertaining of fellow faculty was that even away from the campus the conversations were always about the same things...always about the events, and the students, and the latest crisis at the university. Despite the fact they lived in the West, his colleagues didn't seem to really want to be part of it, at least not Buck's West. Sure they fished, some hunted, and they hiked and skied, but that wasn't the West Buck wanted to be involved in. For him, it was the cowboy west, the west of ranching, old time cattle drives, chuck wagons, good horses, spring brandings, fall roundups and the wide open spaces. It was, for lack of a better description, the romantic west of novels and the movies. Buck was more interested in the writings of Tony Hillerman, Max Evans, J.P.S. Brown, Jack Schaefer, and Elmer Kelton, and the music of Ian Tyson than he was in the Sierra Club. For Buck, climbing aboard a good horse and riding out among his cattle was one of the surefire ways for him to be happy. For Buck, being alone like that was a feeling he couldn't really describe. Buck had heard the stories, maybe far too often and frequently told by cowboys themselves, that if you weren't a romantic to start with, you would never have taken up the cowboy life. The older he got the more he came to believe all of that.

Buck knew the minute he entered Jennifer's apartment that this was going to be a different kind of evening and since he came with no expectations about anything, he was delighted to see that Jennifer's apartment had been decorated in a western style with just enough of a modern touch to suggest the sophistication she obviously had. Her carved, western style wood furniture, along with a few ranch items, including a branding iron from the family's ranch, a small Navajo tapestry, and even a couple of Sioux beaded pieces from her home country, were accented by framed prints from the Museum of Modern Art and Minneapolis' Walker Art Center, a bastion for the very avant-garde. There was also a good collection of books and a quick glance suggested they were mostly carryovers from graduate school. What remained were the most recent volumes for Jennifer's own teaching career and research. What Buck couldn't find was what she read for pure pleasure...he couldn't find any novels or anything even semiserious. After his quick mental examination of the apartment, Buck thought to himself, "So far, so good."

Jennifer offered Buck a drink but to her surprise, Buck was only a beer drinker. He didn't remember the last hard liquor he had downed—maybe it was in college. So beer it was. One good, long necked bottle of Bud was a heavy night's drinking for Buck Cooper.

"I thought all you cowboys were rugged, big time drinkers."

"Well, professor, you were wrong. This isn't some sort of moral crusade. I just don't like the stuff. And have you ever met an interesting or entertaining drunk?"

Jennifer smiled. She'd been around enough liquored up cowboys to know exactly what Buck meant. In fact she seemed a little relieved he wasn't a big drinker.

As the evening progressed it was beginning to dawn on Buck that Jennifer wasn't treating him as a fellow professor but as a cowboy, and he wasn't sure whether that was a good thing or a bad thing. Was it a lack of respect for his academic achievements or was it a desire on her part to be with the kind of guy she had spent most of her life with? He thought he would know before the evening was over.

Dinner was baked chicken with wild rice and a salad, the wild rice obviously a carryover from her days in Minnesota. Dessert was a home made apple pie, probably cooked the day before. This certainly wasn't what Buck would have cooked for himself or for that matter, even knew how to cook for himself. But in his own way he was glad he was able to get away from beef for at least one meal. Since Buck slaughtered one of his own steers once a year, his freezer was loaded with every cut you could get from a beef. Holly had been a gourmet cook and until this dinner with Jennifer he hadn't realized how much he missed his ex-wife's cooking.

During dinner Jennifer put a Mozart piano concerto in the CD and this was just one more part of his past he missed. Buck loved classical music, particularly Beethoven and Bela Bartok, and although he played it regularly at the ranch, this wasn't a joyous thing he could share with many of his cowboy friends. In fact, he couldn't think of a single one of his friends who knew or cared the slightest bit about the great composers. Even some of his so-called sophisticated friends listened to that god awful country music crap that droned on and on about things that all seemed to have their origins in trailer parks in the South. And he really resented all those hillbilly singers wearing cowboy hats and boots. Buck had always felt there was a strong division between country music and western music and it was definitely the country he tried to avoid. And being in Montana it was pretty damn hard to do.

The dinner conversation was generally low key, mostly about Missoula, the weather, the university, and just "get acquainted with" information— Jennifer had a million questions or as she put it, "Tell me everything I need to know to survive here." And she wasn't talking about the weather. There was even a little political talk. Buck was surprised, coming from South Dakota, that Jennifer was a fairly liberal Democratic, but probably she was equally surprised when she discovered that this cowboy/rancher had been doing some work for the Democratic party and some of the environmental organizations that were trying to preserve rangeland and were popping up all over Montana. This wasn't the path ranchers and cowboys usually took although Buck could never figure out what the Republicans had ever done for the ranchers. For Buck, loosening up environmental regulations hardly constituted good stewardship of the land and other than doing just that, the Republicans weren't real friends of the ranchers no matter what the local pols claimed. He thought the constant talk about "preserving private property rights" was just a smoke screen. As far as Buck was concerned, the Republicans were far too close to the mining and timber interests and he didn't think either of the two industries was particularly good for the survival of ranching.

Buck and Jennifer continued to talk about the land and how much ranchland was disappearing all over the West. As they talked, Buck couldn't help but think about Lyndon Johnson's declaration when he signed the Wilderness Act of 1964: "If future generations are to remember us with gratitude rather than contempt, then we must leave them with something more than the miracles of technology. We must leave them a glimpse of the world as it was in the beginning."

That simple statement had so impressed Buck over the years he had it framed and hanging near his desk at his university office and another copy in his office at the ranch. It was one of those quotes he found very easy to memorize. He wished more ranchers actually understood and practiced the ideas behind it.

After Buck helped Jennifer clear the table, she asked him to get comfortable on the couch and she would join him in a minute. She headed to what Buck assumed was the bedroom and he couldn't take his eyes off her. She reemerged with two large photo albums and took a seat next to him, nestled in about as close as she could get. She explained that she hadn't been able to share these family memories, so many of them about the ranch, with anyone since she had been moved to Missoula.

"I hope this doesn't bore you. I thought you'd be interested in seeing the ranch. It has been in our family for four generations and I'm scared to death we are going to lose it. My older brother Nels hasn't made up his mind whether or not he wants to ranch or permanently head to a big city like Minneapolis or St. Louis to make a fortune. He went to college on a rodeo scholarship...he's a helluva calf roper and even did a little rough stock riding. I'd really like for him to stay on the ranch. There are just the two of us but I guess he'll have to make his own decision. My folks don't know what to say to him although down deep I'm sure they'd like him to take over the ranch. I get angry at him when we're together back home because he won't make a decision. I even think about going back myself but since he's the oldest I think it's only fair that he get first crack at continuing the Olsen ranching tradition. I hope you can see this place some time. I haven't met anyone around here, especially on the faculty, who really cares much about ranching. You're the first. The ranch is so beautiful and vibrant when things green up in the summer, when the pastures come alive, filled with cattle, horses, wildlife and beautiful flowers...and yet it's so quiet and almost lonely when it's blanketed with snow in the winter. And then there's that part of winter when it's actually dangerous to go outside for more than a few minutes as the wind comes howling across the prairie, screaming like a

Gaelic banshee warning of dire things to come. It's never boring living out on the prairie of South Dakota."

"Well, let's take a look. I know I won't be bored and I'll bet I've been in that country in my rodeo days. My traveling partner and I spent a lot of time in the Dakotas. In fact, my one serious injury was at Clear Lake, over in the eastern part of the state, in one of the Korkow and Sutton rodeos."

"So you rodeoed!? And you've been to South Dakota. What was your event and how did you get hurt? And for God's sake, please don't tell me you rode bulls."

"Are you kidding? No bulls for me. My injury was the usual kind for a bronc rider. I was the second rider out in the bareback riding on Sunday and I must have hit my head on the gate or something as I came into the arena. I don't remember a thing until the bull riding at the end of the rodeo. My partner says I was never unconscious. Well, they took me over to the hospital and I had a pretty good concussion. An old rancher, who was a widower, whose two sons had left the ranch and gone to St. Paul, invited us to stay with him at his ranch. We stayed there for a few days, until I was feeling a whole lot better. We helped out with the chores as much as we could and he took care of us. He was lonely but he was a wonderful man. He left me with a pretty good impression of the people of South Dakota. After that I stayed off those broncs for nearly six months. I was really afraid I could screw up my head more than it already was and I was actually thinking of my academic career."

"That experience alone should have taught you to stay off those bucking horses. Those darn bareback horses will tear your body apart. I know some bareback riders from back home who are really stove up and they're a lot younger than you are."

She stared at him for a moment with a look that almost asked out loud, 'What were you thinking?' Then she decided to move the conversation along. "Do you want to look at some photographs?" When she asked the question you could see in her smile and the way her blues eyes lit up, the pride she had for the ranch.

"You bet!" was Buck's enthusiastic response.

As Jennifer slowly thumbed her way through the album, explaining each picture, Buck was taken with the beauty of the ranch, how well kept everything was, and how green those color photos made the landscape look. In his own mind, because of his travels during his rodeo days, he always had an impression that the landscape of South Dakota was pretty bleak and bland. He had never met a cowboy who dreamed about going to work in the Dakotas the way they fantasized about going to Montana or Wyoming. The Olson's Double O Ranch was located north of the Pine Ridge Indian Reservation, home of the Ogallala Sioux, north of I-90, near the Belle Fourche River and east of Sturgis. In fact, the ranch wasn't that far west of the southern end of the Cheyenne River Indian reservation. From the pictures Jennifer was showing him, Buck thought the ranch was about as good as a ranch got in South Dakota. It wasn't Montana but still, it wasn't too bad. There were also pictures of Jennifer's family...her mom and dad and her brother...their obviously well bred, good looking quarter horses, the registered and commercial Angus cattle herds, and then the show stoppers—two pictures—one of Jennifer running the barrels and one of her as Miss Rodeo South Dakota.

For a brief moment Buck was really at a loss. He wasn't quite sure what to say or how this all made him feel. A beautiful woman, with brains, and someone who he could actually share the things that were important to him... it was so unexpected it was almost too much to absorb at one time. What had started out as a simple date, as a way to spend an evening with a beautiful woman, suddenly was beginning to take on new meaning. He realized he could definitely get serious with Dr. Olson. Now he was a little confused. This wasn't part of the plan and he wasn't sure he was ready to get seriously involved again, at least not now, less than four months after his divorce was finalized. And besides, why get ahead of the game when he hadn't the slightest idea of how she felt. Maybe she was just a little lonely in a new town, in a new job with new people. Maybe she was just plain homesick for what appeared to be a fairly tight knit ranch family. Or was she interested in Buck for the same reason he seemed to be getting very interested in her? Probably this was just a little innocent get together with two people who had a few things in common.

Buck felt he didn't have much time to sort this all out, and he desperately hoped Jennifer would give him some sign that evening, at least a sign he could understand.

"So you were one of those rodeo queens and a successful one at that. I guess I'm not surprised. I figured you were at least a barrel racer, a ranch girl like you. How'd you do at the Miss Rodeo finals in Las Vegas?"

"Actually, I did very well. I was the second runner-up and I won the horsemanship. I thought that was a pretty solid achievement. Some of those girls had so much money behind them, especially the girls from Texas and

California. All that money makes it hard to compete against them. They can afford the best outfits and some of them actually have coaches to get them ready for all the different events. But it was fun and I made quite a few good friends. And you know what, I'd do it again. In fact, I'd love to do it again."

Buck looked at Jennifer, almost staring. At that very moment he was acutely aware of her beauty and sexuality.

"I'll bet you stood out. I can just picture you in those cowgirl threads, tight and sexy as only barrel racers can look. I wish I was there to see all that. You are a cowgirl!"

Without another word he gently put his arm around her and brought her close to him. She didn't resist, didn't fight him at all, and the next thing he knew they were embracing and kissing passionately, something he didn't remembered doing in a long while. She felt so good in his arms and she seemed to be as involved in this moment as he was. And they didn't just stop all at once and begin to analyze and talk about what had just happened. They just relaxed and enjoyed themselves. And enjoy themselves they did. The longer they stayed close, the more intimate they became, and it soon was apparent the time had come to either move on or stop. They probably needed to let things settle down. Buck would have loved to have spent the night with Jennifer but he knew he would not ask and it was probably far too soon in their relationship for her to offer an invitation. Whatever Jennifer was, despite her obvious warmth, Buck sensed she was a woman with a good deal of reserve about her and she surely was not a schoolgirl.

After some time, and Buck did not really know how long that was, they moved apart and Buck got up and suggested that it was getting late and that he had better head south to the ranch. Jennifer looked at him and for a moment and he was sure she was going to ask him to stay, to spend the night. But she just smiled and told him she really looked forward to their next time together. It was warm and a little bit formal at the same time.

As Buck slowly headed for his car he was still not sure about what had happened or what it all meant. To say he was a little confused was an understatement. On the easy drive south on US 93, passing through Lolo, Florence, and finally on to his own road just south of the Stevensville turnoff, all he could think about was Jennifer Olson and what the future might hold if she was going to be a part of it. Even the mule deer along the road, as he passed the Lee Metcalf Wildlife Refuge, held little interest for him because he couldn't stop thinking about the events of the evening that had just taken place with the beautiful, blonde from the history department. There was no question he was very sexually attracted to her.

When he drove up the dirt road, passed his mailbox, and then another mile and a half up to his lower gate near the headquarters, little pins and needles began to jab at him. Buck figured Jennifer must be more than a dozen years younger than he was and he couldn't imagine that if they got very serious the issue of children wouldn't come up again as it did with Holly. Then he had to pull back quickly because he realized he had taken huge steps way ahead of where the two professors were. What would the second date be like and was this the beginning of a real relationship or was tonight just one of those quirky things that happen between two people for whatever reason? Only time would tell but he knew he could not stop thinking about her and he definitely wanted to see her again and not at the university.

■■■

In the morning, after putting out grain for the horses, he scattered some replacement salt blocks and checked the hay in the feeders that was put out for the cattle. He made sure there was water in the tanks and the drinkers. Back at the house, Buck grabbed his coffee mug and went out on the deck to look around and just enjoy the scenery. The fall was a good time in Montana although it didn't last very long. The ranch's deeded land plus the lease land gave him lots of privacy and from the deck, looking east, he could see down the valley all the way to Stevensville and across to the Sapphire Mountains. At night the lights in town were so surprisingly bright the distances seemed to fade away. Often, as the sun was setting, Buck would look at the mountains surrounding the ranch and the valley and just wonder what sort of secrets those mountains were hiding. He'd sit with his coffee and just wish he could find the key that would release all the stories the mountains kept for themselves.

On the west side of the ranch he shared a fence line with the Bitterroot National Forest, with it's great expanse of ponderosa pine, and just beyond the fence there were over 1.5 million acres for him to enjoy, all the way across the tops of the towering peaks and down into parts of Idaho that included the Frank Church River of No Return Wilderness. Riding that mountain country was one of his greatest pleasures and it was something he didn't think he had the time to do often enough. That was going to have to be corrected.

The Palo Verde Ranch was mostly grass and with some forest, numerous dirt tanks that filled in the spring with runoff from the snow melt and that plus his rights on the irrigation ditch, enabled him to irrigate a couple of small pastures, at least early in the growing season. The timber, mostly ponderosa pine and larch provided shade and wind breaks for the stock in severe weather. Buck always planned to thin some of the timber to improve the pastures but never seemed to get around to what he considered a big chore. The ranch was in a wonderful location except that from late October or early November to the melting of the winter ice, snow and frost, and the increasing mud in late May and early June, it was often a harsh place to live and there were many times when it was strictly a matter of survival. Buck usually shipped his calf crop, both young steers and the heifers in late October so he only had bred cows, some replacement calves, a few bulls plus his horses to care for through the winter. The everyday chores could regularly become dangerous ordeals in the frigid winter so not having most of the calves around made things easier and the fall sale was his only significant paycheck for the year from his ranching. Most of the money from the sale was generally plowed right back into the ranch and the rest invested.

Like all Montanans, everyone had to be prepared for winter. The house had triple pane windows, the exterior walls were wood, board and batten construction, and they were very well insulated. There was enough insulation in the attic so the snow rarely melted off the cedar shingled, peaked roof. Buck was proud of the security the house offered in bad weather. Buck heated entirely with two wood stoves and a good part of every summer was spent cutting enough wood to last him through the winter. There was no margin for error when it came to providing for the Montana winter.

Many times during the winter Buck had to park the truck or the car at his lower gate where he kept a pair of snow boots, an extra jacket, a shovel and even a set of tire chains, all in a wooden box. He frequently walked up the last quarter mile because even with the four wheel drive Ford truck or Subaru he just couldn't make it up the steep dirt road when the snow was deep enough to high center the vehicles. He didn't always have time to clear the road with his small tractor, especially when it snowed during the day while he was still in Missoula.

But this morning, in mid September, the weather was crisp, the sun was already up, and the sky was deep blue punctuated with big fluffy white clouds that just seemed to laze around the heavens. He only wished it would stay that way all year. He knew better but even after all these years in Montana he still wished. Buck liked the quiet of the ranch, with no sounds from town, no cars or trucks or other man made contraptions. All he could hear were an occasional horse or cow, the birds and the whispering songs that came down through the ponderosa pines from the forest above the ranch. Buck knew that the birds, except for the magpies, would soon be gone. Even they were smart enough to head south when winter cast its long, gray shadow over Montana. "Cowboy," his black and white Australian Shepherd was going to be his winter companion, as he had been for the previous six years, since he was a pup. Buck, in one of his lucky moves, had rescued him from the pound in Hamilton. No matter what, "Cowboy" was always good company.

Buck picked up the cordless phone he had carried out to the deck. The wood deck with the three foot railing, wrapped around all but the north side of the house and when the weather permitted, Buck spent as much time as he could out there. Sitting out on the deck with his coffee, the chill of the air so invigorating he favored it over the warmth of the house, he decided to call Jennifer before she had to head off to class. This being Thursday he had no classes and no need to go to town. The phone rang several times and Buck was about to hang up when Jennifer answered. She sounded rushed and almost out of breath.

"Hi. This is Buck. Are you late for class?"

"It's getting that way. Let me call you after my first class. I've got your number in the faculty directory. Okay?"

"I'll talk to you then."

Buck was excited just hearing her voice and knowing he'd talk to her in an hour or so. He sat on the deck, listening to some Beethoven piano music before the cold air forced him inside.

When the Beethoven was over he went inside and switched to the wonderful songs of Ian Tyson. Tyson, more than any of the other cowboy singers, and this was western music, not country, understood what it was like to be a cowboy in the modern world. To Buck, Tyson's songs were like the biographies of his friends and even Buck himself. Tyson wrote about the real, contemporary cowboy world and it wasn't always a very romantic world with all happy endings.

Buck could hear the music throughout the house, as he sat on the couch drinking his coffee and thinking about what the future would bring. He had several problems he knew he had to work out, namely, was he going to stay at the university or work the ranch full time, did he really want to sell this place he had truly come to love and head south to New Mexico, and finally, would Jennifer influence any of these decisions? At this stage of things, he wasn't even sure if last night was the beginning of a real relationship or was he just filled with lust for a truly beautiful woman who for the time being, at least, appeared to return his interest.

He sat in the living room knowing that nothing was going to be decided this morning and all he really wanted was to get her phone call.

Right on schedule, ten minutes after the hour, the phone rang and Jennifer started out by apologizing for her abruptness earlier that morning. After a little small talk they agreed that Buck would pick her up at her apartment in the early afternoon and he would take her up to the Flathead Indian Reservation, past his old ranch and then up to the National Bison Range near Dixon. She hadn't seen any of that country yet and she was eager to take a road trip out of town, or as she put it, "I want to see the land."

■■■

A little before noon, Buck got into his Subaru and started out on the 40 minute trip to Jennifer's. He was surprised by his feelings and how anxious he actually was to see her. It began to annoy him a little because this wasn't part of the plan for New Mexico and the plan seemed so sensible and what he had been dreaming about for years. He already knew down deep he wasn't going to stay in Montana but where did Jennifer fit into all of this if in fact she did?

As he entered Missoula, past Malfunction Junction and over to the river, all the things he hated about the city came to greet him. The noise, the traffic, the dirty streets and the crowds of people scurrying all over town...they began to surround him and it made him very uncomfortable, more so today than usual because he seemed to be in such a hurry to see Jennifer. Overriding all of this was the question of how, for Christ's sake, was he going to resolve the new complications Jennifer was bringing to his life?

Jennifer's neighborhood was relatively quiet. In season there were usually a few fishermen working the Clark Fork and there always seemed to be several couples walking hand in hand along the cottonwood lined banks of the gently flowing river. At this time of the year the leaves had already turned a bright golden hue and some were carelessly falling and covering the ground. It made the whole area seem like the sun had settled there permanently.

It was never difficult to park in one of the lots by the river so he pulled up at the first open spot, got out of the car and headed for Jennifer's apartment. Before he got there Jennifer came out, looking just as beautiful and sexy as he thought she did the night before. He had hoped she would have had time to come home from the university and change clothes. She did. To look like she did now in front of some freshman boys would almost be dangerous if not outright illegal. She gave him a big hug and they got into the car. What suddenly dawned on Buck was that even though they had really just met, their relationship had all the signs of one that had grown and become comfortable and intimate over a much longer period of time. Buck liked all of that but it did make him a little apprehensive. He still didn't actually know who Jennifer was, he didn't know about her past involvements and he really didn't have any idea of what she was thinking and how far into the future she was looking. Maybe she was just lonely in a new place. Buck thought that in all likelihood, he was just plain nuts to even be considering these things. Someone as beautiful and as smart as Dr. Olson, certainly wasn't desperately in need of male attention.

■■■

As they leisurely drove out of town, west on Broadway and then north up the steep Evaro Hill, the conversation was mostly about the countryside, their classes and their students, and Buck tried to describe in his most poetic way, the beautiful scenery on the Flathead Indian Reservation, the Bison Range, and the spectacular Mission Mountains that served as a backdrop to the valley. Jennifer was a good conversationalist and the talk flowed easily. Just a couple of miles or so north of the tiny town of Arlee, inside the southern boundary of the Reservation, Buck pointed out his old ranch with the two classic log barns, buildings erected long before someone had begun to construct those metal buildings Buck felt just junked up the landscape. It was another one of Buck's attempts to push back the modern world to an era he thought for sure was a better time. The fruit trees near the modest wood framed house, the irrigated, lush pastures, all still looked good, even this late in the year. There were a few cattle and three or four horses idly grazing as they drove by. Buck didn't know who was living there or even if they were renting as he did or they were new owners.

Jennifer seemed impressed with the ranch and they continued the drive north, beyond the ranch's main gate. In just a few miles they took the turn at Ravalli west to Dixon, past a couple of ranches owned by tribal members who were friends of Buck, and they finally arrived at the headquarters for the National Bison Range.

Buck knew the range manager and went into the office to see if he was there and just say hi. Jennifer said she didn't mean to be rude but she would wait by the Subaru so she could just look around and try to absorb the surroundings that bordered on overwhelming. Buck returned in a few minutes. Most historians agree that this Flathead country is where the buffalo were ultimately saved from extinction and started back on their journey to safety and off the endangered list. The National Bison Range just verified all that and was a wonderful monument to have on the Flathead Indian Reservation. It was an area of real pride for most of the tribal members.

Buck took the one way drive out on the 19 mile gravel road that wound its way through the rolling grass hills on the range and back to headquarters, always with the towering, already snow capped Mission Mountains off to the east. As they drove they talked about the movie "Dances With Wolves," and the epic buffalo scenes that were all filmed in South Dakota. On the drive, grazing in the open meadows they saw coyotes, antelope, some elk off in the distance, deer, several smaller critters but only about two dozen buffalo. Buck was disappointed that at least a few of the big bulls didn't even make an appearance. The range, nearly 19,000 acres, was home to a controlled buffalo herd of about 500. When they sold off the surplus late each spring...and the buffalo roundup was a big event in the area...several of the area ranchers purchased some of the excess stock at the auction and a few of the locals were building pretty good sized buffalo herds of their own. All the area cafes served buffalo burgers and steaks. It was definitely part of the attraction for the tourists. Buffalo were certainly a very intricate part of the old, romantic West, the West the tourists wanted to see and this part of the reservation wasn't letting them down.

But even without sighting the big bulls, Jennifer just seemed to truly enjoy herself. She was thrilled to be there and see all the wild life after a couple of months of being stuck in Missoula preparing for the start of the academic year, her first as a full time professor. The National Bison Range was as close to home as she had been since she left the family's ranch in western South Dakota.

■■■

As they headed back to town, it was getting around dinner time and Buck suggested they try a restaurant he frequented just east of Missoula. Jennifer readily agreed and they headed back down Evaro Hill, past the Evaro Bar and onto Broadway straight through town. Missoula was growing and even Jennifer commented on the traffic that to Buck seemed to increase substantially each and every year.

When they arrived at the restaurant on the east side of the city, the sun had already set over the mountains that surrounded the Missoula Valley and darkness was enveloping the landscape. Jennifer didn't particularly notice, she was so used to living in the northern part of the country, where fall and winter sunsets happen so early in the day. They took a table for two, way in the back, hidden away from the main flow of traffic and isolated enough from the rest of the dinners so the two professors could have some privacy.

After they were seated, Jennifer appeared very serious as she looked over at Buck. She began very quietly: "I want to ask you something. I know it's probably none of my business but it's something that's got me very intrigued and I want to know the answer. Where the heck did a college professor—and I know you are originally from back east—come up with a name like Buck? What's your real name?"

Buck sort of laughed to himself, almost out loud. He liked being "Buck" because he thought it was so western, so cowboy.

"It's a funny story. Years ago, when I was rodeoing, a few of the guys I traveled with happened to love old western movies. Well, so do I and I guess I started to talk too much about the early movies, especially the movies of old Buck Jones, and I suppose I got too involved—you can guess what an American Studies professor can do with a subject like that. Anyhow, before long they started to call me Buck and much too my embarrassment they passed the word along to several rodeo announcers on the circuit that I liked to be called Buck and from that time forward I was "Buck." And I really do like it. Now, how's that for a good cowboy story?"

"You've left out a big part. What's your given name, you know, your real name?"

"Joel. It's from the Book of Joel in the Bible though I think my parents just liked the name. There's nothing very biblical about me. I actually like that name too, but Buck is so much more cowboy, or at least I thought so when I was a whole lot younger. I'm stuck with it now and I doubt if anyone around here in Montana actually knows my real name. It's interesting that you are the first one to even ask me about it."

She took hold of his hand, gently, leaned toward him and said in what Buck considered one of the sexiest voices he had ever heard, "Well, I'm going to call you Joel sometimes. I like that name a lot."

"When will that be?"

"You'll see. I don't have some plan. I just like the sound of Joel and since you think no one else knows your name, it will be something just between the two of us."

There it was again. It seemed she had a knack of making their relationship somehow very private and intimate without saying so and yet the lure of it was very appealing for Buck. Is this what he really wanted when he knew in the back of his mind, unspoken, that it would mean staying in Montana and maybe even keeping his job at the university? He'd already come to terms with giving up his tenure, with all the fringe benefits that made his life a whole lot easier, and the prestige of moving from Associate Professor to Full Professor next year. Now his plans began to unravel. And yet there was something about Jennifer that remained remote or at least a little aloof and reserved, despite the warmth and intimacy of her conversation, the little touches and the familiarity she had shown in such a short time. Buck couldn't quite understand all of this but knew there was a lot more about this rodeo queen and her world he had to find out, in fact, wanted to find, if she let him. But he wasn't completely convinced she would. He wasn't even sure of how much of his own life he wanted to share with her. There was some kind of barrier with her he just didn't understand and he hadn't yet found a way of breaking through. But to make himself feel better, he just wrote all off to it being so early in their relationship.

It was getting late when they got back to town but Buck drove around a bit, not wanting to have the day end and yet a little afraid to get to Jennifer's place. When they did arrive, they sat in the car, and talked about nothing in particular. Buck used his usually reliable excuse that he had a long way to travel to get back to the ranch all the while hoping once again she would ask him to spend the night. Then he could go home early in the morning when he had to feed. Again, she came close to asking.

"I know you have to get going and I'm going to miss you tonight. It's too bad we don't live closer so you could stay longer."

Then she slid over, wrapped herself around him and they picked up where they left off the night before in Jennifer's apartment. Buck couldn't help thinking the last time he made out in a car like this was when he was in college and making out in a car was considered a big deal. The "pill" and the free wheeling sixties had changed all of that for good.

Buck wasn't sure how long they were together but he knew he had to get out of there and he did. Jennifer, as she had been the night before, was very understanding. When he gave her a very intimate good night kiss, she responded the way he hoped she would.

Just like the first night, as he drove the dark road back down the Bitterroot, his mind was filled with thoughts about Jennifer that brought him nothing but confusion. When he got home, on a whim, he called Jennifer to say goodnight and he was a little surprised she wasn't already asleep. Maybe she was in the midst of some confused fantasy world, too. Buck casually asked her if she wanted to go to Great Falls that weekend for a fairly important horse sale, probably on Friday and Saturday. She answered without any hesitation that she would and they never bothered to discuss the implications of spending a couple of nights away together. Probably that was best and that's how these things are meant to evolve. Buck always thought that too much talk just gets in the way and ruins the natural order of things.

The plan was that they would leave Friday after class, stay overnight for the sale on Saturday and then head home on Sunday. Buck called his neighbor who he relied on to take care of his place when he was gone. Johnny Meyers, who ran a few head of cattle and worked as a successful handyman around the valley, said he wasn't going anywhere and he would be happy to do the chores and keep his eye on things. Johnny and his two sons were good neighbors and Buck always counted on them when he needed help for the branding each spring and the shipping in the fall.

■■■

With this taken care of, Buck began to anticipate the weekend so much he wasn't sure how he'd get through his Friday classes.

Before he left for town Friday morning, he hooked up the white four horse trailer to the 3/4 ton Ford, made sure he had a couple of halters in the tack compartment just in case he actually bought a horse, and threw his overnight bag into the back seat of the club cab truck.

When he got to the university, because the horse trailer was so long, he had to park in the big lot away from his regular spot. It made for a longer walk to his office but the walk in the crisp fall air was good for him. He had a chance to experience the campus again, to meet and visit with more students than he usually did and he enjoyed the extra ten or so minutes it took him to get from the truck to his office.

The day actually passed quickly, and after classes, as he carefully navigated his way down Jennifer's tree lined street with the horse trailer, he spotted her outside waiting for him, again the image of what a beautiful cowgirl should look like in jeans, boots and a gray cowboy hat. After Buck had parked the truck and trailer, she couldn't help from blurting out:

"Good God—you're not kidding about this horse sale. I guess bringing the horse trailer means you're really planning to buy another horse. I didn't realize you were so serious about actually buying something at the sale. Like most cowboys, I just thought this was just another social event for you."

Buck could see the exhilaration in her eyes. "I just thought it would be better to be prepared than buy a horse and have to come all the way back home, hook up the trailer and then head over to Great Falls again for the horse. Pretty damn logical, right?"

"This is a lot more exciting than I thought. I haven't been to a good horse sale in years. Are you looking for geldings, mares, youngsters or is the trailer a 'just in case.'?" Before he could answer, she added enthusiastically,

"Let's get going, cowboy. I don't want anybody to buy a horse out from under us."

Jennifer put her gear in the truck, hopped in and slid up next to Buck, cowboy style. They headed out of Missoula, through Milltown and on toward Potomac and Ovando, one of the gateways to the multi million acre Bob Marshall Wilderness. Buck felt more and more like a travel guide as they headed northeast. Jennifer had a ton of questions as they began their trip over to Great Falls. This was a particularly scenic drive, through the mountains and dense forests and the lush open pastures. It was scenery like this that most people think about when they try to picture Montana. This was another part of Montana Jennifer really hadn't seen yet. The give and take as they drove was real cowboy...there was plenty of horse talk, ranch talk, Jennifer's questions about the countryside, and Buck pointed out several ranches that were owned by friends and acquaintances of his. And Buck couldn't help but needle her about being Miss Rodeo South Dakota. But Jennifer was smart, and instead of getting defensive about her title, she came right back at him and explained how much hard work it took to win and the pride she had because she did win. And she was very quick to explain to Buck that a good part of her education was paid for by the college scholarships she won at the various competitions along the way. At first she did sound defensive until Buck realized how proud she really was of what she had accomplished. This wasn't some frivolous pageant anyone could win and Jennifer made sure Buck understood that. These were real cowgirls, smart and sophisticated. They were not just a bunch of beauty queens who could barely ride but knew how to fill out a tight pair of jeans. These were girls who could actually ride and rope and who knew about ranching and rodeo and they were damn well educated.

As the drive continued they passed through Lincoln, the former home of the Unabomber and a few other Montana nut cases. As beautiful and scenic as the area was it always seemed to Buck it was a little diminished by the kinds of people who chose to live or hide out there. From there it was over the 5,610 foot Rogers Pass and then on to Bowman's Corner where Buck pointed out the large Hutterite Colony with its freshly painted white buildings and well kept grounds.

"You know, on the way home we ought to stop here and buy some of those free-range, fresh chickens that they're so famous for and any produce they might still have. These people are really some of the best farmers in this country. But I don't know...those Hutterite boys will never be the same after they get a good look at you. You're going to upset an age old religion. Not too many blonde, blue eyed rodeo queens have visited the Hutterites. Will your conscience allow that?"

"Will you cut it out?! They've seen outsiders before and besides, it's not like they live in a monastery. I'm sure there must be plenty of good looking Hutterite women."

"But I'll bet that not one of those Hutterite gals has an outfit like yours or can fill it out the way you do."

Buck couldn't help but laugh out loud because the rodeo queen was taking this all so seriously and Buck was just needling her, partially to learn more about Jennifer. He was also aware that Jennifer had probably never been to a Hutterite Colony and didn't realize how close to the truth he actually was about her impact. Although they weren't cut off from the modern world to the degree the Amish were, the Hutterites were still a very conservative religious sect that could hardly be called worldly. But they drove pickups, had cell phones, washers and dryers, very contemporary kitchen machinery and they drove the most up to date tractors and others equipment in their farming operations. It wasn't uncommon to see them socializing in Great Falls, the closest large city. However, very few, if any of them, ever went on to college. Buck hadn't heard of a single case although he couldn't swear that.

Jennifer chose to ignore him and his chatter about the Hutterites and Buck took the cue. Instead, he pointed out the road heading north from Bowman's Corner that led to Augusta, a good old cow town about twenty miles north and one of the entry points on the east side to the vast Bob Marshall Wilderness. Buck used to spend time in Augusta, where he had good friends, but he didn't go there too much any more. He didn't like the way the town was increasingly being taken over by newcomers who were going to bring "culture" to Montana's rural folks and together with their "culture" they would introduce the concept of "big money," just like they were beginning to do in the Bitterroot. Buck had real trouble with all the newcomers heading to rural areas and making them so pricey the new, higher taxes often forced many of the old-timers to leave. This was a problem popping up all over the West, from Santa Fe, New Mexico to the Flathead Valley of Montana. Well, this trip wasn't the time to get involved in these socio/economic concerns. Jennifer was too much fun and he wanted her to enjoy the weekend and not have to listen to his stodgy political views about uncontrolled growth and the evil of developers in the West.

They were soon crossing the Sun River and slowly drifting into Great Falls. The three and a half hours the trip took was a little longer than usual because they were hauling the horse trailer over some curvy, narrow roads, but the drive went along without incident, and as they hit the city limits, Buck started to look for a motel. He wanted something better than a Motel 6 but didn't think they needed a Five Star accommodation, if Great Falls even had one, which it didn't. Somewhere in the middle would do just fine. They decided to go to the Fair Grounds where they were going to hold the horse sale, and park the horse trailer. That would make them a little more mobile driving around town. Jennifer was unusually quiet, just taking in all the new sights.

After unhooking, they drove back toward the downtown part of the city and found a motel that looked pretty good from the outside. As they pulled up Buck asked just a little bit hesitantly, "One room, right?"

"Of course we want just one room. I came along to spend time with you. I hope one room doesn't upset your moral sensibilities."

"I guess that all depends on what you have in mind. A poor cowboy like me doesn't have much of a chance with a beautiful rodeo queen like you."

"Will you please get us a room? I have to go to the bathroom and I'd prefer to use the one indoors."

The room was comfortable, it was clean and it had one double bed. What it lacked was any sense of style or warmth. But then again, it was just an average motel. After bringing the luggage in from the truck, Buck put his silver belly Resistol on the table, sat down on the bed and waited for Jennifer to get ready. It was dinner time and he was hungry. They hadn't really stopped for lunch...they had just snacked along the way. When Jennifer emerged from the bathroom, all fixed up, with her golden hair shimmering in the light, she was gorgeous. They discussed dinner and as they were heading out to the truck, Buck grabbed her and kissed her with more emotion than he probably intended. She reciprocated and for a moment Buck was ready to forego dinner.

"You know I'm finding it harder and harder to keep away from you."

Jennifer smiled but didn't say anything. Fortunately they overcame the immediacy of their emotions and got into the pick up and headed for a restaurant recommended by the desk clerk. Buck was too tired to drive around to find his own eatery and Jennifer was new to town and wouldn't have been of much help.

After dinner they did drive around town a little, took a look at the falls on the Missouri River and even talked a little about Lewis and Clark and the amount of time it took them to portage around the falls on their epic journey to the Pacific. But there really wasn't much to see in Great Falls other than the Charles M. Russell Museum and it was already closed for the day.

They eventually headed to the Fair Grounds to look over the horses that were going to be auctioned off the next day. From the beginning Buck was very impressed by Jennifer's knowledge about horses and the ease she showed around the stables. He was glad she came along to help in case he actually found a horse he wanted to bid on. Her opinion was going to have a strong impact on his decision making. No matter how long he'd worked with horses, he always felt horse auctions like these required all the information and insights he could get. After seeing the quality of the Olson horses in the photographs of her family's ranch, he thought Jennifer just might give him an edge and that made him feel good. Somehow he trusted her and knew when it came to horses she was a serious student. Buck was looking for a mare he could ride, work cattle on, and eventually put into the brood mare band. He explained all of this to Jennifer, she understood, and he did something he rarely did with women he dated—he talked to her about horses, as an equal. There was no talking down to this cowgirl from South Dakota. It never occurred to him to do that and there is no question she would ever have tolerated it if he had. This was something she had grown up with.

As they walked up and down the rows of pens with horses of all colors and sizes...mares, fillies, colts, studs and geldings...they made a few notes in the catalog and marked several horses that might be interesting if the prices stayed within reason. That was always a problem at an auction. If you were looking for a good barrel horse, for example, and somebody's grandpa was bidding against you for his granddaughter, you might as well quit after the first bid. Grandpa was going to get that horse. But they both realized it could be like that for any horse for whatever reason. Buck figured they'd better set a price limit before they even entered the auction barn the next morning. He came up with a figure of $4,000 to $4,500 for a fully broke horse and Jennifer, who had arrived at about the same figure, said it seemed reasonable for the kind of mares they had just looked at.

"Buck, you know we can't predict horse prices and even guess how much you might really want a particular horse. But I suppose the dollar figure you've set is as close as we can estimate. Do you think you can stick to it?"

Buck smiled, mostly because he wasn't sure he could.

They both agreed the horse market was very strong although neither of them was sure why that was. Once they decided on an appropriate price they agreed it was getting late and since there wasn't much more they could accomplish at the horse pens, they headed back to the motel.

Buck took a leisurely route back to the motel...he was a little uneasy. He had no idea of what was going to happen next and the day had gone so well he just hoped it won't get all screwed up in a motel room. Once inside, he turned on the TV, took off his hat and boots and stretched out on the bed. Jennifer went to the bathroom, came out and joined Buck on the bed.

"It's been a long and wonderful day. I'm really tired and dirty." She leaned over, looked at Buck and gave him a kiss. "How about joining me for a long, hot shower—but only if you do great backs."

Buck was speechless for a moment.

"Sounds like a good idea to me. These rough old cowboy hands should sure do a wonderful job of exfoliating your skin." For some odd reason, Buck loved that word, 'exfoliating.'

They got up, headed to the bathroom and as the got there, Buck turned the dimmer switch on the lights down as low as he could get them. No sense in ruining the magic, the mystery of all this or what he hoped this would all be.

He was a little uncomfortable as he took off his shirt, jeans and his underwear. She was doing the same and even in the dim light he could see what a lovely, firm body she had.

As they entered the shower together, they felt the warm water cascading down on their skin as they held one another. They touched one another all over, exploring and enjoying every moment. It wasn't too long before they had both satisfied each other even though they hadn't had intercourse. Buck didn't know what that meant but he felt so good he wasn't going to question anything. He was sure he didn't want to let her go. Jennifer seemed happy and she sure wasn't complaining. Had they passed an important point or had they merely postponed it in a very satisfying way? They lingered in the shower, holding on to each other and touching in the most gentle of ways. Buck just didn't know what to make of all this beyond the extremely sensual pleasure he felt then and there.

Getting ready for bed was very relaxed. As they climbed under the covers, they held one another affectionately and watched some old black and white movie on TV without really saying much. Then it happened. Buck hated these conversations and did everything he could to avoid them but this one was going to happen. Buck could almost feel it coming in the way Jennifer was holding him. She took the clicker and turned off the television.

"Joel, I've got to tell you some things. I know you'll think I'm crazy but I can't be dishonest with you, not now, not after the past few days, and certainly not after what happened in the shower. I think we've gone as far as we can go for a while and I'm not sure what to do." She paused for a moment, almost visibly searching for her next words. "I broke up with my boyfriend just before I moved to Missoula. We were engaged and were supposed to get married last summer. Right before I headed to the university. I think about him sometimes and I really don't know how I feel about him." She paused for a moment then added, "But I do know how I feel about you."

Buck just relaxed as much as he could, already fearing the worst but somehow, he wasn't surprised or even made uncomfortable by Jennifer's heartfelt confession.

"I'm so confused about us and I don't know what I'd do if he called and said he was coming over to see me or if he wanted me to meet him in Minneapolis where he works. I have been thinking about him. I'm also a little embarrassed about how we've acted before I told you all this. I'm sure you don't think very much of me right now. And for God's sakes, please don't think I was leading you on because I was lonely or anything else like that. I really do care a great deal about you. So much that it surprises and unnerves me."

Buck was silent for a minute or two. He had to let this all sink in and figure out how he felt. He wanted to digest what Jennifer had just said and he had to get rid of the thought that this little talk seemed like a very old cliché. All he could think about was these conversations and confessions were the essence of bad movies or romance novels. If real life was imitating bad art he didn't want to be part of it.

At first he didn't say anything. Then slowly—he wanted to make sure what he said actually made some sense—he tried to assure her everything was close to be being alright.

"I don't think you have to worry about us. We've just met, we are very attracted to one another and there's plenty of trail for us to travel before we have to get too serious. You have some things to sort out and now I do, too. Problems like this have a way of working out, on their own. You can't try to manipulate everything. I'll still be here with you, at least until both of us figure out what we want." As he talked he ran his fingers through her golden hair but could feel her body quivering. Buck wasn't sure he believed everything he had just said but at least for the time being, and surely for the rest of the weekend, he wanted things to remain as calm as possible. He honestly didn't know how he felt beyond the incredible lust they obviously shared. And that just wasn't going to be good enough for the long term. Besides, he hadn't told Jennifer the details about his plans to leave the university, head for New Mexico, ranch and write full time. And he certainly hadn't told her how he felt about having children. He couldn't even imagine how she would feel about all of that, but down deep he realized it would really unnerve her and probably push her away and back to her ex fiancé in Minneapolis.

"What should we do? Do we keeping on seeing one another the same way or do you want to end this now? I'll try to understand if you don't want to see me but I won't be happy." As she spoke she seemed so sad.

"Right now I don't know what to say or what to do. You can guess I want to continue to be with you but I think we'll just have to be patient and see what happens and how we feel. I know we can't force this. Jennifer, relax. The world isn't coming to an end and we might as well enjoy the rest of the weekend. Who knows, by Sunday this might all be resolved." He had no idea of why he said that or what he even meant, but it just seemed to pop out of his mouth.

When Buck uttered his last remark Jennifer was a little stunned. How, she wondered, could this all be resolved by Sunday? She didn't say a word. She just stared at Buck. Buck could only muster a weak little smile.

Buck knew this wasn't very reassuring but he was surprised at how she was acting. Where was that sassy, self-assured cowgirl/professor, the one who could really dish it out? Jennifer had become another of those insecure, cloying women he had not the slightest interest in spending time with. Which one was the real Jennifer? He knew he didn't want to just end this relationship but he was absolutely sure there was nowhere for him to go in a relationship that had another man lurking on the edges. He really didn't know what to say to her that would make her feel better or for that matter, even make him feel better. Besides the usual "Don't worry, everything will be alright," he was at a complete loss for words.

He put his arms around his sleeping partner, hugged her as lovingly as he could, making sure the lust that was such an intricate part of their relationship was absent from the embrace. He really didn't want to talk any more. In fact, he wanted her to go to sleep so he could get some shuteye and maybe the morning would get there fast. He was sure the horse sale would distract them both, at least until tomorrow night and already he wasn't looking forward to that.

■■■

They got up early, dressed, took quick separate showers, and headed out for breakfast. Buck knew of a little greasy spoon on the way to the Fair Grounds and they decided that was a good way to start the morning and get ready for a long day of sitting on hard seats in a dreary, chilly building and looking at horses.

Breakfast was steak and eggs for Buck and bacon and eggs for Jennifer. Several cups of hot coffee—that's what it was called on the menu, but it sure wasn't good old cowboy Arbuckles'—and they were ready to see some horses. Not a word had been said about last night and they both acted as if it had never happened. That was probably the best thing. Buck wanted to concentrate on horses and he did have a way of dealing with his own denial. It was hard to tell what Jennifer was thinking. She was still trying to be close. She sat as near to Buck as she could get in the front seat of the pickup with a tight grip around his arm. By morning she had regained the composure of the Jennifer Buck was so taken with.

Once they got to the Fair Grounds they headed directly for the horse pens. They still had some time before the sales was set to begin, so they wandered among the stalls trying to find the horses they had tagged in the catalog the night before. They were also trying to spot any they had missed and all the horses they would potentially bid on. Buck was always excited at this stage of a horse sale because it was so unpredictable. He didn't know how many buyers would be there, who they were or what they were looking for. And he wasn't sure that when push came to shove how committed he was to actually buying one of the mares. He hadn't quite figured out how many horses he wanted to take to New Mexico when and if he left and even the uncertainty of that was a little unnerving. Walking up and down the alleys, he was very serious. But this was serious business. Coughing up some thousands of dollars wasn't something a rancher did easily, especially for horses. It was always easier to figure the return on cattle and watch the daily prices at the cattle auctions. Horses were an entirely different game. Buying and selling horses was much more of a gamble, and you normally had to wait a few years before you could do anything with them—and this was especially true if you started with them as colts or fillies. Ranchers would rather buy well broke horses than babies they had to feed for a year or two before they could get them into training and actually use them on the ranch.

As they continued up and down the alleys between the pens, Buck met a few cowboy friends, introduced Jennifer, saw their reaction to this beautiful woman, as they made some small talk. These were not close friends, just guys he knew from cattle board meetings, other horse sales, the rodeo circuit, and one was even a former student. But they were all from Buck's world of cowboys and ranching and they were all potential competitors once the bidding began.

At about 9:45 the bell rang to announce the beginning of the ten o'clock sale. Everyone out by the pens hustled inside to get their seat in the spacious horse barn. The ring men, all wearing freshly starched shirts with ties, khaki western pants, and even newer looking felt hats, were visiting with some of the buyers trying to get a line on how they would be bidding, and where they would be seating. The auctioneer was testing the mikes. The pedigree announcer, in a corner by himself, was looking over his papers and videos to make sure he had all the information available to him so he could present each horse in the most favorable light. Almost all of the horses in the sale were registered quarter horses so the pedigrees were important. The buyers, and they seemed to be a cowboy crowd, knew all about Poco Bueno, Doc Bar, Doc O'Lena, Smoking Colonel, Easy Jet, Poco Tivio, Quixote, Mr. San Peppy, Music Mount, Three Bars, Skipper W and all the other great blood lines that showed up at the better working cowboy horse sales. It was just a matter of knowing exactly what you were looking for and Buck knew exactly what he was looking for. He wanted a good cow horse that came from cutting stock and with some speed. There seemed to be quite a few horses bred that way in the Great Falls sale. This was not a sale if you were looking for race horses or even gentle trail horses. These horses were performance stock horses—ropers, cutters, reiners, working cow horses and all around ranch horses and breeding stock. Now all he had to do was to figure out how much this was going to cost. He was absolutely firm he would not go over his budget, something he usually did at these good horse sales. He didn't want to be caught in the trap that when the adrenalin started to flow as he bid and then he began to think of the horse as his own. Before he knew it he had become determined not to let anyone else have that horse. It seems so foolish stated that way but that's how things got. And if the auctioneer is good, and "Skeeter" Jones was damn good, Great Falls was going to be a hard sale.

The first horse was a good looking five year old, well bred buckskin gelding with Doc O'Lena and Mr. San Peppy breeding. He had been used on a ranch and roped off. Cowboys liked buckskins because they are reputed to be so tough. Buck thought this gelding would give a pretty good indication about how much the horses were going to bring. As he was trying to figure out what a horse like this would cost, Jennifer nudged Buck to let him know she thought this was a good horse. He was pleased that from the outset they were in sync although he wasn't looking for geldings. At a sale like this, geldings usually brought more than mares because of the old ranch prejudice that no rancher wanted mares for work. They were only for the brood mare band. Buck thought this was downright foolish but that's the way it was and it had been that way for a long time.

The bidding was lively...there were quite a few hands going up and when it was over the horse went for $8,800. Buck and Jennifer had a quick discussion and they agreed that maybe that wasn't a bad price although a little on the high side but sometimes the first horse just releases all the pressure the buyers have, with money burning holes in their pockets, and the prices get a little out of hand. Or, they can go cheap because no one wants to open the bidding. Today Buck thought it went just a bit on the high side.

"Let's see what happens when a good mare comes up. You know how these damn cowboys are. Just rope, rope, and rope. It's either for ranch work or they all think they'll hit the rodeo circuit as calf ropers or team ropers and make it to the NFR. Or maybe they'll be cutters. I guess the dream never dies."

Buck sounded like a cynic but in his own way he actually admired those mostly young cowboys. He had good memories of the parts of seven years he spent on the rodeo circuit and like most former rodeo cowboys he missed the life and would until the day he died.

"Don't be so darn negative. You're one of those cowboys even though you want to sell them horses rather than rope yourself. It's the same with barrel horses. Every girl has a dream and I think it's wonderful." Jennifer squeezed his arm and gave him a quick kiss on the cheek. Buck felt real good for himself and was happy for all the cowboys.

The next few horses brought pretty realistic prices. Those that came with a video showing the horse working either in an arena or out in a pasture brought a little more than those horses without a video but that was par for the course. With the video you got a better chance to actually see what the horse could do and it could really live up to the hype the owner had brought with it. The videos took some of the gamble out of the bidding.

The day passed quickly. Buck and Jennifer bid every now and then but not very seriously. The prices stayed surprisingly strong. The good geldings were averaging a little more than $7,500 and the well broke mares a little less. And the whole time Buck was trying, with all his will to stay at his predetermined price range. By late afternoon the two professors decided that because of the time they'd just as soon leave. There weren't any horses coming up that they had noted in their catalog and they didn't want to buy a horse just out of desperation or frustration. This wasn't the first horse sale Buck had left with an empty horse trailer. It also became very apparent that this wasn't the first horse sale Jennifer had sat through as he watched as she carefully analyzed the stock as each horse was led into the arena by either a handler or the owner. For Buck it was a relief not having to spend any money, particularly on a horse he really didn't need.

When they stepped outside, they were both a little surprised at how dark it had gotten.

"Jesus, I didn't realize how late it was. Where the hell did the day go?"

Jennifer smiled at him. "That's what happens when you become so darn involved in such serious business as buying horses. And you didn't even buy anything."

■■■

The day was over and now Buck had to face that night at the motel. He considered heading back to Missoula but he really didn't want to drive home in the dark, pulling the empty horse trailer on the narrow, windy roads, drop Jennifer off in Missoula and then have to drive down the Bitterroot to the ranch. So Saturday night in Great Falls it was going to be. The thought of another confessional didn't have too much appeal for Buck and he was as sure as he could be that he was going to hear it all over again. Jennifer had been terrific all day and that's what bothered him. Would she feel the need once again to apologize for being so close when maybe she didn't mean to be? Who knew what she was thinking? Certainly it wasn't Buck.

They had dinner at one of those Chinese all-you-can eat buffets. It seemed to Buck that every town in the West, from Montana to the Mexican border, had one of those buffets and they were all about the same. He loved them although it was actually Jennifer who had suggested they head there for dinner.

After a good meal, or at least a filling meal, where Buck really stuffed himself, they headed back to the motel. Jennifer turned on the TV, and for a while they tried to watch some awful sitcom and pretend things were just fine and that there was nothing but smooth sailing ahead for the evening. They both knew it wasn't that way but it seemed neither of them knew exactly how to handle what was inevitable.

The evening drifted by quietly although it could hardly be described as relaxed. After turning off the sitcom they switched to CNN and commiserated with one another about the state of the world, the government, which they both thought was leaning too far to the right, all the strange people that appeared on the screen, and other events that seemed to absorb television news. Finally, it was time for bed and as they snuggled under the covers, Buck decided it was time to do something to break the awkwardness of the moment, even if it went against his best instincts. It would have to be his turn to do some honest talking. It was either that or another wonderful shower. For reasons he did not understand, he chose talk.

"You were straight with me last night and I guess there are things you need to know about me. Maybe this isn't the time or place but it sure as hell will be better than us pretending nothing happened last night. I don't want any more tension building up between us as long as we continue to see one another." He was quiet for a moment, waiting to see if Jennifer was gong to say anything. When she remained silent, he continued, "You know I've been divorced but I doubt if you know the reason. To start with..."

"You know you don't have to do this. It's none of my business and I don't want you feeling guilty because I was a little out of control last night."

"No. Really! I don't feel guilty and I want to tell you. These are things you should know. First, I'm probably planning on leaving the university at the end of the year. I would rather ranch and in all the years I've been at the university do you know I can't remember ever having had more than one or two faculty members to my house for dinner or any other social event. My close friends aren't in Missoula. They aren't at the university. I want to spend more time ranching and writing. I can't begin to tell you how difficult it is for me to leave the ranch and go to Missoula even though now it's rarely more than just three times a week."

"Are you kidding? Why are you telling me this? Do you think it will make me feel better because you want to be a rancher? Are you really going to quit and lose your tenure, benefits, and all the other perks it has taken you so long to get? You're a senior faculty member for God's sake."

"That doesn't matter. The other bit of news is that I want to go back to New Mexico and enjoy the sun and good weather all year long. I've been looking at ranches down there for almost a year and I've got one picked out I'm thinking about seriously negotiating for. I love the desert and I admire the people and especially the culture in the southwest. How would you feel about packing up and heading to New Mexico?"

Jennifer appeared to be a little stunned. Buck could sense the tension in her body as her dazzling blue eyes clouded a bit and she seemed very unsure of herself when she finally spoke.

"For God's sake, I knew you loved New Mexico but I didn't realize how far along you were with your plans. This comes right out of the blue for me. I don't know the slightest thing about the southwest. I've never been there and no, I don't think I want to move there, at least right now."

Buck sat up a little more erect, as if to command the most attention for his next few comments. Then he continued:

"And there's one more thing. This might be the most important and was as much to do with my marriage breaking up as anything else. I'm not good father material. I don't think I want to have children. In fact, I know I don't want to have children. Like the old cowboy saying goes, 'I was traveling fast and light like an old time buckaroo.' I feel like that. I just want to be free to just go where I need to go, whenever I get the urge."

Jennifer sat up and looked at Buck with an almost glazed stare.

"Jesus! That's almost too much to think about and I'm not sure I'm even capable of understanding all of this right now. I guess down deep I knew some of it but to hear it all at once is pretty overwhelming. I don't know what to say or to think. I'm not even sure what it is you're telling me."

"You don't have to say or do anything. I just wanted you to know where I am right now. I could really care for you and I could even envision us being together. But you know as well as I do you want to pursue your career, have children and live happily ever after. And I don't mean that to be funny and I'm certainly not mocking you. I think I know you well enough to know this is what you want and I think maybe I even envy you. I haven't the slightest idea of whether or not I'm doing the right thing or the smart thing. I just know it's just what I have to do. Maybe in a year or so I'll be begging to come back to Missoula. I doubt it but it is a possibility."

You could almost see the fire in Jennifer's blazing blue eyes when she heard that.

"First of all, you don't know what I think or what I want. I'm not sure myself. But I know I can't leave Missoula now to go to New Mexico or any place else. I have other issues to work out. You know that. And God damn it, I do want to have children. Not right now, but I've always wanted to have children."

"There. Now that we've got that all out in the open I feel better and I 'm glad I've seen you with that kind of passion. I think I'm right the way I have all of this figured out. You are a terrific woman and if not me, you sure are going to make some man a very happy fellow."

Jennifer seemed to calm down a little. "You know I adore you. It's just that I can't just shift gears that way you have. I would need so much more time and I don't think you're the waiting type."

Buck was puzzled for a moment. What does 'adore' mean or at least, what did Jennifer mean? Was that a substitute for something else or did it have its own meaning and that's all?

"I don't know exactly what it means, but I guess I adore you too."

Jennifer laughed to herself but decided to let that go. This had all happened in such a short time but they had said what they had to say, there didn't seem to be any anger or animosity and neither of them made any effort to pull away. It would be alright to let lust rule for a time. That was much more than either of them had the right to expect after this weekend and the way they unburdened themselves to each other.

For both Buck and Jennifer it was as if a big weight had been lifted. They really began to snuggle. Buck loved the smoothness and the firmness of her body and the way she made him feel when she touched him. Before the night was over they had actually made love in a way neither of them expected. More intimate and more tender than even before—more intense and more sexual. But underneath it all, there remained unspoken feelings that this was all over. Maybe it was the last time that they would be together like this.

■■■

Early next morning, after they had showered together, and after breakfast at the same greasy spoon as yesterday, they headed over to the Fair Grounds. They weren't in any particular hurry so they had time to visit with a few of the cowboys and brand inspectors doing the paper work for the horses that had been sold. After a while they proceeded to hook up the horse trailer. It didn't take them long to get back on the road and they tried to act as if nothing awkward had happened during the past two days and that everything was fine. Well, it wasn't and Buck just didn't know what to make of it all. Had he just let go of a relationship that had all the potential to be wonderful? He was again brought to the realization that his long held dreams, mostly about New Mexico, meant so much to him had such an impact on his behavior. He was sure time would eventually help sort all of this out and he would have some of the answers but on the trip back from Great Falls to Missoula he felt empty and very alone. Buck sensed Jennifer was feeling something very similar. Neither of them talked about it and they never made that stop at the Hutterite colony to get their chickens.

■■■

They arrived back in Missoula early in the afternoon and parked the rig in a lot near a small picnic area close to Jennifer's and the river. Hand in hand they walked over to Jennifer's car and for lunch they drove to the Missoula Valley Tavern, an old fashioned bar down town. This old tavern served the best hamburgers in the world if you liked them thick and juicy, washed down with a cold, draught beer and you enjoyed sitting at the bar. They both did.

Once lunch was over, Jennifer drove Buck back to the truck and trailer. They hugged and kissed and Buck headed toward Stevensville. They made no specific plans to see one another again, and parted as if they lived just down the street from one another.

■■■

As Buck headed south he couldn't get things squared away in his own head. He missed Jennifer already but sensed somehow they weren't destined to be together. He tried to think about getting home, seeing Cowboy, checking the stock and getting back to his usual routine. He knew he had to be at the university the next day but what he really wanted to do was saddle up and head for the mountain lakes above the ranch. He felt the need to be alone, to think and figure out what was happening to his life. Unfortunately that would have to wait.

When he finally got home he was enthusiastically greet by Cowboy. He was as glad to be home as Cowboy was to see him. Everything looked in order and he thought it was still early enough to saddle up and check the horses and the cattle in the close pastures even if he really didn't have to do it. Unpacking and unhooking the horse trailer could wait.

When he got into the house he called his neighbor to let him know he was home and thank him. Then he checked his answering machine and after a few routine messages from a variety of people, he heard the voice of his good friend, Steve Anderson, a rancher up in the Big Hole country, south of Stevensville, very close to the Idaho border. Steve wanted Buck to come up to the ranch the next weekend and help with the fall gather and shipping. Buck couldn't have been happier. A couple of days in the saddle gathering cattle with some good cowboys away from his own spread—that was just what he needed. He called Steve as soon as the messages were finished and told his old friend he would come up as early on Friday as he could get there and work the weekend.

When he hung up he changed clothes, put on an old pair of boots, his spurs and grabbed his batwing chaps. Cowboy jumped up and down because he was also excited about checking the horses and the cattle. This is what cow dogs were born to do and Cowboy did it as well as any of them. On a ranch like the Palo Verde, Cowboy did the work of two or three cowboys. Outsiders never could figure out why ranch dogs were so valuable.

As the two partners left the house, they headed over to the small horse pasture where Buck kept a couple of saddle horses. He put a halter on a red dun gelding he had raised from a foal and trained himself, led him over to the small barn and saddled him. Once in the saddle Buck and Cowboy trotted over to the lower pasture where some heifers were grazing and everything looked just the way it was supposed to. There were no new signs of bear, or mountain lion or even a coyote. Next they headed to the horse pasture where everything seemed normal. It was still too early in the season to be winter feeding full time although Buck grained the horses he used regularly and was beginning to put out hay and even a little cake, to the cattle. This had been a mild year and there was still plenty of graze in the winter pastures. The horses were showing the beginnings of their heavy winter coats and Buck knew it wouldn't be too long before he'd be putting hay out on a regular basis. Winter was still going to come to Montana with a vengeance. This year he had gotten his hay in big round bales from a good rancher friend across the valley, over by the Sunset Bench. With the addition of the metal round bale feeders, Buck was looking forward to only having to put new hay out every few days instead of every day. The big, round bales lasted much longer than the smaller, two strand, rectangular bales he had been using for years. Of course he had to make sure the tractor would start because moving the round bales without it could be a pain in the ass. In fact, without the tractor it would be impossible. But anything was better than trying to feed in 30 below weather and Buck had actually faced 70 and 80 below wind chill at the ranch several years ago. He had never forgotten that time and how difficult everything was. In those conditions the good life rapidly became a trial for survival. There was a very small margin for error. Maybe that's what was making New Mexico so appealing.

The more he examined his pastures and thought about the coming winter, the surer he was this was going to be his last one in Montana.

Getting back to the barn after a short but therapeutic ride, he unsaddled "Poco," turned him out and made sure the gates were closed. In the house again, after starting a fire in the living room stove, Buck realized he had to think about dinner and doing some preparation for his classes on Monday. The preparation was easy. He had his undergraduate courses in Regionalism and The Western in Film and Literature, and his graduate seminar on The Art of Russell and Remington that was very popular with both art history majors and students of the West. He just wished he had his own graduate students in American Studies so he could explore more sophisticated subjects at a higher level. But he also knew budgetary considerations made that impossible, at least for the short term. Fortunately he had selected all the slides he'd need for his classes last Friday morning so he was all set. He had taught all three classes before and knew the material very well. It was dinner that posed the problem.

He prowled around the kitchen, took out a couple of eggs and some bacon and salami and went to work. Cooking was not Buck's strong suit. If it was up to him every meal would be either breakfast or some sort of beef cooked outside on the grill. But he had to eat so he turned the TV on to the new Encore Westerns Channel as he prepared his "breakfast," and got himself involved in some old Randolph Scott movie from the 1950s. He loved the old westerns, even the ones that were made before they became "adult westerns." Mostly he enjoyed the beautiful and rugged scenery and trying to figure out where the movies were shot and in times of stress he appreciated the fact that the good guys always won. It was reassuring.

After dinner and the conclusion of the movie, Buck settled in with Elmer Kelton's novel, "The Time It Never Rained," a good warm fire in the wood burning stove and some quiet. He debated about calling Jennifer but he didn't know what he actually wanted to say and he was fairly certain whatever had to be said next should be said in person, not over the phone. Maybe she would call him. But he couldn't get over his feelings of lust or of his desire t o make love to her again. He was sure if he didn't see her again, he would miss their new sexual intimacy as much as anything.

By the time he was ready for bed there had been no phone calls—incoming or out-going. That was probably just as well.

At the university the next day, Buck met his classes, and he managed not to run into Jennifer. He knew neither of them could keep avoiding the next meeting but it wasn't something he looked forward to. He still didn't know what to say or how he felt. He assumed she was having the same problems.

After meeting with several of his students in his office, Buck left his work study gal, Nancy Lundgren, a sophomore from Havre, a small town way up near the Bear Paw Mountains and the Canadian border, in charge of the office and he high tailed it out like some sort of thief in the night. He got into his car and headed for home. He knew this kind of sneaking around couldn't go on for very long and he determined to call Jennifer that night. It just seemed too awkward to see her on the campus where they would have no privacy to discuss whatever it was they had to discuss and yet he still felt awkward about having a serious conversation on the phone.

Settled in at home and finished with his chores, he just plopped down on the dark brown leather couch and sat there, staring out the big windows at the glorious Bitterroots with their early coating of snow way up on the peaks. It was scenes like that that gave him pause about moving to New Mexico or anywhere else. The longer he sat there, almost in a lingering reverie, the surer he was he should call Jennifer and just see where that conversation would go. He knew he could only put it off for so long. He took hold of the phone, held it for a minute or two and finally dialed her number.

"Hi. I'm sorry I missed you on campus today. I was so darn anxious to get home and catch up on my chores I tore out of there right after my classes."

"I thought you were avoiding me. I looked for you but I guess I wasn't fast enough."

There was one of those long, awkward pauses before Jennifer said, "I was just getting ready to call you. I really want to talk to you. Can I come down to the ranch? You know I've never been there and I'd love to see it. And down at the ranch we can have some privacy and quiet. I won't be coming to the lion's den, would I? No kidding, I want to see you and I want to come down to the Palo Verde Ranch in Stevensville."

Buck was completely caught off guard. Before he could answer, Jennifer added, "Don't be a chicken. I won't bite."

"Okay. We've got a date. When do you want to head on down? Why not make it Saturday and then we'll be free and I'll have plenty of time to show you around. And bring some riding cloths. I do things horseback down here."

He went on to give her directions and added some small talk to try and ease whatever tension had built up.

As they were about to hang up, Jennifer said ever so softly, "Thanks, Joel. I can't wait to see you."

"Wait. Wait. I just forgot. I can't see you Saturday. I told a friend of mine I would go up to the Big Hole and help with the fall round up and shipping. I'm leaving early Friday as soon as I get home and get packed. Shit, I'm sorry."

"Are you avoiding me or are you being honest with me?"

"Honest, that's the truth. Why don't you come down on Thursday? You're finished your classes in the morning and if you can get here early enough we can still ride. I'm really sorry but I just plain forgot."

"Okay cowboy, I'll see you Thursday. I should be there a little after twelve."

"Good."

Buck repeated the directions and when they hung up he laughed, told "Cowboy" they were going to have guests and headed off to bed. He was sure he wanted to see Jennifer and it definitely was going to be safer to see her at the ranch than somewhere at the university or anywhere else in Missoula.

■■■

The week went along without incident. Since it was the beginning of hunting season, Buck locked all his gates as he usually did each year to keep the stray hunters and the poachers off his place. Many were out of staters and they usually had no regard for the ranchers, opening gates and leaving them opened. Closing gates didn't seem to be a priority and Buck sure didn't want any of his cattle or horses shot by "mistake," mistaken for a mule deer or some other critter.

■■■

At the university, Wednesday was a teaching day and he did his job and headed home. It seemed that more and more he wanted to be at the ranch and spend as little time in Missoula as he could manage—only what was absolutely necessary. And since he enjoyed teaching he wasn't sure why. He couldn't figure out if Jennifer had something to do with it or that since he had definitely decided to leave the university, for all practical purposes he was already gone.

On Thursday Buck had finished his chores by a little after nine o'clock and was sitting on the deck having a cup of coffee with Cowboy, who was enjoying himself alongside Buck. It was a chilly and slightly overcast day but in the mountains that wasn't uncommon for that time of the year.

By around 12:15 he could hear Jennifer coming up the dirt road well before she arrived at the lower gate which he had unlocked for her. She was kicking up just enough dust so he could follow her trail and when she had to stop, get out, and open the gate, Buck felt badly because he had always wanted to replace that gate with a cattle guard.

As she closed the gate behind her, got back in her car and head up the last stretch of road, she was coming through a 30 acre horse pasture that was one of Buck's favorite places on the ranch. It had good grass with enough trees to create shade in the summer and form a wind-break in the winter so the horses didn't have to be put inside a barn each night. It was very much a protective barrier around most of the headquarters and it also created a private sanctuary for him.

When Jennifer arrived at the house she parked between Buck's two trucks and the Subaru and as she got out she couldn't help repeating herself. "This place is so beautiful. I can't believe you actually want to leave here." She must have said that several times before she added, "I'm so glad you invited me, even if I kind of invited myself."

They hugged, gave one another gentle kisses and just stared at each other for a brief moment.

"Very few people are invited here. This really is my private world and this isn't a place for drop-in visitors. The Palo Verde Ranch is off limits to virtually everyone. I know that probably sounds a little odd but that has kept me sane. It's never lonely for me up here. Come on, I'll show you around. But you know all about ranching and how things are set up."

"Not like this I don't. Back home, the only mountains we see are the Black Hills, and they are way off, far off on the horizon. To us the horizon just provides a vague reminder that the mountains actually exist. We're out on the prairie. Here you're an intricate part of the entire landscape and you're right in the heart of the whole environment. You really do belong here. Now I can understand and I can see why you don't want to come to town any more than you have to. This is a very impressive place."

Buck didn't say anything. Then, "Come on, hop in the truck. I'll show you some real scenery."

"Cowboy" jumped into the front seat of the red Dodge ranch truck with them, Jennifer sitting next to Buck and "Cowboy" taking over the partially opened window. They headed out the west gate near the house, up over Kootenai Creek on a bridge Jennifer was sure wouldn't hold a horse and rider no less a pickup, and drove up an old logging road until they got to a sign announcing they were only a short distance from the Selway-Bitterroot Wilderness boundary. Buck turned around and as they headed back to the house they could see across the valley, through the gray sky and the menacing clouds, to the Sapphire Mountains over on the east side. With the open meadows and trees in front and the towering Bitterroot peaks with their early season white snow caps reaching nearly 10,000 feet behind them, Jennifer was completely overwhelmed.

Back at the house, when they got out of the truck, Buck went inside to get Jennifer a jacket. At this time of the year and this late in the afternoon, it usually got pretty chill in the mountains. Today was no different. When she had left Missoula it was fairly warm and it never occurred to her it would be so much colder at the ranch. They walked around the outside of the house and the over to the barn and looked at some of the horses grazing in the horse pasture. Buck could see how relaxed and happy Jennifer was to be on a ranch again, at a place where she really did feel at home.

When the brief tour was over, they settled in the living room and Buck put on some Ian Tyson music. Jennifer strolled around the house, looking at a few western paintings and sculptures by artists who were members of the Cowboy Artists of America, some limited edition prints, several by Tucker Smith, a few finely woven Two Gray Hills Navajo rugs, and a fine collection of "cowboy collectibles," including an antique 1890s saddle on a stand by the big picture window. And of course, there were photographs of Buck on bucking horses from his rodeo days and at work doing a variety of ranch chores and with other cowboy crews. There were also photos of his parents, his sister and her husband and their two sons, plus shelves of books. Even as the sun was setting, Jennifer was aware of how light and open the house was and how the environment protected it.

In some ways Jennifer thought that this is exactly how Buck would live, what there would be in Buck's home, and yet she was surprised. She didn't know why but she began to realize that Buck talked about a lot of things but very little about his private life or the personal things that meant so much to him. Other than wanting to ranch, move back to New Mexico, and not have children, there were so many pieces missing from the puzzle he had created. He was someone you knew but you didn't really get to know very well, at least she hadn't been able to in their relatively short time together. That bothered her but she knew there wasn't anything she could do about it.

By then it was getting late in the afternoon and Buck asked Jennifer if she wanted to stay for dinner. She laughed. "Are you cooking? Is that safe?"

"Hell, I cook for myself every day and I'm still here. I'll show you how to cook on that grill out there. But it's up to you."

"You know darn well I'm going to stay. I wouldn't miss this for anything."

They had a beer, listened to more Ian Tyson and talked easily, a good deal about ranching, and without any tension. But that would all come later, Buck was certain of that.

He went out to the deck, put on the coals and came inside to get things ready. He took two thawed steaks from the refrigerator—he had taken them from the freezer that morning just in case—along with a couple of late season ears of corn and he was ready to go.

"What about a salad?" Jennifer got no answer so she went to the refrigerator and took out the makings, placing everything on the spacious countertop, and began to create one herself. She was a little surprised Buck even had the ingredients, or the salad bowl or the utensils.

Buck knew it would be a while before the coals were ready so he turned off the stereo and put on the TV on to see if the evening news and weather were on. After Jennifer finished with the salad and put it in the refrigerator, she joined him on the couch and even though she cuddled up in his arms, they both got slightly depressed watching all the murders, rapes and other hostile acts of civilization while they were comfortably settled in an area that was far removed from all the danger in the cities. They were in a place many would consider a sort of paradise. This was the part of his romantic world Buck never wanted to leave.

When the coals were ready, Buck put the steaks and corn on the grill, cooking the one way he actually knew and enjoyed. As the sun went down it got cold outside but that didn't dampen his enthusiasm one bit. Jennifer ordered a medium rare and since Buck liked it the same way it made his cooking job that much easier. Inside, the roaring fire in the wood stove kept the house warm and comfortable.

When everything was ready, they sat down to a dinner in a house warmed by the wood stove and filled with the aroma that came both from the wood stove and the grill fired up with real coals. Buck wouldn't have one of those "fake" propane gas grills on his place. Somehow it just didn't fit into his lifestyle.

After the two finished their dinner, Jennifer insisted on washing the dishes. Buck let her take command of the kitchen and he took up the role as wiper. They worked together like a real team and the chores were done in no time. Buck said he had to go out before it got pitch dark to check on things and just give the horse pasture a once over. He probably didn't have to do any of that but he did want to get out of the house to postpone whatever was next in coming. Jennifer insisted on joining him and they completed the evening outdoor look over fairly fast and with a very easy feeling that had surprisingly come over both of them.

Back in the house, as they settled in, Jennifer went over to Buck's extensive record collection and pulled out some Mozart and put it on the old stereo. Now was a time to sit back and to just relax. Everything that had to be done was completed and the evening was free. At least Buck hoped so.

But it didn't turn out that way. As the music took over the room, Jennifer slid closer to Buck on the couch and softly asked:

"Buck, are we going to talk? I came down because I wanted to see you but there is also so much we have to talk about, so much hasn't been said, starting with our future together or if there is even going to be one. I don't know what to do or what to say and I definitely haven't resolved any of my own problems. We never finished talking when we were over in Great Falls."

Buck was absolutely certain he wasn't going to let this get out of hand. Before Jennifer could say another word, he interrupted:

"I think there are certain things you know already but really don't want to face. Let me start at the beginning, again. First, I told you I was planning on resigning from the university. I want to give President Gaines my letter next week. I also plan to leave for New Mexico as soon as the school year ends and my obligations at the university are over. When the spring branding is completed I'll be gone. I've had several serious inquiries on this place and I've been in negotiations for a place in very southwestern New Mexico, the area they call the Bootheel. A lot of that will depend on money and how much I can clear when I sell this ranch. The prices here are so much higher up here than in very southern New Mexico that I should be able to take the money from this place and buy just about anything I need down there."

Jennifer sat on the couch not knowing how she felt or what to say. Buck sounded so cold. He sounded like a real estate agent. And there didn't seem to be any role in these future moves for her, even if she wanted one, and she didn't know if she even did.

"But Jen, you know the rest. I'm not getting any younger and things haven't changed about me having kids. They just don't fit into my plans. Even if I wanted to have kids, I'd be in my mid 40s by the time one arrived and who wants their father to be in his late sixties when he graduates from college? And what about our own age difference?"

"You are being so damn foolish. I didn't know we were planning on having children? What has all of this got to do with anything? Why are you trying to put so much distance between us?"

"It's got everything to do with us. I know you want to have children. And I doubt you want to give up your promising academic career to go traipsing off to the desert. You're starting your career as an Assistant Professor and do you want to just forget all the hard work you've put in to get where you are? I've asked around, I've asked some of the students, and they say you are a good teacher. You know, sometimes romance has to come to grips with reality, and in the end reality always wins. You are being romantic but not very realistic."

"Look who's talking. You're the romantic. I don't think I've ever met a real cowboy who wasn't. You all live your life with those romantic dreams, about life as you want it not as it is. How it was hundred years ago. When was the last time you were very realistic?"

"I guess right now!"

Neither of them said anything for a long few seconds and Buck could see Jennifer was becoming a little teary eyed. He felt badly because he cared for her but he knew, down deep, he was right about all of this.

"Joel, I told you I adore you and I don't want tonight to be our last time together. Why can't we continue to see one another, at least until the end of the school year, and see what happens?"

"What happens? How about when you have to make a trip to Minneapolis, when you're ex calls, or you realize how badly you really do want children, or how much your career means to you? These are big deals. How do we handle all of this when you know my mind is made up about the future and for me there is no turning back?"

"I don't know. Right now I couldn't decide whether or not to wear a coat outside in below freezing weather. I admit I'm sort of a mess but I want this to play out. Will you give it a try?"

"I'm not even sure what that means. What do think can 'play out?' And give what a try? That we continue to see one another even though we both know how it will end?"

Buck tried to be calm and let Jennifer know he cared for her but he was determined to get down to the basics so there wouldn't be any confusion about his goals and his immediate plans.

Jennifer was silent again. She was crying now because she sensed he was right and she didn't want him to be. Buck sat and looked at her, wishing she'd go home and wanting her more than he ever remembered wanting a woman in a long time. He had no better idea of what to do right then and there than she did. He really was bewildered with how this was turning out.

She wiped her eyes, sat up and aimed those blue eyes right at Buck. "I think I'm going to stay with you tonight."

"You're what?" Buck felt his body react with all the excitement of a high school kid about to have his first sexual encounter.

"You heard me. Since we are going to take this step by step, at least I hope we are, and not worry too much about what's going to happen tomorrow, I thought I'd like to stay over. I want to see you get out of bed in the morning when it's so cold and build a fire. I want you to make me coffee. And I just want you right now, tonight. Who knows what will happen tomorrow?"

"What the hell. I'd be one big ass liar if I told you I didn't want you to stay. This is going to be a helluva night." He paused for a moment and then with a big smile he added, "And why do you think I'll get up and make the coffee. I can show you how to work the coffee maker now so you'll be very comfortable doing it in the morning."

"Not on your life. Lend me a tooth brush and a t-shirt and let's go to bed." When she got up and started for the bedroom Buck thought she just might be one of the most beautiful women he had ever known.

They made love that night for what seemed like hours. There wasn't a part of her body he didn't want to touch or taste. It was as if a dam had broken. Maybe they just had to get past tonight and relax and there was no question about them having relaxed. Neither Buck nor Jennifer got much sleep and they both had to be in Missoula early in the morning to meet their classes.

■■■

When the sun began its slow rise over the Sapphire Mountains and eased its way thru the large windows on the east side to light up the house, they were both happy and groggy. Jennifer got up first, put on Buck's heavy blue and white bathrobe, the one with the hood, and sat by the big window in the living room with her freshly brewed coffee. She watched the red glow of the early morning come up over the mountains across the valley and gradually light up the forest as it rose above the broad horizon.

Once Buck had gotten up and stoked the wood stove and they were both up and moving, it was rush, rush, rush. Buck had the earlier class but they left the ranch at about the same time.

■■■

Late in the morning, when he finally got back home, he took a quick look around the ranch to make sure everything was secure before he left. Although he hadn't gotten much sleep the night before he was alert and ready to go and he collected the gear he had assembled for his weekend up at the Anderson Ranch. If there was ever a time Buck needed some time in the saddle with his cowboy friends, it was now. And Steve Anderson was the only rancher who let Buck bring Cowboy when he went to work. Most of Buck's other rancher friends, and it was true all over the West, didn't want another cowboy's dog around. They can cause trouble, particularly when the owner has his own dogs and they become territorial. But Buck knew the ranch and usually Steve had him work alone or with just one other cowboy for a good part of the gather. Steve's own cow dog was old and had arthritis so he wasn't much help on the roundups any more. In fact, he mostly stayed around the house and slept. Steve was in the process of getting a couple of new dogs but he hadn't made any decision yet. Cowboy would be alone with Buck and would be a big help and he was always a good companion.

Buck didn't have to bring a horse to the Anderson ranch. Steve's remuda was replete with good quarter horses, all raised in open pastures and trained working with cattle. Because he had been to the ranch so often, Buck had a couple of favorites he liked to ride when he was up at there. The Triangle A horses covered lots of miles each year chasing cows in the hilly and mountainous country and they were always in shape.

Buck was anxious to get going. He threw his duffel, a good warm winter coat along with his saddle, chaps, and some dog food into the pickup, called Cowboy to jump in and off they went, down the bumpy dirt road and finally onto the smooth paved highway that would lead them south to Lost Trail Pass. Then it was east to the Big Hole. The Anderson's Triangle A was about four miles from Wisdom and then down a dirt road for about half a mile to headquarters. The ride was glorious at this time of the year. The air was quiet, the aspens had turned golden and were already shedding their leaves, the skies were a deep blue and all the large beaver slide haystacks in the fields were full and were fenced off to protect them from the deer, the elk and the occasional moose. The Big Hole country was already feeling the early stages of winter—they already had had some snow—and the Big Hole seemed to be from a different time, a time Buck was desperately trying to hold on to. There weren't many places left where the ranchers still put up the hay, stacked and fed it out in the winter with horse drawn equipment. They never baled their hay and they rarely, if ever, used tractors. This was cowboy country the way it was supposed to be.

The late Montana fall was Buck's favorite season, especially in the Big Hole where winter seemed to come at a least a month earlier and lasts a month longer than down in the Bitterroot. He had been part of both the Triangle A's spring branding and fall roundup crews for several years and during that time he and Steve had become good friends. Steve's wife, Mary Ann, was a wonderful woman...she was bright, attractive, a terrific conversationalist, very funny and a gracious hostess. Like many of the ranch women, she always treated the cowboys with respect and offered them the kind of warm hospitality so common on the good ranches. There wasn't a cowboy around who didn't want to work for the Triangle A.

Usually Buck stayed in the bunk house but on this trip Steve invited him to stay in the large main house with the family. Buck wasn't sure why he got the invitation because of all the bunk houses he had ever stayed in, the Triangle A's was by far the cleanest and best maintained. It had TV, got clear radio reception and there was a shelf of good books and magazines. The bathroom was clean and there was always plenty of hot water and the bunk beds were actually comfortable. But a couple of nights in the main house didn't seem like a bad idea. The bunk house was sure to be full considering the size of the crew Steve needed for the fall works.

As he was getting ready for dinner, Buck found the bowl he had brought and loaded it with food for Cowboy. He knew his good canine partner would be very content just sleeping in the room after he finished his dinner.

From his room Buck slowly ambled down the hallway toward the mess hall attached to the main house where dinner was awaiting the cowboys. Carol Jones, the cook, was a young gal, probably in her early thirties and fairly attractive, although her appearance was clearly not her top priority. She looked like she had put in a long, hard day getting the food ready for a crew of big eating, hard working cowboys.

Carol was an enigma of sorts. She had just showed up at the ranch one day several years ago and asked for a job. After a few trial meals she was hired but she remained something of a mystery woman. No one knew where she came from or what she was doing in the Big Hole. But she was one helluva cook and she ran a tight kitchen. During dinner the cowboys knew they had to take off their spurs, chaps, and hats and they had better watch their language. Carol wouldn't tolerate a lot of foul mouth cowboys in her mess hall, being disrespectful while eating her good food.

Among the cowboys seated around the large wood trestle table was Cody Jacobson, a cowboy who worked for Steve full time and who was rumored to be dating Carol. Cody lived in a refurbished historic log cabin down by a pond about a quarter of a mile from the main house. Although he grew up on a ranch in North Dakota, he thought the Triangle A was the best job he would ever have. He loved the country and working for Steve was a damn good deal for a cowboy. From the day he arrived, after drifting through several ranches in eastern Montana, Cody felt he belonged and wasn't looking to leave the Triangle A anytime soon.

Also seated around the table, getting ready to chow down, were the cowboys who came for the weekend—Dave Bradshaw, whose dad owned a good size cow/calf outfit over by Dillon, Bobby Trujillo, a top hand who worked many of the area ranches but seemed adverse to settling down anywhere, Phil Shaw, a kid from a good college back East who wanted to be a cowboy and had turned into a pretty good hand during his short time in Montana, Clint Henderson, a rancher's son from the Bitterroot who had finished junior college on a football scholarship and was getting ready to go to school at Montana State in Bozeman the next year to play football and finish his four year degree. Clint planned on returning to the family ranch after he finished at Bozeman. The last cowboy, TJ Parsons, a professional cowboy who had been doing this work most of his 56 years, was on loan from the Circle H ranch, one of Steve's Big Hole neighbors. TJ was a widower, his wife of 25 years, Peg, died of some sort of cancer a couple of years back and he went to work for Bud Hoffman at the Circle H. TJ was a throwback to the old time iterant cowboy. He had his first paying cowboy job when he was just past ten and most of his life as a cowboy he did seasonal work, moving all over Wyoming and Montana, even traveling to Arizona and New Mexico for winter work. He was good, so good in fact, that he wound up making a very good living doing day work and he was seldom without a job. Peg had helped out financially by doing some cooking at the various ranches they worked. What made it doubly good for the cowboy and his wife was that TJ and Peg got to travel and see country that otherwise they would have missed. He knew and Bud Hoffman both knew old TJ wasn't going to stay at the Circle H very long. It just wasn't in his nature to settle down like that.

By Buck's count, including Steve and his two teenage sons, there was going to be a crew of ten riders, a good number although Buck wouldn't have minded if there had been a couple more savvy hands. The guys Steve brought in for the roundup were all top cowboys, even Steve's two sons and Phil Shaw, the college cowboy. They were all experienced and the type of guys you could count on when you were riding in rough country and the Triangle A was a good test for both horse and rider. There were cattle up on the Forest Service lease and this crew would work hard getting them all down to the shipping pens, sorted, and ready for the trucks by Sunday afternoon. There really wasn't any margin for error. Steve, his two boys, and Cody had already spent the last couple of weeks driving the cattle out of the most inaccessible parts of the lease land so that the full gather could be accomplished in a weekend. The agreement with the Forest Service called for all the cattle to be out of the Beaverhead Forest by October 1.

These cowboys would be gathering somewhere around 550 pairs, cows with their calves, and once they had them in the pens the calves would be weaned, sorted and shipped. The mother cows would be sent back to winter pasture to calve in the spring, usually early April in the Big Hole, and then this would all happen again next year. The calves had been branded, inoculated, dehorned, and castrated in the early summer and then sent out to spend the next few months on the open range with their mommas. Once the fall roundup was over they would be leaving home, probably for a feed lot and eventually someone's dinner table. The rhythm of a ranch was so much like the waves on the ocean. It was perpetual but once you understood the rhythm it was extremely relaxing and very satisfying.

■■■

Carol's steak dinner lasted more than an hour, mostly because the cowboys enjoyed one another's company and the conversation was just as Buck expected. It started out as cowboy talk always started out—about horses, cattle, girls, trucks, guns, and the weather. It seems this conversation had been going on in some form among stock growers since the first teenagers, with switches and sticks in hand, herded their cows on foot in New England in the 17th century. These were the first cowpokes. But here at the Triangle A, since most of these guys knew each other and hadn't been together for a while, the talk eventually became more personal...who had a new girlfriend, a new horse or who bought a new truck. And everyone wanted to know how Steve's two boys, Josh and Brent, were doing in school, and what their plans were after school. Josh was a sophomore and Brent was a senior. Brent was headed off to college next fall and was excited about leaving home and being on his own. Josh at least for the time being, just wanted to get through high school. Beyond that he hadn't made any specific plans about college although college was definitely in his future. Both boys had said repeatedly that they wanted to come back to the ranch and eventually take over for their folks. You could just feel how pleased Steve and Mary Ann were to know the ranch would stay in the Anderson family if this all worked out.

During dessert of fresh peach cobbler, Steve laid out the plans for the morning gather. Breakfast was at five thirty and right after that everyone was to be saddled and ready to go. Buck was paired up for the gather with the college kid from the East, Phil Shaw.

The horses for the next day's work were already penned in the corral near the barn. Most of the cowboys had brought their own mounts and they were corraled with the ranch remuda. As soon as dinner was over, Buck dropped off his saddle and gear at the barn and went back to the house. He put his bag in the bedroom he had been assigned earlier in the evening and was greeted rambunctiously by Cowboy. Within a few minutes Steve came by.

"If you have a few minutes and I can drag you away from that dog, I'd like to talk to you a bit. It won't take long. I can only guess you're plenty tired and could use some sleep so we won't be long. Come on down to my den."

"Sure. I'll be right down."

Buck thought mostly about sleep and although he was tired he was also filled with anticipation and energy looking forward to the work for the next couple of days. He was also wondering what Steve wanted to talk about. They had been friends for some years after they initially met at a cattleman's meeting over in Big Timber but because of their work and the distance, they didn't get to see one another often as they both would have liked. Steve had gone to Montana State and even received his Masters there after he decided he wanted to come back to the family ranch. The ranch had been started as part of a homestead by his grandfather and there was a lot of Anderson history in this land. At college Steve had been a one of the top saddle bronc riders on the school's rodeo team and that's where he met Mary Ann, who was also on the rodeo team. She had been a pretty good barrel racer, breakaway roper, and she tied goats.

Mary Ann came from a ranching family over in the eastern part of Montana, somewhere around Glendive, not too far from the border with North Dakota. She and Steve appeared to have a good life in the Big Hole. But it was so cold here in the winter and that was really an understatement. Buck knew he wasn't man enough to live in this ice box. Too often Wisdom, Montana was listed in *US Today* as the cold spot in the nation. During the winter the few high school kids had to go to school in Dillon, where several families had apartments and the adults took turns being the house parents during the week. Wisdom was far too small to have a high school of its own and Buck figured it was also too damn cold.

When Buck entered Steve's den, a warm room with shelves of books and a variety of plagues and photos commemorating some of the ranch's history, he was drawn to the fire in the wood stove. Steve was settled in a big leather chair reading the paper.

"Do you need a beer?"

"No thanks. I'm not sure I could get anything in me after that dinner. I don't know where Carol came from but there are a lot of cowboys around here who are real glad she showed up and you were smart enough to hire her."

"You know, it's a funny thing. I've tried to pry some information about her past from her but she's as tight lipped as she can be. But I agree with you, she sure can cook and she's been great around the ranch. She keeps Cody close to home and that by itself is a big plus. He doesn't have the need to go to that old bar in Wisdom any more to have fun and get into trouble. Things are a lot calmer around here. And as much as I need him I surely do need some calm."

Steve paused for a few seconds and looked directly at Buck. "But that's not what I wanted to talk to you about. Rumor has it you are leaving this country pretty soon and heading down south, Arizona or New Mexico? Do I have that straight?"

"You've got it. I'm off to southwestern New Mexico, way down south— the Bootheel—right on the Mexican border. I was planning to fill you in this weekend but I guess the rumor mill beat me to it."

"Are you taking that good looking, blonde professor with you?"

"Jesus Christ! How did you hear about that? I guess you still have all those contacts at the university. And no, I'm not taking her with me. She is very special but it won't work out for me or for her. When we have a lot of time I'll give you all of those sad details about my love life."

"Have you bought a place in New Mexico? They say it's really good ranch country. It's just that you need so much more land down there to run any size cattle operation. They say the carrying capacity is pretty darn low, at least compared to most of western Montana."

"I've got my eye on a pretty nice spread but I can't finalize anything until

I sell the ranch here and I know exactly what kind of cash I have. But I'm kind of close on both ends. Fortunately it's mostly a buyer's market in the Bootheel. You know me, I'm always the optimist."

"It must really be something down there to drag you away from this country and the spread you've put together. Are you going to stick with the cattle business or just stay with horses? I know how you love those horses and from what I hear I guess the horse market down in the southwest is as good as it gets, especially for good roping and cow horses. At least it's better then up here. With the weather being so mild in Arizona and New Mexico I suppose they can rope all year, even on the ranches. Down there they must just love to drag the calves to the fire. I guess they don't use the squeeze chutes as much down there as we do up here in the north country."

"I think eventually I'll get some cattle. That's up in the air right now but you're right about the horses, roping and the weather. And you're right about dragging calves to the fire. They sure do hate to use the chutes. But you know how all cowboys like to live in the past and do it the way their grandpas did it. Steve, why do you have all this interest in my move to New Mexico?"

"I'll try to be as direct as I can. Have you ever thought about having a partner? Mary Ann and I have talked about going south for the winter but it's always been sort of a family joke. I don't have to tell you how cold it gets here during the winter and winter in the Big Hole just wants to go on forever. How long do you think I want to ranch at 30 and 40 below zero? I'm getting older and both the boys will be gone in a few years. I'm kind of hoping they'll both come back and take over for us. That's what they say they want to do. By that time I want to be somewhere that's warm. You know what it's like to feed here once winter sets in. And you've been here on the calving crews when we calve in April and its still can be below zero. It seems you're always freezing your ass off."

Steve paused for a minute to see how Buck would react. Buck remained silent, knowing Steve wasn't finished.

"I haven't checked into it in any detail and I don't have any figures worked out, but suppose we shipped our cows south to New Mexico for the winter, after the fall works, and either calved in New Mexico or brought them back up here to calve in the spring? It would mean we don't have to put up so much hay and after we ship in the fall, we could send all the mother cows south. With your place and probably some leased pasture we could probably find enough graze and feed for the winter months. I don't know if it would fit into your plans or if it even makes any sense financially, but it was an idea I had and before I got too involved in the details I wanted to ask you how you felt. I was just curious if it had any appeal to you. It would sort of make me a 'snow bird', at least for the first few years. Who knows, maybe Mary Ann and I would eventually decide to settle down south after the boys are settled here. I've done a little research and it doesn't seem like a bad idea."

Buck looked at Steve for a minute without saying anything. It was if he had to gather his thoughts.

"This sort of comes out of nowhere. You know how I feel about you and Mary Ann and if I was to do something like this I can't think of anyone I'd rather do it with. Steve, give me some time to think this through. First I'll have to see what I eventually can buy down there and then we'll talk some more. The idea actually is fascinating to me. A lot will depend on how big a place I get and if there really is any lease land available and the size of the herd I'll want. Down there it's all state or BLM land, almost no forest land. There's plenty of BLM land all around but I don't know how it's tied up. And I sure don't know if any of the locals would want to lease out their own ranges or give up their leases."

"That sounds fair enough. Give it some serious thought. Mary Ann and I would really like to do something like this."

Steve got up, went over to Buck and put his arm around his shoulder.

"Now go back to that dog and get some sleep. I'll make sure you're up in plenty of time for breakfast."

"I'll see you then, boss."

As Buck headed down the hall to his room his head was reeling with all the possibilities Steve had just introduced. This move south to the New Mexico Bootheel was becoming more interesting every day.

■■■

When the five cowboys from the bunkhouse drifted in to the mess hall and approached the table with Steve, his two boys, Cody and Buck, they all looked like they could use about eight more hours of sleep. Buck was sure the bunkhouse crew had spent most of the night gabbing away, catching up. Buck didn't know how he looked but he sure felt like he could use that same extra eight hours.

After taking off their heavy jackets and putting them on hooks lining the wall behind the table, Dave Bradshaw and Bobby Trujillo gingerly seated themselves at the bench table, followed in slow motion by Phil Shaw, Clint Henderson and TJ Parsons. They seemed drawn by the aroma from the huge breakfast served for round up crews, not only on the Triangle A but on ranches all over the west. There were plenty of eggs, bacon, toast, sausage, orange juice, flapjacks and more hot coffee than they could ever drink. It was a great way to get started on a day that was going to be cold, cloudy, long and hard.

They all knew there were going to be many hours in the saddle.

There wasn't much talk at the table but as the cowboys finished eating, Steve told them he wanted them to bring their gathers to a central point, the big dirt tank at the head of Horse Canyon. They would all meet there and then they would bring the entire herd back to headquarters together. He wanted everybody to be at Horse Canyon by noon so they could water the cattle before the afternoon drive. Lunch would be waiting for them at the Canyon and then the drive home would take them till just about dark. Everybody nodded as best they could.

It wasn't quite light yet when they headed into the cold, overcast morning air, to the barn to saddle up. Buck always used one of the ranches good cutting horses and today was no exception. "Buster" was experienced and Buck liked his gate and his mental attitude. "Buster" knew what a day's work was. As they grabbed their saddles, Buck got hold of Phil Shaw and they talked over how they would approach High Lonesome Draw, the brushy foothill country that they were assigned to gather. Phil had only been on the ranch once before so just by rights of experience, Buck took charge. The young cowboy was eager to learn as much as he could and he was sure Buck would be a good teacher.

By the time they were in the saddle the sun was just beginning to creep up over the mountains, and as it found its way through the scattered clouds, it cast an eerie light over the entire valley. The cowboys walked their horses together at a pretty good pace for more than a mile. Then the small groups began to peel off as they approached the area they were assigned to make their gather. Buck and Phil would be the farthest out from headquarters and eventually they were riding alone. They covered the last mile or so at an easy trot, their horses, both from the ranch string, seemingly knowing the country and anticipating the day's work.

When they approached High Lonesome Draw, Phil could see that the terrain was small canyons, hills, and a scattering of stunted trees, bushes and even some cacti that could hide cattle. There was even some leftover snow from an early storm in the shady areas. This was country that made you glad you had a good pair of chaps and a warm coat and gloves. The ground itself was pretty rocky. Fortunately they weren't in the dense forest country that covered some parts of the ranch. Buck, who had worked this section of the ranch before, suggested they split up, each working a side of their area and pushing what they gathered down into the middle of the draw where they had a natural alley way to drive and control whatever cattle they were able to find.

This was pretty dry country and there weren't any water holes Buck remembered except for a small one way down at the bottom of the draw. Buck was certain they would pick up a good part of their gather at the water that at this time of day was surely still covered with a skim of ice.

Buck and Phil took off to different sides of the draw and each headed over to the hill tops, hoping to spot some cattle among the foliage from high on the ridges. When they each reached their highest point, Buck signaled over to Phil to start to move and as they headed down, they picked up pairs along the way as they fought their way through the rough brush. Buck's gelding had done this work many times and the ride never got out of control. It didn't take them long to reach the bottom of the draw and they picked up nearly two dozen more pairs at the water. At that point they had their cattle assembled for the drive to Horse Canyon and Buck made a quick count and came up with 59 pairs of Brangus cattle. There didn't seem to be a dry cow in the bunch. He felt they had done a pretty good job and came as close as they could to what Steve had estimated would be scattered in their area. Although the terrain was rocky and covered with brush and small trees, the gather had gone smoothly. Buck was impressed that Phil had learned so much in his short time doing day work on ranches in Montana. Phil had a good seat on his gelding and he worked quiet and easy, not getting frantic as so many young cowboys seem to do. He knew how to make the most of it as each situation developed.

It was closing in on ten o'clock and both Buck and Phil knew they would have to get their drive going to reach their destination by noon.

As the cattle were bunched up for the push to Horse Canyon, Phil heard mooing and bawlin' coming from the east side of the draw and heading into their herd were two more mostly black cows with their calves, breaking through the brush, intent on making sure they wouldn't be left behind. Cowboy, who up to this time had been pretty quiet, sprinted over and got behind the two cows, nipping at their heels and encouraging them to join the herd as Buck and Phil just watched.

"Maybe we can pick up a few more as we head out of this area. We'll just hope that if we missed any more they'll find us."

"Buck, you give these damn cows way too much credit. They aren't the smartest animals on the face of the earth."

"Well pardner, for someone that's only been in this country a short time, you're catching on very fast. Now let's head for home."

■■■

The drive to meet the others was fairly long and tiring but not too difficult. For a good part of the way they had a fence on one side that let Buck and Phil push the herd along on a fairly straight line at a good pace. They had to be careful so as not to go too fast so the calves wouldn't be able to keep up. There was only one wire gate to get through and didn't present any problems. These cattle had been worked before and they knew the routine as well as the cowboys did.

The two cowboys didn't talk much now or on the way out earlier in the morning. It was just a habit Buck had picked up over the years. He was always quiet in the saddle, trying to absorb as much about the country as he could. And when he was riding like this he enjoyed the quiet and the time he had to reflect on things, whatever they might be. He loved being in the saddle and partnering with his horse. He enjoyed having Cowboy trot along beside him and he mostly treasured being in this kind of cow country. Buck on a horse pushing cattle with his dog alongside was as good as it got for him. Maybe Jennifer was right, maybe he was all romantic.

As they came over a low ridge the herd just seemed to freeze and so did Phil's and Buck's horses. So did Cowboy. As Buck stood in his stirrups to see what the hell was going on, he spotted two coyotes just over on the next ridge. Neither of them moved. Buck slowly pulled his Winchester out of the scabbard and told Phil to stay as quiet as he could. Buck slowly urged "Buster" forward toward the coyotes, rifle at the ready. He didn't want to shoot if he didn't have to—he sure didn't want to stampede the cattle.

As he moved forward the coyotes stayed where they were, like they were frozen in time. Suddenly Buck gave a loud yell that could be heard in every corner of the valley. He didn't think it would scare the coyotes but he did want to draw their attention and distract them if he could. At first the two coyotes didn't move but after a moment, almost as if they were thinking out what do, they looked back at Buck and just trotted off, almost as if they were just giving him a shrug of their shoulders. Buck actually thought they were sneering at him. He loped over in their direction, just wanting to be sure there wasn't a whole pack of coyotes lying in wait for his herd, particularly the calves, and the two he had seem on the ridge were actually gone. When he got to the crest of the ridge, to his relief, there were no coyotes in sight. They had disappeared as quietly as they had appeared.

When he got back to where Phil was holding the herd, he tried to explain to his young partner that seeing coyotes like that was not very out of the ordinary but you always had to be careful. Phil just nodded. He didn't really know what to say.

■■■

It was just about noon, the clouds were beginning to part and the sun was warming everything up when they finally got a glimpse of the dirt tank at Horse Canyon. Already waiting for them was a good part of the herd. They pushed their cattle until they mixed them with the others already settled by the water which by now was all thawed out. Cody Jacobson was sitting his horse watching the herd along with Josh and Brent Anderson. Everything was under control. Before long the others brought in their gathers and the full herd was assembled, right on time. As the cattle ambled in the cowboys let them drink at the dirt tank.

Just about the time they got all the cows settled down, they heard the Chevy pickup rattling its way down the bumpy dirt road carrying the lunch Steve said would be waiting for them. It was, as most things were on this ranch, on time. As they came into view, Buck could see that Mary Ann was driving and Carol was riding shotgun.

Steve wanted two cowboys to hold the herd and Buck and Phil took the first shift as the others ate. By the time the meal was finished—hamburgers, potato salad, even some peach cobbler, and soft drinks and coffee—and everything packed up and back in the bed of the pick up, Mary Ann and Carol finally got a chance to sit around for a few minutes as the crew relaxed. The cowboys spun some tales of their morning work, Buck made light of the coyote encounter, and several of the hands kidded Phil about being so far away from his east coast upbringing and having his first face to face coyote experience. The one thing each and every cowboy agreed upon was that they all looked forward to the big meal Carol had promised them once they got back to headquarters that evening. Food always seemed to be on the mind of these cowboys. They always seemed to be hungry.

Mary Ann talked in private with Steve for a few minutes but never spoke to her two boys who were obviously trying to avoid her. She made sure they were treated like all the hands and none of the cowboys wanted their mom on the drive, even if your parents owned the ranch.

Once the cowboys finished their meal, they all knew the afternoon drive was going to be a good time on the roundup because from here on in it was just time in the saddle with enough riders to insure that the big herd was easily controlled. The drive home was over fairly flat grass country, slightly down hill, and they would go slow and easy, the way Steve liked his cattle worked, especially when driving cows with calves. No yelling or roping along the way. No chousing the cattle. Steve made it clear that this was the Triangle A, not some old cowboy movie. All the hands on this roundup knew what he expected and behaved accordingly. They did it the same way for themselves with their own herds when they were working on their own spreads. That's probably why Steve tried to hire these same guys each year.

■■■

After lunch the cowboys tightened the cinches on their geldings, adjusted their tack, climbed back into the saddle and the drive was on. Cody took point along with TJ, and being the youngest, Josh and Brent were assigned drag. Bobby Trujillo volunteered to ride with them. It made it easier with a big herd like this one to have three riders spread out at the back of the drive. They were lucky though since this was mostly grasslands and the dust and dirt was not nearly as big a factor for the drag riders as it was in some dry pastures or during the more arid summer months on the ranch.

Dave Bradshaw, Clint Henderson and Phil rode the flank on one side of the herd and Steve, Buck, and Cowboy took the other.

Steve and Buck talked just a little, mostly about the country and how lucky they were the weather hadn't turned bitter cold yet. It wasn't uncommon for the Big Hole to be below zero at night and barely into the thirties during the fall roundups. Winter often came too early in the Big Hole and as they rode Buck's thoughts kept drifting to the warmer winter days he knew he'd have in New Mexico. For this year's drive the weather in Montana had been relatively mild. As the two ranchers rode side by side, tending to the herd, neither Buck nor Steve brought up the idea of the cattle partnership.

Except for an occasional cow and calf breaking from the herd, the drive was uneventful. As the sun was beginning to set, creating a beautiful crimson sky over the Bitterroot Mountains to the west, they spied the holding pens and corrals at headquarters. The cattle smelled water and the entire herd seemed to pick up the pace and the bawlin' grew increasingly louder. Buck was always surprised at how much more noise there was in moving a herd of cows and calves then there was in driving a herd of steers. The cows, who were constantly seeking out their own babies and the babies not wanting to be separated from their mommas, created a racket as each searched for the voice of the other.

Cody rode on ahead and opened the gate to the small pasture where they would be held overnight. As they pushed their way through the gate to get to the water, Cody and Steve both counted the number in the drive. They both came up with the same count of 523 cows and Steve was pleased. He knew a few pairs had been missed but they could be rounded up later and taken to the local livestock auction. There were only a few dry cows, cows without calves, and that always made Steve happy. Dry cows didn't earn him any money.

The cattle were watered, the gates were closed and the cowboys headed back to the barn to unsaddle and take care of their mounts. After a while, after they had finally settled down, all the cows and their calves would pair up and there would be a little less noise coming from the pens.

Once the horses were watered and hay pitched into the horse corral, the crew drifted to the bunk house to clean up and Buck headed to the main house with Steve, Josh, Brent, and Cowboy. All he could think about was what a tiring and satisfying day this had been. Buck had been a little worried that for this large a herd in fairly rugged country, they might have been short a couple of cowboys. But as usual, Steve knew what to expect from this crew and what troubles might come up on the Triangle A. These guys, including his two sons and the cowboy from the East, were experienced riders and handled the job without any mishaps. Whatever the other problems Buck had, they had melted away with the daylight. He kept thinking about that old saw, "The best thing for the inside of a man was the outside of a horse." He didn't know who had said that first but he was dead certain whoever said it was absolutely right. At that moment it was hard for him to imagine a better life than that of a cowboy.

■■■

As the roundup crew reassembled in the mess hall, they were far more animated than they had been at breakfast, partly because they were wide awake and partly because they knew the roundup had been a good one. Steve made sure all the hands knew how pleased he was with their work. A cowboy, like any other working man, enjoys some praise when he does a good job. Too often, taciturn cow bosses never bother to praise the cowboys for a job they had done well because that was what was expected of them and that's what they were getting paid for. Cowboying could be tough!

■■■

Carol outdid herself for dinner. When everyone was seated and the meal was started it was Thanksgiving a month or so early. There were two of the biggest turkeys most of the cowboys had ever seen, with all the trimmings—

yams, stuffing, gravy, cranberry sauce, coleslaw, hot rolls and even a salad. Everyone dived in like they hadn't eaten in a month. Once again the talk just sort of disappeared as it seemed all the crew could concentrate on was eating. Their faces showed how good they felt.

When the main course was finished Carol brought two large pumpkin pies to the table and a couple of cans of whipped cream. Life really didn't get better than that. Buck knew that for this crowd there weren't words to describe how good they all felt. This day surely gave meaning to why they were cowboys and why they took such pride in the life they had chosen. All the money in the world couldn't influence this crew, not now. These guys were cowboys doing cowboy work and they were so damn proud of it. It just wasn't something they had to or even wanted to talk about. And they always knew outsiders would never understand them or their lifestyle.

After dinner everyone stayed at the table, had a cup of coffee and unloaded all the conversation that had been pent up all day in the saddle and even at dinner. The talk was free, funny and very warm. These people were friends and it was apparent in the way they interacted with each other. There were no off color jokes, mostly in deference to Mary Ann and Carol, but there was great humor and everyone was included. There were stories about roundups from the past, adventures that had occurred over the years, some real "windies" and stories and wise cracks about one another, all with a general good feeling. This was a comfortable group of compadres.

Before the dinner was over and everyone headed to get a good night's sleep, Steve laid out the plans for the next day, not the most appealing for the cowboys because so much of the work would be done on foot in the sorting pens. This was a crowd that felt most comfortable and liked being in the saddle. There was good natured moaning as the boss assigned jobs and set the time for breakfast. It would be later than it was today because they just had to walk over to the shipping pens and except for Bobby Trujillo and Buck, the others didn't even have to saddle a horse. Besides, no one expected the cattle buyer to show up at the Triangle A as the sun came up. In the sorting pens Steve would get the final and accurate count of the herd.

After the bunkhouse crew headed over to their "home," Buck plopped down in the living room where the TV was on. He didn't realize how tired he was until he was able to relax. Brent came in to say hello and Buck asked him about his plans for his education.

"Well, Dr. Cooper, I think..."

"Wait a minute. At the university or in town you can call me Dr. Cooper. Here on the ranch while I'm working for your dad, it's Buck. Got it? Now, what about your plans for next year? It's just so darn hard for me to realize you're a senior this year and that you'll be off to college next year. Everyone will miss you at the spring brandings and fall works."

"Yes sir. I'll miss all of that too. But I think I want to go to college back East. I really like that American Studies stuff you and dad talk about. I like history and reading and going back East would give me a chance to learn a lot of things about America and meet new people and see some new places and a whole new way of life. I had a few schools picked out back East and I've finally made my decision. It was hard because I haven't really seen any of them first hand but I did as much searching on the internet as I could."

"Brent, I thought you wanted to come back to the ranch after college and eventually you and your brother take over for your mom and dad?"

"I do. I thought after college I could come back to Montana State and get my Masters in Ag Economics or Range Management and then come back home. That's still my plan."

"Damn. For a young guy you've really thought this out. Where are you planning to go to school?"

"Well, I want a liberal arts college, small enough for me to fit in. I've never been to a big school. Even high school in Dillon is pretty small. I looked at quite a few and picked a school in Virginia, Washington and Lee University. Did you ever hear of it?"

"Are you kidding? It's a top flight place. It's always rated one of the best liberal arts schools in the country and it's an absolutely beautiful campus right in the middle of horse country in the Shenandoah Valley. It's also one of the oldest schools in the country. I was there a couple of times for meetings when I was teaching in Virginia and I was impressed. I think you've done well. And I know you'll love the Shenandoah Valley. Have you heard from them?"

"I got an early acceptance and I was even given a partial scholarship. I don't think they get too many kids applying from Montana."

Buck stopped for a minute and looked intently at the young Anderson. He then continued, with a mock smile and a grin he hoped Brent would understand.

"Brent, I think that's wonderful. They are lucky to have you. And I guess you know they don't have a rodeo team back there."

Buck smiled and was pleased that Brent shared that smile.

"Keep me posted and if I can help you in any way don't you hesitate to ask. I think this is pretty exciting news and I'll bet your folks are thrilled. And I'm sure you know the former all men's college is now coed. That should add some extra fun."

For a moment Brent almost blushed but he gained his composure and went on as if he had never heard the last part of Buck's comments.

"Thanks Buck. I think my folks are happy. I even think they'd like to come to Virginia and visit me in Lexington. I don't think mom or dad have ever been to that part of the country and you know how much dad loves that Civil War history."

From the expression on his face Buck could tell how pleased and excited Brent was about his college decision. Sometimes you just know the right decision has been made, and this was one of those times.

"Well, it's getting late and I'd better hit the sack."

Brent left and Buck sat there with his coffee, thinking again about his decision not to have children. Having kids might be okay if you knew you were going to have a kid like Brent. That thought passed quickly. He turned his attention to the TV and tried to pay attention to the news from CNN. He just wasn't able to concentrate so he got up, headed for the kitchen but instead went outside. This time Cowboy followed him. The air was cold the way it's supposed to feel in Big Hole in the fall, and the sky was clear and saturated with stars. He just stood there a while, letting thoughts drift in and out of his consciousness. No big deals, just random thoughts. He was happy and the stress he had been experiencing for the past several weeks was gone. He particularly enjoyed thinking about Brent's decisions concerning college and his future.

As he stood outside, he heard the screen door slam. Steve came into the light cast by the kitchen window.

"It was a good day today. The guys did a fine job and I think we did a pretty complete job gathering those cows. I don't think we missed too many. The boys and I and Cody should be able to find any we didn't get. We'll ambush them at the water holes and take them to the livestock auction in Dillon. How are you feeling? You're not getting too old for this kind of work are you?"

Buck waited a moment before he said anything, knowing Steve was actually a few years older than he was.

"Pretty damn good. I'm sure glad you called me for the roundup. It was just what I needed. And to change the subject, that son of yours is really something. He just outlined his college plans to me and it's hard to believe a kid so young can think so clearly. It's a real credit to you and Mary Ann."

"I appreciate that, Buck, but sometimes I think Brent gets along so well despite us. Sometimes it's not easy being a parent."

Buck was quiet again. He was getting very confused about this parent thing and he couldn't get a clear picture of his own thoughts.

"You know I've met some professors from Washington & Lee at national conferences and when I was teaching in Virginia and the one thing I remember most is that it's a teaching school, not a research mega university. I just think Brent will be a wonderful fit, for him and for them. They have so much to offer one another."

"I'm glad to hear you say that. We researched as much as we could on the internet and Mary Ann and I sort of came to the same conclusions you did. We're very happy for Brent. He's really anxious to see a new part of the country and meet people from all over. Growing up in the Big Hole can be a little bit isolating. We're glad he's getting out of here for a while."

Buck and Steve were quiet for a minute, just letting the glow of the day settle.

"Well, it's about my bedtime. I'll make sure you're up with the sun again. It's supposed to be a little warmer tomorrow, especially in the morning, and lots sunnier. Good night and thanks for coming up this weekend. I didn't mean to tear you away from that blonde professor of yours."

Buck was going to say something but decided to keep quiet.

"See you in the morning, professor."

■■■

As the sun was creeping up over the mountains and beginning to flood the Big Hole with a golden light, Steve knocked on the door to Buck's room just as he was starting to wake up.

He dressed, brushed his teeth, pulled on his boots, fed Cowboy and headed to the mess hall. He could smell breakfast before he got there and couldn't wait for a big cup of hot coffee. This was going to be one of those necessary days but not one nearly as enjoyable as yesterday's gather. The sorting pens and the alleys were going to be dry and dusty. Not the scenic trip a horseback through the hills and forests of the first day. Not the kind of work most cowboys look forward to although they all realized how vital it was to the success of the ranch.

As the preliminary work was being done out by the pens and these pens were all welded pipe, the kind that made the work easier and safer, each of the cowboys had taken his assigned place.

Steve waited at the scales for Joe Bob Oakes, the cattle buyer to arrive.

Once the steer calves and the heifer calves were sorted and placed in different pens, any slick calves, the ones they had missed during the spring branding had been separated, the dry cows isolated and probably readied for sale, and the bulls separated from the rest of the herd, the day's work was nearly done. That would take most of the morning and into early afternoon. The trucks were supposed to arrive a little after three o'clock and if there is one thing the ranchers don't want to do is make the trucks wait. The drivers expect you to be ready and they get pretty damn surly when they have to sit around with nothing to do. Steve was sure that with this crew, everything would be ready on time.

Buck and Bobby, saddled and mounted, headed into the big corral where all the cows and calves were milling around, making a thunderous amount of noise that was only going to intensify as the cows and calves were separated. Steve was in the alley with Cody. They would be identifying the cattle and calling out to the other cowboys who were manning the various gates, and they in turn would let the right animal into the right pen. Steer calves here, heifers there, unbranded calves over yonder, bulls to the right, cows to the left, and so forth. Buck and Bobby had to keep the herd moving so they could get a good number into the alley when Steve called for them. Once the operation was in progress the work went smoothly. This was an experienced crew, they had all had done this work many times and they all knew their jobs.

Joe Bob Oakes arrived just about the same time as Pat Wrightson, the brand inspector. Joe Bob was a jovial sort and most of the cowboys knew him well enough to like him and well enough not to completely trust him. He wasn't there to give his money away. Besides, the cowboys rooted for Steve and wanted him to have a good sale at the highest possible prices.

Finally everyone was ready to begin. After some pleasantries with Steve and some joshing with the cowboys who all knew Joe Bob and Pat, Steve and Cody were ready to get the work underway. Buck and Bobby started the herd toward the gate. After some prodding from the cowboys on horseback, the cattle moved rapidly into the alley.

When all the sorting was finally completed, the heifer calves and the a few rejects were isolated, the steer calves were herded in small groups, about twenty head at a time, toward the scales. After the weighing was completed the prices were calculated so the only thing remaining was to get all the calves loaded.

By about three o'clock, right on schedule, the job was done, the dust was settling, and after double checking the weights at the scales, Steve and Joe Bob had agreed on prices. This was a good year—the calves were in top shape and prices were high. Steve was happy and Joe Bob knew that every year he was going to get good cattle at the Triangle A. This was always an important time for a rancher. It was, in many cases, the only paycheck for the year and there were no do overs. Once the price was set and the cattle were sorted and ready to be shipped and then loaded, that was it.

▪▪▪

Right on schedule the trucks rolled in and the first one set up at the loading chute. Today was going to be a late lunch for that crew of dirty, dust covered, and parched cowboys.

Soon after the details and the ground work was completed, after Joe Bob Oakes and Pat had driven off and the trucks were headed out to the highway for their trip to the feed lot, Steve called the crew together before they sat down for their meal and thanked them all for the work they did. He let them know he was going to give everyone a little bonus. This wasn't a usual practice but the sale had gone far better than even Steve had anticipated. The cowboys thanked Steve one by one. The Triangle A was a good place to work probably because Steve selected the cowboys so carefully and treated them appropriately. They all knew the rules about drinking in the bunkhouse and the general conduct on the ranch and Buck noticed not one of the crew smoked or chewed. He wasn't sure whether that was just a coincidence or it was intentional, but it was definitely unusual for a bunch of cowboys.

By the time late lunch or early dinner was gobbled up—nobody knew what to call it or cared very much—Steve had each of the cowboy's checks ready and the crew began to drift out, each of them heading back home to his own place. Steve took Buck aside, told him to think about the partnership deal and not to get too involved with that pretty professor unless he wanted to marry her. Buck grunted, said that he would give serious thought about the partnership and that he had no marriage plans. Before he left, Buck found Mary Ann helping Carol in the kitchen and had a few words with her, mostly to thank her.

"You know Buck, as Steve and I get older we think more and more about warmer weather. I can't even imagine what a winter would be like without it getting below zero every night and never really warming up during the day. I envy you a little, going to the southwest."

Buck smiled at Mary Ann as he gave her a hug but didn't say anything. In his own way, he envied Steve and Mary Ann...their marriage, their two boys and the Triangle A. Buck wanted to settle down but he couldn't find a way to get all three things lined up at once. Right now all he was concerned about was the ranch part. The marriage had to wait and he just didn't see where children fit in. Without any regrets, he honestly believed it was too late in his life to even begin thinking about that.

As he loaded his gear into the bed of the pickup, he gabbed with the other cowboys as they got ready to leave and Buck could tell they were all feeling the same way that he was. The camaraderie among this group of cowboys was one of the elements that made their work, as tough and dangerous as it was physically, so enjoyable. It was hard to have it end. They were leaving but each one wanted to stretch the weekend out and continue riding for the Triangle A. Even Bobby Trujillo lingered at his pickup, just palavering away. No one was in a hurry to leave. But they all eventually got into their trucks and headed for their respective homes. Cowboying, even on your own place with your own family, can be a lonely life and the camaraderie of a weekend like this one meant a lot to the cowboys.

■■■

As Buck and Cowboy drove west to Lost Trail Pass, past the Big Hole National Battlefield where in 1877 the Nez Perce Indians and the U.S. troops had fought a ferocious battle, won by the Nez Perce as they attempted to escape to Canada, Buck couldn't stop thinking of what a satisfying couple of days he had. His thoughts kept drifting to ranching and cowboys, about the past and how things had changed but stayed the same. The cowboys of the past spent most of their time in the saddle but now days they probably spent as much time in their pickups as they did horseback. What really bothered Buck was how many ranches used four wheelers and he knew of some big outfits that actually tracked their cattle with helicopters. But he knew that in the end, ultimately cowboys still had to control cattle and that part of ranching hadn't changed all that much. On any outfit, big or small, good horses were still irreplaceable. He thought about the times long ago, in the era of the open range, before barbed wire, when the chuck wagon went out twice a year—nearly three weeks in the summer to brand the calves and then again for more than a month for the fall works when the ranches had to gather the cattle from the summer ranges that were going to be sold by shipping them on the railroads to the stockyards scattered throughout the West and even the Midwest. With fenced ranges the big roundups weren't a part of the yearly cycle any more except on some very large outfits.

Buck wondered how he would have done in the "good old days," when he imagined cowboys were a lot tougher than they were now. How would he have survived living in a teepee tent for weeks on end with no plumbing, no hot showers, and none of the other modern conveniences he was so used to having, even at his own ranch. So often, he thought, the romantic past is far more fascinating than the reality but he was also intrigued by a rash of recent articles he read, about how some ranches in Texas, Montana, Wyoming, Nebraska and even New Mexico, were starting to take out the wagons again. They justified it by saying it actually saved money but Buck was sure it was just the cowboy way of not letting the past get too lost in the hustle and bustle of the modern world. He also knew cowboys are by nature romantics...he heard cowboys say time and again, that if you weren't a romantic you could never be a cowboy or even want to be a cowboy. Was this Buck? Buck realized for good or bad, he was probably born a hundred or so years too late, at least that's what he wanted to believe.

As he drove on home, his thoughts turned to his more practical side, as he thought about how much he didn't want to get back to the reality of the university, Jennifer, and facing his own future. Maybe working for someone like Steve Anderson was a good way to go. He knew the minute he had that thought that it was ridiculous and it would never happen, but he was trying to find a way to get his life smoothed out. He knew working for someone else wasn't the answer now or would it ever be.

As he arrived at the 7,000 foot Lost Trail Pass he looked north, down the Bitterroot Valley and despite how beautiful it was, and it sure was that, he knew his time here was on a short string. He couldn't stop thinking about the old days, the way it was when the ranges were unfenced and cowboys devoted twenty four hours of every day to the brand. He headed down the twisting road to Stevensville, down to about 3,300 feet and then his turn off west and back up to the ranch. As he drove through his pastures to his lower gate he took great pride in what he had built and he knew that in New Mexico he could do it all over again. In fact, he would have to do it all over again in the desert, but it was something he wanted to do.

Once the Ford was parked, he did a quick check of the place and everything seemed to be in order. In the house he called Johnny Meyers to thank him and tell him he was back, he reviewed the messages on his answering machine and there were the usual messages from neighbors, businesses, and hang-ups. Mixed in was a message from Jennifer telling him she hoped he had a good weekend. There really was nothing urgent. Since it was early in the evening and there was some sunlight left, he went out and fed the horses in the near pasture, just a little grain, and just leaned against the split rail fence and let his mind wander. At the conclusion of his evening reverie, he then went back into the house and thought about dinner. But he couldn't make a decision about what to eat so he decided to take a long, hot shower. The shower was another good place to think and a good place to loosen up and relax. The more he thought about it, Buck realized how much he had missed working with a good crew of cowboys. He felt increasingly isolated at the university and he was absolutely certain where his future was. He knew he was on the right track. Getting to New Mexico and the problems that posed along the way were what had to be solved. And as complex as he thought they were, he knew they would be solved.

After a dinner of leftovers heated up in the microwave, Buck settled in his big, comfortable chair and watched some police drama on TV for about an hour. He was restless. He got up, went outside and took a quick stroll around the house and the corrals. He was just passing the time. There was nothing specific he was looking for and there was nothing out of the ordinary he found.

The next morning he was up early, did the chores, took a brief look at his notes for those Monday's classes, and then cooked up a big breakfast of bacon, eggs, toast and orange juice and coffee. He ate slowly and thought about having to go into Missoula and what to do about Jennifer. Their schedules were different enough he could miss her and that's what he wanted to happen. And luckily that's how it turned out.

When he got home that evening, though, he called Jennifer and they talked easily but made no plans. That would have to wait. Later in the week they talked again and they decided to have dinner together Friday night in Missoula.

Dinner itself was uneventful. Jennifer wanted to know all about the roundup, and at one point asked, "How are things coming in New Mexico?" Buck was surprised she asked and he danced around his answer in the most general of terms. Jennifer was savvy enough not to pursue the topic. But things went well enough so that Buck did spend the night at Jennifer's. They still enjoyed one another's company and the physical relationship remained intense. But he was sure the entire relationship had changed. It was as if they were both just indulging themselves until something different or maybe, even better, came along. They didn't talk about the future, they didn't implore one another to make some kind of commitment, and they didn't even talk about their careers. They just had fun, made love very intensely and Buck went back to the ranch.

For all he knew, Jennifer had been in touch with her former fiancé and they were working things out. For the first time, it didn't really seem to matter to him.

■■■

Several weekends later he headed down to Dillon to work the fall shipping for Dave Bradshaw and his dad. Dave had been at the Triangle A and in addition to Buck, Bobby Trujillo and Phil Shaw were on the crew along with several of the Bradshaw neighbors who Buck didn't know. Buck liked the way Dave Bradshaw handled himself. He was sure that eventually Dave, who was an only child, would take over the ranch and that it would stay in the Bradshaw family. Shipping in Dillon, which was a good 2,000 feet lower than the Big Hole, came later because winter arrived later. It was the same routine except the ranch was a little smaller than the Triangle A and they didn't have to scour nearly as much rugged mountain terrain to find the cattle. The Bradshaw ranch was on flatter ground with big, wide grassy valleys and rolling hills, and it was easier country to gather than the steeper mountainous pastures up in the Big Hole.

By Sunday night Buck was home again and ready for another week at the university and the self indulgence of his own problems.

One week later it was Buck's turn to ship. Since he only had 91 cows to gather and just 85 calves to ship, both heifers and steers, he didn't need a big crew and the work would go fast. Buck was proud he had been having around a 93% calving rate for the past few years. And it was at least a couple of years since he had a prolapsed cow he had to doctor.

Bobby Trujillo and a friend from down in Victor, Ike Clarkson, came to the ranch to help out and along with his neighbor Johnny Meyers, Buck figured they were all the crew they would need. Ike was in his early sixties but still slim and fit and had been a good cowboy most of his life. Now he lived on about twenty acres and ran a few steers and sold meat to his new neighbors who had come to Victor, mostly from the cities. Ike had grown up near Lusk, Wyoming and he and Buck had met at branding nearly ten years ago. Buck always liked his sense of humor and the work ethic he brought to all his cowboying.

They had Buck's herd gathered early in the morning, and with the help of the Meyer's two teenage sons, the pairs were quickly sorted. Since Buck leased his bulls each year, they didn't add an extra sorting problem during the fall shipping. The leased bulls had already been shipped back to their owners. For the past week or so Buck had been bringing the cattle in off the lease land and his own outer pastures, keeping them closer to headquarters to make the day's work easier and far less labor intensive.

Because Buck's ranch was too small to have their own scales, the crew had to load and truck the 85 calves to a set of scales just north of Stevensville. The small number of calves made the job easy and by 2:30 the cattle hauling truck arrived in town, the cattle were loaded and that part of the ranch's work was done for another season.

Joe Bob Oakes was again the cattle buyer and after Buck concluded his dealings with no rejected calves, just as it had been done at the Triangle A, he was extremely satisfied with the money paid for the calves and Joe Bob appeared equally happy. But the entire time they were negotiating, all Buck could think about with a big grin was that Joe Bob reminded him of Jim Ed Love, the wheeling, dealing rancher from Max Evans' comic Western novel *The Rounders*, someone you sort of liked but you weren't sure you could ever trust. Buck finally figured as long as the check didn't bounce it was just his own little humorous insight.

As they were concluding their business and Joe Bob was getting into his shiny new red Dodge truck, he asked casually, "I hear you're leaving this country and going to the southwest. Is there any truth to that?"

Buck smiled trying to act low key. "That's my plan right now. I guess I'm getting too old for these Montana winters."

"Well, that's too bad. I've enjoyed doing business with you and I'll miss the good cattle I could always count on up here. But I'm sure I'll see you before you leave for good. Have you actually sold this place yet? I sure do hope whoever you sell to is someone I can do business with. And for Christ's sake, invite me down south when it gets 25 below up here."

Buck smiled at Joe Bob and explained to him that he hadn't sold the place yet but that he'd sure as hell try to find him a good client. The one thing Buck didn't want to do was sell the ranch to some city dude. But he knew he had no control over that. Buck and Joe Bob talked a little more, shook hands and Joe Bob was off.

After cattle buyer drove away, Buck signed all the papers for the brand inspector and paid the Meyers and given the checks and said his farewells to Ike and Bobby. As they got into their pickups, Buck just stayed put and began to reflect on the year's work. Cattle prices had remained strong and although all the ranchers realized what a yo-yo the cattle market was, in the good years they all enjoyed the riches, paid off loans and made whatever improvements the rest of the money would cover. Buck banked most of his cash this year because he had only a small loan on the ranch—money he had to borrow to give to his ex wife as part of their divorce settlement—and since he was in the process of selling the place, he didn't want to make any major improvements. That was for the new owner and the more he had in the bank the more he could do on the new ranch in New Mexico. Buck was actually beginning to think like a businessman.

■■■

With the fall work completed, the season eased into winter, darkness came earlier each day, the nights were colder and the snow levels in the mountains slowing inched their way down to the valley, driving most of the wildlife ahead of it. Each year it seemed as if winter was sneaking up on you a bit earlier. Before he realized it, Thanksgiving was only a little more than a week away. He had been seeing Jennifer on a fairly regular basis and they had been enjoying their time together. Buck was trying to figure out what they would do for Thanksgiving when Jennifer, a little hesitantly, informed him over lunch at the university cafeteria she had to go home for the holiday and be with her family in South Dakota. She mentioned something about Buck going with her but he quickly explained why he couldn't be away for that long. Now was not the time for Buck to start getting involved with Jennifer's family. Their relationship, he was sure, wasn't going in that direction. He was disappointed though that Jennifer had to leave and that he would be alone for the holiday but he understood.

His own parents had passed away far too young. Buck's father died of cancer in his early seventies and his mother died a couple of years later of what he could only describe as sadness. He never could come to grips with them both dying so young and it left an emotional hole he hadn't ever been able to fill. The women he had known since then certainly weren't helping to fill that void.

Buck's sister, Emily, lived on the east coast so he had no family to spend time with, at least not for just an extended weekend. But being alone or spending Thanksgiving with friends in the area was okay with Buck. He sure wasn't interested in becoming friendly or entangled with Jennifer's family. He did spend the Monday night before the holiday at Jennifer's, and she promised to call him as soon as she got back from South Dakota.

As it turned out, Buck actually wound up spending the holiday with a retired couple who lived down on the valley floor, a few miles from his ranch. They regularly invited him for dinner but he hadn't accepted the invitations as often as he should have. It made him feel good to say yes for Thanksgiving. Mr. and Mrs. Mahoney had lived in California and retired to the Bitterroot about four years before. Mrs. Mahoney was a retired nurse and Mr. Mahoney had owned a large machine shop. Buck first met them at a café in Stevensville and he frequently saw them around town. What he could never figure out was why they ever came to Montana. Mr. Mahoney had terrible arthritis and the winters in the Bitterroot were tough on him. The Mahoneys claimed they thought the Bitterroot was so beautiful and the people were so friendly but that seemed so simplistic considering the pain Mr. Mahoney suffered once the cold weather settled in.

The retired couple were living in a double wide that was very homey and extremely well kept on about one acre near Kootenai Creek. They had obviously put a great deal of effort in landscaping their grounds and you had to look closely to realize the building was actually a double wide. As far as Buck knew they had no children. When they were with Buck they were always asking questions about horses, cattle, ranching and mostly about being a cowboy. They were almost childlike in their interest and Buck often thought they were living a little vicariously through him. He sort of liked the attention and occasionally embellished his stories to make them more exciting for the retirees and maybe to romanticize his own life. To hear Buck tell it Wyatt Earp and John Wayne and Randolph Scott and The Virginian were just a stone's throw away. The Mahoneys didn't ever seem to tire of the tales about ranching and roundups and the cowboys Buck knew and some he didn't know.

Mrs. Mahoney, and Buck still respectfully called her Mrs. Mahoney, was a wonderful cook and the turkey dinner couldn't have been any better. In fact, the entire afternoon and evening was very enjoyable. Buck even had some wine with his hosts, something he very rarely did. By evening, after a big hug, a solid handshake and the promise to return more often, Buck headed back up the mountain to his retreat and some much needed time for himself.

■■■

When he got home he checked the answering machine and other than his sister who he talked with regularly, there was apparently no one who wanted to hear his voice. Just as well, he thought. He was a believer in the old cliché, "No news is good news."

By Sunday night he was ready to return to the classroom. He had spent a good part of the holiday preparing and updating his courses and looked forward to getting back to work. He was also waiting for Jennifer's call that never came.

He'd see her on Monday so he wasn't overly eager to call her to make sure she got back. This wasn't the time in their relationship to be too aggressive. He was trying to be careful as to what signals were being sent and he didn't want to send the wrong message. He was leaving and she wasn't going with him. There was no changing that.

After his Monday classes he decided to head home instead of chasing after Jennifer over at the history department. He thought she'd call that night.

She did call, about 7:30, and told Buck she was sorry she hadn't called on Sunday but her plane was delayed for several hours by snow over in Rapid City and that's why she got home so late. She was sure he would already be asleep. She wondered if she could come see him tomorrow, at the ranch, since she knew it was one of the days he wouldn't be coming to town. He told her to come down after class. Buck didn't ask why she wanted to come down to the ranch but it did intrigue him.

When she arrived the next day, after driving up Buck's lightly snow covered road, she looked nervous and Buck knew right away something was wrong. They went into the house and as soon as they were seated, Jennifer began:

"Buck, I'll get right to it. I got together with my ex fiancé over the holidays. I didn't plan it and I didn't even know he was going to come to the ranch, but he did. We talked and I guess what I want to tell you, is that we are going to give it another try. I still adore you and I think we could have had a wonderful life together but you aren't going to commit to us being together unless it is 100% on your terms and you know I can't do that—at least right now. And I know you'll be leaving and I can't go with you. I don't know what else to say. I know I will really miss you. In many ways I don't think any man has ever made me feel the way you do."

Buck thought a moment to try to see how he felt and if there was a strong emotion it was almost one of relief.

"If you are sure this is what you want I guess all I can say is I want you to be happy. I know I've been a hard ass about myself and what I want but you are right, I've wanted everything on my terms. I plead guilty to that. And Jesus, I'm going to miss you, you must know that. Are you going back to Minneapolis or is he going to move here?"

"I think I'm going to move back to Minneapolis at the end of the school year and try to get a teaching job at one of the schools there. The Twin Cities area is loaded with colleges. If not, I'll do some research and maybe write. I really don't yet know how this will all turn out."

"Before you resign from the university or make some kind of big move, make sure he is the one you want to be with. Make sure! Divorce is a messy thing, trust me. It's never good, there are no such things as "friendly" divorces and you rarely remain friends after you are separated, unless, maybe, there are kids. And then you have no choice. Don't do this because it's the easy way out or because I've acted like a jerk. And for Christ's sake, don't settle for second best."

Jennifer seemed edgy but in control.

"I've been thinking about it and I was awfully glad to see him when he surprised us by showing up at the ranch. I think I'm doing the right thing. He loves me so much and I love him. We would have gotten married last year except I was leaving and he couldn't give up his business. I think maybe I made the mistake. Then you came into the picture and that messed me up. It felt good to be with Lars when I was back home."

Buck began to realize he truly wanted her right now and that he would have given anything to make love to her. After some more talk, she got up to leave and as they hugged it was more intimate than they had been for some time. She pressed her body all over Buck and before either of them knew what was happening, they were in bed making love, maybe for the last time. They didn't talk very much, what was there to say? It was best they just enjoy their time together. She stayed until early morning and when they kissed they both knew it was over. Nothing more had to be said. Buck wasn't sure he was very proud of what had happened. Besides, what was done was done and he felt free to get on with his own life and his own future.

■■■

The more he considered his entire relationship with Jennifer the more it dawned on him what actually kept them apart was that she was going to be fine with contentment and he wanted happiness. It seemed like a subtle difference but to Buck it was the difference between night and day. He was willing to gamble on the ups and downs, the highs and lows, the excitement that goes with being happy and she was willing, maybe even needed, to have the stability that comes with being content. Those were two different worlds and they required two different mind sets. Buck never seriously considered himself a gambler or a risk taker but when he gave his life the introspection he tried to do, he realized he was, in fact, very much a risk taker.

He was dead certain there wasn't much life without risk and it's the risks that wake you up to life—it's the risks that keep you energized. Even the move to New Mexico, he knew, was all about taking risks.

Jennifer was not a risk taker. She was ready to take the more conventional path that would offer her a large dose of security. Buck needed the sense of adventure Jennifer apparently did not want or need. Maybe it was something she couldn't handle. He didn't think one direction was any better than the other—they were just different, very different, and the gap between the two approaches was probably too large to bridge. He knew his life now and for the foreseeable future was just going to be too chaotic for Jennifer.

When she got into her car, their goodbye was almost formal and they made no mention of seeing one another again. They both knew their schedules were so different it would be rare that they would accidentally run into one another on campus, particularly since they would both probably try and avoid that. Buck was spending less and less time in Missoula and except for his classes, meeting with students, and the monthly department and committee meetings, he was hardly ever around.

Everyone seemed to know he had resigned and even President Gaines had met with him to find out the real reason for his leaving. They met for nearly an hour and President Gaines, who Buck truly admired and respected, wished him well, told him he would certainly give him any reference he wanted and that he too, loved New Mexico, except his view of New Mexico was mostly Santa Fe and Taos, two areas Buck liked and was familiar with but not at the top of his list of places he wanted to ranch and spend the rest of his life. To Buck, Santa Fe and Taos compared with the rest of New Mexico, weren't cowboy country, at least that's what he thought. What he didn't know was: he was wrong.

■■■

It was early December and winter had tightened its hold on the valleys of western Montana. The mountains were covered with their mantle of white although this year the valleys stayed fairly mild and most of the game had already been driven down from the high country. The year, both socially and educationally, continued to move forward without too many snags. Buck did miss Jennifer, at least the physical relationship, and although he dated there was no one of any particular importance in his life. The last thing he wanted to happen was to get involved with someone. He often felt he was just biding his time and he would soon be on the road. The negotiations for his ranch were going well and he kept in touch with Ann Lewis, his real estate agent in Hidalgo County in New Mexico, to make sure the ranch he was interested in down there was still available. These two issues were now the most stressful things in Buck's life. He needed to sell his place in Montana and buy a place in New

Mexico and the timing had to be fairly simultaneous. By Christmas, with his usual optimism, he was sure things were going to work out. God, he sure hoped they would.

At first he thought he'd go see his sister back East, but getting someone to look after the ranch at this time of the year, while he was gone, was far too complicated during the holidays and the cold weather. Besides, he wanted to stay in Montana, maybe have a white Christmas for the last time and visit friends he might not see again for years. He had friends and knew people in Bozeman, Great Falls, Big Timber, Kalispell, Livingston, even way out east in Glendive—just about all over the state. Going back and forth would be fun. He arrogantly came very close to thinking of it as a farewell tour. Most of his friends never did believe he was going to leave for New Mexico, no matter how much he talked about it, so delivering the good news first hand would let him do a little gloating. And he wanted to do that. It was sort of a good natured pay back. And he looked forward to having Christmas dinner with the Mahoneys. It seemed important to them since they still really didn't know a great many people in the Bitterroot and apparently had no close family members nearby. Buck liked them both and enjoyed the relaxed, pressure free time he spent at their house down near Kootenai Creek.

The holidays were uneventful. He did some visiting, exchanged gifts here and there and had, by any criteria, a cheerful and exhilarating good time. New Year's Eve, on the other hand, which never meant much to Buck, was an evening that turned out to be much more interesting than he had anticipated. He spent it up in Bigfork, on Flathead Lake. His date was a slim, pretty, dark haired gal he knew from graduate school, who was recently divorced and getting ready to leave Montana for California. They had run into one another a few weeks earlier in a Missoula cafe and since neither of them were attached, they decided to spend New Year's Eve together in Bigfork. When Buck picked her up at her place on the east side of Flathead Lake she was in heels and wearing a tight fitting black dress. Buck though she looked sensational. Karen, who was a financial consultant and very sophisticated, suggested they go for dinner at one of the trendy new restaurants popping up all over the Flathead country. After dinner they danced to the kind of big band music you just don't hear much any more. When they got back to Karen's place, she put on a Sinatra CD and they danced some more.

In the morning, as they got out of bed and had breakfast, they both knew it was one of those evenings they both needed and they both knew would probably never happen again, at least not together. But it had been wonderful.

■■■

After the holidays Buck felt no particular pressure either socially or about his move. The real estate agent in Stevensville and the one in New Mexico both kept assuring him all the negotiations were going well. A Californian had visited the ranch several times when Buck was in Missoula and he was apparently representing a buyer from Hollywood. And Buck actually looked forward to meeting his classes again. He knew that after he left the university he was going to miss teaching, especially the interaction with the students, although he wouldn't miss all the meetings, bureaucracy, politics and other nonsense that comes with being a faculty member. Buck wanted some freedom to come and go as he wanted and ranching seemed to be the perfect vehicle. He was having less and less self doubt about leaving university life.

When school resumed he was anxious to get back to work. He ran into Jennifer the first week back and fortunately their meeting was extremely friendly. They hugged, this time more platonic than the last time, and he realized she had probably spent the holidays with her fiancé in either Minneapolis or at the ranch in South Dakota. She looked great and seemed happy. They even talked about having dinner together in Missoula but it was more like one of those "let's get together sometime." Very vague and you could only wonder whether either of them wanted to try it. But lust doesn't go away very easily.

■■■

The first week back at school Buck had a knock at his office door. Standing there was a good looking young woman, too old to be an undergraduate but he was certain she wasn't faculty.

"Hi. Come on in. What can I do for you?"

"Professor Cooper, my name is Rebecca Walker and I'm your new work study person."

Buck was a little taken aback. "You're my new what? Where's Nancy? She wouldn't have quit without talking to me first."

"She didn't exactly quit. Over the holidays someone died in her family and she had to go back home to Havre. She dropped out of school and she's not sure if she's going to return this year or whenever."

"Wow, I'm sorry to hear that. I really counted on Nancy. She is...was one of the finest work study people I've ever had." He stopped for a minute to look over his new employee.

"Well, come on in. If you're going to work here you'd better tell me all about you and then I'll fill you in on the job. I don't mean to be too abrupt but I have things I have to do this afternoon. I just want you to know I'm not easy to work for. I'm sort of a perfectionist about what goes on here in the office. But I'm sure you already know all that."

"It can't be all that bad. Lots of people wanted this job and the chance to work for you. You're very popular and I had to use all my wiles to get this job."

Buck looked at his new work study girl, Rebecca Walker. She was about 5'7", with silky chestnut hair and she had a sparkling smile and the smoothest, almost olive skin. She was very attractive, wearing a fairly tight, straight blue skirt, hemmed just above the knee, low heels and a white blouse that was tight but not too tight. She had a helluva figure. At least, he thought, she doesn't look tacky. In fact, he was taken with how classy she really looked. After seeing most of the women on campus, particularly the students, wear nothing but baggy old jeans and sloppy sweatshirts, it was a pleasure to see someone so feminine and so clearly proud of it. From the start Buck knew Rebecca Walker was not your average college student.

"Everyone says you are actually easy to work for and that you aren't even here as often as most professors. People who have worked for you like the freedom you give them."

"So you've been checking around. I don't know what you've heard but don't confuse freedom with this being an easy job. I expect you to keep the slides and the books in top notch order. That's your primary job. And when I send you over to the library to do some research I expect the same level of work as though you were a graduate student. I know that sounds a little unfair but that's how I do business. Is that okay with you?"

"It really is. This job probably won't get boring."

Buck looked her over again and was glad she seemed a little older and a little more mature than some of the students that had worked for him over the years.

Buck was becoming intrigued by this young woman. Why would someone so much older than most undergraduates and with an obvious touch of style, be part of the work study program? He thought he'd better find out.

"If you don't mind me asking and I'd prefer this to be off the record so you can't accuse me of sexism or asking some other inappropriate, personal questions, I'd like find out something about you and they might be personal. Okay?"

She smiled. She took a seat, crossed her very shapely legs, and sat there and waited for the inquisition, knowing full well she would be able to handle this. It wasn't the first time she had to answer questions because she appeared to be the wrong person in the wrong place.

"Go ahead. I'll try to answer your questions. I know this must be a disappointment now that Nancy's gone. Everyone told me what a good worker she was and how you relied on her when you were out of the office."

Buck liked her style. She was full of self assurance, she knew how to handle men and she certainly knew how to flirt in the most subtle way.

"Tell me about yourself. Where are you from, what year are you in, how did you get to the University of Montana, what are you majoring in—you know, the usual stuff. I like to know who it is that works for me."

Rebecca took a deep breath.

"I'm nearly thirty, I'm a junior, I'm majoring in American literature and I'm originally from Seattle. I came to Montana to get away from the big city and Seattle in particular. I did a very foolish thing when I was younger. I thought I fell in love when I was a freshman. Then I got pregnant, got married, had an abortion and got divorced. That's it in a nutshell. I had to quit school at the University of Washington and earn a living. That's why I'm on work study and that's how I got here. What else would you like to know?"

Buck was speechless. In a few sentences Rebecca Walker had told a life story that would have made a small movie. What surprised him was she did it with no embarrassment and with no particular sense of self pity.

"Jesus, that's a full biography. Is there anything you've left out? What kind of work did you do when you left school?'

"I was a paralegal at a pretty good size law firm in Seattle. They sent me to school to learn to be a paralegal after I was there a few months and I just loved the work. They were the ones who encouraged me to get out of Seattle for a while and go back to school and get my degree. I'd like to go to law school after I get my BA. If you really want to know about me I'll tell you honestly I'm a darn good student, I am very, very motivated and I guarantee you won't be sorry that I'm the one that got the job to replace Nancy. You can trust me and count on my ability to do whatever is needed around here."

Buck wasn't even sure what all that meant, if anything. He was sure that on the one hand he wasn't going to regret having Rebecca work for him and on the other hand he was absolutely certain he was going to regret having Rebecca work for him. This girl, or rather, young woman, was going to be a handful! But since he knew he needed someone he could rely on for his remaining months at the university, she actually seemed like a good fit.

They talked for a while, mostly about the job, her adjustment to Missoula and the university and what Buck actually expected of her. They set up Rebecca's schedule—she had to put in at least 12 to 15 hours a week—and agreed she would start that week. She thanked him and left the office. Buck was a little nervous and a little excited. He had just been through one of those flirtatious situations with Jennifer Olson that had gotten way out of hand, and he didn't want to start down the same road all over again. All he wanted was for the year to be over and for him to get relocated down in New Mexico. He had to make sure that was what was going to happen and that nothing, absolutely nothing, was going to get in his way.

Buck spent the rest of the afternoon running errands in Missoula, a chore he never enjoyed. When he finally got back home the first thing he did was take off his boots, light a roaring fire in the wood stove, grab a volume of Max Evans short stories, get himself a cup of coffee and settled in his favorite chair to just relax and read. With Carl Nielsen's Third and Fourth Symphonies on the turntable, Buck was ready for some peace and the type of quiet only a great symphony could produce.

An hour or so went by when he heard Cowboy barking as if the place was being invaded. Buck wasn't sure whether it was some coyotes, that in the last few months had become more and more bothersome, or deer, but he got up, took a look out the window and there by the main hay stack near the horse corral was a big antlered buck. Buck kept some of the smaller two strand bales in a small stack near the corrals where they were easy to feed to the horses. The deer often came down and dined on his winter hay and there wasn't too much Buck could do to stop them. His first instinct was to grab a rifle and restock his freezer with venison. But he knew there was already a beef in the storage so there was no sense in shooting one of these creatures. In fact, Buck hadn't hunted in several years. It wasn't a moral decision. He wasn't even sure it was actually a decision. He wasn't a member of PETA or any of the "Save the Coyote" groups headed up by women who came from the east. He just didn't enjoy hunting any more and since he only hunted for meat there was no real reason to continue since he had no use for the meat and he wouldn't throw it away or let it rot. Even giving it away didn't make much sense because anyone in this area who wanted wild game already hunted. Maybe hunting was too easy, living where he did. All his friends hunted and he always enjoyed getting a few good elk or moose steaks from them.

It was the same with fishing. Buck was sure he was the only adult male in Montana who didn't engage in the state's official religion, fly fishing. That was one of those things that just bored him. He enjoyed floating the rivers with his friends and he always volunteered to row the big rubber boat while they fished the Big Hole, the Beaverhead, or any of the other prime trout streams in western Montana. He let his compadres provide dinner when they made camp and he usually even offered to do the cooking. He could never get enough of the scenery on the rivers and he actually liked eating trout, especially when it was cooked over an open fire.

■■■

After a few minutes of watching the deer he decided to do nothing except let Cowboy out to chase the buck back to his home in the forest. He enjoyed watching the muley sail over the five strand wire fence as he headed back into the thick forest, to his refuge deep in the Bitterroots.

Buck added a little wood to the fire and took up his Max Evans. The Nielsen was wonderful and he sat there, his feet up on the ottoman, book on his lap, his eyes closed and he just listened as the music soared and filled the house. For the first time in a long while he felt fully at ease with himself and once again he was looking forward to the future with all the anticipation and excitement he had before he met Jennifer. She had put a real crimp in his plans although he had never wanted to admit it. Now that their relationship was over he knew every thing had worked out as it should. They were both headed in the direction that would bring them the most gratification for each of their lives. He was absolutely sure of that. Maybe doing nothing and just letting events take their natural course is the best way to handle life. It gets very hard trying to manipulate reality, if in fact you can, and Buck was convinced you couldn't do it, no matter how hard you tried.

It was three A.M. when he woke up. The fire was down to red hot coals and there was a Montana chill in the house. The stereo had shut itself off and the open book was still on his lap. Cowboy had come back in through the doggie door and was fast asleep in his usual place on the couch. It took Buck a few moments to focus and get his bearings before he got up and put a couple of logs in the stove, turned off the lights and headed for the bedroom and to bed. It had been a good day.

PART 2

HEADING OUT

By Montana standards the winter was turning out to be fairly mild. There wasn't nearly as much snow on the ground, or even in the mountains, as Montanans normally expected. These mild conditions actually began to pose a problem for Buck, for many of his fellow ranchers, and all the farmers who relied on the spring snow melt for their irrigation water. The mountains looked white but according to the official snow survey reports, the snow pack was barely half of normal.

Well, maybe there would be a late set of storms. It wasn't uncommon for March and even April to be wet and snowy months, often bringing in the biggest storms of the winter. But since there was not a damn thing anyone could do to change things Buck tried not to think about it too much. He was getting ready to head to a desert where drought was the normal condition. This was probably going to be his last winter when he had to worry about snow and the spring runoff and that didn't bother him one bit.

By the middle of February things hadn't improved at all and the long range weather forecasts weren't proving to be very encouraging. Although the temperatures were cold, often well below zero, the Montana winter drought was the main topic of conversation at all the cafes and the feed store in town. Nearly everyone who put up grass hay or purchased hay locally for their stock was concerned that if the irrigation water which came from the melting snow pack was cut off too early, the problems could be severe. There surely would be no second cutting and next year there would probably be a very critical hay shortage. Of more immediate concern was that there would be little summer pasture. To top it all off, the price of hay would sky rocket, the talk around town being that it would go up by a third or more. This was going to be one of those wait and see situations that was out of the control of the farmers or the ranchers. "Don't mess with Mother Nature," made sense to the people of the Bitterroot.

But on the other hand, as the end of February approached, Buck kept hoping any big snow storms would hold off, at least a little while, since the Palo Verde was about to begin calving. This was always an iffy time for ranchers in the Bitterroot and all over Montana, because if they had waited to breed their cows to calve in warmer months it would have made branding and then the fall roundups too late in the season to capture the top of the cattle market. If the weather helped out, calving wouldn't be too tough this time around. Buck only had to pull a few calves over the last several years and he was hoping that since he had so few first calf heifers, he wouldn't have to pull many, if any, calves this season. And without too much snow on the ground or very severe cold weather, the calving would be easier. And that meant there wouldn't have to be many calves brought into the barn to survive. For a small rancher like Buck, every calf represented a major investment and he didn't want to lose any because each one represented significant part of the herd's income. He always assumed there would be a few dry cows but losing a calf was something that could be avoided, he hoped, with good care and lots of hard work. During the calving season he hired his good neighbor, Johnny Meyers and his two sons, to ride the herd while he was at the university. The entire herd had been brought into a pasture closest to headquarters and the barn in case there were any problems and it sure was a lot easier to keep an eye on them. Buck got very little sleep during those weeks as the temperatures continued to hover close to zero or below. Often when he had to venture outside, it felt like someone was rubbing ice cubes over ever exposed part of his body.

"Damn", he thought, "how in hell do you keep warm?" It was times like this he felt fortunate to have Johnny Meyers to help him.

■■■

At the university everything was going well. Rebecca turned out to be as good as she said she was and Buck enjoyed having her around the office. It was a relief after all the very young men and women that had worked for him. Rebecca was much more sophisticated than his other work study people and she was a good conversationalist and easy to be around. She had a sense of humor and maybe more importantly, she had a sense of herself.

Then one afternoon, in late March, out of the blue, Buck got the call he had been waiting for. His real estate agent informed him that a deal had been made for the Bitterroot ranch and that he wouldn't have to endure people coming there to look the place over. Buck really hated those visits—the idea of people wandering through his house and ranch made him uneasy—but he knew he had to put up with them to make the sale.

The buyer accepted the original selling price and other conditions and there wasn't any real need for any negotiations. This was a done deal. Buck realized that now he could call New Mexico, actually buy a little more land than he had originally figured on and start planning his move. With the good prices he got for his cattle in the fall, and the high end sale price for the ranch, Buck was flush with cash and ready to spend it on his dream. The more he spent, the less he would have to pay in taxes, or some such formula, he thought. The closing on the ranch would be near the end of the school year and the buyer was some Hollywood type—not a movie star but some part of the film business. It seemed they were the only ones who could afford to live in Montana, primarily because they didn't have to make a living there nor did they have to live there all year, or even for more than a month or two, if even that long. Buck recalled talking to one of the Hollywood crowd who was already a "ranch" owner in the Bitterroot who said he was rarely there for more than ten days a year. Buck had no idea what the new owners planned for the Montana Palo Verde Ranch.

■■■

Buck got right on the phone to Lordsburg, New Mexico and told Ann Lewis to get him the ranch they he had been looking at with the 50 sections. About a third of the sections were deeded and the rest was mostly BLM leases with about two sections of state land on the east side. All the other leased land adjoined the deeded land on the north. He knew that the slightly more than 32,000 acres could only support somewhere around ten head per section year round. But it was his plan to eventually run around 350 mother cows and a fairly good size horse herd with fewer cattle, if that's what it took to get the balance he wanted. But he was sure he could maintain a cow herd of about 320 mother cows without over grazing or taxing his land. Of course, all of this planning was predicated on having normal rain years and in the Bootheel of New Mexico, that could be pretty iffy.

He explained to Ann that he would fly down in a week or so and if everything was in order they could go over the contract, he could inspect the ranch again and arrange the closing. And for the first time, Buck was even considering getting some more government lease land if any was available. It would be all BLM and state land and although he hadn't dealt with them before in Montana, as usual he was optimistic. In the back of his mind was the offer

Steve Anderson had made about their partnership and Buck knew any such deal would require additional graze land...maybe up to 35 sections...22,400 acres...to support Steve's herd for just part of the year. But he also knew how difficult it would be to get hold of any lease land. It wasn't something ranchers gave up readily.

After he hung up the phone, Buck just sat down and was almost dazed. Could this really be happening? He felt a little scared but it was the kind of fear that got your adrenalin flowing far more then it was causing you to become paralyzed. He had some serious logistical problems but they could all be solved. Primarily he would have to sell his cows and calves, and terminate his lease for the bulls or offer them to the new buyer at the going price. He wanted to take eight horses with him and that would mean at least two trips hauling horses to New Mexico, finding someone to care take his new place while he was still in Montana and tend to the stock, and just sort of be his hired hand, his cowboy. When he finally did move south he thought he might need someone full time. In the meantime, he had things to do in Montana to get ready for the move. He decided to take his retirement out of the university account and use that money, his cattle money from the fall, his savings and the nest egg he had inherited when his parents died, together with the money from the sale of the ranch and cattle, to give him the flexibility to put a fine ranch together in New Mexico. He knew he wouldn't make any money for a year or two but he was certain he could eventually make a go of it. He would count on the income from writing, something he wanted to do more of, and some investments he had made to help carry him the first couple of years. He saw a rosy future and he just hoped he was being realistic. But it didn't actually matter because he was going south, and what was going to happen, would happen. He was ready to head to "The Land of Enchantment" as soon as he could get packed.

As Buck tried to grasp the reality of the moment, he became acutely aware that he didn't really have anyone to share all this good news with. Not a wife, not a girl friend, not his parents and not even the kind of close friend movies and books always romanticize about. He knew a ton of people but they just were never completely allowed into his life. But he decided he had to tell a few people who mattered to him. He took the phone out of the cradle and started to dial.

∎∎∎

The first call was to Steve and Mary Ann Anderson. It was 28 below zero in the Big Hole in late March, and after explaining how envious they were of him for being able to head to sunny and warm New Mexico, they conveyed their excitement for his success and they promised they would call him the next time they headed down to either Stevensville or Missoula. They wanted to know all about the New Mexico ranch and Steve still hadn't lost his interest in pursuing the cattle partnership idea. In fact, he seemed even more eager now that Buck was actually going to make the move to New Mexico.

Next he called a friend in the English Department. Steve Harrison was relatively new to the university and Buck had talked to him about offering a course together about western American literature and art of the 19th and 20th centuries. Buck knew he had better tell him about his future now that it was a fact and that next year there would be no new course. He also called an old bronc riding partner in Great Falls and one or two other cowboy friends. He even contemplated calling Jennifer but decided a call to her was a bad idea. He started to dial the Mahoneys down in the valley but put the phone down before the call was connected. He knew they would be happy for him but he was aware it might also seem like bad news. Someone they liked and often counted on would be leaving and they didn't have too many friends in the area. He figured that conversation would just have to wait, although Buck had no idea when it would be an appropriate time to call those good neighbors.

He was a little wiped out after digesting all the news and retelling the story on his various telephone calls, so he decided he'd go to bed, get up early and since he had to teach tomorrow, he'd see what happened when he hit town. He would go to the Credit Union, the bank, and talk to some people in the administration building about his retirement funds, final paycheck and things like that.

Buck knew he would also have to tell his Dean, who in Buck's view was a pompous ass who Buck felt never did fit in at the university. He was an easterner who related everything to his dismal life in Rhode Island and somehow Montana and the West always came in a poor second. Buck actually disliked even having a conversation with the man. This was the man who needled Buck about being a rodeo cowboy because he had such little respect for the sport or the athletes who participated. In fact, most people around the campus who knew Dean Graybill thought he was just frustrated at being in Montana rather than at some eastern school where he thought he belonged. Buck looked forward to telling him he was leaving and that he could go to hell.

When he got to his office Rebecca was working at the slide table, organizing and sorting the slides he had used the previous two classes and pulling the ones he had listed for the coming week. At first she pretended she didn't see him. But she finally said, very quietly, "So you really are leaving. I've heard rumors for a couple of months but I thought you would at least tell me yourself. When are you going? Are you at least staying to teach summer school?"

"How do you know all this? I'm sorry I didn't tell you but you weren't at the top of my phone list."

He quickly regretted saying that. It sounded harsh and Rebecca didn't deserve any smart ass comments.

"Rebecca, I'm sorry but this has been in the works for many months—more than a year. Way before you came to work for me. Don't worry about your job. I guarantee I'll give you the best damn recommendation I can write. You'll have a job."

"I wasn't thinking about my job."

She didn't say another word and continued working on the slides. It was close to the top of the hour and Buck had to get to his seminar so the rest of this conversation would just have to be put on hold.

When he returned to his office after his class, Rebecca was already gone, off to one of her own classes. Although he felt he wanted to clean up this little mess that he unwittingly created with his senseless comment, he knew it would have to wait until Wednesday. He had to meet his other class and then he wanted to head right home. He thought he had so much to do and so little time in which to do it. In his own head it was as if the move was going to happen tomorrow and he wasn't ready. Everything about his life was suddenly truncated and he was beginning to feel the pressure.

The drive home took longer than it ever had. It seemed like hours instead of forty minutes. He did remember to stop at the liquor store in Lolo to pick up some boxes. He had always been told that liquor boxes were somehow stronger than the regular boxes he could get at the super market. He really didn't know if this was true but if the liquor store had boxes he would get them. He was lucky that Paul's Liquor Store was just restocking and had an almost unlimited supply of boxes in a variety of sizes. They were glad for him to take as many as he wanted. He flattened the cardboard boxes and filled up the Subaru Forester until it was almost impossible to see out through the rear view mirror. Then he headed for the ranch. He made arrangements with the store owner to stop by again if he needed more boxes.

■■■

When he got settled in at home, he tried to make a rational plan for packing, getting rid of things he didn't want or need, and some type of schedule for the move. He knew it would take several trips—some with horses, some with furniture and other belongings, and one or two just to get things ready at the new ranch. Buck was going to do the move himself with a U-Haul, not hire some professional moving company. He also wanted to see if the five acre piece on his west fence line in New Mexico was available. The land itself wasn't of any particular value but it did have a house, its own well, a small barn, and a good set of pipe corrals that were all in pretty good shape. Buck was sure he could get it reasonably cheap. No one was living there and although it wasn't really rundown, it certainly wasn't what someone who was looking for a retirement home would pick. And besides, the Animas Valley wasn't exactly known as a place for retirees. But it could be just the place for a cowboy, if he had the chance to hire one for the ranch. If not, after some work, it would make a good guest house. Buck liked the idea of the guest quarters being a distance away from the ranch's main house.

His next move was to call two of his Bitterroot neighbors, neither of them really friends but they shared Buck's north fence line. They had only been in the valley a little over a year and they stayed pretty much to themselves. One was from Chicago and the other from Richmond, Virginia and from what Buck heard around town, neither of them had families. Buck had no idea what they did for a living and he wasn't even sure if they lived there full time or just came for the summer. Neither had any stock so closing their places down when they left posed no particular problems. Over the past year Buck never had any social contact with either of them. In fact, he had never actually met them. He was surprised that when he called he was able to reach both of his neighbors. He explained that he had sold his place to someone from Hollywood and that he would gladly give them any information he had if they were interested. Neither of them seemed to be remotely concerned.

Buck next called his Stevensville realtor, Helen Ostegard. He wanted to make sure the new buyer was aware that the Palo Verde Ranch in Montana had been put into a conservation easement, one of the first in western Montana, and that such an easement could not be broken or that it was not an option for the new buyer to decide whether or not he wanted to maintain it. The land Buck had nurtured for so long was going to remain open and natural. He had always been adamant that the place not be sold to a developer, the kind of person he considered lower than a used car salesman or TV evangelist. The conservation easement insured that. In the Bitterroot Valley, the word "developer" had come to mean about the lowest of the low. Yet they appeared to be all over the place and ranchers were selling out so people could build million dollar second homes they rarely used. It didn't make sense to Buck but many things that were happening in the modern west didn't make sense any more.

■■■

Helen assured Buck this had all been made clear to the new buyer and that it had actually been an asset in making the sale.

Next he put in a call to New Mexico and arranged a quick trip down to see the new place, go over some details and get an estimate of what it would take to have the main house made as livable as he wanted it to be in the shortest possible time. In his calmer moments he knew he still had about three months to get organized and moved, so he began to think more rationally and plan more carefully. He got on his computer and set up a flight to Tucson, the closest major airport to the ranch, reserved a rental car and realized he would have to cancel one day of his classes. So be it.

He then went out to the barn to inventory all the odds and ends that accumulated there over the years. For the first time he admitted to himself that some of this was junk and that it had no good use now and never would. After he took into account all the stuff he had, all he could think about was that he could sell most of this at a garage sale. He was also aware, after a quick look around the house and barn, that he could have one helluva garage sale. On his list of things to do, the garage sale quickly emerged close to the top. He was also concerned about the number of books he had at his office and at home. They could fill up dozens of boxes, far too many for him to move south to New Mexico. When Buck realized he would have no further use for so many of the volumes, he decided to sell some and donate the rest to a library or school.

Buck was beginning to take things in a rational order and although the job of moving almost overwhelmed him, he knew in the end it would all get done and everything would fall into place. He trusted to the "moving Gods" to help him out because he wasn't sure exactly what came first. He just knew he had to go to New Mexico and find out what the conditions of things were down there. He had to check the water, the perimeter fencing, the corrals, the barn, and especially the house. He remembered they were all in good shape on his last trip there and Ann Lewis had double checked before he made his offer, but it was best to check everything again, certainly before he set a closing date. He wanted to find a local fix-it guy who could do work for him while he was still in

Montana and have everything ready when he arrived to settle in permanently. It had to be someone who was good at his work and someone Buck could trust.

■■■

By Wednesday he felt he had things under control. As he headed north to Missoula, he realized that one of the things he would miss when he left Montana was the drive up and down the Bitterroot Valley, at least to Lolo, where everything began to merge into the Missoula traffic. The valley was truly a beautiful place. When he got to the campus he parked farther away from his office than he usually did because he wanted to walk. It was very cold. The wind was blowing through the canyons that surrounded Missoula and the sky was its usual overcast gray, but the walk was what he needed. He just wanted to get energized.

Rebecca was hard at work when he entered his office.

"Hi. Any calls or other annoyances?"

"Good morning. I guess no one wants to see you or talk to you."

"Is that a personal comment or just a general observation? It sounded a little bit of both."

Before another word could be said, Rebecca started out on a long rambling explanation of her own feelings.

"You know I'm going to miss you. I've learned so much from you in the past several months. I think I've got my own future straightened out and I feel so good about things. I guess I did know you were thinking of leaving when I took the job. The lady at the work-study office told me that. I just didn't think it would really happen or it would happen so soon. One of the things I've wanted to do was take some of your classes. I guess now that's out of the question. So I've decided to go back to Seattle after this year and reenroll at the University of Washington. You know, "Go Huskies." I hope it will make it easier to get into law school there and that's what I really want to do. I'd stay if you stayed but since that isn't going to happen I might as well split while I can. I have no real ties here. I don't have any real close friends and I don't even have a boy friend."

Buck was glad she paused to take a breath.

"I'm a little surprised. I thought you liked Montana. But I do understand. It gets pretty dreary here in the winter, particularly in Missoula, and the winter isn't the best time to make rational decisions. Getting out of here would be at the top of anyone's list of things to do. But going back to Seattle? I'm glad you still want to be a lawyer. I think you'll be terrific. And for what it's worth, you've been about as good working here as anyone I've ever had. You're very smart and talented. But mostly, you know how to make decisions and I put a high premium on that. If you were going to go to graduate school and I was still teaching, I'd love to have you as my TA."

She tried to hide a smile but then got serious again.

"What I don't understand is why you're leaving teaching. Everyone says you are one of the best lecturers on campus and they all want to take your classes even though they all say you are one of the toughest graders. I can see how you interact with students when they come to see you here in the office.

You leave and we're left with some real asses and they are the ones with tenure. And I don't mean just here. I had some terrible professors over in Washington. What is it about being a cowboy that is so fascinating you are giving up something you have such a talent for? And why are you going all the way to New Mexico? You have a ranch here and from what I hear it is a beautiful place. Isn't it too hot and dry down there in the desert?"

Now it was Buck's turn to smile. He stood up and walked over to the window.

"I'll tell you a quick story and then you'll understand or maybe you won't. Some years ago my traveling partner, Ab Northway, a top flight bareback rider from Idaho, and I were rodeoing in west Texas when we decided we'd better head north. We crossed the border into New Mexico, down by Carlsbad, and soon we were we in the Sacramento Mountains over by Ruidoso. I remember telling him this is where I belong and this is where I was going to live. I had never even been in New Mexico before. But I just knew. We headed west and when we hit the desert country west of Las Cruces and the Rio Grande River, I knew I was home. I just knew it. I can't explain it any better than that. And for the other part, about being a cowboy, haven't you ever heard the Willie Nelson song, "My Heroes Have Always Been Cowboys"? I guess I just want to be somebody's hero. Being a cowboy is something I've wanted to be since I was a little boy growing up in the East."

"I think I'd better shut up. Maybe I've said too much already."

"Have you ever been to the southwest, to New Mexico?"

"Never!"

"Well, some day if you get there you might understand. There is no better weather and they say you either love the desert or hate it. There doesn't seem to be any middle ground. I guess you know how I feel." He paused for a minute. "I don't mean to change the subject, but I have to fly down to look over my new ranch next week so I'm going to cancel my Friday classes. You might as well take a little break yourself. Over the next couple of months I'm going to be making a few more trips down to New Mexico, eventually taking some of my horses." He waited a second to let this all sink in. He looked at her and realized how really disappointed she was that he was leaving.

"Come on now. You can smile and don't be angry at me. This has been my dream. Don't ever, and I mean ever, give up your dreams. Be a lawyer, and be a damn good one. When you give up your dreams, you might as well shrivel up and die. Just look around, you can almost tell without asking, those who still have their dreams and those that have stopped dreaming."

He waited a few seconds to see what Rebecca was going to do or say. He remembered a quote from Edmond Rostand, the 19th century French writer: "The dream, alone, is of interest. What is life, without a dream?" Then, as if to break the mood, he quickly added:

"Let's get to work."

"Thanks." She said it quietly and he wasn't sure what Rebecca was thinking. He didn't think she was still angry but what other thoughts she might have would just have to remain a mystery.

That afternoon, as he was heading for his car, he ran into Jennifer. He hadn't seen or spoken to her in nearly a month and the unexpected meeting was a little rattling. She looked sensational, as usual, and she seemed glad to see him.

"How are you? Did you forget I existed?"

"You know better than that. But I've really had my hands full. I sold the ranch and I'm in the process of buying the ranch I've wanted in New Mexico. Now I'm going full speed ahead with the move."

He then gave her a short list of the details and sort of a schedule for his departure. She seemed surprised and a little uncomfortable. When he looked at her she had a hint of sadness in her eyes but he knew that was temporary and that she was going back to Minneapolis. She was beautiful but lacked a certain fire, a certain kind of sexuality he had never noticed or missed before. Maybe that was what allowed her to settle for a comfortable, conventional life rather than the longer and harder search for happiness. Because he didn't want her asking too many questions—Buck didn't want this conversation to get very personal—he decided to jump in with his own.

"When are you leaving? Have you told your department yet? And what are your wedding plans? I'm sure this is all very exciting and I know it will work out for you."

"I haven't told anyone yet except you and I actually haven't made plans. Lars might come out here in a couple of weeks. Would you like to meet him?" She was almost sorry she asked that question before it was completely out of her mouth, but Buck took her off the hook.

"I'll be traveling back and forth to New Mexico so I doubt if you'd even find me. I'm feeling real pressure to get organized, get packed and I still have to get my place down there fixed up, get the horses moved, and then be ready to close on time. Moving is so damn stressful, even when it's the move you really want to make."

Here it was. They both were talking about their future and there wasn't room for either of them in the other's plans. That's the way it should have been from the beginning and Buck was glad it all worked out reasonably right. They made some small talk and as they were leaving, Jennifer gave him a big hug and a kiss on the cheek. Buck never knew what those cheek kisses meant but he didn't take this for anything more than what it was—a fond farewell for today if not forever.

When he arrived back home he started to do an inventory of what he had. It really surprised him but he had always been accused of being a pack rat. He was that! He made a list of things to take to New Mexico, of things headed for the dump, and of things that could go in a garage sale. Unfortunately, the "things to take" list kept getting longer and longer. He organized the boxes, made some plans for his trip that coming weekend, and then put Beethoven's Seventh Symphony on the stereo. Once again he realized the only thing missing was someone to share all this with. Well, he thought, "I'll have to find one of those dark haired senoritas somewhere around the Animas Valley." The idea actually had some real appeal to him. He needed something new in his life and that would definitely break new ground for him.

■■■

Rebecca volunteered to take him to the airport but he decided to just park his car in long term parking. That way he could come and go more easily and if the plane was late or really delayed in getting back to Montana—and that wasn't unusual during the winter in Missoula—he didn't want to have the hassle of someone else having to wait for him. The airport was west of Missoula and adjoined the Smokejumpers Fire Depot, where they trained all those extremely tough and courageous fire fighters who parachuted into fires and then had to hike out. The Missoula airport was small although he had seen it grow over the years. There still weren't too many flights and almost nothing that was nonstop unless your destination was Great Falls, Salt Lake City, Denver or Spokane. On this trip he had to change planes in Salt Lake City.

The flight was nearly full, uneventful and boring. Because the legs of the trip were so short there was no food served on the flight and small bags of pretzels hardly sated a cowboy's appetite. He planned to grab something to eat at the Salt Lake City airport, where he had almost a two hour layover.

It was dusk when the plane finally landed at the Tucson airport that was just being rennovated. The new facility was very modern, clean, spacious, and empty. It must be hard, he thought, to compete with Phoenix, which is just a little less than two hours up the road, even though the city of Tucson was growing at an almost unmanageable pace. "Maybe," he thought, "someday they'll catch up and really ruin this place, too."

He went to the Alamo rental car desk, got his vehicle and headed for I-10, which was a straight run to Lordsburg that was just across the border into New Mexico. He figured it would take him a little over two hours to get to Lordsburg where he was going to meet Ann Lewis. He called from the airport and because it was so late she said she would meet him at her office at 8:30 the next morning.

The drive wasn't too bad. He headed east to Benson, wound his way through Texas Canyon, an incredible array of rock formations, over to the old ranching community of Willcox, and then it was an uneventful run to Bowie, San Simon and finally the New Mexico border. The entire drive was through open ranch and farm country with mountains in the near distance, no matter what direction Buck looked. Lordsburg was at milepost 22 in New Mexico and that's where he got off the interstate and took a room at the newest looking motel. After checking in he drove around town, once again just to get a feel for the little town that was going to be the closest real town to the ranch. Even with the darkness settling in and hiding most of its obvious flaws, Lordsburg, which was the Hidalgo County seat, wasn't a very impressive place.

He had dinner at the first restaurant he could find that wasn't fast food and then headed back to the motel. It had been a long day and he was surprised at how tired he was. He wanted to get a good night's rest and with all the anticipation of what the next day was going to be, Buck wasn't sure he'd even be able to fall asleep.

By morning he could barely wait to get to Ann's office at the agreed upon time. She was waiting for him and after a few pleasantries they decided to head to the ranch. Ann was very attractive, probably in her mid forties, and you could tell she must have been a high school cheer leader. She seemed smart and because she was the third generation of her family to live in Hidalgo County, she knew almost everything about the area and just about everybody in the sparsely populated community.

It took nearly thirty-five minutes to drive down to the ranch in the Animas Valley. The ranch was on the east side, in the foothills of the Pyramid Mountains. Across the valley were the Peloncillo Mountains, whose name probably comes from the Spanish word that means "little baldy," right on the Arizona border, and towering behind them were the impressive Chiricahua Mountains in Arizona. This was a stark and beautiful place, in sharp contrast to the far greener and lush Bitterroot Valley but as he did in Montana, he wondered again what secrets the mountains were hiding. Looking south you could see Animas Peak, located on the legendary Gray Ranch. That was just north of the border with Mexico and the beginning of the Sierra Madres. Buck knew this valley was where he wanted to be.

Hidalgo County had fewer than 6,000 people, which came to less than two people per square mile, not a single stop light in the entire county and a history that was rich and diverse. For Buck this was an American Studies treasure trove. Mining, ranching, and the railroads were dominant but this was also the historic home of the Apaches. Names like Cochise and Geronimo were frequently mentioned and they were an intricate part of the history of the region. Just over the mountains to the west was Tombstone, the "City Too Tough To Die." The Bootheel of New Mexico was going to be an entirely new area to investigate to satisfy his academic and personal interests in American history and the West. He knew he wouldn't be bored.

Lordsburg, though, had the look of a dying town. It had been bypassed when the Interstate came along and it just never had recovered. All the empty cafes, run down motels, and closed buildings spoke to another time. Supreme Court Justice Sandra Day O'Conner spent time there when she was growing up on her family's Lazy B Ranch just across the border near Duncan, Arizona. But no longer did the town resemble the place she would later describe in her memoir.

Buck had hoped it would.

Lordsburg seemed to represent so many small towns in the West that are hanging on for dear life with no real prospects for the future. If the railroad ever pulled out, it would be hard to imagine there would even be a Lordsburg. The town had been founded in 1880 when the Southern Pacific Railroad arrived from the West. It was quickly populated by railroaders, freighters, cowboys, miners gamblers, prostitutes and merchants. It just seems that its time had slipped by and no one had a good idea of what to do about it. All the usual things were discussed—economic growth, tourism, and even more trade with the towns across the border in Mexico. But those schemes take money and leadership and no one knew where either was going to come from. It was obvious there was virtually no new construction going on in town—maybe a new motel near an interstate exit—and no indication that any new businesses were setting up shop. Buck just shook his head and felt a little sad.

■■■

Buck and Ann drove south in her SUV and talked about the details of the sale and the general area. People weren't flocking to Hidalgo County so it was very much a buyer's market.

When they arrived at the ranch and drove across the cattle guard and up to the house, Buck was almost shaking he was so excited. Was this for real? All he could think about was the years he had fantasized about living back in New Mexico and now it was actually going to happen. The house needed a little more work than he remembered but the barn, corrals, fencing, and other parts of the ranch were in good shape. He could, if worse came to worst, move in tomorrow and work on the house while he lived there. He didn't want to do that and because of the time frame for the move, he was sure he wouldn't have to. Most of the work could be done while he was still finishing out the school year in Montana. He could see he wanted to knock out a wall here, put in a better door there, sand and redo the hardwood floors, put in a new window in the living room, and probably upgrade a good portion of the kitchen. The bathrooms were surprisingly modern and in good shape although he ultimately wanted a hot tub. He could do all the painting himself. The house had three bedrooms, two full baths, a screened in porch and a smaller room with a window facing the western sunsets. That could easily be Buck's office. The living room was large and had a pass through to the kitchen and dining room. There was no heating system in the house but the small southwestern fireplace in the dining room and the new wood burning stove looked like it could heat the entire interior. To Buck, a wood burning stove was just a natural, particularly in the southwest where he wouldn't have to endure any more below zero temperatures. As he stood there in his new home he could almost smell the mesquite and the piñon burning in the stove. The exterior was stucco and needed a fresh coat of painted but otherwise was in good shape. The area's typically green metal roof was less than five years old and looked even newer. He had no immediate neighbors, at least none he could see, but the views to the west, in the direction of the Peloncillo and Chiricahua Mountains were staggeringly beautiful, the kind of scenes romantic landscape painters understood. The sunsets, he guessed, would be beyond anything he could imagine.

Ann didn't say very much. She could tell how much he was enjoying himself and she actually felt talking to Buck right then would be an intrusion. Ann had seen others come to the desert and be completely captivated by its beauty and even its loneliness.

They drove over some of the fifty sections. Most of the land that bordered the ranch was more BLM although Buck knew there was one neighbor to the south. But it was some of the BLM land Buck hoped he could lease one of these days. There were dirt roads and cattle and wildlife trails on his land, no matter what direction they traveled. They checked a couple of the windmills and several of the dirt tanks and Buck was surprised at how much water they still held, even in this very dry season. When they got to the extra five acres with the house, Buck got out and examined the building. He thought it would work and was a bit surprised it would need so little fixing up. Ann followed him and told him the owners had agreed to sell. Buck was glad to have the additional house, corrals, and barn and especially the extra well.

Ann was quick to identify all the wildlife on the ranch, in the Pyramids, and across the valley. She explained that there were mountain lions, mule deer, Coues' white tailed deer, antelope, coyotes, javelina, jack rabbits, a variety of smaller animals and so many species of birds—song birds and raptors, and road runners—that Buck couldn't keep track of them. There were even Desert Bighorn Sheep across the valley near Granite Gap, and to the south just past the tiny town of Animas. The mountain lions and coyotes concerned Buck but everything else was just a bonus.

■■■

It was still early when they headed back to town so they went directly to Ann's office to sort through the paper work. Her office looked like a bomb had hit it. Her computer was surrounded by papers, brochures and all manner of literature. He wondered why, since this was certainly not a booming area for real estate, but he decided it was better to not ask. He just concluded that Ann was not a good housekeeper.

The contract seemed in order. It was surely was what Buck had expected. The price was correct and even with the additional five acres and the house it was still well below what he had originally budgeted for and expected to pay. The difference in land prices and particularly taxes in Hidalgo County and in the Bitterroots of Montana made the move a good one, at least financially. He was sure his attorney back in Montana would find the document in order and ready to sign.

"Anne, do you know someone from around here who I can trust and can do some of the handyman work while I'm back in Montana? I'll want some things done to the house before I move in. I don't want to make too big a deal of this. Is there a local guy you can recommend? You know the type—someone who doesn't need daily directions to get the job done?"

Ann didn't have to give it much thought. "I think I know someone. There's a fellow who does a lot of work around Animas and I haven't heard any complaints. He isn't very expensive and I know you can trust him. I just always assumed you wanted whatever work had to be done finished while you were still in Montana. "

"That's right. I'll set out the plan and then check back with him every week or so. I don't want to wait until I get here to get started. How do I get in touch with him? What's his name?"

"His name is Tommy Sanchez. He was born and raised right in the area. I'll find his number here somewhere."

Buck wasn't sure she could find anything on her desk but she came up with it in no time at all.

"Here's his number." She handed Buck a yellow post-it-note with Tommy Sanchez's name and number and Buck thought he'd give him a call before he went for something to eat.

"Ann, I can't thank you enough for all you've done and for all your patience. I know I've put you on hold too often but I couldn't be happier with all the arrangements. I doubt if you can even imagine how much I want to move down here."

"I glad we did this deal, Buck. You are the kind of person we want to move into this valley. We don't get many new people so a few bad apples moving in could really do some damage down here. I was talking with Clay, my husband, and he agreed. He wants to meet you as soon as you are here and settled. Or better yet, why don't you have dinner with us the next time you come down?"

Maybe Buck was becoming too suspicious with all the developers and new people he had seen moving into the Bitterroot Valley but he was wondering exactly what Ann meant by telling him he was the kind of person they wanted to move in down here. Exactly what kind of person was that? He was hoping all she meant was they wanted another rancher, another cowboy. He knew she didn't know his politics which he wasn't sure would fit in with the prevailing attitudes in the Animas Valley.

"That sounds good to me. I'm going to head over to the motel now. Call me as soon as we can close, as long as it's at least a month or so away. I want to make sure I have the money from the sale of my Montana ranch all squared away and in the bank. I know that down here there doesn't seem to be any rush. Ann, thanks again for everything. I'll call you from the airport on Sunday or when I get back to Montana. I'm really sorry this was such a short trip"

They shook hands and Buck went to the motel and called Tommy Sanchez. He wasn't home but his wife said he should be home any minute. She'd have him call Buck at the motel.

Buck was dozing when a half hour later the phone rang and it was Sanchez. Buck explained the situation and since it was still early in the afternoon with plenty of daylight left, they agreed to meet at the ranch in an hour. Sanchez knew exactly where it was and even seemed to know who Buck was or at least that someone from Montana was buying the ranch. Buck just marveled about how news travels in small ranching communities.

Buck was the first to arrive at the future Palo Verde Ranch. When Tommy showed up, they shook hands, chatted a bit and then they took a tour of the house. Ann had given him the keys to both houses.

Tommy was in his late thirties, nearly six feet tall, dark haired with a small moustache. After a go through of the house, he made some very innovative suggestions and Buck was impressed about how much this local handyman knew. They talked about fees, about how long the various projects would take and how Buck would set up a charge account at the Animas Valley Feed Store so Tommy could get parts and materials as he needed them. Buck said it would be okay with him if the Feed Store would open a charge account. Tommy thought they would since Ann Lewis had already told people in the area all about him.

"And don't worry, it was all good stuff. We're always glad when another cowboy moves in here. We get so much crap from the environmentalists and the people with way too much money and not a clue about how to actually make a ranch work. But they never last. I think you'll fit in fine. Are you married? Do you have any kids?"

"No wife and no kids. And I'm glad people are willing to give me a chance.

I want to make it work down here. I haven't come down here to change anything. In fact, I don't want anything to change."

After Buck and Tommy agreed on the work schedule and the priorities, Buck asked Tommy to follow him over to the Feed Store. He thought it would be easier to get things done in person there since they all knew Tommy.

Tommy led the way in his Dodge truck and Buck followed in his white rental car. When they got to the Feed Store, about a twenty minute drive, Buck liked the old fashioned look of the place with its wood floors and tin ceiling. A quick look around led Buck to believe they certainly seemed to have enough stock—everything from lumber, paint, fencing, all sorts of plumbing and automotive supplies, tires, veterinary provisions and feed and hay—everything you might need in a ranching community. It was also the only store in town.

The building was large and old fashioned yet it had what any modern rancher would need. The people running the store greeted the newcomer warmly, were incredibly helpful and very talkative, the way they were supposed to be in a small town. Setting up the account was easy. All they wanted was an address so they could send the monthly bill and permission for Tommy to charge on the account. No fancy forms to fill out. The simplicity of it all seemed to be from another era and to Buck's way of thinking, that era was a far better time.

As they were about to part ways, Buck gave Tommy a set of keys. Tommy wanted to know how he got the keys and was anyone going to care that he was working there since they hadn't closed yet. Buck explained that he had put down enough money so that the deal was essentially done and that Tommy should know how things work down here. Ann had negotiated all of this all and for Buck there was no backing out now. The people who were selling Buck the ranch were an older couple, Marge and Willy Gilbert, who were retiring and apparently had no heirs. They hadn't actually lived on the ranch for a little over a year and all they wanted to do was travel in their RV. They were just happy they didn't have to sell to a developer although Buck couldn't image what a developer would do with land in such a remote location. Throughout the area the Gilberts were apparently known as good ranchers and good neighbors and from the looks of things they had been good stewards of the land. Buck was lucky to be getting a place that was in as usable condition as the Gilbert's Bar G ranch. This was as close to a turnkey operation as he could have hoped for.

Buck told Tommy that if there were any immediate problems and if for some reason he couldn't reach him in Montana, he was to call Ann. She'd certainly know what to do.

Tommy said that was good enough for him.

The next day Buck headed over to the Feed Store, bought some light bulbs, a couple of padlocks, some chain, a few odds and ends and then headed to the ranch. He checked the barn and the corrals and then went back to the "guest" house to double check everything there. It had its own barn and corrals and was ideal for what Buck wanted. As soon as he realized what time it was—it was nearly four o'clock—Buck remembered he had barely eaten all day so he decided to head back to Lordsburg and get something to eat. Later that evening he drove around the area, just trying once again to get a good feel for the country.

Hidalgo County was sparsely populated but despite the apparent run down condition of Lordsburg and the surrounding country, there was a feeling of warmth and community he couldn't explain to himself.

■■■

In the morning Buck was back on the road to Tucson. He returned his car at the airport, checked in and had about a forty-five minute wait. The flight was again uneventful and when he got back to Missoula he was a little surprised at how cold it was. New Mexico was shirt sleeve weather—Montana was damn cold, even late in March, and Buck was glad he always kept a heavy jacket in his car. He couldn't wait to get home but once again he had an empty feeling because he had no one to share all this excitement with. For a brief moment he wanted someone. But he knew that would pass and he would get on with his planning. His main job now was to figure out how to move the horses. He was going to take eight with him and he wanted to make that move in two trips. Almost more importantly, who would care for them once they were settled on the Palo Verde in New Mexico and he had to head back to Montana? Buck had an idea.

When he got home, he looked around the ranch, checked waters and gates and made sure the horses and cattle were all where they belonged. Then he headed for the telephone. He called Bobby Trujillo.

After some small talk, Buck explained his situation and offered Bobby a job in New Mexico that included a pretty good salary and a house. Bobby was unattached and there wasn't anything Buck knew of that was holding him in Montana.

"Buck, thanks for the offer but I've got to say no. Don't think because my last name sounds like it's from New Mexico that I want to live down there. My folks have been in Montana for at least three generations and I just don't know anything else. I'm not so sure I want to. The cold up here doesn't bother me and you know I don't like to get attached to one place for too long. Maybe someday I'll get married, settled down and I'll have a place of my own but not right now. When I'm not doing day work I help my family on our own ranch over by Deer Lodge and they still need me here. Right now I can't see myself settling down and working for anyone else full time. Not even a good old boy like you."

"Well, I thought I'd try. I really need someone I can trust and someone who knows what he's doing. You just happen to fit the bill. If you change your mind, give me a call. I'll probably see you at the Bradshaw's down by Dillon for the branding in a couple of months and if I'm still around, up at the Triangle A for the spring branding. Drop on by when you're over here in Stevensville."

"Will do that and thanks for the offer. I do appreciate it. I'm just sorry I can't help you out."

When Buck hung up the telephone he sat by the table for a minute or two. Buck was disappointed, but calling Bobby Trujillo was worth the try. This problem was now going to take some thought. Maybe Ann and Clay Lewis would know someone or maybe they had a bulletin board at the Feed Store or the Post Office down in Animas where guys placed ads for jobs. He didn't want to wait too long to get someone.

■■■

On Monday Buck got to his office a little early and there already hard at work was Rebecca. She gave him a big hello and after he settled in at his desk, his work-study girl started to pump him with questions about his trip. He was a little surprised by her interest but he was glad to see her. Over the few months she had worked for him he had gotten used to talking to her about some personal things, things he really had no one else to talk to about. Buck was a little surprised she had become such a good friend and that he trusted her to keep her mouth shut about whatever they talked about. Trusting people like that was something Buck didn't do with people very easily.

"It was beautiful. I haven't seen the ranch in a few months and I was afraid I had romanticized it in my own mind but I didn't. It was just as I remembered it. You'd love all that sun, the blue skies and the desert plants. I know they call Montana "The Big Sky Country," but I honestly think New Mexico has it all beat. Someone like you would really appreciate it after all those depressing, rainy winters you've had to put up with in Seattle. Don't you ever want to just get away from that?"

Rebecca smiled at him.

"Oh, you get used to it. I've lived there so long I don't even know what it would be like if it wasn't rainy all winter. And the gray days lets you save so much money on sun glasses and sun screen. What's your next move, cowboy?"

Buck was a bit surprised by how familiar this conversation had gotten but it really didn't bother him.

"I'm planning to start bringing horses down to the ranch as soon as I can hire a good cowboy. Once that's done I just have to finish here and then I'm off to the desert, for good, probably in late June."

Rebecca didn't say anything for a moment. It seemed she was searching for the right words.

"You're going to the arid, sunny desert and I'll be off to a place where for half the year it never stops drizzling and you're never able to dry out. This is a heck of a country. We ought to switch for a year and see what happens. Good God, I could never survive in all that sun. I'd get wrinkles around my eyes from squinting and you wouldn't want that to happen to me. I'm way too young for lots of wrinkles."

"Don't worry about it. Even with wrinkles you'll do just fine. One of these days we'll just have to find you a boyfriend." Buck smiled at her and didn't realize how she would react to his little quip. It was always clear to him that if she wanted a boyfriend she could probably have anyone she wanted. She was so good looking—and smart and amazingly sexy. Maybe that was exactly what was keeping her from finding a good man—she was too smart and too sexy.

"Why do you think I want a boyfriend? I like things just the way they are and this gives me time for my studies. You know how important that is right now." She had gotten very serious and Buck was worried that maybe he had hit some nerve. He needed a quick recovery.

"To celebrate my return and my new ranch, let me take you to lunch. We'll even go off campus so you can get some real food. What do you say?"

"Okay. But no more talk about my love life or lack of it. Is that a deal?"

"It's a deal. I'll meet you back here after my class and we'll have plenty of time before your afternoon class. Think of where you want to eat."

Rebecca lit up with her mischievous smile. "I know already. Let's go over to the Sheraton. Everyone says they have a really nice dining room and it will cost you a lot of money, Mr. Big-Time rancher. Are you sure you want to be seen in public with me? You know how it is with all that teacher-student stuff?"

"I can't think of anything that I care less about than some Missoula gossip. Besides, being seen with you will only improve my reputation. What are they going to do, fire me at the end of the year? Besides, the winter is always slow here and a little gossip about the two of us will give the locals something to occupy their time."

For one of the first times, Buck realized how little he cared about what people in Missoula thought about him or what he did or how he acted. He was, at least in his own mind, already gone.

■■■

When they entered the Sheraton it was fairly quiet. There were a couple of men dressed in suits sitting in the lobby, probably businessmen, one or two others just scurrying around and a couple of well-dressed, middle-aged women over by the gift shop. Buck and Rebecca headed straight to the dining room and where they were promptly seated by the young, far too perky hostess. Most of the tables were occupied and as they took their seats, Buck realized that there were eyes turning to get a look at the new couple. He was known around town but Rebecca was the wild card. He was very proud of being seen with Rebecca and that surprised him. He hadn't thought much about it until the eyes started to follow them. Once they were seated Rebecca just laughed.

"Did you see all those old ladies and horny businessmen looking us over? I'm sorry that I'm dressed so conservatively. It would be more fun if I looked like one of the high priced hookers who hang around here. Maybe they think I am one of them anyway, here to entertain one of the local college professors."

"How the hell do you know about that? I thought that the hookers here were Missoula's little secret. I've never seen one of them but then maybe I have and wouldn't even know that I did. The word is that they dress pretty well, and you're right, they are supposed to be expensive. That puts them out of the range of an underpaid college professor like me. And from what you hear around town, they sure don't look like the hookers you see on TV. They aren't nearly as slutty."

"Are you kidding me? You really mean you don't think you'd recognize a hooker in a place like this?" She laughed out loud. "And don't tell me you've never participated in the pleasures of cheap women."

"Cheap women...well, maybe. But I've never had to pay for my little sexual pleasures."

He paused for a moment. He truly wanted to change the topic.

"Let's order before this conversation gets out of hand. You are an inquisitive young woman. And, most of this is none of your damn business."

The new couple had an enjoyable lunch filled with easy conversation that was mostly about school, Rebecca's time in Missoula and Buck's ranch. And yet there was barely a mention of each of their impending moves. When they left the Sheraton Buck dropped Rebecca off at the university and from there he headed downtown to run a few errands and do a little grocery shopping.

The more he thought about lunch the more he realized what a good time he had with his work study girl. He had trouble thinking of her that way. She was becoming more and more of a friend. There was no question in his mind that she was a challenge, but she was sure an enjoyable challenge. She didn't seem to have any excess baggage beyond what she had already told him and he wanted to believe that she was what she appeared to be. And he wanted to believe that he could keep his relationship with her on a friendship-only basis and not let himself get crazy. Or let her get crazy, for that matter. She was tempting and he was leaving. And that should be the end of it.

■■■

When he got home and finished with the evening chores, he took off his boots, put on his comfortable sheepskin lined slippers, and settled on the couch to just relax. Cowboy jumped up on the couch and got comfortable too, his head nestled in Buck's lap. Buck was thinking again of who he could get to work for him on his place in New Mexico. He went through a list of names in his head until he faced the fact that it would have to be someone from New Mexico, not Montana. This was a problem that was beginning to get to Buck. He couldn't think of an easy solution but he knew that a solution had to be found.

He was about to get up and investigate the kitchen and prepare some dinner, when he had a new idea. Why not try Phil Shaw? He was single, unattached, he wanted to see the West and be a cowboy. What could fit the picture better than that? And he was smart. All that Buck knew about Phil was that he had graduated from Amherst College in Massachusetts, an expensive, first rate, private liberal arts college. He had been an excellent student and left the east to follow his dream. Buck sure understood that. And the more Buck thought about it the more convinced he was that Phil must have money or at least come from a well-off family. He couldn't possibly be driving his new truck and living on the money he made doing occasional day work on the ranches in the area. Although Buck didn't know him very well, he remembered working with him and that had left him with a good impression of the young easterner. He didn't know where he lived or even his phone number but he knew he could get that from Steve Anderson up in the Big Hole country.

After a call to Steve, Buck learned that Phil lived over by Whitehall, just north of the Tobacco Root Mountains and just off I-90, east of Butte. To Buck, that seemed a strange place for the young, single cowboy to live. It was pretty isolated, and it surly didn't provide much in the way of a social life for someone Phil's age, but Montana wasn't overrun by interesting cities, at least not for a young, good looking, single guy.

Whitehall was a very small town, on a busy day maybe you could count 1,000 people, surrounded mostly by ranching country nestled between Butte and Bozeman.

Buck sat on the couch thinking about calling Phil and then he finally decided that he had nothing to lose. He might be offering the young, college graduate just the right opportunity. He dialed the number and got Phil's answering machine. Buck asked him to call back and later that evening, the phone rang. It was Phil.

After some preliminary conversation, renewing their brief friendship from their work together at the Triangle A, Buck got to the point and asked Phil if he was interested in moving to New Mexico? Phil asked a few questions about the ranch and the type of work it required.

Mostly he wanted to know how close Animas was to Santa Fe and Albuquerque and what kind of country it was. Buck filled him in as much as he could and explained that the ranch was just north of the Mexican border and closer to Tucson, Las Cruces, and even El Paso, than it was to most of the New Mexico towns that he might have heard of. Phil said he was definitely interested and that he was coming to Missoula next Friday and if Buck was free they could get together and talk more about the job. Buck was pleased with himself for making the call and his intuition told him that this might actually work out. He arranged to meet Phil for lunch at the old One-Eyed Cowboy Cafe in the old part of downtown Missoula.

In the meantime Buck had more planning to do. He even called Tommy Sanchez to make sure that progress was being made on the renovation of his future home. Tommy assured him that he was on schedule and that the place was beginning to look "pretty damn good." Buck told him about the possibility that he might need the other house ready even sooner than his own and to get a key from Ann, look it over and make sure that it was livable. Buck then gave him a tentative schedule for his next visit and when he hung up, he had a good feeling about Tommy and how things were beginning, finally, to shape up on the new Palo Verde Ranch in New Mexico. It seemed that all the pieces were beginning to fall into place.

The ensuing days in Montana went along without incident. Buck enjoyed seeing Rebecca at the office and he couldn't help but anticipate his lunch with Phil Shaw. Being an optimist, Buck was sure that this was all going to work out and become a positive move for both of them. He liked Phil's enthusiasm and what he had seen of his work ethic and he knew that he was smart and independent, both good traits for the work ahead. And no matter how you cut it, what Buck was going to offer him was significantly more interesting and certainly economically more rewarding than what he was making doing day work over near Whitehall, Montana. And besides that, day work in Montana pretty well dried up during the long winters.

When they met at the One-Eyed Cowboy Cafe, in an older part of town, Phil and Buck greeted one another like long, lost buddies. They took a seat in one of the dimly lit heavy wood booths, close enough to the pool table to hear the constant clicking of the balls.

As they settled in, Buck thought that it was a good sign that Phil had driven all the way over from Whitehall. After they had ordered some burgers and fries, Buck proceeded to explain the "job" offer and give him as much of an overview of the ranch, Hidalgo County, and the surrounding country as he could. He even mentioned, though just in passing, the possibility of partnering up in the cattle business with Steve Anderson for part of the year. Phil paid close attention, excited by the possibility of having a full time cowboy job, but he didn't ask too many questions. In fact, he wasn't even sure of what to ask since he'd never been to the Bootheel of New Mexico or for that matter, any part of New Mexico and for all intent and purposes, knew almost nothing about it.

When Buck was finished, Phil sat up, looked at Buck with a big smile and said, "Let's do it. I just wonder if you can ever image how much I've wanted a job like this. I just didn't know exactly where to look or who to ask. It's hard for an eastern dude like me to always feel that I fit in out here. I'm never sure what these old timers are thinking. I know you came out here from the East a long time ago and have owned your own outfits, so I guess it's different for you. And I should tell you, I am intrigued with you being a PhD and a college professor. I guess that's part of my background that I can't escape. I'd rather be around someone like you than some dummy that is hard to have a conversation with. Jesus, that sounds pretty damn eastern, doesn't it? When will you need me? I've always heard that New Mexico is as cowboy as it gets and I guess it's time for me to go down there, see it and get started if I'm ever going live the cowboy life."

When Phil finished he felt a great sigh of relief. He had just committed to doing something he had dreamed about for years and he had the opportunity to do it with someone who he knew he could admire and learn from.

"Phil, I can't tell you how good this makes me feel. From here on out everything else will be a whole lot easier for me. I know that you'll work out just fine. When can you be ready to go?"

Buck was so elated that he thought he must sound like a kid who went into the living room and got everything he wanted on Christmas morning.

"I can be ready tomorrow. I've got nothing holding me here. I'm living in a cabin that I'm renting from an old cowboy who needs some help with his place. He's pretty stove up and we trade some work for rent. He'll understand why I'm leaving. He's been encouraging me to go find a real ranch job, something full time. I almost think that this will give him a boost. He is a fine old guy and it's just too bad that his wife died when she did and his two boys went off to Denver. He's like so many of those old timers that I've met so far—they just don't want to sell out and go live in a nursing home or in some city where they don't know anybody. I guess he could go to Denver to be with his boys but he sure doesn't want to be a burden on them and their families. It's really sad but you've got to admire and respect people like that. They've a put in some hard years. But, I guess it really is time for me to move on if I'm going to learn anything. And New Mexico seems like it'll be a great adventure. You'll be a good teacher."

"Well, we won't be moving tomorrow but it should be in a week or two. I'll have to make some calls to New Mexico and check my schedule here. Why don't you come down to Stevensville tonight and stay over. We can talk and get to know one another a little better. And you're sure right that this is going to be one helluva of an adventure for the both of us."

"That sounds fine to me. I'll just follow you home."

■■■

Phil was easy to be around. He was upbeat, seemed sure of himself and apparently he knew why he came west and what he wanted to do out in the country that was so different from where he had his roots. Buck admired his obvious drive and his determination.

When they arrived down in Stevensville and got settled in the house, they talked a little about the weather, Montana, New Mexico, cattle and horses—nothing important, and nothing specifically having to do with either of their moves south. Finally, Buck asked Phil to tell him more about himself.

"I'm from the east, but you know that. I'm an only child and I grew up in Connecticut, went to a fancy prep school, then to Amherst where I was an American History major and I played varsity lacrosse and I was pretty good. I'm sure you're one of the few people out here who knows what lacrosse is. After college, instead of graduate school, I just packed up and headed west. It was something I wanted to do since I was a little boy. My first stop was Wyoming, down around Laramie. I'm not altogether sure why I picked that place. Maybe it was just because it was Laramie. I really didn't know anyone there and I couldn't find anyone that wanted to hire me because I had no experience. I understood that so I eventually left and came up here to Montana, not that I knew anyone up here. I was just drifting around trying to see the West. I was at a college rodeo over near Bozeman and I was lucky enough to meet this old cowboy whose ranch I'm living on now. He helped me get some day work. I've been here almost a year and it's all I wanted it to be except that I'd rather be on some place full time, doing the work every day and being around for a full year's cycle. Doing day work is kind of incomplete. You never settle into a routine and the style at each ranch is really very different. That surprised me. It's just something I never fully realized before I started doing day work."

"Phil, I need to ask you some pretty personal questions. They are probably none of my business but I'm going ask them anyway. First, do you have a girl friend that you are going to haul south?"

"I wish. I date some but nobody seriously and definitely nobody I want to take south with me. Next."

"This is a little touchy. I know you don't live on what you make doing day work so I assume you have some money put away, maybe for a rainy day or hard times or some other emergency."

"I do. I don't come from poor people and I was able to save an inheritance that I got when my grandfather died. I don't tap into it very much but it helps to have it there. Don't worry about my finances. Besides, what you are offering to pay me is more than I need to live on. I'd like to put some money away and eventually have my own place. My dad's a lawyer and my mother teaches history at the local community college back in Connecticut. They both think I'm wasting my education but I don't see it that way. I'm assuming that you understand that part of me."

"You bet I do. Probably your folks will never understand what you're doing, but you have to do things your way. If it doesn't work out your education won't disappear and you can always go back to grad school, get a good job in corporate America and then make lots of money."

"Buck, I wish you could explain all of that to them. But I won't get you involved in my private family affairs. It's hard enough for me to have to deal with all that crap. Hell, my folks are concerned that I can't get the New York Times every day."

After a filling steak dinner cooked out on the grill, the two cowboys sat around listening to Ian Tyson and Don Edwards CDs, and just talked as if they had been friends for years. Buck liked Phil more and more as the evening progressed, and was pleased that they were able to hook up. They agreed that they would head to New Mexico with four horses in a couple of weeks and that Phil would stay down there and start work, checking fences, water, and repairing whatever needed repairs. He was going to have to get a hand on the general lay of the outfit. Buck wanted Phil to know his way around the ranch, what the environment was like, and to meet some of the people in the area before the new Palo Verde Ranch began to put too big an operation on the ground. The first few weeks down in Animas, by himself, were going to be a very big challenge for the young cowboy but it never occurred to Buck that Phil wasn't up to that challenge.

Before they headed to bed, Phil appeared a little uncomfortable and seemed to want to talk about something. Buck wasn't sure what this was all about but he didn't want any loose ends so early in his relationship with Phil.

"Is there something on your mind that you want to talk about? You seem a little edgy."

"Buck, how the hell do you learn all that you have to know to be good at this cowboy work?"

Buck smiled at the young cowboy. "Phil, it isn't very complicated. In this world you learn more with your ears than you do with your mouth and when you have a question you ask it. And I stress this—you almost never offer advice unless you're asked. Most guys you'll work with want you to be a good hand and they'll help all they can. It makes their job easier and safer. Now that isn't too hard is it?"

Phil paused for minute. "To you it doesn't seem too hard but for a dude like me...just for an example, what the hell do you do in a stampede like we could have had when we faced the coyotes over at the Anderson's if you had to use your rifle? How do you learn that?"

For the first time Buck smiled."I don't know. I've never been in or seen a stampede. I guess we'll learn that one together."

Phil gave a sheepish grin and knew that whatever it was he had to know he'd have to figure it out and it was going to be a whole lot of on the job training.

Before they hit the sack the plan for their future travel to the Animas Valley was set.

The two of them would go south during spring break at the university and Buck figured that the trip would take three or four leisurely days. He would have places all set up along the route to put the horses up each night. In the meantime, the electricity, phone, and gas would all be turned on by the time that they arrived. Between Tommy Sanchez and Ann Lewis, he knew he could count on all this being done. He'd sign whatever papers the utilities required when he got down to Animas.

By the time Phil got ready to leave in the morning it was as if two young boys were getting ready to go off to summer camp. They were almost giddy in their anticipation of the adventure ahead. Buck was never more sure of a decision that he'd ever made than he was of hiring the aspiring cowboy from Amherst College.

■■■

When he arrived at his office the next morning, Rebecca was already at work and Buck was particularly happy to see her. Before he could even say hello, she uncharacteristically jumped in with:

"Guess what? I've got some great news." There was a moment of silence. Buck wasn't sure how to react. She seemed uncharacteristically girlish, sort of like a little school girl who was just invited to her first prom.

"Well, aren't you going to ask me what it is?"

"Okay. I give up. What is it?"

"I've been readmitted to the University of Washington for the fall semester and all my credits will transfer. I was hoping for this but I'm still going to be sorry to leave and not have you to harass me any more."

"Rebecca, that's wonderful news. I want you to get on with your career. And you know that I'll miss you. Having you working here in the office this semester has been more fun than I ever imagined it would be."

Buck had a big grin as he settled into his desk chair.

"In a way I'm glad I'm leaving too. It would be very difficult to replace you. Now I don't even have to try. And I have some good news. I was able to get a good cowboy to work for me in New Mexico. He's living here in Montana but he wants to go south and try being a cowboy full time. I guess things are working out for both of us. Maybe it's because we're good people."

Rebecca chuckled at the last remark and could see that Buck still had a big smile on his face.

"You know what? I don't have to be back in Seattle until fall and I want you to take me to New Mexico with you on one of your trips down there. I've never seen that country and to hear you talk, it's the new Garden of Eden. I don't know when I'll get a chance to see it if you don't take me."

Buck was thrown off balance by her request. He didn't know what to say or how to answer her. He just smiled, looked at her and was sure that she was at her usual game of trying to shock him. This time, without question, she had definitely succeeded.

"Well, professor? What do you say? Will you take me? Maybe I can seduce your cowboy."

Without giving it any more thought, Buck answered her:

"You're on. When do you want to go? We are heading south during spring break and that would be a good time if you really want to come along. And you'd better promise to leave my cowboy alone. What do you say?"

"We've got a deal. And as a way of saying thank you, I want you to come over to my place for dinner sometime this week. I'll even cook for both you guys when we get to the ranch in New Mexico. How about coming over for dinner this Wednesday night? I know you'll be in town to teach that day."

"Okay. But you'd better be able to cook."

She smiled the smile that comes from great self confidence. She didn't have to say a word.

Buck looked forward to Wednesday night. He wanted to learn more about this future lawyer and he knew that he had learned about all he could at the office. He wasn't sure what the fascination was but he knew that her place would provide an easier environment and he was anxious to see her away from the university.

■■■

Wednesday couldn't come fast enough for Buck. Everything seemed to have speeded up since he hired Phil and by Wednesday's dinner he had taken care of all the details for the first trip to New Mexico. He was also able to arrange for stopovers on the way down to stable the horses at night and that was his major concern. The trip would take about three and a half days without pushing it very hard. Buck wanted to give the horses plenty of rest along the way with periodic stops and he wanted to enjoy the scenery and the trip, particularly now, since Phil and Rebecca had never seen the southwest. It was barely two weeks until spring break and Buck could feel the anticipation growing in him every day. He was the one who felt like the school kid who just got his first date for the prom.

■■■

By the middle of the week and his dinner date, the American Studies professor was feeling less and less like a professor and more like the full time rancher that he was about to become. He couldn't wait for the complete changeover and he thought that dinner at Rebecca's would be an interesting and relaxing diversion.

He arrived about ten minutes fashionably late. She lived in a better area of town than he had expected. She certainly wasn't in the heart of the university community or where so many of the undergraduates congregated. She lived in a nice residential area surrounded by big trees and plenty of lawns. When he arrived at the house, he found that she had the basement apartment. He had no idea who lived upstairs.

Buck rang the bell and when Rebecca answered the door he couldn't even muster a hello he was so stunned. She was wearing a T-shirt with no bra and a mini skirt that helped define the genre. She wasn't wearing any shoes. Buck couldn't believe her body. Her breasts were full and firm and her nipples almost pushed through her T-shirt. Her skirt revealed incredible legs and thighs and Buck thought that he had never been so easily captivated by a woman in his whole life. Jennifer was extremely beautiful but Rebecca's sexuality was overwhelming. In the months they had worked together he had never seen her with her chestnut hair as loose and flowing, her dark eyes so sultry, her body revealed in the most suggestive way, and her demeanor that of a woman— she was no longer one of his employees or a student at the university. He had difficulty maintaining any semblance of dignity or sophistication.

"Hi." Rebecca's greeting was very casual.

Buck didn't know what to say.

"Hi. What am I supposed to say next? You do look fantastic."

"I didn't want to shock you but I wanted you to see me in a way that you don't get to see me in the office."

"Good heavens, Rebecca, I can see most all of you right now. If I had to look at you like that in the office both of us would have gotten fired months ago. If you are trying to seduce me instead of my cowboy, you are well on your way. I don't know what to say or how to act. You didn't expect me to just come on in as if you were dressed in jeans and a sweatshirt. What do we do next?"

"I am trying to seduce you and I am glad that you find me so seductive. Come on in and I'll try to tell you what I have in mind. Or don't you want to come in?"

"Just close the door and let's get in the house. I'd hate for your neighbors to see you like this. They'd never get over it. This is a very sedate part of town and you'll get thrown out of here."

As Buck eased his way into the house, he still was a little shaken. Rebecca led him into the small living room that was dimly lit with a couple of candles burning on the coffee table. It was easy to tell that this was a furnished apartment—there was very little that spoke of Rebecca. It was pretty nondescript. As they both sat down on the couch Buck wasn't sure what was going to happen next.

"I know you aren't a drinker but I want you to have a glass of wine with me so we can both toast the future and toast tonight. There are a lot of things that I have wanted to tell you, and tonight might be as good a time as any. I'm going to get up and go get us a couple of glasses of wine."

As she got up and left the room, Buck couldn't take his eyes off her and he was sure that she knew that. She returned in a minute and handed Buck a glass and she raised hers as if to offer a toast.

"To the future and to good times with people you care about."

Buck raised his glass and then took a sip. He stared at Rebecca. He was still off balance and wasn't sure yet what was in store for the evening although his imagination, which was running wild, probably wasn't too far off the mark. This could be a once in a lifetime evening or it could be a once in a lifetime evening. Buck was beginning to feel that so many of his decisions and experiences lately had all been this close. The differences between good and bad, between right and wrong, were becoming too blurred far too often.

"Sit down so we can talk. I wanted you to come over because I couldn't think of any other place where we could be alone and I could tell you all the things that I want to. We don't have a whole lot of time left together here in Montana and I didn't want the time to slip away and then be gone before we could talk."

"What is so important that you have to go through all of this? Don't you think I'd talk to you if you were just casually dressed? Damn, Rebecca, you are beautiful and sexy and don't you think that I've noticed that before. Do you think that I just float in and out of the office in some kind of fog? I'm a man and you're a very desirable woman. How in hell do you think that I could miss that? There is probably nothing that you are showing me tonight that I haven't probably fantasized about. One thing for sure, looking at you now is definitely not disappointing. Well, I guess you'd better talk and say whatever is on your mind. I'm not quite sure what I want to say or how to go about saying it. You've really caught me off guard."

"I will be leaving Montana either late in the summer or very early in the fall. You know, I think, how I feel about you. I'm very infatuated and I want to have a relationship of some kind before I go. I don't want us to feel that we have to make all kinds of commitments and I am definitely leaving for the University of Washington, but I think that I will probably never meet a man like you again. I don't necessarily mean romantically, I mean a man that has your values and your determination to live life to the fullest on your own terms. I just want to be a little part of that before I go. I want to make love to you, I want to travel with you and I want to be around you. It really isn't any more complicated than that."

"Are you kidding? That isn't complicated? For God's sake, Rebecca, what do you want me to say? I'd be a flat out liar if I told you that I didn't want to make love with you or that I don't enjoy your company, but to put a time limit on all of this makes it more mechanical than I think that I'd want it to be. I'd love to be close to you and I have no doubt that I'm a little infatuated with you, too. But do we get close, share all of whatever it is you want and then just say, 'bye'? I'm not sure that I can do that. Can you? Somebody is going to get terribly hurt and I sure as hell don't want it to be me. Have you thought about that? Can you really just walk away from whatever you are proposing at the end of the summer? What if the relationship changes and we just can't walk away? What then? What about all of your plans, your dreams?"

Buck couldn't help but think that he had this conversation not too long ago with Jennifer and he remembered all too well how that had ended.

"I've thought about all of that and I have no answers. I honestly want to get back to school, to Seattle, and you know how much I want to become a lawyer—and I really want to be with you. How everything moves along will just take time to determine. I guess I want it to actually take its natural course. I'm not a kid and you know that I've had my share of real life experiences, so for me to want to do this is sort of out of character. Maybe tonight I'm the woman I sometimes want to be but never am. I think you are the only man that I know who I could comfortably show this side of me."

Rebecca didn't say anything for a moment. Buck could see that she was thinking over what to say next.

"Now that you're actually here, I'm beginning to think that maybe this wasn't the smartest thing that I've ever done. But that doesn't change how I feel about you or what I want for the next few months. Probably I haven't handled it well but at least you know how things are for me."

Buck wasn't sure what to say either. Rebecca's scenario was overly romantic and at the same time it was so cold and calculating that it almost offended him. He was sure that the way things were going tonight and how Rebecca explained her aspirations for their short term future was only a part of the real Rebecca. Buck began to understand how much he desired her and how much he didn't want her to get hurt or for that matter, how much he didn't want to get hurt. And he was sure that if he let this happen the way Rebecca had outlined her plans, someone was in for a bad fall—a very bad fall. Buck couldn't help but think again about Jennifer and how that had all turned out. Was this going to be another one of those relationships?

"You know, Buck, I'm not a college aged kid who wants a fling with a professor. I see those girls all over on campus, flirting and trying to tease the young professors. They kind of make me laugh. I'm a grown woman who has found a real man that honestly interests her."

Rebecca slid over to Buck and put her arms around him and kissed him. He answered her with a kiss and it didn't take them very long before they were embracing and touching each other all over. Soon Rebecca's T-shirt was off and she had begun to take off his belt and open his jeans. He couldn't believe the sensuality of her sculpted body and how good he felt as she ran her hands down inside his jeans.

"Rebecca, let's do this like adults and go to the bedroom so we can get in bed. This is like the back seat of a car."

As soon as they were in bed, under a light cover, wrapped in one another's arms, and completely naked, they began to share the most intimate of moments. Before long they were embracing one another in so many positions and so intimately that Buck didn't want this to ever end. He felt his lips go all over her body and when he felt her lips and tongue on him he was completely under her spell. Her skin, and the warmth of her body, was more enticing than he could ever have imagined it would be. Soon they were making love and after they both were both satisfied, they just held one another and didn't say a word. Buck thought of a million things to say but not one of his thoughts seemed appropriate. In fact, he really didn't know what to say.

After a while Rebecca broke the ice.

"That was very nice, wasn't it?" Buck thought that her comment was one of the greatest understatements he had ever heard. Rebecca waited a second not knowing whether Buck was going to say something. He didn't even try so she continued.

"It's early and I've made a good dinner so I hope you still want to eat. What do you say?"

"I think that's a good idea. I'm hungry and if we stay here much longer we might never get out of this bed."

After dinner, they went back to the living room and just talked like the good friends Buck has assumed they were before tonight. They talked about Rebecca being a lawyer, of Buck's ranch and how lucky he was to have Phil going to work for him, about living in Seattle and what the desert was like on a hot summer's evening as the brilliant red sun set over the western mountains. Most of the conversation was about things they had talked about before but this night they were sharing thoughts and feelings instead of descriptions. The evening went by so easily that it was well past 11:00 when Buck realized that maybe he should be heading home although he wasn't quite sure that he truly wanted to do that.

"I want you to stay here tonight. You don't have to teach tomorrow and my first class isn't very early. I don't want tonight to end, at least not now. Please, stay."

Buck wasn't sure what to say. He knew what he wanted to do but he wasn't sure what was right. He knew that he had to say something.

"I can't think of anything I'd rather do but do you think that this is the best way for us to be? How often will we be doing this? I don't know, Rebecca, but we seem to be getting in very deep in a very short time." Buck hugged her, almost to let her know that he wasn't pushing her away and that he also wanted her.

"Stop thinking so much and just stay with me tonight. You don't have to analyze everything to death. We can worry about tomorrow, tomorrow." She kissed him and held him tight. Buck thought there was almost a quiet sense of desperation in all of this and he frankly didn't know what to make of it or what to do. He had no idea of what was motivating this beautiful woman who said she was still planning on heading back to Seattle in the fall.

"It's late and I guess I really do want to stay. Rebecca, I think we are heading into water over our head. I hope you can swim better than I can."

Once they were in bed they made love again and finally fell asleep nestled next to each other. About six in the morning Buck woke up, wrapped himself around Rebecca, who was also awake, and again they made love. They didn't say a word and they didn't have to. The way they touched and the way they held each other made words superfluous. It was as if they wanted one another so much that it was impossible to be satisfied. It made trying all the more intense.

They stayed in bed, still not speaking but just letting the moment take care of itself. Neither of them could imagine what the rights words would have been and neither really wanted to break the spell of the evening and early morning. Finally, as the morning sun came up and broke through the small window on the east side of the bedroom, projecting eerie streaks of light into the cozy bedroom, Rebecca broke the silence:

"I've got to take a shower. Come on with me and wash my back and just hold me. After that I'll make you breakfast."

■■■

At a little before nine o'clock, Rebecca left for her class and Buck headed back to the ranch in Stevensville. He couldn't believe how good he felt and he wasn't sure whether he had just become so horny after he stopped seeing Jennifer or that Rebecca had introduced something into his life that he had never had. He didn't know what the next step would be. Infatuation is a tough thing to overcome particularly when it's accompanied by maybe the best sex he had ever experienced and driven by uncontrollable lust. Was Rebecca playing a game or was she serious? Could she really break this off in time for her to go back to Seattle and school in the fall? Would she? Could Buck and would he want to?

As he drove south he remembered all the way back to high school when he had a mad crush on a pretty gal a year behind him who would have nothing to do with him. As he looked back he kept focusing on the chase and how unfulfilled he was. And then he thought about the really cute girl with the long raven hair and dark eyes who claimed that she was in love with him and who he would have nothing to do with. The same kinds of scenarios repeated themselves through college and graduate school. This dating business all appeared to be some sort of game and eventually a winner emerged, usually after a lot of damage has been done. After all these years it still seemed that way. Did he really want to get any more involved with Rebecca? Who was going to emerge from this relationship without getting hurt and who was going to be the winner? Maybe that's what it had become—a case of winners and losers. Was it necessary to even think in these terms? He couldn't figure this all out. If he tried too hard he was sure that his head would explode and he couldn't even decide if there had been a winner and a loser in his relationship with Jennifer or if there even needed to be.

■■■

He tried to redirect his thoughts to New Mexico and all the work that had to be done to get

the impending move south smoothed out. He had already called Helen Ostegard, his real estate agent in Stevensville, to remind her that even though the closing for the Montana ranch was soon, the new owners couldn't take possession until mid summer. To his relief, that had all been agreed to. The Hollywood people didn't care when they finally got to Montana although they claimed it was going to be their permanent home, not some weekend or summer getaway. Buck laughed when he heard that because the same explanation always seemed to surface, whether it was in Montana or with the celebrity crowd in Santa Fe, Jackson Hole or Sun Valley, Idaho. Ultimately, most of them drift back to the area where they feel comfortable and that is with their own crowd in their own environment. And the rural West is definitely not their usual environment. Buck could never figure out why all these people wanted to have ranches in places like Montana, Wyoming, or even New Mexico. Everybody said it was for a tax right-off but Buck never believed that. It was something much more basic. He figured it was more of a social thing like keeping up with the Joneses or even some far fetched romantic idea about cowboys and horses and the wide open spaces. Do we ever outgrow our cowboy heroes? He had even heard some of that celebrity crowd talk about rediscovering their "inner cowboy," whatever that meant. Comments like that made Buck laugh because even with his limited acquaintance with these people, he was sure that they didn't even have an "inner cowboy." He just didn't know for sure what it was that motivated these kinds of people. For now all he wanted was their money— nothing else. He would leave all the analysis to someone far wiser and someone who actually cared about all these newcomers. Buck was sure that wasn't him.

Home again, he called Phil and told him to come over the day before they headed to New Mexico so they could load his truck with boxes and other belongings that they might as well move now. And he reminded the young cowboy that he needed to bring all the gear he had since he would be staying down south permanently.

Phil assured him that all he had was his saddle, his rifle, some books and his personal things and clothing. He didn't have any furniture or a whole lot else and he hoped that the house on the ranch had some furnishings. Buck explained that what it lacked they could buy in Lordsburg, Silver City or Deming although he was sure that both houses had a few chairs, a bed and appliances—at least enough to get them by until everyone was really settled in. For the time being all they needed was a couple of beds, some bedding and towels, a chair or two and a table, a few lamps, plus utensils, pots and pans, and some dishes for the kitchens. For Buck it was all pretty basic and not very artistic.

Now it was up to Buck to figure out what he should take on the first trip of the big move south. He packed bedding and towels and he had already packed many of his books and given away or sold several pieces of furniture and some odds and ends. Although he thought that he had way too much of everything, when it came time to actually taking an inventory, he found that in many areas of his household goods, his holdings were pretty sparse. He kind of looked forward to buying news things and eventually redecorating his house in the desert, possibly with a southwestern flare. Maybe it was a cliché, the kind of decorations you see in all of the hip western magazines that seem to devote far too many pages to newcomers building multimillion dollar homes in Jackson Hole or Santa Fe, or outside of Bozeman, but he was sure that he could personalize his own place enough to make it fit his lifestyle.

Even more importantly, as the time for the first leg of the move approached, he just felt his excitement grow and his anticipation almost overcome him. Making dreams come true was surely one of the great experiences that anyone could have, and he was about to have that experience for himself. Buck was beginning to think of himself as one very lucky guy.

∎∎∎

That afternoon he called Tim Stewart, a good friend who lived across the valley over by the Sunset Bench. Buck and Tim had often neighbored together on their own ranches and other outfits around the Bitterroot and they had always gotten along just fine. Tim knew that Buck was leaving and had already told him that he was going to miss his company. Like many people who live on ranches, getting together is not something that happens as frequently as it does in the city. It's never a five minute drive and rarely is it a drop-in call. When they weren't working together, Tim and Buck saw each other most often at one of the cafes in town, where they had coffee and caught up on the news from around the valley. Every so often Buck had dinner with Tim and his wife at their ranch which was only about forty minutes away. Today the two ranchers made a date for lunch at the Bugling Elk Café in Stevensville.

When they arrived at the café on Main Street, almost simultaneously, they shook hands near the entrance and went inside and took a table. There were about ten tables, all fairly close to one another and the atmosphere was definitely casual, certainly nothing fancy. Most of the clientele were ranchers and cowboys from around the area and some of the local businessmen. This was not a place that drew the tourist crowd that prowled around the Bitterroot Valley. The Bugling Elk was a place for the locals.

After they ordered the day's special—meatloaf, mashed potatoes, peas, lots of gravy, and coffee—it was Buck's turn to answer all kinds of questions about the southwest. Tim, like so many people in Montana, talked a great deal about moving to a warmer climate as he got older, but had never made the trip to see what the southwest was actually about. Buck knew that their dreams were just dreams—it was just talk. Tim and his wife were both born and raised in the Bitterroot. They met in college over by Dillon and after graduating they headed back to the valley for Tim to take over the family ranch. Now with their own two kids in college—his son was a senior at Colorado State and hoped to get into vet school there and his daughter was a sophomore over in Bozeman—Buck was sure that the Stewarts knew that they weren't going anywhere. Despite all the changes and new people moving into the Bitterroot over the last decade or so, changes that they weren't too happy about, their roots were just too damn deep for them to ever pick up and leave.

After a good lunch, Tim looked at Buck very seriously. "You know something. I've known you for almost ten years and when I get to think about it I don't really know you at all. Yet I know that you are a good friend and someone I can always count on. All this really confuses the hell out of me and I don't know why it does."

"I guess, Tim, that's how I want things. I'm pretty internalized and feel awkward talking about things that are very private. I don't want that to put my friends off but that's just how I am. Not much I can do about it. And besides, there's not much about me that you'd really want to know that you don't already know."

"If you say so, but it was just an observation." Tim's comment was not intended to be critical. In fact, it was just what Tim meant it to be, an observation. Buck had heard all of this before. He heard it from college friends and he even heard a little of it from his ex-wife. If he wanted to change, he probably didn't know how. And he wasn't altogether sure that he did.

The two ranchers lingered over lunch and coffee and Buck had a chance to visit with other cowboys and ranchers he knew in the café. It was very relaxed. After Buck assured Tim that he would see him again before he was gone for good, they shook hands and Buck got into his truck and headed back up the dirt road to the ranch. As he left he felt a little loneliness because his time here in the Bitterroot had been good times with good people and they were fast coming to an end. All he could hope was that he would have some of these same experiences in New Mexico.

■■■

The next time Buck headed for his office in Missoula, he did it with some trepidation. He was a little worried about how Rebecca would act after their night together and even more so, how he would act. When he finally got there, Rebecca greeted him as if nothing much had happened, like they just had been on an innocent dinner date. Buck was glad and chided himself for not realizing that Rebecca had enough maturity and sophistication to not act like a little school girl. Was he mature enough to not act like a teenager in heat? Christ, he hoped so.

They greeted one another and the only difference that Buck could sense was that there was a little more warmth and familiarity than there had been before they had shared a bed. After class, Buck had some work to catch up on and he waited for Rebecca to finish her class and come back to the office. When she finally returned, she again brought up the notion of going on the trip to New Mexico with him. He wasn't sure that she had been serious about joining Buck and Phil on their journey when she first mentioned it but now she made it quite clear that she still wanted to go.

Buck took her at her word and despite his better judgment they made all the arrangements. She would drive down to Stevensville, spend the night, along with Phil (that concerned Buck but who was he keeping all this from? And why?), and they could get a good early start the next morning. He wanted to make the northern border of Utah the first night. He had made arrangements to use the local fair grounds at Tremonton, Utah to stable the horses. Tremonton was a small town, not even eight thousand people, but the fair grounds were secure and the guy who ran the grounds had been very generous and accommodating. And they had several very good motels right on the main highway.

■■■

Phil arrived about three o'clock and Rebecca had said that she'd come down after dinner. By the time she did arrive, the horse trailer was hooked up and both the pickups were loaded, including enough hay to get them through the trip. Buck also loaded a couple of his saddles and other horse gear, along with buckets, brushes, some veterinary supplies, and even some shoeing equipment, just in case Phil might need any of it in New Mexico. Buck was surprised when Phil mentioned that he had learned how to shoe a horse from the old cowboy he was staying with over in Whitehall. Now all that they had to do was try to get a good nights sleep, load the horses in the morning, and make sure that they got a fairly early start.

■■■

Buck's neighbor, Johnny Meyers, called that night to double check everything and to find out if Cowboy was going south or staying. Buck let him know that Cowboy was traveling south and that all the rest of the chores were the same as usual. He thanked him again and when he hung up he knew he was going to miss the Meyers and their two teenage boys. They had been good neighbors, very likable people, and over the years they proved to be friends that he could count on no matter what the situation was. It's not always easy to find neighbors like that.

Rebecca had never been to the ranch before and when she drove up the road from the lower gate it was already getting dark. What was left of the sunlight was still poking through the trees casting an eerie light, and there was still the lingering red and yellow glow that washed over the peaks to the west. She had a very good feeling when she saw the warm lights shimmering in the windows in the house at the end of the dirt road. Tucked away in the forest the way the house was, it was reassuring to find that beacon at the end of the very rough, lonely road.

Rebecca didn't bring very much. She had a canvas duffel bag, the kind that everyone seemed to be using, and she said they could throw that in the truck in the morning. After Buck introduced her to Phil, he was surprised to see how animated Phil became. It almost appeared that he was trying to impress Rebecca the way a high school kid tries to impress the head cheerleader or prom queen that he has a crush on. Although Phil was by far the younger of the two, Buck knew immediately that Rebecca was also enjoying herself. She smiled and only slightly flirted but her sexuality couldn't be hidden. She actually made poor Phil blush a couple of times. But they got along fine and the evening was casual and friendly, the way it should be for three people who were headed for a big adventure. Although each one of them was on a very different track with separate expectations and very specific personal views of the future, the three of them all seemed eager to get the adventure started.

When it was time to hit the hay, Buck showed Phil where some towels were and then he headed to one of the guest rooms. Rebecca and Buck went to the main bedroom. Once the door was closed, Buck told Rebecca that he thought the walls were pretty thin and that they'd probably better be good tonight. She laughed a little and told him that he had no faith in their ability to make love quietly and that was, indeed, being good. She put her arms around him and pulled him close, brought their bodies together and gave him a long kiss. Not a word was said. There was no need to.

"You see. We're quite capable of being close without making a racket. I just hope that the bed doesn't squeak too much. I'll bet you we could make love all night and never say a word or make a sound. Would you like to try that?"

"I would definitely like to try that, but it'll have to wait. We have a long trip ahead of us and we'll need all the damn sleep we can get. You'll just have to fantasize about us until we get to the motel tomorrow night. And because you mentioned it, you've made me horny as hell."

"Good. I'm going to brush my teeth and get some sleep."

When they were finally in bed together, they actually did make love, once and quietly, and then fell fast asleep, their bodies remaining intimately close together all night long. Intimate time with Rebecca was beginning to feel so very natural.

Everyone was up and dressed before the radio alarm went off. Although the sun was just beginning to come up over the Sapphire Mountains, the coffee maker had gone on automatically, and Rebecca was up and making bacon, eggs, and toast. Buck kind of chuckled to himself when he saw the "domestic" side of Rebecca.

By the time Buck and Phil got back inside the house, after feeding the horses that were to stay in Montana and putting some hay in the manger and in the hay bags in the trailer, breakfast was ready. Instead of there being lots of talk about the trip, they ate quietly and there was actually very little conversation. The three travelers seemed edgy and about ready to jump up and head for the trucks. At the breakfast table, you could just feel the anticipation the three of them had, filled with some real trepidation, for the trip to New Mexico. At least for Phil and Rebecca, this was all unknown territory, on many levels.

Buck rechecked his briefcase to make sure all the traveling papers for the horses were in order. He had the Coggins Tests, medical certificates, and the brand inspections all ready to go. He even had the registration papers for the four quarter horses that were headed south. He didn't think they would be stopped as they crossed state lines but it was a possibility and he wanted to be ready, just in case. The western states had gotten quite serious about the transportation of livestock, especially cattle and horses. If they were stopped without the proper papers, it could cost them days of hassle getting things cleared up and back on the road.

Loading the horses took no time at all. They placed two up front and two behind the mid-trailer divider and it was done. These were four dependable horses that had been hauled many miles while Buck worked on the Palo Verde and the other ranches all over western Montana. The rear gate was secured and Buck's and Rebecca's gear was thrown in the back seat of the club cab truck. Cowboy jumped in and nestled in the back seat, just as relaxed as if he and Buck were headed for the feed store in town.

Phil said that he would follow them down the ranch road to US 93, over Lost Trail Pass, and down to Salmon, Idaho. They agreed if they got separated they would meet on the north side of Salmon near the big highway Chamber of Commerce sign. Even though they had new cell phones, nobody was sure where they could get a signal and where they would have dead air.

Buck liked this drive. It wasn't too long ago the road had been narrow, steep and windy, full of s-curves and so dangerous that if it hadn't been straightened out, for this trip he would have headed over to Butte to pick up I-15 heading south. But now that US 93 was straightened a bit and widened, on both the Montana and Idaho sides, the trip was safer and just as beautiful, as it headed over the pass, the Continental Divide and down through the dense Salmon-Challis National Forest and on to Salmon.

Even though they got a little later start than Buck had originally wanted it didn't seem to bother him. He knew that each of the days would be relatively short so there was no pressure to meet a deadline. Within a couple of hours they were cruising south, on their way to North Fork and it wasn't long before long they arrived in Salmon. Phil had been able to stay close behind so there was no need for either vehicle to stop and wait for the other. Buck had given him a map and if need be, he had the entire route right up to the ranch gate in Animas. Once they got to Salmon they took State Road 28, a road declared a scenic highway on all the maps, south east, down to Mud Lake. From Mud Lake it was an easy fifteen miles until they approached the ramp that led them onto I-15. The trip so far was relaxed for both the passengers in the trucks, Cowboy and the horses, as they cruised easily along the interstate. And although they had snack food with them, they had agreed to stop for lunch at a little café that Buck had frequented over the years just north of Idaho Falls.

Once they had finished their meal and brought a little snack for Cowboy, they were back on the road. They drove through the Fort Hall Indian Reservation, the home of the Bannocks and Shoshones, and it didn't take them too long to cross the border into Utah. They were in Tremonton long before dinner time. It was almost too early to stop but Buck had planned the first night in this little Utah town and he wanted to stick to his slow and leisurely schedule. But more important to him was that this trip stay totally stress free and if that meant stopping earlier than later, that was fine with Buck.

When they were finished checking into one of the newer motels, Buck went to his room and called Alan Jessups, the fellow who was in charge of the fairgrounds and the one who had given Buck permission to stable the horses there for the night. With the permission confirmed, Buck and Phil drove the horses over to the fair grounds where they unloaded, fed and watered the critters. Buck let Cowboy run around the grounds until he had used some of the pent up energy that he had gathered being in the truck all day. Buck had also brought along a chain and lock and fastened the gates where the horses were stabled and after one quick check around the horse pens, the two cowboys headed back to the Silver Saddle motel to pick up Rebecca and find a spot for an eagerly awaited dinner.

There weren't a whole lot of options in town but the café they found was air conditioned, unusually clean and the food was pretty basic and damn good. They weren't looking for a gourmet restaurant nor could they have found one in Tremonton.

They were in no hurry to get back to the motel so they lingered at the café a while, drinking coffee. After an hour or so Phil joined Buck and Rebecca back in their room at the motel. They talked some, dabbled in a little political talk that wasn't very contentious, and watched part of an old Glen Ford western on TV. Phil then headed back to his room with the understanding that they would get going at about eight, and then try to find a place to have breakfast somewhere around Brigham City. They would pick a place while they were on the road and coordinate things over the cell phone. Buck then went out and loaded the hay in the manger and hay bags in the horse trailer that was parked at the motel. It was only then that he and Rebecca settled in for the night.

Rebecca had been very quiet all day and Buck wasn't sure why. When he asked her about it she said that everything on the trip so far was all so new to her that she could barely take it in. She had never seen country like this—some extraordinarily beautiful and other places that she felt were as boring and dull as anything she could imagine. She was particularly taken that once they were out of the forest and had hit the Interstate, this was mostly dry, open country, not at all like what she was accustomed to in Washington or even Montana.

"Which is the real thing? Does one kind of scenery begin to dominate the other? Is it mountains or desert or grasslands? Does it vary like this all the way down to New Mexico?"

Buck had no answer for what were honest questions. In his own mind, he thought that it was all wonderful country—either scenic or suited so well for ranching—and for him that balanced everything out. He had been along this route so many times that he didn't have a very objective view of what they were seeing, certainly he didn't see it with the new clarity that Rebecca was bringing to it. Nonetheless, he enjoyed Rebecca's observations and tried to explain to her that she would ultimately have to deal with the scenery in her own way. And for whatever reason, he did hope that she would come to love this country.

Once they had brushed their teeth and Buck had made sure that Cowboy had eaten all his food, the cowboy and the future lawyer headed for bed. Rebecca wasn't wearing anything at all and Buck got undressed and slipped into bed with her. The night proved to be everything that he had been thinking about all day and Rebecca once again let her sexuality take over and control them both. Buck didn't care a bit and couldn't have been happier.

They were both up at a little after seven, showered, dressed and ready to go, right on schedule. After a quick breakfast at the same café where they had had dinner, Buck and Phil got into the Ford with the horse trailer and went to the fair grounds to load the horses. When they came back to the motel, Phil headed for his truck and Rebecca and Cowboy got in with Buck. Within minutes they were off on the second day of the "big move." Their goal for the second night was Monticello, Utah, just south of Moab and Arches National Park. It wasn't going to be hard day, certainly not any harder than day one, and Buck thought that it would be best for the horses and the crew if the entire trip was easy rather than rushed. He wanted to be sure that each night they stopped and unloaded the horses well before darkness set in. And maybe the move even scared him just enough so that he didn't want to get to the new ranch too soon.

■■■

Day two was going to be a scenic drive once they got past the traffic of Salt Lake City and he didn't want to zip through country that neither Rebecca nor Phil had ever seen. As they drove during the day Buck called Phil, when it was possible on the cell phone, to point out something of interest or give him a little history lesson. Phil often returned the calls with some questions of his own but most of the time they couldn't get any cell phone connection at all.

There was an older motel in Monticello where Buck wanted to stay. He had stayed there several times before. It had an indoor pool and a big hot tub, and that was a goal that was worth shooting for. They could then make Reserve in Catron County, New Mexico the third night and from there they had less than 200 miles south to the ranch. The trip was easy so far, just the way Buck wanted it. They usually stopped in the middle of the day, found a side road off the highway and unloaded the horses and that also gave the three travelers a chance to stretch and talk as the horses grazed and Cowboy ran around. Phil used the stops as a chance to discuss the trip and talk about the journey with his traveling companions from the other vehicle. Buck, Phil and Rebecca were becoming very close as the trip took its course. It made everything so much easier, especially for Phil and Rebecca who were entering into such new territory, both physically and emotionally.

Once they left I-15 for Provo they wouldn't have very much more Interstate to travel and the driving would get a little more difficult and much, much slower. The roads would become narrower and not nearly as straight or as fast as they had been on the first couple of days of their journey.

Despite all the traffic, they were able to navigate through the morning traffic around the Salt Lake City area and were driving into Provo when Buck asked Rebecca, with a serious voice and a straight face, to keep an eye out for any of the Osmonds. Rebecca gave no reaction and the journey continued as they headed for the nearly 7,500 foot Soldier Summit where Buck had bad memories of a winter crossing of the pass some years ago in a raging snow storm and howling winds with near zero visibility. He was thankful that during this trip all he would see was the rustic mountain scenery and canyons set off by a dazzling clear blue sky and an occasional white puffy cumulus cloud. For this time of the year there was very light traffic.

When they got to Price, an old mining town with just over 8,000 people, they decided to stop and eat. Buck knew of a restaurant that served both Chinese and American food and where they were pretty good at both. It certainly wasn't some chain restaurant and that was his destination. Fortunately there was a big parking lot in the rear so parking the trucks and horse trailer didn't become a major ordeal. Price was a mining town where the railroad, coal, and then uranium, helium and natural gas discoveries have brought new life to what had been a town that was struggling to survive.

After a leisurely meal—Buck had Chinese and Phil and Rebecca American—the threesome ambled back to the trucks, once again bringing a snack for Cowboy. Then it was back on the road. As they drove south and headed into Moab, Buck explained as much about the scenery to Rebecca as he thought she could absorb and she loved every minute of it. She seemed to be completely involved in the surrounding country of red rock formations and green, tree lined waterways.

Moab had become known as an outdoorsman's paradise, partially because there was easy access to Arches National Park, the famous Dead Horse Point State Park and the Colorado River, and just a little to the west was Canyonlands National Park, where the Colorado and the Green Rivers converged, forming some of the best rapids in the southwest. Despite all the natural beauty of the surrounding countryside, including the striking red cliffs and the La Sal Mountains, Buck wanted to get through Moab as fast as possible. Although the town had lost its agricultural heritage with the discovery of uranium in the 1950s, the town's major industry now, it seemed, was tourism. Buck thought, from his own visual sightings, that Moab had more motels per capita than any town in America. For a town with a listed population of a little less than 5,000, Moab had an abundance of motels and restaurants that catered to an enormous tourist trade generated by all the scenic grandeur. But Buck much preferred Monticello, named after Thomas Jefferson's Virginia home, with its smaller population of about 2,000 and only a little more than a scenic hour directly south of Moab.

Moab represented so much of what was happening to the West and to Buck's way of thinking it wasn't very positive, either in the short term or for the future. Moab was another of those places that seemed to actually be taken in by the Chamber of Commerce myth that "bigger was better," while at the same time they paid lip service to protecting the environment and keeping the "small town feel." But even he couldn't deny the beauty and the incredible recreational opportunities that the area had to offer. It was easy to understand why people flocked here.

After negotiating the traffic through Moab, they headed south on US 191 for Monticello. When they got near the north side of Monticello, Buck had to locate an old ranch road on the east side of the highway just before they entered the town. He had made arrangements with the owner, an old friend from his rodeo days, to put the horses out in a ten acre pasture. The pasture had abundant grass, a water tank powered by solar panels, and the size of the pasture provided an opportunity for the horses to run and get some exercise. It proved to be everything that Casey Hawkins had said it was when he talked to Buck on the phone. Just as it was when they stopped the evening before in Tremonton, it was still relatively early in the day and the trio of travelers wanted to stop and relax as much as the horses probably did. Buck eagerly looked forward to the pool and hot tub at the motel.

The directions Buck had were good and locating the pasture and unloading the horses for the night was completed without any problems. Casey Hawkins had been a pretty darn good bareback rider in his day, on the professional circuit, but now he was taking tourists on trail rides in the Abajo Mountains over in the Manti-La Sal National Forest, just to the west of Monticello. If all things were equal he would have chosen to stay in the ranching business full time but the economics of it all said take the tourists. He still ran a small herd of mother cows, only about thirty, but now that was almost a hobby for this former full time cattleman.

Unfortunately, in the screwed up world of ranch economics, these trail rides were more profitable than raising good cattle and horses.

Buck knew that Casey wasn't going to be around when they arrived but his friend had given him the combination to the lock on the gate. After the horses were watered and a little grain was put out for them, the travelers headed south into town to find the old motel. Buck was taking something of gamble because he hadn't made reservations but he liked the old mom and pop motel where he had stayed years before mainly because it wasn't one of the newer national franchises. He had stayed there several times during his many trips to the southwest and remembered with great pleasure the pool and hot tub. When they signed in at the desk he found that the rates weren't mom and pop any more but Buck figured that's what happens when you're in a growing tourist area like this part of Utah.

Some miles west of Monticello was the edge of Monument Valley and if they weren't pulling a loaded horse trailer, the extra miles through that overpowering landscape would have been well worth the side trip. The scenic route where John Ford's movies with John Wayne had been made would have been a highlight of the trip south. The magnificent scenery had helped to create for many people a somewhat distorted idea of what all of the west looked like and this made Monument Valley a major tourist Mecca. All Buck could hope for was that it wouldn't be ruined by too many people having to see it, and all the greed that went with that. But he knew better. The one saving grace was that so much of it was owned by the Navajo Nation and he was sure that they would protect what they could.

There was an old cowboy café just south of Casey's pasture and the crew headed there for an early dinner as soon as they got parked and settled in at the motel. They took one of the round tables over by a large picture window with a wonderful view of the mountains. The table was covered with a fairly new oilcloth that was illustrated with western scenes. Rebecca commented on all the western and cowboy "stuff" that seemed to take over the walls of the small café—old saddles, branding irons, spurs, reatas, beat up old hats, chaps, boot jacks, and lots of other cowboy memorabilia. And the food was even very filling, particularly the chicken fried steak with all the trimmings, although Buck was a little surprised that someone with a figure like Rebecca's could pack it away with such enthusiasm. He wondered how she did it. He concluded that it was her high energy and a metabolism that probably topped the metabolism scale.

After dinner they went back to the motel, changed into swim suits and just sat around the pool and hot tub. Rebecca looked sensational in an off white bikini. All Buck could think about was how she just seemed to know how to present herself. He couldn't help but notice that Phil had trouble taking his eyes off her. She kidded him about not having a girl friend to take to New Mexico and Buck just sat there and wondered what was going on in the mind of the young cowboy who was so obviously infatuated with Rebecca, an infatuation probably comparable to his own.

The next morning they had a big breakfast at the same cowboy café where they had had dinner the night before. Rebecca asked questions about some of the artifacts hanging on the walls and scattered about, and Buck and Phil tried to explain to her the use a cowboy would have for each item. She became completely engrossed and the two cowboys appeared eager to impress her with their knowledge. Once a leisurely and filling breakfast was over, they headed back to Casey Hawkins' pasture to gather and load the horses.

The horses were easy to catch and the loading went without a hitch.

They were soon on their way southeast to the New Mexico line and then they'd head south to Shiprock on the Navajo Nation, with their next major destination Gallup. Rebecca's appreciation of the scenery seemed to be increasing. She fired questions at Buck as they drove through starkly beautiful scenery, much of it important farm country, particularly around Dove

Creek, the self proclaimed "Pinto Bean Capitol of the World." Buck was glad that she appeared to be so interested in the countryside and involved in her surroundings. She even commented every now and then how much fun they were having together and how glad she was that she had invited herself on this trip.

When they got to Gallup, Buck actually drove around town a little before he headed south on State Road 602, down through the eastern edge of the Zuni Indian Reservation toward Fence Lake. This was mostly open ranch country with no towns and very little obvious impact from people. From Fence Lake it was a little over an hour on windy State Road 36 to Quemado. The quiet old village of Quemado was easy to navigate and after that it was a beautiful scenic drive through the Apache Sitgreaves National Forest. At the small and rustic Apache Creek store the crew loaded up on snack food and gassed up the vehicles. It was only a slow nineteen mile drive to Reserve, the county seat in the heart of huge Catron County, along the San Francisco River. Reserve was also the town that made Elfego Baca famous after his shootout with the cowboys from the Slaughter ranch in October, 1884.

Catron County was big enough to hold Rhode Island, Delaware and Washington, DC, almost 7,000 square miles, but it had barely 3,000 people. To Buck, that was how he wanted the entire state of New Mexico to be. Growth was not an appealing concept to one of New Mexico's newest permanent residents. Buck didn't quite get the irony of all of this. Catron County and Buck's new home, Hidalgo County, both had fewer than two people per square mile and neither of them had given up the old frontier spirit. These were not places that wanted to change very much and newcomers came at their own risk, particularly if they wanted to change things. "If it was good enough for my grandfather...,"or, "I like it just the way it is and if you don't...." were phrases you heard often in this part of New Mexico. They offended some people, mostly the urbanites from Albuquerque and Santa Fe, and the increasing number of California and Midwestern immigrants who ventured into this frontier environment, but to the locals, this part of western New Mexico was their home and it was just the way things were. This was one of those places where the people wanted time to stand still if not actually go back a few decades. It was Buck's kind of place.

Sure everyone in the area talked about economic development but Buck wasn't sure himself what that actually meant. Was it industry, tourism, subdivisions, or something else? Why wasn't it bigger and better ranches? The government had just reintroduced the wolves back into the Gila country, and the uproar from the locals made it seem like they had brought in a band of terrorists. To the ranchers and some others in the area, the wolves actually were terrorists. Since the people of Albuquerque and Santa Fe seemed to be the ones who were the most vocal and seemed to want the wolves back the most, the locals just didn't understand why they weren't being reintroduced where they were really wanted, up in northern New Mexico and away from their ranches. They sure weren't very welcome in Catron County. And like it or not, that's the way it went on the New Mexico/Arizona border.

After getting a couple of motel rooms at the only place in town, they put the horses up at Denny Skelton's, another of Buck's rancher/rodeo friends. Denny was getting ready to head to a roping just across the border near Springerville, Arizona so their get-together was brief. Denny told Buck how glad he was that his friend was moving to the Land of Enchantment and that it would give them a chance to see one another more often. Buck looked forward to that.

After the brief visit with Denny the trio decided to head for a café on the main drag. Since it hadn't been a long day on the road, they took their time eating, surrounded almost entirely by locals. When they finished the meal they had several cups of very strong coffee and just visited. Reserve was in the middle of the Gila National Forest, all 3,321,000 acres of it, and to Rebecca it didn't seem too different from western Montana with its own towering peaks and large Ponderosa pines. The Gila's summits reached some nine and ten thousand feet in altitude, and were green and covered in dense forests. This wasn't the desert, at least what she thought the desert was, and she wasn't too sure how you got from here to the "real" desert.

At dinner Buck suggested that Rebecca ride part of the way with Phil on the last day of their drive and when he made that suggestion he could see Phil light up. He was sure that the young cowboy already had a big crush on Buck's traveling companion. Rebecca smiled in her usually low-key provocative way and Buck thought that if there had been any doubt before, Phil was gone now. Buck hoped that these new, temporary traveling arrangements were going to work out. But if there was anything that he was certain of, it was that Rebecca knew how to take care of Phil and herself, and all at the same time.

■■■

In the morning they were all up early and eager to cover the last 200 miles. They knew the routine and since there weren't too many places to stop along the way, they had a hearty cowboy breakfast in Reserve, picked up the horses at the Skelton ranch and they were on the road.

The final leg of the trip was a beautiful drive, the first part of it in the national forest and through old historic villages like Alma and Glenwood. Buck felt a little lonely but he still had Cowboy as his companion. He was surprised at how much he missed having Rebecca next to him but he was sure that Phil and Rebecca would have a good time together. The two vehicles headed south and spent a considerable part of the day going through canyons, towering forests, lush open graze land and driving the winding roads along the west side of the Gila Wilderness, the first wilderness area in the world. When they hit the little Mormon towns of Cliff and Gila, just north of Silver City, Buck, to his surprise, was able to reach Phil on the cell and told him to pull over when Buck did. After they had both stopped, they all got out of their vehicles and Buck explained that this was really an historic spot.

"Gila was once the headquarters for the Lyons-Campbell Ranch. In the mid 1880s the place was advertised as the largest ranch in the world, stretching some sixty miles from north to south and another forty miles from east to west. Thomas Lyons, a Scotsman, always thought that he could make Grant County the biggest cattle market west of Kansas City. Well, it never happened. In fact, he was killed in El Paso by a mob in 1917. He was one tough son of a bitch and the story goes that he was actually beaten to death by some squatters who he had run off the ranch. Running off squatter was something he did with great pleasure. Some of those squatters actually waited for him in El Paso and that was the end of Thomas Lyons."

Rebecca looked at Buck. "How do you know all of this? You don't live here and you don't even get here that often."

"I guess you can attribute that to my academic background. I love all the history and the stories and folklore of this area. This is cowboy country, pure and simple. Honey, this is the real west."

Phil smiled at his boss and added: "You know Buck, with the way you're invested into this area you're never going to leave. You're sure out of Montana."

"That's the way it's supposed to be. It's what I've always thought about and tried to make happen. Who knows what the future has in store but for the time being it feels real good and sweet."

Phil grinned and was silent. This is what he always had dreamed about, too, but he had never been sure that he actually was ever going to be part of this kind of an environment—the real cowboy world. Each day it looked better and better and he felt more comfortable as he thought about adapting to his new life. He also felt lucky to be doing all of this with someone like Buck.

■■■

By the time they hit Silver City, a town of nearly 11,000, Buck knew that they were almost home. After negotiating through Silver, they took the forested road that led them down from around 6,000 feet, over the Continental Divide, through the Big Burro Mountains that were part of the Gila National Forest, until they hit the desert floor at 4,000 feet with the various mountain ranges creating an almost surreal, blue and gray layered backdrop in the distance. They could easily see the ranges looming over and behind the Peloncillos to the west in Arizona and by looking as far south as it was possible to see, they actually had a view of Mexico. The trio arrived in Lordsburg, turned right at the underpass, got on I-10 and headed west for about nine miles to Exit 11, south for Animas. As soon as they got off the Interstate and were on state Road 338, Buck pulled over and reclaimed Rebecca. Phil looked disappointed but Buck was sure that he would survive. Rebecca was her playful self, making several off-handed comments about being the chattel of the two cowboys. She sure was fun to be with.

■■■

As they headed for milepost 13 on the road south to Animas, the yuccas along each side of the road appeared like sentinels, guiding the travelers to their new home. And miles to the south, almost acting as a welcoming beacon was Animas Peak. Although it has an elevation of only 6,482 feet, it stood by itself and Buck knew that was the direction he had to head.

With cattle and horses grazing leisurely in the open pastures that led all the way to the base of the mountains on each side of the highway, the road lead the vehicles down a straight path to their long awaited destination.

They arrived at a place called Cotton City that had no post office, no school and no longer produced any cotton but now had chili fields and a chili processing plant and a several good sized alfalfa farms. The old cotton gins were idle and rusting, just metal ghosts from the past. What few stores were still standing along the main road were either boarded up or just deteriorating in the bright sun with peeling paint, broken windows and doors on wobbly hinges that kept nobody out. From Cotton City they headed east, toward the Pyramid Mountains, all on a washboardy dusty dirt road that looked liked worn out tan corduroy guarded on each side by ditches filled with empty beer cans and all sorts of debris blown in by the winds. The irrigated chili crops in the fields on both sides of the road gave the wide open areas their only sense of color and life.

It took them about twenty minutes to arrive at the ranch headquarter below the Pyramid Mountains. As they parked their vehicles at the main house and got out in the hot sun, Rebecca was the first to speak or more correctly, burst forth, "Wow! It's beautiful, just like you said it was. I didn't really think that I could ever feel good about this desert country but I guess the last three days have introduced it to me in such a darn subtle way. I had no idea that this kind of harsh environment could get to me so quickly. I was so sure that this was going to be lonely and unforgiving country and for some reason it really isn't. I'm really am glad that I conned you into taking me along on this trip."

Buck didn't say a word. He was glad to see Rebecca so animated and eager to express her feelings about the country and especially glad that she was so enthusiastic. Buck was still a little overwhelmed that he was actually here, home, and that this was all his. He was equally glad that he had Rebecca and Phil along with him to share this with. It was one of those moments when everything seemed so good, so complete, that you just waited for the other shoe to fall.

Phil remained quiet. He was looking around, wanting to take it all in at one viewing.

"Well, what do you think? Are you going to be able to survive down here after that time in Montana? How do you like the desert?"

"God Buck, I just don't know what to say. This place is really something. It's so open but yet there are mountains all around and the sun and sky are so big. No kidding, I really don't know what to say. Rebecca's right. This is harsh country but it's what I always pictured a good ranch in the old West would look like. I can't wait to get in the saddle and cover some ground around here. I think this is going to be just fine. Yes sir, this is going to be just fine."

Buck smiled. "I'm damn glad that's how you both feel. I tried to tell you about it as honestly as I could and I guess I got it pretty close. Phil, let's get over to your house so you can see your new digs and we can start to get you settled in. It's still early enough to get some unpacking done and we'll put the horses over in the small pasture or the corrals by your place. When I was down here last time I checked the fencing and the water and that's all set and ready to go. There's a big tank in the corral and we can fill that. Let's start ranching."

While all this was going on, Cowboy was off chasing rabbits, roadrunners or any of the little critters that were so abundant in the area and anything else that moved. To Buck, this was the way life was supposed to be. Maybe dreams do come true. Now what was going to happen? How would all this turn out? There were the three of them—Phil, Rebecca, and Buck himself, on the new ranch, all in a kind of limbo. But Buck knew that at least for the short term, getting the ranch in operating shape and teaching Phil how ranching is done in the desert and especially on the new Palo Verde, would take up a majority of his time, even if initially most of that would have to be over the phone and during a couple of short trips back and forth. It was only going to be a few months before he would be here full time and that's all he could contemplate as he looked over his new ranch. The thought of going back to Montana to finish out the school year wasn't something he was looking forward to. That was going to be harder than he ever imagined it would be. What to do about Rebecca was another whole story and one that he didn't really want to think about right now but he knew that he would have to deal with that sooner or later.

***

After getting the horses unloaded and settled with a little hay, Buck took a quick tour of the house where Phil was going to live and realized that it would need a woman's touch or at least a good paint job. But it seemed structural sound and he figured that Phil would do quite well in his new digs. Since there was no woman he'd just fix it up the way he wanted to. Buck next set out to take care of all the little details. He plugged in one of the cordless telephones with an answering machine that he had brought from Missoula's new Walmart. There was very sporadic cell phone service out on the ranch, mostly dead zones, and Buck wasn't sure that these cell phones were going to be a permanent part of everyday life, at least not on the ranch proper. Then he gave Phil the new phone numbers that he had gotten from the local phone company, the mailing address for the post office boxes in Animas, called the DISH TV network and ordered service that they could get connected at both houses, making sure that they got the new Encore Westerns channel as part of their package. He finally talked to the phone company about getting high speed wireless because he wanted the computers to be functioning at their maximum. The three newcomers were all a little surprised that the area even had the high speed service way out in the middle of nowhere, but it did. In fact, it was less than three months since all the new cables had been buried, all the way to El Paso.

The phone service was very important to Buck. He had to have some way of keeping in close touch with Phil while he was back in Montana and Buck still wasn't a big fan of E-mail. Somehow he always wanted to hear a voice and actually have a conversation. It was just another one of his fights with the modern world and one that he was absolutely convinced he was right about. E-mail seemed so impersonal, so distant, and so incomplete. Buck didn't think that was the way to run a ranch. He wasn't stupid and he wasn't naïve so he knew that he couldn't keep the late 21st century from eventually taking over. He was sure, though, that he could keep it from completely taking over his own life all at once. That's all he wanted to do.

Finally, they all pitched in and did what they could to help make Phil's house as comfortable as possible. Once they unloaded the truck, Buck got some bedding from one of the boxes and they began to set up real living quarters. It didn't take long for Phil to get settled. Tommy Sanchez had cleaned the place so it was quite livable and he had fixed all the obvious problems. He had even left a small shop-vac in case Phil needed it. The stove worked and seemed fairly new, the gas was turned on and the refrigerator was humming away. Phil would be able to cook and he had hot water. And there was a double bed for him to sleep in. Any other problems would take time to solve but they would eventually all be solved.

After making sure that they had all done what they could to get Phil settled in, the trio and Cowboy headed back over to the main house and did many of the same little chores. Buck and Phil unloaded everything from Buck's truck while Rebecca went for a walk in the hills around the house. This was all so overwhelming for her. She wanted to see everything first hand and just get a more intimate feel for the desert. She wanted to feel the ground and touch things, almost to prove to herself that this was all real.

Buck and Phil didn't actually need her help to unload all the stuff they had brought so Rebecca and Cowboy just disappeared for more than an hour. When she returned it was as if a new person had surfaced. She was calm, very introspective and just had a smile that both Buck and Phil found so damn appealing. Cowboy, on the other hand, couldn't contain himself. All the new smells and sights were just about too much for him. He ran here and there, chased whatever moved, sniffed at everything and then did it all over again. All Buck could think about was how happy all of this was making him feel. It's what he had been dreaming about for years. And probably not coming as too much of a surprise after spending three days with her on the ride south, he was able to see another side to Rebecca, a woman who was so complicated and yet so natural.

Once everything was unpacked, the three of them sat around and had a cold beer from one of the coolers. Buck suggested that they go into Lordsburg for dinner since they hadn't had a real meal since breakfast. They could make whatever plans for the immediate future while they were there. After the horse trailer was unhooked and parked down by Phil's barn, along with Phil's truck, they hopped into Buck's Ford and headed back down the dusty road to town. Cowboy stayed inside his new house and seemed content to be alone to explore whatever he had missed on his first go-round.

When they arrived in town they drove around a little until they found a restaurant close to the Desert Sunset motel on Main Street. Buck figured that in all likelihood it was probably the best place in town—at least it looked that way. The entry way had T-shirts, postcards, terrible pottery, and all the other trinkets that restaurants like this sold to the tourists—nothing very expensive and nothing very valuable. Of course, there was the local art work on the walls, all for sale. It appeared as if it had all been there for months, if not years. Buck wondered if they had ever sold a painting off the wall and if they did, who actually would be the buyer and why? And who were the artists?

Once they were seated in the non-smoking section by the smiling, young hostess, no one took the lead in making conversation. Each of the three was locked, at least for a while, in his own private world, trying to absorb the events of the last few days and at the same time making some kind of assessment for their own future. Seated at the dinner table were three people, each experiencing the same physical world and yet each perceiving that world, their future, and their own situation in the most personal of terms. And the three were all significantly different.

Then out of nowhere, before they had taken their red cloth napkins out the glasses that were their temporary holders, Buck just jumped in and aimed a few comments directly at Phil. He spoke quietly because the other tables were so close but that just added to the serious tone of what he was obviously going to say.

"Phil, as soon as Rebecca and I leave here and head back to Montana, you'll probably go to Silver City to do some serious shopping. While you're up there, make sure you stop by the local animal shelter and pick out a dog for yourself. You'll need a good companion and you know what they say about a cowboy without a dog—that he isn't a real cowboy. They must have some good cow dogs up there and I'm sure you'll find one you like. Make sure it's spayed or neutered and you'd better give him a good home. And the second point. You know the ranch and this whole area is right in the middle of the trails that the illegals and the drug smugglers and all the others coming up from Mexico use. I want you to be alert and a dog will sure help you." He waited a minute before he continued.

"Do you have a gun? You're going to need either a hand gun or a rifle to help protect the ranch. If you don't have one or the other, you'll need to get one or both. Do you know how to shoot?"

Buck seemed so serious and it caught both Rebecca and Phil a little off guard. From what they had expected to be just a light, pleasant dinner the conversation had changed to dogs and an old Wild West shoot out. Phil didn't say anything for a minute but Rebecca jumped in, visibly agitated.

"Buck, are you kidding? Who, in God's name, is he going to shoot? Do they really do that stuff down here? My God, what happened to the beautiful starry summer nights and the clear skies and desert winds and all the other things that were so romantic? Is Phil actually expected to start shooting at someone?"

She seemed so confused and agitated by the conversation Buck had started. The city girl couldn't quite comprehend the rugged and volatile nature of the desert country in the Bootheel of New Mexico.

Phil thought he had better get his two cents in before things got out of hand.

"Buck, I know how to shoot and I do own a rifle. I don't own a hand gun and I don't think I'll need one, at least I hope I won't. Besides, once the Border Patrol and the sheriff know who we are, and that the ranch is inhabited again, I think they'll be keeping in closer touch with us and having us there should help keep some of the traffic away from the ranch. You were kind of confusing me for a minute but I really do understand what you're saying. I'll definitely get the dog. That's something I had been thinking about and wanted to do anyway, but shooting illegals or drug smugglers—that just seems so damn crazy."

Just as Rebecca seemed about to enter the conversation again, Buck gently grabbed her arm in order to keep her quiet. He sensed that this was all getting out of hand and he wanted to put a stop to that before it was too late.

"Jesus Phil, I don't want you to shoot anybody. The gun is for mountain lions, rattlers, coyotes and any other damn predators that will invade the ranch. I just wanted you to be fully aware of where you live and what the potential risks are. If you ever see any illegals, always, and I mean always, call the Border Patrol or the sheriff's department. I'm not kidding about that. I've heard that there's a deputy that lives right in Animas. Those guys get paid for what they do and they're good at it despite what some of the critics say. The Border Patrol until very recently has been undermanned but that's because the people in Washington are too full of crap to really help them out. The politicians talk a lot and do a lot of posturing but don't seem to get anything done. They do some hotdogging for the folks back home and they think that's enough. I'm not even sure that they know what to do. Our local Congressman is probably the worst of the lot. All we get from Washington is a lot of patriotic talk about securing our borders and then more talk. Nobody seems to know what to do or how to do it. Or what "securing the borders" even means. But we're on a main trail coming up from the Southern Cross Ranch and they come over the border there pretty frequently."

Buck was quiet for a moment. It was as if he wanted all this to sink in before he started something new. Then he continued.

"I'm sorry I just injected my political views into all of this, but honestly, I don't want to sound like doom and gloom. You both know how much I love this place. But with all the trails on the ranch, you know, the cattle and wildlife trails, there are also trails made by men. Those trails are littered with empty plastic water bottles, soda cans, used toilet paper and diapers, condoms, and small, empty tins of sardines, tuna and things like that. Even clothing! These are left by the illegals and the smugglers coming up from Mexico. It's as simple as that. And just so you know, the border from the Arizona line to almost a third of the way across New Mexico is nothing more than a seven strand barb wire fence. Nothing fancy, no big walls or steel fences, at least not yet—just barbed wire although they say that they are going to improve that. If you get a chance to see it up close, parts of it looks like macramé it's been repaired so many times. When they'll make some changes...well, nobody seems to know but everyone says it will be soon and you have to realize that the Forest Service has actually put up signs just across the valleys in southern Arizona that read: "Travel Caution: Smuggling and Illegal Immigration May Be Encountered In This Area." That's pretty defeatist for them. It's as if they can't do anything about the problem so they just warn you to be alert. They're telling you that you're on your own or at least, be careful. Maybe it's the ultimate government disclaimer and it sure doesn't solve anything. All I want you to do is keep your eyes open and if the trails look really fresh, call the Border Patrol. I haven't talked to them yet but I'm sure they know, better than we do, where the trails are on our ranch and they probably patrol them periodically."

Phil was very attentive and seemed to be absorbing everything that Buck had to say. He didn't say anything but he knew that what Buck was talking about would affect him every single day he was down here. He waited, anxiously, for Buck to continue.

"Now the next thing you have to do is to start thinking like a rancher. There really are rattlers, coyotes, mountain lions and all sorts of varmints that can screw up our operation. I don't want any of our foals or dogs being chewed up by one of those critters. I do expect you to shoot them if it becomes necessary. And later on, when we add cattle, the same dangers lurk for any calves or heifers. The mountain lions and the coyotes are pretty thick. The reason you think that this is such colorful cowboy country is that it is still harsh, and rugged, and uninhabited. No two bit developer has got his hands on this country yet and probably never will. But you have to be there for your animals and you are the best protection that they have. I do worry a little that you'll be here alone for a few months, until I get back, and I just want you to be aware of what lurks out there. It's important that you get to know the few neighbors that we have as soon as you can. You'll make lots of contacts at the Animas Valley Feed Store. And there must be a café around where the ranchers and cowboys and the other locals go for coffee in the morning. We'll have to find that. There isn't anything you can't handle as long as you're aware of what the options are. And I know you'll be just fine."

Rebecca sat there a little amazed and a little amused. She was definitely a city girl and had never been exposed to this kind of country and she surely had never become part of the ranching world in Montana. This whole conversation surprised her so much and she didn't know for sure whether Buck was being overly dramatic or realistic. The more she listened to the conversation she was sure that Buck was being as straightforward as he could be. She was convinced, in fact, that he was trying to alert Phil to things that might happen, not scare him. Never having been in this kind of environment, Rebecca was a little scared herself and wasn't sure how to react. She was trying to bring an abstract idea about the "old West," in line with the reality that Buck was outlining for Phil. What she didn't understand was whether or not she could ever fit into a world like this. In fact, she wasn't quite sure that she wanted to.

Finally she began to speak quietly.

"You know, Buck, the sorts of things you're talking about are mostly the kind of stories you hear about on the television news, or read in the papers, but no one I know actually takes all this seriously or has actually been exposed to it. It's hard to identify with these kinds of border problems when you live in Montana, Wyoming, or Washington and the border problems are Canadian and not Mexican. The problems you hear about on television are always the ones along the southern border."

She stopped, not knowing exactly what else to say. To Rebecca the difference between the Canadian and Mexican borders seemed immense but to Buck she seemed very naïve. And that surprised him.

In Rebecca's head she was in the middle of a real war. Her first impulse was to want to get out of there, as fast as possible, but she also felt a deep sense of security with Buck. She liked the way he talked about the border, that he seemed to know what was going on, and that he appeared to not be hesitant to defend what was his. This really was the old west and every inch of Buck was part of it. He was doing all he could to make sure that Phil had a place right in the heart of things. She admired him for the way he trusted Phil and the way that he wanted to prepare the young cowboy for the potential dangers that might await him in the country he was just beginning to embrace. But mostly she understood that Buck was willing to protect him. It was so clear to her now that Buck would not linger in Montana one day longer than was absolutely necessary. Animas, New Mexico, from this day forward was his home and if she hadn't fully understood that before, finally Rebecca was never so sure of anything in her life.

Buck stopped his discussion of what life might be like on the Palo Verde Ranch and just sat in his chair, fidgeting with the silverware. It was hard to tell whether he was just waiting for everything to sink in or waiting for someone to make a comment. He kept looking over at Phil to see what kind of reaction he would get from the young college cowboy.

Phil wasn't sure what to do. He had all sorts of thoughts running through his head and even some questions but for the time being he thought silence might be his best, immediate reaction.

Rebecca was almost in another world. This was so new and in many ways, frightening to her, she also chose silence. Luckily for everyone, the waitress showed up just about the time that the awkward silence might have reached a deafening roar in the dining room.

Once the three silent partners got back to their menus, a more normal conversation returned about choices for dinner and other trivial matters. You could almost hear their audible sighs around the restaurant.

Buck was the first one to speak after everyone put in their order.

"Rebecca and I have to leave the day after tomorrow so we'll probably have to do some shopping and such before we leave. Phil, I'm going to open a ranch account at one of banks in Lordsburg that's connected to my bank in Missoula. I'll set up a substantial credit line. Then I'm going to give you a month's advance on your salary so you have some walking around money. When I get back to Montana I'm going to get us a credit card for the ranch. I'll make sure that you'll have one. That will make record keeping a whole lot easier. Until then, just be certain that you keep pretty good records and receipts on things you buy for the ranch out of the bank account. And by the way, how would you both like to go to Silver City tomorrow? It's a pretty good town and since we just breezed through it on the way down I thought you might like to take a closer look. It will probably be where you'll do most of your shopping. Besides, as you saw today, the drive to Silver City is pretty scenic. Most of it's off the Interstate and every now and then you'll even get to see deer when you drive up through the Big Burro Mountains."

"That sounds like it could be a good day. I'd like to see more of the country before we head back to Montana."

Rebecca was glad that the conversation was lightening up and that the mood was about having a good time and not about the more serious problems that had dominated the earlier part of the dinner.

Phil was eager to let Buck know that he felt the same way.

"That sounds good to me, too. I'll need some supplies and a few odds and ends to just get settled in. You know what I'm talking about, basic things like food. And maybe we can find out where the animal shelter is. It's going to be a little lonely without you, Rebecca, and Cowboy. I probably shouldn't admit it to you but I really look forward to getting that DISH TV installed."

Buck smiled. This is how he wanted things to wind up. All the seriousness from earlier was now put on the back burner and the three friends could settle in and enjoy their dinner. He felt he had made his point and there wasn't any reason to pursue the line of conversation that had started the evening. Dinner was going to be relaxed and he wanted the table talk to get back to the concerns and interests shared easily by friends, particularly as they all embarked on a new segment of their lives.

The food turned out to be better than they expected but that isn't saying too much since the expectations were pretty low. And as they chatted they even had an interesting conversation about the possibility of stocking the place with cattle, and whether to go cow/calf or yearling steers. Buck once again brought up the proposal from Steve Anderson about wintering the Montana Big Hole cattle in the Animas Valley. It was getting to be a progressively interesting idea for Buck, and Phil appeared to be intrigued with the idea because it would give him an opportunity to work a good size herd full time. Buck knew it would take a year or so to get into a position where he could honestly explore the possibility but it was something he wanted to do.

Phil was pleased that Buck seemed to be involving him in the planning and Rebecca enjoyed seeing the friendship that was so obviously growing between the two cowboys. She was also becoming increasingly aware that there probably wasn't a place for her on the Palo Verde Ranch—at least not now. It came as something of a jolt because she hadn't planned that there would be a place for her or that she even wanted to be involved. Her plans had been firm about returning to Seattle and going back to school. She wasn't sure herself why the feeling of being left out affected her so much. But she knew how much she was becoming attached to Buck and how much she even admired Phil. Mostly though it was about Buck and leaving him, if that's what the future held. Maybe this wasn't going to be as easy as she had expected. All the conversations they had in Missoula about their future and their little fling now sounded downright foolish to her. She knew it wasn't going to be anything like that at all.

After dinner they took their time as they drove back to the ranch. It was almost their way of announcing that all was well with the world and that they were in no hurry. It was also one of those clear desert night skies, about a day or two away from a full moon, the kind of sky that seduced you into believing that every star in the heavens has been gathered directly above for your own personal enjoyment. When they arrived at Phil's house, they all got out of the truck just to look at the sky and it was so overwhelming that there wasn't much for anyone to say. The big golden moon had just come up over the Pyramid Mountains and there was enough light to give everything an eerie glow. The three of them stood there in silence until Rebecca made the only comment when she sort of uttered, "Oh my gosh!"

After Phil went into his house to spend his first night on the Palo Verde, Buck and Rebecca got back into the Ford and headed over to headquarters where Buck was about to spend his first night on the ranch. He had been thinking about this all evening and although he realized it was foolish, he actually looked forward to it as a major stepping stone to settling into Hidalgo County. When they parked at the house they could hear Cowboy barking and Buck enjoyed the thought that Cowboy was already protecting his new home. He was sure that he would soon become as comfortable on his new ranch as Cowboy seemed to be.

Hand in hand Buck and Rebecca walked to the front door and after they were inside and let Cowboy out for his evening constitutional, they put on a couple of lights and Buck got some sheets, pillow cases and towels out of one of the boxes that was scattered around the living room floor. They took the bedding into what was going to become the master bedroom and Rebecca started to make up the old double bed. Buck looked at her and realized that if he was going to share his first night with anyone, he was glad it was Rebecca.

"How about we take a shower before we head for bed? All that dust and grime needs to be washed out."

He smiled when he finished his transparent request because both he and Rebecca knew that it wasn't about the dust and grime that had prompted his invitation.

"I'm all for that. I can't wait to wash you all over and feel your hands all over me. I've been thinking about how I was going to convince you to take a shower with me since dinner. We must really be a horny twosome."

Buck smiled but didn't say a word. He headed for the bathroom and turned on the lights. Tommy Sanchez had installed the dimmer switch that he had wanted and Buck turned the lights down to what he hoped would be a romantic level. Then he went back to one of the boxes in the living room to find a couple of candles. He lit two of them in the bathroom and decided to turn the lights completely off. It wasn't long before Rebecca joined him and after undressing they stood outside the shower, naked and both very excited.

"Do you realize that all these firsts—the first shower, the first night actually sleeping here, the first meal—all the firsts that I've thought about for so long, are now going to be shared with you. You are now part of the legacy of the Palo Verde Ranch."

Buck grinned, almost laughing out loud, and gave her a big hug. Having her so close to him at that moment, couldn't have been more satisfying.

"Well, other than you being a little too dramatic, I guess I'm actually honored. Stay here and hold me so you can add the first kiss in the bathroom to your long list of firsts. I think that feeling you against me here is among my firsts and part of my legacy."

The shower exceeded anything that Buck might have wished for. Their intensity and affection seemed to rekindle thoughts that for at least a few days, Buck had put aside as much as he could, as he concentrated on the ranch, getting settled, and making sure that Phil was feeling comfortable in his new home. Being with Rebecca again, alone and with nothing interfering in their relationship, made Buck remember how much he cared for Rebecca and how much he was physically attracted to her. The passion of their physical relationship continued to overwhelm him. Rebecca seemed to want to let him know that maybe she didn't want to leave him. Buck just wanted to be as intimate and physical as he was possible of enduring. That was pure lust.

For some reason, as close as they were and as intimate as they were, they were on different wave lengths. Rebecca didn't know how to communicate all that she was feeling. All she knew was that it could not be done physically. And Buck, he was enjoying the physical moment at a level that he found almost mesmerizing. He had never known a woman like Rebecca and he was bound and determined to enjoy every minute of their time together. He had become so self-absorbed that he was completely unaware or maybe even uncaring of Rebecca's needs. He had taken everything at face value...that his time with Rebecca was temporary, that she was going back to Seattle and school, and once he was settled in New Mexico, he would just pick up his life from there. He had blocked out any thought that they would be together. He wasn't even sure now that he was in New Mexico that he wanted them to be together. He had great doubts that Rebecca could fit into the lifestyle of Hidalgo County and he was afraid to open himself up to a major disappointment. Buck was becoming increasingly damn good at denial.

After the shower, they climbed into bed and Buck announced that one of his first purchases would be a new spring and mattress set. They laughed at how lumpy and uncomfortable the bed was and they agreed that's probably why it was left in the house when the original owners moved out. They were sure they couldn't even give it away. Its future was at the dump. But they managed to be close and fall asleep holding one another affectionately, despite the mattress. Buck felt like a ton of bricks had been lifted from his shoulders. He had actually made it to New Mexico, to his new ranch, and he was completely relaxed and happy. His cynicism was gone, at least temporarily, and he was on cloud nine to know that dreams, at least his dreams, were coming true.

Rebecca wasn't sure of exactly what she was feeling. She didn't really have any expectations when all this started, beyond her plans of going back to Seattle and her own future. Now she wasn't even sure that she should have been so aggressive in pursuing Buck. It wasn't supposed to be so serious. She never intended to feel so deeply about him and at least for the time being, she didn't know what to do about it. Now there was a problem as she began to give more serious thought to her own future. Seattle, law school, a career as an attorney, the rainy winters, what was left of her family in the Pacific Northwest...were all these to be left behind because she was beginning to care more for Buck Cooper than she was for her own future and her own dreams? This was not the Rebecca Walker that she had always envisioned herself to be—strong, in charge, and usually one step ahead of the game. What had happened to her?

PART 3

THE FIRST DAYS IN NEW MEXICO

B/C

Phil had been alone on the Palo Verde for two days and the adjustment wasn't nearly as easy as he thought it would be. Buck and Rebecca had headed back to Montanan with the empty horse trailer a couple of days before and Phil was left alone, with no friends, no specific contacts and not anyone to share his day to day cares with. He really didn't even have anyone to talk to. He felt very isolated and wasn't quite sure how to take care of that. He did make a list of things that had to be done immediately. Some for his own needs and some were requests from Buck. All would keep him busy for the short term.

Everything, from putting food in the cupboards, getting the odds and ends he needed for the house, checking the ranch so he knew where he actually was, to finding and meeting the local vet in Lordsburg, those were things that had to be done. But mostly Phil wanted to get that dog that he and Buck had talked about and he anxiously awaited the arrival of the DISH TV man the next day. Even his own reading material wasn't what he wanted but he found a good book store in Silver City the day he explored there with his two pals from Montana. That was one place that he wanted to spend some time. He had realized from the start that this was lonely country and that it would take some time to have even the vaguest sense that he belonged in the Animas Valley. He was right about that. Buck had called from the road and for the time being the telephone land line was Phil's link with the outside world. The computers were all hooked up and he was trying to create some format to keep track of ranch business. Buck had asked him to keep a thorough record of the weather, including the amount of rain, temperature, and general conditions. He also wanted him to keep a diary, or at least a daily record of the goings on at the Palo Verde. Phil wasn't sure whether Buck really need all of this or if it was his way of keeping Phil busy. Ultimately it didn't matter because Phil was enjoying the record keeping and the diary was developing into a full blown narrative. The more he wrote the more he realized how complicated the daily goings on at the ranch were. That actually surprised him.

Phil made two trips to Silver City before he found the dog he wanted, a year old Australian Shepherd/Border Collie cross that he named Cactus. Phil loved the dog from the minute he saw him and since he was already spayed and had all his shots, for a very minimum fee Phil was able to take him home right then and there. When he got into Phil's Dodge, Cactus was clearly scared and nested on the floor. By the time they had made the 70-mile trip back to the ranch, the newest member of the Palo Verde family was sitting up, poking his face out the partially opened window and taking in the countryside. All Phil knew about the dog was that he had been brought to the animal shelter by a young couple at the college in Silver City who didn't think that they were able to care for him and that they wanted "a good home for the dog they just loved." Phil was going to make sure that happened. Cactus made an easy adjustment to the ranch and instantly became devoted to Phil, just the way it was supposed to be.

The young cowboy also visited the bookstore and picked up an armful of books, mostly good western literature and histories of the southwest and the Apaches, and several novels by J.P.S. Brown, Elmer Kelton, Tony Hillerman, Jack Schaefer, and Max Evans, authors that had been recommended to him by Buck. His DISH was working and he made a point to saddle up each day and ride the ranch, gradually working his way deeper and deeper into the Pyramid Mountains, now with his new partner Cactus at his side.

■■■

There really wasn't a whole lot of pressing work to do on the ranch. All the fencing that he had been able to check was in good repair, although he did find one spot where it had been cut some time ago, probably, he thought, by people heading north. The pipe corrals and pens certainly needed some paint, the water systems were in fine working order, and so far he hadn't found any leaks in the miles of water lines that were buried all over the ranch. Phil realized that for the next few months, until Buck came back permanently, his main responsibility would be to see that things were maintained and repaired when necessary, the horses were fed and cared for, and that he got a foothold in the area, meeting as many people as he could. He needed to gain some visibility in the community and learn what it took to have a good life in Hidalgo County. If nothing else, he had the feeling that his own roots were being planted.

Buck had encouraged Phil to select one of the young horses they had brought south and to think of it as his own. After riding all four of the horses they had moved down from Montana, Phil selected a four year old bay mare with Doc O'Lena, Doc's Sug and Sugar Bars blood lines. Buck had obviously got her for the brood mare band because of her breeding and Phil knew he'd have to get a second horse because it was just a matter of time before "Canyon" would be bred.

Phil had been on the ranch nearly two weeks when he decided to go to Lordsburg and introduce himself to Dr. Browning, the local vet. Phil needed to know what shots were appropriate for the horses in New Mexico and anything else that might be different from what he knew about in Montana. Besides, it was always a good idea to have contact with the local vet. Dr. Browning was originally from Wyoming and had gone to school at Colorado State University in Fort Collins. Both Buck and Phil thought they were lucky to find him because they had such respect for the equine vets that came out of Colorado State.

Bob Browning was in his mid to late forties, a little over six feet tall with graying hair around the temples, and had the trim build of a man who obviously did hard physical work. He had been in Lordsburg about six or seven years. From the little that Phil could pick up at the feed store, Browning was very well respected and a "good guy." Although he specialized in large animals, mostly horses and cattle, he also took care of household pets. He would become Cactus' doctor as well as the ranch vet.

It was a warm Wednesday morning when Phil drove to Lordsburg and picked up several newspapers, including *USA Today*, the *Albuquerque Journal*, and the local weekly. Getting a daily paper was hard and Phil wanted to figure out a way to make this a regular feature of his life, whether the paper came by mail or he had to run into town to buy one. It was either that or get all of his news and daily dose of crossword puzzles from TV and the papers that were available on the computer. The more he thought about it, the newspapers on the computer seemed to be the best alternative since he wasn't going to be in town on a regular basis and he picked up his mail in Animas where newspapers weren't that readily available. Besides, he only picked up his mail in town a couple of times a week.

The rest of the Lordsburg trip was to see the vet, get acquainted, and just sort of look around and see what was what in Lordsburg. Phil really had no particular expectations or goals.

Dr. Browning's Lordsburg Animal Clinic was on the east side of town and was a fairly new facility with outside pipe pens for horses surrounded by large shade trees and a waiting room that was spacious and decorated with western art prints, mostly scenes of working cowboys. His receptionist was a gray haired middle age woman, very friendly, and clearly knowledgeable about everything that took place at the clinic. Phil explained who he was and what he was doing in the area and then asked if he could meet with the Dr. Browning. He was told that he would probably have a fifteen minute wait. Phil took a seat, grabbed an eight month old issue of Western Horseman Magazine and just relaxed. When Dr. Browning came out to the waiting room, he greeted Phil and invited him to come back into his office, where they visited. The vet assured Phil that he was available day or night and that he knew where the ranch was and had in the past been out that way preg testing cattle and caring for a variety of animals. After about twenty minutes, Phil got up to leave and as he was heading out he ran into a stunning dark hair young woman, obviously the vet's assistant.

Phil was stopped in his tracks. The woman was so beautiful and a quick glance didn't reveal any rings on her left hand. Phil thought that maybe he had hit the jackpot but then he couldn't figure out why someone so beautiful would be unattached. He doubted that she was just sitting around waiting for him. As they passed one another he nodded to her, said hello, and he tried to forget the whole thing as he headed back to his truck. But on the drive home he couldn't get the picture of the dark haired senorita out of his head. He would definitely have to find out more about her. Phil hadn't had a date in a long time and he was beginning to think that maybe he just missed spending time with a female companion. He thought that maybe he ought to put "getting a date" on his list of things to do, and soon.

■■■

The next morning, Phil was riding on the east side of the ranch, in the foothills of the Pyramids, with Cactus at his side, when he saw a small pile of trash neatly piled along an old dirt road nestled under some old oak trees. The road didn't look like a vehicle had been on it in years but the trash, a plastic water bottle, some used toilet paper, a Coke bottle, and a small tin can, all appeared to be very recent. He climbed down off "Canyon" to take a closer look and as he did he realized that everything that Buck had told him about the illegals crossing the ranch was probably true. Not that he actually had had any doubts. There were several tracks, easily identified as sneaker prints, so he immediately called Cactus over to his side and steered "Canyon" out of the way so the Border Patrol would be able to have the site as pristine as possible, just in case they thought they needed to track this guy, or guys.

When he got back to the house he called the Border Patrol who seemed interested but expressed no great urgency. They did assure him that they would be out to look things over. Phil gave them as precise directions as he could and they told him that one of the agents would give him a call if anything turned up. Phil was glad to have made the contact but he knew that this wasn't going to be the most urgent or biggest or best trail that they'd see that day. After he explained where he found the trash pile, he even introduced himself to the operator at the Lordsburg station and told him to tell the guys on duty that they were welcome to stop by for coffee or just a place to hang out. Phil hadn't expected to be confronted with this kind of illegal activity so quickly but in a way he was glad that he had seen, first hand, what a crossing point and camp would look like. And he was glad that he had a chance to make his initial contact with the Border Patrol. He was sure that he would eventually become friends with some of the crews who worked the area and that he would see them maybe more often than he really wanted to. New agents were coming to the Lordsburg area on a regular basis as the Border Patrol continued to beef up its presence along the border that at least for the time being was damn porous.

About an hour later one of the younger BP agents, Rudy Medina, knocked on Phil's door, introduced himself and asked the young cowboy to fill him in on what he had seen earlier in the day. When Phil was finished the agent thanked him and headed out to the spot where the camp site had been found. Phil just assumed that whatever had to be done would be done.

■■■

Within a week Phil had the house feeling fairly homey. He had made another swing up to Silver City to pick up some of the things he had forgotten on his first trips and he was beginning to feel like he actually lived at the Palo Verde. His house began to take on some of his own personality as he scattered a few family pictures and even one of him in his lacrosse uniform, around what was becoming a very comfortable living room. He had picked up a small table, an easy chair, a colorful area rug with a southwestern design, and a good reading light, all at a second hand store.

He didn't, however, completely forget the raven haired girl at the vet's. He was trying to figure out how to meet her, or at least see her again, when he decided that maybe Cactus needed a once over to make sure that he was as fit as they told him he was in Silver City. He called the clinic and they told him no appointment was necessary, just come on in. Phil decided that the day after tomorrow would be the ideal time for a trip to Lordsburg.

■■■

That night Buck called and Phil told him about his first encounter with the illegals and Buck let him know that he thought that he handled it perfectly. Other than that, they just exchanged some chatter about the horses, life at the ranch and in Animas, the weather—Buck was always asking about rain or the possibilities for some moisture—and that was about it. Buck had nothing specific he was calling about, just checking in, but Phil was always glad to hear from him. Buck still remained Phil's main lifeline to the outside world.

Early the next morning, after Phil had fed the horses, he got into the pick up and rode over to his closest neighbor, an ex rodeo cowboy who was ranching about seven sections to the south of the Palo Verde. The old cowboy, probably in his late 50s or early 60s, was a little crippled up but certainly able to get around. From what Phil could tell, at best his place was a marginal operation with somewhere around 40 or 50 mother cows. When Phil drove over the cattle guard and up to the single story, tan stucco house with the slightly pitched roof, the old cowboy came out. He had a dog by his side and a pistol on his hip and it appeared that he was as surprised to see a visitor as Phil was to have a neighbor. He invited Phil to get out of the truck and as he did, he came over to Phil and introduced himself. Phil, in turn, explained who he was, where he was from, and what he was doing in the area. The cowboy, Guy Halsey, invited him into what was obviously a bachelor's house, filled with old magazines and newspapers and used glasses and dishes. Clearly, housekeeping was not the top of Guy Halsey's list of priorities.

Before Phil was even seated, Halsey offered him the choice of some coffee or a beer. Because it was still pretty early in the day, Phil decided that coffee was probably the best choice so Guy did the same.

Phil learned that Guy Halsey had been living on his ranch for about fifteen years and at one time had been a full time saddle bronc and bareback bronc rider on the Rodeo Cowboys Association (RCA) circuit, the major league of rodeo. It was now known as the Professional Rodeo Cowboys Association (PRCA), the name that Phil was more familiar with. Guy had done pretty well, just missing out a couple of times of making the National Finals Rodeo when it was still held in Oklahoma City, but he did well enough to put some money away and buy the ranch. He had even spent a couple of seasons on the Old Timers Rodeo circuit and made their finals one year. Scattered throughout the living room were photographs of Guy on bucking horses in all sorts of almost impossible configurations from the major rodeos at Cheyenne, Pendleton, Prescott, Salinas, Houston, San Antonio and others that Phil couldn't identify. Guy also explained that he had an interest in a couple of oil wells in West Texas that he had inherited and that sure helped to pay the bills. He loved to spin some yarns and he appeared to be as glad to have someone to talk to as Phil was. He obviously didn't have many visitors and Phil kind of got the idea that Guy didn't go into town very often. Not that he was a hermit or anything like that. It was just that he seemed to enjoy his time on the ranch and had no particular need to go to town to socialize. What surprised Phil was the number of books scattered around the living room. Guy was obviously a voracious reader.

Phil was there for several hours and as the conversation rambled on, Guy told his young neighbor that he was born on a ranch over near Roswell, New Mexico, had been divorced for about fifteen years and that's when he bought the ranch, that he had a 36 year old son who managed a pretty good sized cow/calf operation in the Texas Panhandle, north of Amarillo, and that he had no particular lady in his life right now.

From their first hand shake, Phil had the gut feeling that Guy Halsey was someone that he was going to like and see quite a bit of. It was one of those situations where you have an immediate reaction, either positive or negative, and in this case, it was definitely positive.

Somehow, Phil sensed that Guy was going to be a good neighbor and that he had a lot to learn from this old cowboy. In a way, Guy was just the kind of neighbor that Phil hoped he would have—a living part of the romantic past that he envisioned the first time he laid eyes on the Animas Valley and the Palo Verde Ranch. Guy was a cowboy who was a part of all the local ranching traditions and was actually for real, not someone from books and movies, not someone playing a part and dressing up for the local rodeo. Guy was just what Phil needed and someone he wanted to get to know. He was, as the old saying goes, "More cow than hat."

When Phil got back to his own place, he sat outside on one of those white, molded plastic lawn chairs you can buy for practically nothing at WalMart. As he ate his salami sandwich he was feeling the need to stop, think and plan for the next few days. But mostly he wanted to reflect on his life and the decisions he had made in the last year or so. Things were going well, he was beginning to settle into his new home in New Mexico, although he did feel a bit of isolation, but the future seemed to offer a lot of opportunities. Phil had to try and figure out what they were and how he could take advantage of them. He knew that he wanted to stay at the Palo Verde, he knew that he loved this new country, and he was beginning to warm up to the people he was finally meeting. He was also certain that when Buck eventually arrived to stay, things would get even better. He wasn't nearly as clear about how to meet that girl at the vet clinic, he wasn't sure what the long term on the Palo Verde offered him, and he wasn't sure if and when he would ever get his own place. But everything seemed to suggest that eventually getting a place of his own some day was a real possibility, not some unrealistic pipe dream. As much as he liked and respected Buck, he couldn't envision working for Buck or anyone else for the rest of his life. He knew he couldn't settle for that and he was almost certain that he wouldn't have to. But he also knew that he had so much to learn in the interim.

That evening, before the sun set, Phil saddled up, and along with Cactus, took a ride south in the direction of Guy Halsey's ranch. Their shared fence line was several miles from headquarters and on the other side of the fence it was nearly a couple of miles to Guy's house. That kind of distance made good neighbors. Phil hadn't yet been on this part of the range and he was surprised at how much grass there was. He was sure that in a wet year those sections would hold a good size herd of mother cows. It appeared that cattle had grazed on the land fairly recently—maybe a few years ago and there were still some old, dried up cow pies—but it was not overgrazed. Phil thought that when Buck arrived they would surely have to do an inventory and figure out what land could be used immediately and what land had to be rested, and then they would have to wait for a wet summer monsoon season to use the entire ranch. According to Guy, the last several summers had been dry and the winter rains were almost nonexistent. The local ranchers were beginning to compare conditions to the drought of the1950s. Phil could only hope that the weather would return to a more normal pattern. The weather forecasters weren't very clear about the next few months and what this year's monsoon season were going to bring. They were all hoping for an El Nino weather pattern to shape up since that would mean good summer rain and wetter winters. But time was running out for this year. Ranching in desert country wasn't easy. It occurred to Phil that keeping the diary, as Buck had requested, was probably a part of trying to figure all this out. Without water there wasn't going to be any cattle and it would be next to impossible to make this ranch pay for itself with just a small horse herd. Having to buy great quantities of hay to replace the grass that wasn't there, could break a rancher in no time at all. That was something to be concerned about. This was very fragile country and very different than what Phil had experienced in Montana.

▪▪▪

Phil was up early the next morning. It was a typical late spring day at the ranch. The sun, with its warm glow, was coming up over the Pyramids, the air was still and by 7:30 the temperature was already warming up. Cactus, who was now used to sleeping inside, on the bed as often as Phil would allow it, which was pretty much all the time, was eager to get outside and Phil, still in his pajamas, let him out and joined him in the small front yard. Phil looked around, not anticipating seeing anything in particular, but he just enjoyed the view...to the west, out across the valley to the Chiricahuas and to the east, just behind the ranch, he looked up into the Pyramids. Phil still was on a high, knowing that this was his home and that this is the way it was supposed to be. So far there hadn't been any disappointments. He went back inside, poured himself a cup of coffee, got dressed and headed right back outside to just enjoying his new surroundings.

Today was the day the young cowboy was going to take Cactus to the vet with the hope of meeting the young woman who had drawn his full attention the first time he was there.

Phil decided to take the old back road into town. This road had probably been an old ranch wagon road that was now used almost exclusively by the locals. The ride on the dirt road into town took a little longer but it was relaxing and Phil enjoyed the scenery. Cactus took his usual position by the window that Phil kept partially opened, and the young cowboy just relaxed as he made the drive to town. He was becoming increasingly familiar and comfortable with the countryside. By the time he got to the Lordsburg Animal Clinic he had an uneasy feeling with the anticipation of seeing his "dream girl" again. But since he didn't have any idea of when she worked, or how he would get to visit with her, or who she even was, he almost felt foolish, like a real young kid. But he figured, what the hell, he really had nothing to lose.

▪▪▪

After he signed in at the main desk, he had been waiting about ten minutes when the "dream girl" came into the waiting room and asked for Mr. Shaw. Phil somewhat awkwardly introduced himself to Selena Maria Bradley, and she led him and Cactus into one of the examining rooms in the back. Selena asked a few questions about Cactus and had her back to Phil as she filled out some forms. Phil gave her a full look over. Her raven hair, down below her shoulders, glistened under the fluorescent lights, and although she wasn't wearing very tight jeans, they were tight enough for Phil to see what a good figure she had. Once again he checked her left hand and there wasn't a ring. He was really at a loss of what to do or say.

Selena Maria Bradley asked him about the ranch, the horses and was making small talk while they both waited for Dr. Browning. Selena did tell Phil how much she liked to ride but since she lived in town she didn't have much chance to get into the saddle. As they talked Phil was almost staring at her. She had smooth, tan skin, and beautiful dark eyes. Phil was sure she must be Hispanic and was just about to pursue her interest in horses when Dr. Browning entered the room.

Bob Browning greeted Phil. "Are there any problems with this little fellow?" and asked him about Cactus. Phil explained that he just wanted a check-up to make sure that everything was okay as they started their life together. Browning smiled and so did Selena. They both liked the idea that Phil cared enough to bring Cactus in for the exam. The exam itself didn't take very long and Dr. Browning gave Cactus a clean bill of health.

Now came the hard part. How was Phil going to pursue Selena Maria Bradley and not seem like a teenager doing it?

As Dr. Browning was about to leave, he shook hands with Phil and told him that Selena would finish up with a few details and a little paper work. Phil was elated. When they were alone, Phil brought up the horses again and Selena told him that she would really like to find a place to ride. Without thinking things through, Phil invited her down to the ranch. To his surprise and joy she said she would love to do that and since she was off this Thursday, how would that be for her to come on down to the ranch? Phil readily agreed to the day and they made their date. Phil gave her directions, set a time and he couldn't wait to get out of the clinic. He was so excited he just needed to get away to take a deep breath.

■■■

Thursday morning arrived bright and warm. Phil had ridden one of the extra horses on Wednesday to make sure that the mare wasn't going to be broncy. He was ready for the arrival of Selena Maria.

Selena drove up in an older green Jeep, and as she parked and got out of her vehicle, Phil felt more excitement than he had since the first time he was introduced to Rebecca. He was again staring at Selena as she walked over to him, this time in tight jeans, a light blue button down shirt, boots, and just a hint of makeup. She looked even better in the bright sunlight than he thought that she did under the fluorescent lights at the clinic. As she approached she greeted him warmly and he welcomed her to the Palo Verde Ranch.

"Hi. I guess you didn't have any trouble finding this little hideaway. I know it's pretty isolated. I'm really glad you wanted to come here for a ride. I'm out here alone so much that it's gong to be fun to see the country with someone else. Do you need to use the restroom or anything?" Selena let Phil know that she was ready and eager to ride.

Phil thought he'd better explain to her that this wasn't some kind of competition. "If you're ready for a big ride we can started right now. Just remember, we can go as long as you want but don't be hesitant to tell me if you are getting tired or sore. I ride every day so I'm not a good judge of when to stop."

"I'll let you know. I really do appreciate you asking me out here. As close as it is to town I'm even surprised that I haven't been down this way in years, not since I was just out of high school. I had a friend who lived down here in the Pyramids but her family has been gone for a long time. It still is so empty in this country—still not too many people. I was surprised when I drove out how little this area has changed over the years. I really wasn't even sure what I was going to find once I got down this way."

She waited a minute and Phil didn't say a word. "I guess you can tell that I don't get down here very often. It's so close to Lordsburg but there really isn't anything that draws me here."

"Well, I hope this won't be your only trip. I think you're going to like riding in the Pyramids. I was surprised when I first came down from Montana to see how rugged this country is. But it's so darn open you can see forever."

Selena smiled. "You know, growing up around here you sort of take things for granted. Sometimes it's nice to see the country all over again through someone else's eyes. And do you realize that I've never actually been in the Pyramids, not even for a hike?"

"Have you ridden very much?"

"When I was younger my uncle had a ranch up at Red Rock, near Silver City, and I used to ride there a lot. Sometime I'd go up for the weekend and my cousin and I would ride every day, down by the Gila River and way up into the hills. It was a good time." Selena looked off into the hills as if she was reliving a fond memory from an earlier and maybe better period of her life. She smiled and Phil just couldn't help giving her the once over again.

"Well, let's head over to the corral and saddle up. We'll have to adjust a saddle for you and then we can be off. Do you have a hat? That sun can get pretty strong up in those hills and today is supposed to be a bright day. But then again, isn't every day a bright day down here?"

"I have a baseball cap in the car. Wait a minute and I'll get it."

When Selena returned, wearing the red baseball cap, she was putting on some sun screen and she looked absolutely enticing. Phil thought that some women look good in hats and others don't. Selena was one of the ones who did. The more he looked at her the more he hoped that this ride would be the beginning of something that would last. He was really taken with Selena Maria Bradley.

After they had saddled up and Phil finished adjusting Selena's stirrups, they headed east into the foothills of the Pyramids. They rode slowly and Phil kept an eye on his partner to make certain that she could ride. She had a good seat and Phil was a bit surprised at how relaxed and very sure of herself she seemed to be in the saddle. Phil relaxed. As they rode, Phil casually asked, "Tell me all about Selena Bradley."

"Well, I'm married, I have two sons, one in college and one in high school. You know that I work at the clinic and I've lived here about all of my life. That's pretty much it."

Phil could almost feel the pain of an arrow going through his heart. Married and with older children. How old was she and why was she here if she was married? He was so confused that he was almost looking for an excuse to turn around and end this ride before it got started. He hoped that the disappointment wouldn't show in his face.

"Wow. I had no idea. You don't look old enough to have two boys as old as your sons are."

Selena was beginning to understand what was happening and she was a little uncomfortable because the last thing she wanted to do was lead Phil on. She knew he was barely older than her oldest boy and all she wanted to do was ride a horse again. She wasn't sure how to handle this.

"Phil, I'm a lot older than I look. I'll be forty in a couple of months and I've been married for nearly twenty-one years. Kind of makes me an old lady to someone your age. I thought you knew I was married."

She didn't say anything else, waiting to see how Phil would respond. She hoped that she was wrong about his intentions, and that they could continue the ride. Until she climbed into the saddle this morning she hadn't realized how much she missed being around horses and getting out to see all this old country again from the back of a horse.

Phil quickly regained his composure and decided that even if this was a one time only ride, he was going to enjoy it and not act like a fool. He changed the subject as fast as he could, talking instead about the landscape, a little of the area's history, and even the local flowers and the wildlife. He wanted the conversation to be about nothing and definitely not personal. Although there were a multitude of questions he wanted to ask Selena, he was afraid to ask and he wasn't certain that he even wanted to know the answers. He was just guessing that she was Hispanic, that she had married an Anglo, and because she had married so young, had little or no education beyond high school. He had no idea how long she had worked for Bob Browning and what she did before that, if anything. And it was killing Phil to know what her husband did and who he was.

"Well," he thought, "maybe that will all come out later and without too much questioning." But he was curious.

In fact, the conversation went in the other direction. Selena questioned Phil all about himself—where he was from, why was he here, did he like it, and was he planning to stay, who owned the ranch, what was the owner like, and was he planning to live here full time or be one of those absentee owners? Was he very rich?

Phil had no trouble answering her questions and it made the ride a lot more comfortable for him. But as he answered, Selena seemed to be fixed on Buck. As she explained it, "It's hard to imagine a college professor down here, owning a ranch and thinking that he can be so at ease that he'd fit in. He must be a terrific guy or just plain crazy. What's his wife like and how many kids does he have?"

After Phil explained that Buck was divorced and never planned to have children, Selena expressed some surprise. "God, how old is he? He must be over the hill or some kind of real loner to want to be here. You know, Phil, we don't get a whole lot of new people moving in down here and the ones that do come here usually don't want to hang out with the locals or even be part of the community. We never know why they come here and when they try to explain it to us it just seems like nonsense. I hope this Buck guy isn't like that."

Being loyal and not wanting any rumors to start before Buck even arrived on the scene full time, Phil tried to explain his boss to Selena. "First of all, I think he's only in his early or mid forties, he's surely not some old guy and he wants to be a big part of the community. This place has been his dream for a long time. Don't let the college professor thing bother you. He's as regular a guy as they get. He's been ranching for a long time and I'd say he's more cowboy than anything else. I'll bet you and your husband will really like him. He's an easy guy to be around and he is smart but not a smart ass. I haven't known him for that long but he's treated me damn well. And you know, I can't think of anything bad to say about him."

Phil waited for Selena to say something. She was quiet, as if she was thinking this all through, so Phil added, "The Palo Verde Ranch should be a real asset down here. Buck wants to do things the right way and he wants to get to know all the folks around. I'm hoping we have a good, old fashioned open house once he gets settled in. He should be here in a month or so."

"Phil, you're very convincing. At least I'll want to give him every benefit of the doubt. It's just that we don't get newcomers very often. We almost don't know how to act. Too bad my husband isn't much into ranching or the cowboys. He works for a trucking outfit and he's usually home every night and likes to watch sports on the weekends. He doesn't do those long haul jobs very often. I guess he likes it although there really isn't any future for him beyond what he does now unless he got transferred or something like that. It seems pretty boring to me. He's fifty-five years old and has been driving for the same company since before we were married."

Phil was a little surprised by Selena's description of her husband and his work. There didn't seem to be any affection or tenderness in her comments. And the age difference came as a surprise. All he could think about was that this guy got a young girl pregnant and they had to get married. He tried to do the math in his head, but it was all too confusing, and Phil wasn't sure that he even wanted to know the answers.

As they rode further east into the mountains, the conversation was casual, Phil still trying to stay away from the personal. Selena, though, was interested in Phil and his background and kept asking questions that suggested she had rarely known anyone from the East. She truly appeared to have trouble trying to understand why he was working on the Palo Verde Ranch with his education and family background. Phil figured that she must not have too much respect for cowboys or maybe just hadn't been around them very much. That surprised Phil a little because he just assumed that everyone in this country was ranch and cowboy oriented. Obviously they weren't.

Phil pointed out one of the trails coming up from Mexico but did it without any accusatory tone or language. He just pointed out a physical feature. He was sure that Selena, as well as everyone else in the area, knew everything that was going on with illegals in this country, certainly more than he did. All they had to do was watch the local television news each night from Albuquerque or El Paso to know that illegal drugs were a large part of the local economy. And you'd have to be almost blind not to notice the Border Patrol's presence in Lordsburg and the roads all over Hidalgo County because it was so very pervasive, particularly of late.

"You know its funny how things change but stay the same. My great grandfather came here from Mexico, and this is where he met my great grandmother, who was also from Mexico. He was a miner and a rancher and they had five kids but only two lived to be adults. My family has been here for over a hundred years and the Lopez name has been a fixture in Hidalgo County for a long time, although virtually none of my family lives in the immediate area now. They weren't too happy when I married an Anglo. This whole thing with all the illegals crossing over here is hard to take and I don't know how I feel about it or what we should do. I'm an American and although my roots go back to Mexico I'm not a Mexican any more than you're a citizen of wherever your family is from. When my family gets together at the holidays we have real fights over this. Sometimes I hear really ugly things said about the Hispanic people around here. You'd be amazed what I hear in the waiting room at the clinic when some of the locals don't know that I can hear them gossiping."

Phil was certainly getting an earful, far more than he had anticipated. He couldn't help but wonder, no matter where the conversation went, why Selena Maria Lopez had married the Anglo truck driver.

After nearly two hours, Phil suggested that they get down and take a short rest. There was a small grove of trees, mostly oak, so they could get out of the sun and Phil had brought a water bottle in his insulated saddle bag. It had been solid ice when they started so he knew that the water would be cold. Selena dismounted at the rest area Phil had picked out although she hadn't complained once about being tired or stiff. She was much more of a hand than Phil thought she would be which only made his frustration with her marital situation and age even more difficult. He just couldn't get over how beautiful she was and she sure as hell didn't look her age.

When they finally returned to their starting point at the corrals, Selena was still full of energy and Phil could tell what a good time she had. It was written all over her face. She helped Phil unsaddle, water, and turn the horses out into the small horse trap. As they walked over to her Jeep, she told Phil that she'd like to do this again and, almost as an aside, added, "Sometimes I wish I had married a cowboy or a rancher. I love it out here in the country. Let me know when that professor gets here. I want to meet him and see if he is the real thing."

Phil assured her that he would let her know and as she was about to get into the green Jeep, she gave him a kiss on the cheek and said very quietly, "I'm really sorry."

As Phil just stood there watching Selena drive away he was a little depressed. He had looked forward to their ride together with such expectations, and although he had a good time, it wasn't the way he had wanted it to be. There certainly was no future with her. He knew he would have to get Selena out of his head but he was at least committed to the idea of finding someone to date. He concluded that he'd better get out more, maybe to Tucson, Las Cruces, El Paso, or the college in Silver City. He didn't want to be some lonely, stove-up old cowboy, living alone, and telling stories about what the country was like 100 years ago. He laughed when he thought about this because he was only twenty-four and the world was hardly passing him by. He was, in fact, just starting out on what he hoped would be the adventure of his life and as far as he could anticipate, the future held out unlimited possibilities.

■■■

A few days later, Phil was reading the local weekly paper and saw an ad for a jazz festival in Silver City. This was just what he needed. He wanted to get off the ranch more often and see what was going on around him. He thought it might be fun to see if he could meet more than just the ranch people from the immediate Animas Valley. He knew his own contacts were very limited. He hadn't lived in the West long enough to have a network of friends. But maybe Silver City would be a good place to start. He was also planning on going to the horse races at Sunland Park, a major track between Las Cruces and El Paso. He hadn't even begun to explore Tucson yet and that was something he was anxious to do. What gave him pleasure in making all these tentative plans was finding out that there were so many options and so many possibilities out there. The ranch would take up a good part of his time but when he wanted to get away, there were things to do and places to go. He was very encouraged.

First he went to the races over at Sunland Park and although he went by himself, they turned out to be a lot of fun. Phil had never seen quarter horse racing before and he found the sprints exciting and so damn unpredictable that he hardly knew how to bet on them. The longer thoroughbred races were far more familiar to him. He had been to Saratoga, Pimlico, and the tracks around Massachusetts, but he had never seen the sprints. He found it far easier to bet on the longer races. By day's end, he had met some interesting people down on the rail and in the betting lines and he thought that he was actually a few dollars ahead. But when he started to factor in the costs for his gas, food, and the racing program, it turned out that he was in the hole. He rationalized all of that by deciding that the overall cost for that much entertainment was cheap. He was smart enough to stay away from the casino at the racetrack. As he found out, the casinos were a dominant feature at every track in New Mexico because that was what was keeping racing alive and the purses healthy after some pretty lean years.

The next weekend was the jazz festival at the college in Silver City. Phil wasn't the world's greatest jazz fan but he did like that music more than he liked rock and roll or country, which he disliked. He was also getting hooked on cowboy music: Ian Tyson, Don Edwards, Chris LeDoux, Cowboy Celtic, Marty Robbins and the rest. Buck had lent him some tapes to play on the drive down from Montana and he found that so many of the songs captured the lifestyle that they were both going to live on the Palo Verde. But he liked some jazz, particularly the vocals of Diana Krall and Marian McPartland, Ella Fitzgerald and Dinah Washington, and all the great jazz singers, some going all the way back to the forties and fifties, even before his parent's generation. He wasn't the most hip devotee but he did enjoy the more traditional forms.

The cowboy from the Palo Verde wanted to make an evening of going to Silver City for the concert, but since he was alone he couldn't get too excited about eating out and doing all the other things that would have been fun to do with a date. So he ate at the ranch and drove up to Silver in time for the start of the concert. He was surprised by the size of the crowd. He wasn't sure until he got there that Silver City had that many people. Another thing that struck him was that it wasn't primarily college aged kids. These were mostly "townies," as they called them at Amherst, even though the concert was being held at a campus auditorium. He waited in the lobby of the auditorium, just looking around and trying to get a fix on things. This was his first big social event since he came to New Mexico and he was interested in seeing what the social scene would be like. He noticed immediately that wearing a big hat made him part of a very small minority. This sure wasn't a cowboy crowd.

As he stood off to one side, just gazing at the crowd filtering in, a very attractive young woman dressed in a skirt and heels came over to him. At first he thought she might be an usher but as she approached he quickly realized that she was coming over to talk to him.

"I don't mean to be too nosey but you look a little lost. Maybe I can help you. I'm a graduate student here so I have a pretty good idea where everything is. My name is Marina Talbot."

Phil was surprised at how direct this young woman was but he was happy to have someone to talk to, someone around his own age. In turn he was as open and as pleasant as he could be.

"Hi. I'm Phil Shaw and I'm not actually lost. It's just that I've never been here and I guess I'm just crowd watching. I've been down on the ranch so long I suppose I'm not used to being in crowds of people any more."

Marina smiled at him as if she understood and maybe had gone through some of the same experience herself. Phil and Marina talked a little and then she asked, "Well, if you're alone and you don't think I'm too pushy, why don't you sit with me and I'll fill you in on where things are and how they work around here. I'd hate to see a cowboy all alone. I'll even show you around a little bit. I've only been here a little more than a year but this place isn't so large that you can't feel comfortable in a very short time. This is a small school and the campus isn't overwhelming. It's pretty and it's easy to navigate. And Silver City is a nice place. As you can see, most of the crowd is from town, lots of retirees, and a few are from the small Mexican villages around the area. It would be hard to get big crowds if they just relied on the college students. This really is a small school."

"Thanks. I think I'd like to have some company. I'm pretty new to this area myself. I just came down from Montana a couple of months ago and I'm still feeling my way around. I do like this country and I must admit that the people are turning out to be pretty interesting. Where did you come from?"

Marina looked at Phil, decked out in his cowboy duds, not a traditional college student any more. There was 6'1" of him plus his cowboy boots, his silver belly Stetson, and his freshly starched white shirt and jeans. He was a good looking guy, by anyone's standards, and Marina thought that since she didn't have a date maybe she could hook up with Phil, at least for the evening. She didn't know very many cowboys and she surely didn't know any as good looking as this newcomer.

"I'm glad you don't think I'm some kind of weirdo approaching you this way. I don't know a lot of people here myself, and I don't really know any cowboys at all. I'm a little like you. I don't get to too many social events either. Not that Silver City has them every night. But I've never even been to Tucson or even Albuquerque. I'm originally from northern California and after I graduated from Berkeley, I came here to get away from the crowds and all the noise and congestion. I thought Silver City and all of New Mexico would be a real change for me and it sure has been. I want to be a teacher and I don't want to teach in the inner city or some other urban area. I want to teach in a more rural setting and this school has a good program for that. And I wanted to see some new country. I'll finish my MA this year and see if I can get a teaching job somewhere around this part of New Mexico. From what I've seen so far, I really do like it here. I want to see a whole lot more, though, before I make any final decisions." Then she quickly changed the subject. "Where do you ranch and have you been there a long time?" She clearly was a little nervous and had obviously not heard him when he told her that he had just come down from Montana. Phil kind of liked that.

But Phil did laugh out loud at that last question. Here he was, living in Hidalgo County for a just a couple of months and being taken for a local cowboy. He was very flattered even if the observations were coming from a real newcomer herself.

"Why are you laughing? Did I say something foolish?"

"No...not at all. It's just that I've been here just a short time and I am flattered that you think I'm a native or at least that I seem like a local. Actually I'd like that."

Without going into too much detail, he filled Marina in on his background, his time in Montana, Buck, and the Palo Verde. He tried to explain where the ranch was but Marina hadn't traveled around enough, certainly not down into Hidalgo County, to have much of an idea of where he was living. Phil was finding it easy to talk to his new friend and after they were able to sort out whom each of them was and where they were from, they were able to relax and just be themselves.

When the concert started, they found seats in the middle section and settled in, hoping to enjoy some good jazz. The program was mostly regional ensembles and although Phil thought it was okay, it wasn't something he would race to see again. Marina, after telling Phil that she wasn't a great jazz fan and that she had only come to the concert to "get out," she also suggested that she might try something else the next time she had the urge to socialize.

It was still early in the evening when the concert ended so the two college graduates headed down town to a little café Marina knew about and had coffee, dessert and continued to get to know one another. When it was time to leave, Phil took Marina back to her car. As they arrived at the campus parking lot Marina asked Phil if he would like to come over to her place that was off campus, for a nightcap. But Phil explained that he had a long way to go and had to feed early in the morning. As he explained all of this, he couldn't help thinking that he sounded just like Buck trying to get out of Missoula for Stevensville. He did get Marina's phone number and promised that he would call the next time he was coming up to Silver City. He had had a surprisingly good time and was sure that he wanted to see her again. He just thought that it was smarter not to rush things on their first meeting even if she seemed to be as eager to follow up this relationship as he was.

■■■

It was a very dark night, there was no moon, and as Phil drove home the countryside had an eerie feeling to it. Phil tried to think about his work at the ranch and he thought that he owed Buck a phone call, but as he drove south he had almost no sense of the surrounding landscape. It was as if it wasn't there. There were so few houses or ranches along the road that there were no lights, just the dense forest and the sporadic open meadows. The headlights from his truck revealed very little. This was indeed, a lonely road at this time of night. It wasn't until he was past the border between Grant County and Hidalgo County and out of the forest that he could finally see the lights of Lordsburg as the road dropped down to the desert floor. It created a sense of the unreal because during the day Lordsburg seemed so small that the intensity of the lights at night, with the dark sky as a backdrop, made it appear two or three times larger than what he would have expected it to be. In its own way it was beautiful and was another one of those sights that he was almost coming to expect in this desert country. Even in the pitch darkness of night, in the loneliness, he couldn't get over the spaciousness and the vistas that he knew were always there, eventually all backed up by mountain ranges that were scattered in all directions.

Phil slept well that night. In the morning Cactus was the first one up and Phil had to let his partner out. It was then and there that he thought what he really needed was one of those "doggie doors" so Cactus could get in and out on his own. Before he got back into bed he took his pad with the list of things to do and added "doggie door" to the growing list. Maybe another trip to Silver City and some shopping was needed to cut into that list. He played with the idea but decided that he'd better stay at the Palo Verde and get some work done. He wanted to do some painting inside the house and ride one of the fence lines that he had been ignoring. He didn't have any reason to think that there was a problem but he hadn't been there yet and it was time to see more of the ranch and more of the country.

After breakfast Phil ambled down to the corral, saddled a horse and along with Cactus it didn't take much time before he was headed to the most northern of the fences. The ride was easy, the sun had warmed everything up, and it was turning into one of those days that most cowboys just dreamed about—warm, sunny with a deep blue sky, a few scattered cumulus clouds, and just a hint of a breeze. Phil always marveled at the land; the ruggedness, how harsh it seemed and yet, as he rode it day after day, he realized how very fragile it actually was. No matter where he rode on the ranch he could see vestiges of an old cattle operation. There were decaying cow pies all over, and he found dried, crumbling dirt tanks that obviously hadn't held any attention or water in years and every now and then came across a strand or two of rusted barbed wire. He even discovered the remains of old, metal liquid feeders that hadn't been used much on this range in quite some time. The former owners must have given them a try some years ago, decided they weren't going to be part of his operation and then just abandoned them.

After a good long ride, he approached the northern fence line and was surprised to find that the fence had been cut. It didn't look like it had been done recently and there were no obvious new tracks, so Phil climbed down off Booger, took his fencing tool out of his saddle bag and went about patching the five strand barb wire fence. It didn't take him long but as he worked Phil wrestled with calling the Border Patrol but decided against it since this seemed like a very old crossing. He was certain that this had happened months if not years ago.

Before he climbed back into the saddle, Phil stood at the fence and just looked around, trying to image who the people were that crossed here and why and where they were going. For some reason Phil wanted to put a human face on all the illegal activity he had seen on the ranch. He wasn't sure why. After a few minutes of this he did resolve to spend more time checking fences, especially at the more remote areas of the ranch.

By the time he returned home and finished a late lunch it was painting time. Darkness had begun to settle in by the time that chore was accomplished and as he washed up and looked his house over he felt pleased that it was beginning to look like it was his home. He had, over the weeks, bought a few more pieces of furniture and even a nice limited edition western print of a Fred Fellows painting that he found at a framing shop in Silver. Yes sir, this was beginning to look like home.

That evening he decided to called Marina. He didn't want to let their relationship her slip away and they arranged to meet for lunch the next day at a little restaurant in Silver. Phil wanted to get some of his shopping done and seeing Marina again would be make the journey to town very enjoyable. She was the first girl his own age that he had met in New Mexico and he enjoyed the idea that he could have a friend and a female one. Besides, Marina was obviously smart, very good looking, and he found her easy to be around. Nothing about her indicated that she was shy or indecisive. Phil liked the fact that she had approached him and did all she could to make sure that they would at least get to know each other. When he was alone at the ranch, Phil thought about Marina quite a bit.

For Phil, life in the Animas Valley was going along just fine.

His lunch with Marina was truly enjoyable, he got his shopping done, and he returned to the ranch happy and realizing for the first time that he actually liked being at the ranch, alone, and with plenty of time to himself. He couldn't explain that and he would have argued with anyone that tried to suggest that he would be this way, but that is what was happening. He did some reading and found himself becoming fascinated with the history of the area. He watched a little TV and rode with Cactus as often as he could. He worked with all four of the mares although he thought of Booger, a seven year old red dun as his primary mount. He began to think that he was so happy because this is what he had always dreamed being a cowboy on a big ranch in real cowboy country would be like. He was overwhelmed that all this was happening the way it was supposed to. He didn't think that dreams like this usually came true in real life but now in Hidalgo County, New Mexico, they were coming true, at least for him.

■■■

Over the weeks Guy Halsey had introduced Phil to the Cotton City Café, a small place just south of the old, deserted village, owned by Eva and Pacho Gomez. They kept the café open only for breakfast and lunch, usually until about three o'clock, and it was a hangout for several of the local ranchers, a few cowboys who had to come to town on ranch business, and some of the guys who worked for the power company or the phone company. There were rarely any women in the café and almost never a tourist. Phil usually met Guy Halsey there once or twice a week, the day they each picked up their mail in Animas, and it had become a good place to meet people, get to be known, and keep up on the local gossip. Eva and Pacho were known for their pies and anyone who stayed for lunch usually indulged. Pie was one of the few items on the menu that wasn't laced with chili. Phil and Guy often spent several hours at the café, sometimes having breakfast and sometimes just drinking coffee and gabbing. Phil loved to hear some of Guy's rodeo stories. For Phil, to spend that kind of time with his neighbor, a veteran cowboy and someone who had lived in the area for so such a long time made it almost an educational session. Phil really looked forward to his coffee and breakfasts days with Guy. In an abstract way, it made him feel more a part of the community.

The two waitresses, both in their mid thirties and fairly attractive, were wives of cowboys. Doris' husband was the cow boss on the Southern Cross and Yvonne's was the horse breaker for the Lazy Double D. With pickups, this was a different era for the cowboys and their families. Their wives could get off the ranches and the children could go off to school in Animas where they had an opportunity to socialize and even play sports. The big ranches didn't have to provide little school houses for the kids or hire a teacher or some tutor. For the wives there was a new found freedom and many of the wives had careers as teachers or nurses, a few ran small businesses or worked for the county, and several even did hair and nails. Some of the wives actually used their computers and worked right out of their ranch homes. This sure wasn't the romantic past or the way most outsiders perceived ranching or the way ranch wives were portrayed in the movies. What it helped do, among other things, was to increase the family bank account and the ranch owners liked it because it made the cowboys more reliable and less likely to just pick up and leave as they did in the old days. Hiring married cowboys, particularly ones with children, was now the way to go.

After dinner that evening Phil called his folks and just tried to make some small talk. He was bound and determined not to get into the specifics of his "career" decisions and he just wanted them to know that he was safe and very happy. Despite their education they had no clear idea where the Bootheel of New Mexico was and what he actually did there. At first they thought he was in Old Mexico and that really seemed to bother them. Phil wasn't sure that they would ever understand even if he sent them a map or tried to explain it all in detail. So he didn't even try. To them he was in some parallel universe. When he hung up the phone he was relieved that nothing catastrophic had occurred between them during their brief conversation. He surly wanted to keep it that way.

The next call was to Buck and Phil brought his boss up to date on the cut fence, the general condition of things on the ranch, including the lack of any kind of moisture throughout the area as the ranchers anticipated the monsoon season, the time he spent at the Cotton City Café and the good pie that they served, Guy Halsey, and he mentioned, in passing, his friendship with Marina. Buck grabbed onto that nugget of information as if Phil hadn't even mentioned the rest. He was glad that Phil had a "girlfriend" and that he wasn't lonely on the ranch all by himself. Buck had worried about Phil's isolation and was glad that he no longer had that to consider. All he had to think about now was getting to the Palo Verde himself. He was getting awful antsy up in Montana.

■■■

It was a slow process but Phil was beginning to know people in the valley. Ann and Clay Lewis had invited him over to dinner and he learned quite a bit spending time with these two natives even though the conversation was often pretty gossipy. He was becoming good friends with Guy Halsey and he had met a few other people at the café and at the feed store. He wanted to take it easy, to let people get to know him and he didn't want to be overly aggressive, a trait not particularly admired in outsiders settling in the Animas Valley. These people were going to be slow to accept a newcomer and Phil understood that. But he was certain that it was just a matter of time before they would. The longer he was in the Animas Valley, the more convinced he was that he wanted to stay and that the two cowboys from the Palo Verde would be an established part of the ranching community in this isolated part of New Mexico.

PART 4

THE LAST DAYS IN MONTANA

B/C

Spring was gradually gaining some control over western Montana and the Bitterroot Valley. The cold winds and snow of winter were giving way to warmer breezes and patches of green grass were beginning to inch their way out of the cold ground. There were more hours of daylight and the days, and even the nights were getting warmer. The snow was melting, at least in the lower areas. The isolation of winter was finally yielding, although not without a fight, to the new season that would let Buck and the other cowboys move around again without the constant daily fight for survival.

But the new season was not without its trials. Winter never gave up easily in the Bitterroots. There was mud all over the place—on the roads, in the pastures, and around the house. The spring mud in Montana was hard to avoid. And despite the physical surroundings Buck couldn't have been happier. He was only a little over two months from finally leaving and he was all packed and ready to go. He had already sold what had to be sold and he had even given the Dodge truck that he used around the ranch to Johnny Meyers as a sort of thank you for all the years of being a good neighbor. And now he had just four horses and the household goods to move. He wanted to take the horses down in one trip, as soon as classes were over in late May, and then make the final move in a U-Haul towing the Subaru. First he would take the horses, trailer and the Ford down to the ranch, leave them there, and then fly back to Montana. He had it all worked out and at least on paper, it seemed like a good plan.

■■■

He was still seeing Rebecca but they didn't much talk nearly as much about the future. They were, as the new hip expression of the day seemed to express, "living in the moment." In fact, they were both in denial and the time was getting away from both of them. Buck knew that a decision about their relationship had to be made and made very soon. He just didn't know what he wanted to do, and he didn't know what the right thing was for either of them. All he hoped for was that they would decide soon and that they wouldn't make a big mistake. He certainly enjoyed his time with Rebecca but was moving south to the new Palo Verde Ranch the best place for her? And was he prepared to spend the rest of his life with her, if it came to that? Was giving up all that she had hoped for the best decision Rebecca could make? Well, time was running out and they would have to know soon enough.

Buck was spending more and more time in his office at the university, primarily to see as many students as he could, especially his advisees, and working his way around the campus saying goodbye to his friends on the faculty. These were tough days because he didn't feel that he was leaving Montana nearly as much as he was going to New Mexico. He had enjoyed his time in the Big Sky and at the university, and under almost any other circumstances he could have seen himself living there and enjoying the life that he had settled into for a long time. But he couldn't resist the call of New Mexico.

With a little more than a month left before he was to leave, he finally had his meeting with his dean. Although everyone on campus, including the president and vice president for academic affairs, seemed to know he was leaving, the dean never bothered to call Buck and have a conversation about it, even after he had officially resigned months earlier and a search had already begun for his replacement. He finally called Buck and the meeting went as Buck had expected it would. Buck was sure that they would never meet again and that suited him fine. He truly disliked the man from Rhode Island and by the time their ten minutes were over Buck was positive that the feelings were mutual. If there is such a thing as burning one's bridges, in this one ten minute meeting Buck had done that with his dean. Buck had no regrets.

■■■

All the details about the funds in his pension account, final check, insurance, checking and savings accounts, and even his fairly significant stock portfolio, were taken care of so another set of the big headaches were relieved. He had transferred his money, insurance, and stock to agents in New Mexico, and tied up a few other loose ends. He sold his cattle, including this year's calf crop and extra horses because the new owners weren't interested in buying them. Obviously the old Palo Verde wasn't going to remain the kind of ranch that Buck had worked so hard to create. But he had done extremely well financially with the sales of his stock and that helped. He had been lucky because the markets for horses and cattle remained very strong. So all he had to do now was finish teaching, get in his truck and leave. Time was flying by. It was just going to be a little over a month before he left but he didn't want to think too hard about it. He thought that too much thinking would make it seem like a hundred years and each day he got more edgy about leaving.

Much to his surprise, he was feeling a little sad about actually moving away from Montana. That sure as hell caught him off guard. It wasn't just that he was leaving friends, or a good career, or any of the things you could actually quantify. It was just that he was making a big change after living in a place for a long time and it was a place that he actually liked. The more he thought about it the more he realized that he had been reasonably happy in Montana and enjoyed his years at the university. He was just hoping that this move south wasn't some big mistake, some romantic fantasy of his. His sudden lack of certainty was another surprise. But he was sure that in the long run this was all part of making a major change in your life. The regular reports from Phil were always so optimistic that they always buoyed him up if he was a little unsure of himself. In fact, maybe he was actually a little scared and it wasn't easy coming to grips with that.

And then there was Rebecca. Thoughts about her were always lurking in the background and creating even more anxiety. This was a situation that just had to be resolved, one way or another, and damn soon. He knew that they could only put this off for so long before it became an extremely serious problem for the both of them. But at least for the time being, he still didn't know how to handle their dilemma or if he ever would. He wondered if she did.

■■■

Buck and Rebecca had planned to have dinner one evening in Missoula and Buck was ambivalent about the whole night. He wanted to stay with her but he wasn't sure that it was the smart thing to do. He wanted to end their relationship, or at least put it on some kind of hold, so that they could both move forward but he didn't want to close a door that might be hard to reopen. Rebecca wasn't the type of women who would sit around pining for a New Mexico cowboy while he tried to get his priorities in order. And she also wasn't the type of woman that a man gave up very easily. No matter how things turned out, Buck knew that he would never entirely forget Rebecca or completely get her out of his system.

When he arrived at her basement apartment in town, she greeted him like a long lost lover. Buck hugged her tightly and kissed her like it might be their last kiss. The tension in the entry hallway was thick and they both sensed that tonight was the night to settle all the issues between them. Buck was heading south permanently within a month and that was that. All the loose ends had been tied up at the university, he had said his goodbyes to everyone he intended to, everything from the ranch, including all the horses and cattle, had been sold or moved south without any problems and all he had to do was load the last of his personal things into the small U-Haul truck, hook on the Subaru, and head south to his new home in New Mexico. When he thought of it in those terms it all seemed so simple, so clear cut. Buck knew better.

Because Buck hadn't said anything to Rebecca about her coming along to New Mexico she went about her business with every expectation of moving back to Seattle. It was difficult for her because she was so confused and she didn't know exactly what she should do. She wasn't even sure of what she wanted to do, except she knew that she didn't want to lose Buck. What she couldn't figure out was how to make this all work. She understood that she couldn't go to the ranch and just live there with nothing to do. She had no idea of what kind of a contribution she could make, if any, and she wasn't going to be just a ranch "wife" with little else to do but cook and take care of the house. That just wasn't Rebecca's style and she still had her own hopes and goals.

"I've missed you," was all that she could say when they moved apart.

"I've missed you too. I just don't know what we're going to do. Come over here. Let's see what we can come up with."

Rebecca didn't say a word as Buck gently took her hand and led her to the couch. They sat, almost facing one another and again there was silence.

Finally, Buck decided that he had better begin. He was a little unsure of himself and of where this conversation should go but he knew that he had to say something. It was clear that Rebecca, who was usually so talkative, wasn't going to start this discussion.

"I'm not going to go into a long spiel about how much I care for you. You know all that. It's just that I have to get the ranch in shape—I can't afford to fail—and if you came with me and had nothing to do it would only be a matter of time before you would resent me, the ranch, and hate yourself. You can't give up everything you've dreamed about for years to go to a place where there isn't anything for you right now. You can't quit on your education or your hopes of becoming a lawyer. And think about it. Do you want to just sit in Animas and hope something comes along? What if it doesn't? And what would it be? Rebecca, I'll miss you more than I can ever express to you but the Palo Verde

Ranch isn't the place for you—at least not now and you know that I can't give it up."

Buck stopped, hoping Rebecca would say something. She just sat there, looking at Buck with a glazed stare. He wasn't sure what to do or what more he could say. Finally, after a few seconds of total silence, he added, "I don't want to lose touch with you. I'm not trying to end any future we might have. I just want to postpone things and let us each spread our wings and if we want to get together we could do it later as equals. Do you understand what I'm trying to say?"

Finally, Rebecca hesitantly began to speak. "I guess I know everything that your saying is right and it's been tearing me up for months. I don't want to lose you either but I do think I would wind up hating you and the ranch if I went there and just sat around. I know that I have to go back to school and get my law degree. But we can still see one another on vacations, the summer or any time we can get together, can't we? You know, Buck, I don't want to end this either."

As she finished they held one another again and there was a feeling of relief that made the moment as intense as any Buck had experienced with Rebecca. What they seemed to be agreeing to, although it was filled with a certain element of sadness, lifted the weight off both of them. At the same time it gave them time to let things simmer down and see what the future would hold for them individually and if there was a place for them with each other. Given their history together, it was probably the best either of them could hope for.

Buck spent the night with Rebecca and they continued to see each other regularly as they both made plans to leave Montana for good.

■■■

Buck was now talking to Phil nearly every day and continued to be pleased to hear what Phil reported and the way he spoke about the ranch and the people in Hidalgo County. All that was lacking was some good talk of rain although there was some optimistic talk about the coming monsoons. Phil was proving to be all that Buck had expected and hoped for and Buck felt good about having him along on this exciting new journey. It was clear that Phil had made a good beginning in his new home and whatever difficulties Buck thought he might have just never seemed to have happened. If anything, Phil seemed to have made it much easier for Buck to enter the scene in New Mexico.

As the time was winding down in Montana, everything that needed to be had been finalized, and the situation with Rebecca had been taken care of as well as it could be. With telephones, E-mail, and airplanes they were going to be able to keep in touch and see one another when the timing was right. That was the plan.

On his next to last night in Montana, Buck spent it in Missoula at Rebecca's and they decided that it was probably best that she not come down to New Mexico until she was settled back in Seattle and he was well established on the ranch. Getting together at Thanksgiving seemed to be a good date to shoot for and that's where they left things. Their passion and intimacy was still at peak levels and when he left in the morning, Rebecca cried and Buck wasn't sure what he felt. He hurried out to the car and drove straight down to the ranch where he would spend his last day and night after all the years in Montana.

Since everything in the house was packed and he had hooked the car on to the U-Haul when he got back to Stevensville he felt a deep sense of loneliness that night. But all Buck had to do in the morning was roll up the sleeping bag he had used since all the remaining furniture that wasn't already packed was gone, make sure he had some dog food for Cowboy, lock the house and get in the U-Haul truck and head out. Breakfast would have to wait—maybe a quick meal in Hamilton or even down at Darby or Sula. The trip would only take a little more than two days pulling the Subaru behind the U-Haul if he drove hard and late. And that was his plan as he headed down the dirt road for the last time. He wasn't sure what his emotions were and all he hoped for was that he was making the right move. He kept trying to reassure himself that he hadn't fantasized about a life that wasn't going to be there. Phil had been so upbeat about the new Palo Verde and that helped but he knew that he was going to miss seeing Rebecca and the Montana ranch and all the privacy he had built for himself in the foothills of the Bitterroot Mountains. Could he really reestablish all of this in the Animas Valley of New Mexico?

As he headed on out to pick up US 93 to Lost Trail Pass, he seemed to have an exceptionally sharp focus on things he had seen every day for years. Every house, every ranch, every meadow, every detail along the highway brought back a flood of memories and he knew that once he left he would probably not be returning, either on a pleasure trip or even for business. Buck was not someone who liked to look back. The future was where things were going to be happening and that was all going to be in New Mexico at the Palo Verde Ranch in the foothills of the Pyramid Mountains.

PART 5

THE PALO VERDE
AT LAST

B/C

When he arrived at the top of Lost Trail Pass, Buck pulled into the turnout and got out of the truck. He looked back down the valley and took a deep breath, letting a flood of memories filter through his head. He just stood there, leaning against the truck, letting his feelings move at random. From the ranch the ride to Lost Trail Pass had been all up hill and but from here on out he hoped that it would be an easy downhill journey, both literally and figuratively. After some minutes and lots of uncertainty, Buck finally decided it was time to get into the U-Haul. He knew it was time to get going and start the drive to his new life in a new part of the country. "Wow," was the only emotion that he could easily identify for himself.

The drive wasn't difficult since it was one he had made many times although this time Buck didn't feel that he was ever completely relaxed. All sorts of things went through his head—about the new ranch, the people he would get to know, how he would get along in his new surroundings, what his relationship would be with Phil, would he continue to think so intensely about Rebecca, and had the two of them made the right choices? He even wondered about Jennifer. He hadn't seen her in some time and he wasn't quite sure whether or not she had actually resigned from the university and moved back to Minneapolis or somehow changed her plans. Since he hadn't heard from her he was fairly certain that she had left and was going ahead with her plans to get married. Buck had been out of the gossip loop at the university for so long that he was surprised at how little he knew about life in Missoula. But the thoughts about Jennifer passed quickly. She, at least, was completely out of his system.

There were a million little things about his new life that he seemed to be apprehensive about. He even wondered if he'd like living in his new house.

After a few hours of this Buck began to think this was all very funny and he tried to loosen up. He put some Ian Tyson and Don Edwards in the CD player in the U-Haul and decided that for the time being he would rather live in the world of their songs than his own thoughts.

On the morning of the third day he began to feel the tension again as he cruised out of Silver City and entered the last leg of the trip to the ranch. For reasons he didn't understand, he decided he didn't need to get a real early start and it was just after nine when he called Phil on the cell phone to let him know where he was and that he was a little over an hour to "home."

To most people Cotton City is barely a blip on the map. Hell, it's not even on the New Mexico state map. But to Buck it was an oasis in the desert. It was getting near 10:30 in the morning when he finally arrived and took the rutted dirt road east to the ranch. As he made the turn off the main paved highway, he seemed to relax and was eager to see Phil and the Palo Verde. Even Cowboy, sitting in the front of the U-Haul cab, perked up and started intently looking around. When they got within sight of the ranch Buck started to honk the horn like he was at some wedding or a Friday night high school football victory celebration.

For whatever this country was, this was, indeed, Buck's country!

Buck spotted Phil as he came out of his house and after he stopped and let Cowboy out, the two cowboys embraced and started to jabber at one another. They were both so excited that it was one of those rare times when the joy of the moment overrides everything else. Finally Phil said, "Welcome home. I've been waiting for you and it's so damn good to see you." Just then there was some barking from around the side of the house and at that moment Cowboy and Cactus began their friendship.

"Phil, come on over to my place and join me in a beer to celebrate all this. I want to hear about everything that's been going on. There are so many questions that I have and the sooner I can get this U-Haul unloaded and returned to Lordsburg the sooner I'll be able to feel like I really belong. It's been a fast trip down this time and it couldn't go fast enough for me." He waited a minute, looking around, and then added, "Things look great and I can just sense that you're really settled in."

Phil smiled. "The house is coming along. Since you were here last time I've added a few things, done some more painting, and even made a little patio out back. By the way, is Rebecca coming down?"

Buck was quiet for a few seconds. "No. Not right now. I'll fill you in on the whole story once I get unpacked and we go into Lordsburg for dinner. Besides, we've got a ranch to run and right now we don't need any distractions. But you don't have to fret. She'll be coming down for visits. You'll get to see her."

Phil was close to blushing. It seemed that Rebecca or any discussion about her could do that to him. He never realized that his attraction to Rebecca was so obvious although anyone within a mile of him would have known how he felt. Phil sensed that it was just about the right time to change the subject.

"Let me put a few things away and we can head over to your place and get you unpacked.

Christ, I'm glad you finally got down here. It'll sure make things easier and a whole lot more fun. You realize that there are some major decisions that you're going to have to make pretty quickly once you get settled in."

Over at the main house, Buck and Phil did a quick job of getting the U-Haul unloaded and they decided it was still early enough to head to Lordsburg to return the truck to the dealer and get something to eat. Buck was truly glad to see Phil and to see how the young cowboy was prospering at the ranch and in such a completely new environment. Buck was actually beginning to relax.

After unhooking the Subaru and returning the U-Haul to a dealer north of the railroad tracks, Buck and Phil got into the car and headed over to a little Mexican café. It didn't take them long to go over the menu and after they had ordered, Buck asked Phil to just begin at the beginning and bring him up to date on everything that had gone on at the Palo Verde since Phil's arrival several months earlier. He even admonished him "to not leave anything out."

Most of what Phil had to report Buck knew from his visits and their telephone conversations, but he wanted to hear it all again in case there were things that he had overlooked.

Buck was particularly interested in the people Phil was getting to know so Phil gave him a run down on Guy Halsey, Marina Talbot, Doc Browning, Selena Maria Bradley and some of the crowd, mostly the cowboys and ranchers, who he had met over at the Cotton City Café, the feed store or around town. Phil added some solid observations about the area, Silver City, and even his relationship with the Border Patrol, which he felt was good. And Phil was even able to give a fast rundown on the area ranches and how they conducted their business. Buck was fascinated that Phil had gotten around and learned so much and that he appeared to have made some solid and useful contacts in such a relatively short time.

"You've done a wonderful job down here getting us settled in. You seem happy and from what you say it looks like we might have a pretty damn good setup here. At least you haven't told me anything that makes me nervous."

Phil showed a wide grin because he was sure that Buck would fit in and even in his short time in his new home he too believed that they might just have a "pretty damn good setup."

After finishing their meal the two cowboys headed back to the ranch and Buck was unusually aware that this was the beginning of a whole new phase of his life. The anticipation was becoming very exciting.

■■■

Within a few days life at the Palo Verde Ranch had settled into a routine that was both leisurely and efficient. Buck and Phil usually had morning coffee together over at Buck's so they could plan out the day's schedule and make some decisions about the future and just visit. A couple of times a week Buck joined Phil on his sojourns to the Cotton City Cafe where he met Guy Halsey and some of the other regulars. This had become very important to Buck because he wanted to meet as many of the ranchers and cowboys as he could and he wanted a place to hang out, a place where he could be relaxed and know most of the people. In a small town, especially a ranching community, there is nothing like the local café.

It wasn't uncommon for Buck and Phil to saddle up and ride together as Phil pointed out little things he had found on his rounds. Together their lives were solidly centered on the ranch. Buck enjoyed throwing himself into the Palo Verde full tilt and Phil, who had been alone for several months, enjoyed Buck's participation and companionship. Even though Phil naturally deferred to Buck without speaking about it, both men were aware that they made a good team and that they felt comfortable with one another. They knew that at least that part of the Palo Verde ranch was going to work out well.

Buck had been at the ranch barely two weeks when he told Phil that they needed to set up a plan for the coming year—from fall to next summer and that they had better include some solid long range planning. They didn't talk much about the monsoon that was due to arrive very soon. Like everyone else in the valley, what talk there was centered mostly on their hopes that there would be a monsoon and that it would be a good one. All the weather forecasters on TV at last had said that this summer's rains were going to be at least average with a good possibility that they would even exceed that. All the ranchers could do was hope that they were right.

"We probably should talk about a breeding program for the horses and decided what we want to do about getting some cattle and what kind. The planning will take us until next spring and then we have to make things operational. Damn it Phil, I just wish I knew if we were going to get some rain for the rest of this summer and then this winter. God almighty we need the summer monsoons. It would make planning a whole lot easier." He waited a minute and then added with a grin, "Isn't this ranching thing fun?!"

Phil smiled. "Boss, let's assume we don't get the normal amount of rain and go from there. Anything else will be a bonus. All the guys I've been talking with said that we are in a drought and we'd better learn to live with it. Most of the locals are cutting their cattle herds and that's something we should keep in mind. From what I've heard around here the cattle prices are dropping a little because there are so many cattle on the market. It's really become a buyer's market. If you are going to buy, now is probably a good time. And that's true unless you factor in the lack of grass and what the price of hay will be. If I've learned nothing else, I've learned how god damn complicated this all is."

Buck sat and listened. He nodded silently as Phil tried to explain the local situation and then Buck added, "This all goes to prove how little control we have over our own lives. We're just kidding ourselves if we think otherwise. But, that all said, I think we ought to pay attention to what the locals say. They've all been in this place a helluva lot longer than we have and they seemed to have made a go of it. They seem willing to help as much as they can but we have to ask, they'll never volunteer anything. You know that's the old cowboy way."

■■■

The first summer on the Palo Verde, despite the early lack of rain, was turning out to be a good one. Phil was seeing Marina on a pretty regularly basis and she had spent several weekends down on the ranch, seemingly enjoying, what was for her a new lifestyle.

A good deal of Buck's spare time was spent glued to his computer trying to work out a manageable plan for the future of the ranch. He found it even more challenging than when he did the same thing at his much smaller ranch in Montana.

Whenever he could, he found time to write. That was something that he didn't want to get away from him. Professor or not, Buck hadn't lose his interest in history and uncovering new information. And Buck actually liked the process of writing.

As the days moved on, to nearly everyone's surprise, by early July the monsoon rains had begun and the weather people on the TV said that it would be a very productive, rainy summer. Buck and Phil couldn't be happier. And each day, as the afternoon storms came rumbling through, the ranch began to take on an almost verdant appearance. The more Buck and Phil rode their range the more grass they found and even at the few places that had looked burned out or even had been slightly over grazed, a new crop of grass rose steadily from the soil. Maybe the drought wasn't completely broken but at least for the time being the desert was blooming. The browns and tans were becoming rich greens. Because Buck hadn't put any cattle on his range there was no fear of over grazing or even making a dent on his pastures. Buck and Phil had crossed fenced some of the range into several 80 or 160 acre pastures so they could move the horses around and that left most of the ranch idle. Buck wanted to make sure that his land was what he anticipated it would be and leaving most of it alone for a year would give him some indication of what he could do in the future. Buck was working on a plan that fully anticipated the yearly summer monsoon and so far everything was working out according to plan. He wasn't kidding himself, though. He knew that he had to have a contingency plan based on little or no rain. This was the Chihuahuan Desert.

All this time he was still either emailing or speaking to Rebecca by phone several times a week. She had settled into her life in Seattle and was back in summer school, trying to get a good head start on her fall classes. The more that they talked it slowly began to dawn on Buck that Rebecca wasn't coming back to the Palo Verde. It wasn't something that she said as much as it was just a feeling Buck had. Maybe the old cliché, "Out of sight, out of mind," was working its magic here, for both of them. It was easier and easier for Buck to find reasons why Rebecca would never fit into the lifestyle of the Bootheel of New Mexico and he was sure that she was beginning to realize the same things. But for the time being at least, as their lives were developing separately, neither Buck nor Rebecca were making plans to see one another any time soon.

■■■

Early one July morning, as the sun was slowing coming up over the mountains and releasing itself from the almost unbelievably bright red morning glow, bringing with it a warm, rich golden warmth to the valley, just as Buck was climbing out of bed, the phone rang unexpectedly.

"Buck, we've got trouble. Two of the horses are missing from that little horse trap just south of my corrals. And there isn't any open gate. I don't..."

"Hold up a sec Phil. Go slow and start over."

"Okay. When I got up to check things I noticed something kind of odd. The door to the tack room was open. So I went in and found some of my stuff was missing and it didn't take me much looking around outside to realize that two horses were also missing. To top it off there wasn't any fence down or gate open. They had to be stolen and you can only guess who did it. And surprisingly, they took several of the newer bridles and other gear but they didn't take any of the saddles."

Buck knew that this was serious business and actually this was going to be his first encounter with the kind of border activity that he had thought about and anticipated for a long time. He was angry, as a matter of fact damn angry, and surprisingly a little bit nervous, all at once.

"I get you. I'll saddle up and we'll go looking for our horses. And we'll find them! I'll be at your place in about fifteen minutes. Get your rifle and get saddled."

By the time Buck arrived at Phil's, the young cowboy had Booger saddled and was mounted. He had already found the tracks leading out of the small horse pasture. After Buck locked up Cowboy and Cactus in Phil's house, since they would probably cause more trouble on the trail than any help they could give, the search for the horses began. A few days ago Phil had shoed one of the missing mares so the tracks were crisp and clear. The two cowboys slowly followed the trail that the thieves had made no effort to hide. It led directly southeast toward the mountains and was probably going to intersect with one of the trails that headed straight south to the Mexican border. These were not illegals heading north to find work. These were probably drug mules heading back south after having delivered a load of marijuana in Lordsburg or points north and found going back home horseback much easier than walking.

Once they had determined the direction that they would take, Buck decided to cut to the south and try to pick up the trail where they might find the thieves. In all likelihood the horse thieves had nearly an hour head start but the thieves were riding bareback and going at a fairly slow pace, probably not anticipating that they were already being followed. Sensing this, Buck thought he could make up quite a bit of time on them by cutting their trail.

The two cowboys traveled hard and in just a little under half an hour Buck's and Phil's intuition told them that they were very close to their two stolen mares. The dirt trail wove through small brush, mesquite and scattered oak and cactus and it appeared to be very fresh. And their own mounts almost seemed to sense their pasture mates were close by. There was no indication that the thieves were in any hurry. The country was rugged and far off the beaten path and they knew that the chance of anyone running into them accidentally was very remote. Even though they did cover this terrain, the Border Patrol's attention to the area was considered less important than on some other parts of the ranch. This was true all over the Bootheel—the terrain was so rugged— good for the bad guys and bad for the good guys.

Phil, who had been over this part of the ranch several times, explained to Buck that there was a wind mill that pumped only about a gallon or two per minute and an old tank not too far ahead. It was a fair guess that the thieves were headed for that spot. In his rides Phil had come across activity at the old well and was pretty certain that they were on the right track. It was a good source for water to fill up their water jugs, there were a few old oak trees for some shade, and most importantly, it was isolated. And Phil could tell from some of the trash that he found there that it had been used before and pretty recently.

As they approached the wind mill the two cowboys dismounted, tied up their horses and took their rifles from the scabbards on their saddles. Buck was surprised at how jittery he was. Phil wasn't feeling any calmer. But slowly and quietly they worked their way through the brush and mesquite and sure enough, just resting as casual as if they were at a Sunday picnic, there were two young boys, just barely into their teens, eating tortillas and small cans of sausage, and quietly jawing away in Spanish. The two stolen horses were tied to a couple of trees about twenty yards away. Right next to the bigger of the two boys was a couple of knapsacks that probably contained all the gear that they had stolen from the tack house. The two didn't seem to have a care in the world as they ate and relaxed in the morning sun.

In a low whisper, as they both squinted in the rising bright and glaring sun, Buck and Phil made their plan for the horse rescue. Buck looked at Phil and cautioned him as the two were getting ready to move, "Be damn careful and for Christ's sake, don't let this get too western." And then Buck warned Phil that these two "kids" could easily have guns hidden somewhere. Because the cowboys both had jingle bobs on their spurs, they removed them so they wouldn't make any noise as they moved through the brush.

"Phil, be careful, will you," Buck warned again as they began to make their way through the brush. Spread out by about ten yards, they slowly walked into the camp, rifles at the ready. As they got in sight they told the two young boys to stay quiet and not move. Phil did the talking because his Spanish was better than Buck's but he was not sure that he was really communicating in the most articulate way. Despite the fact that he felt that his Spanish stunk, he turned to the smaller of the two and asked, "Como se llama, muchacho?" The youngster, in a blue sweat shirt and dirty jeans and dark hair that looked like it hadn't been combed in a week, without any visible expression on his face, answered, "Humberto." Phil turned toward the other. He looked liked he was just trying to grow his first beard and mustache. He just smiled and also answered in one word, "Jesus." He was wearing a Baltimore Orioles baseball cap and appeared just as disheveled as Humberto. They obviously had been on the road for a good deal of time. Their sneakers were just about worn out and their cloths were pretty tattered. But it was the irony of the American baseball cap that almost made Phil smile.

The two youngsters, seeing the rifles pointed at them, must have gotten the picture, because they just raised their hands and made no move to escape or engage the two cowboys. Thankfully, after a quick pat down, it became clear that they weren't armed and they didn't seem the least bit combative. It was obvious to both Buck and Phil that they were resigned to their fate and they weren't going to challenge their predicament.

"Shit, these two are just kids. Phil, I'll cover these guys. Hop on your horse and get to the first spot that you can get cell service and call the Border Patrol. I'll hold these two here. You'll know how to give them directions to this spot."

"Okay. It can take a while but I'll be back as soon as I can. Do you think we need to tie these guys up first?"

"No. I'll handle this. I don't think that they're going anyplace. They really look beat. They just want to rest. You just get to some phone as fast as you can."

Phil returned in less than twenty minutes and was glad to see that nothing had changed and he brought the good news that some agents were already in the area. The two Mexican boys, Humberto and Jesus, were sitting in the same spot as when he left and Buck still had his rifled trained on them although the scene seemed less tense than when they first encountered these two young drug mules. About fifteen minutes later two veteran agents, Oscar Ibanez and Peter Wilson of the Border Patrol showed up in their new green uniforms and both were wearing dark glasses to protect themselves from the blazing sun. Buck turned his prisoners over to the two agents who came in the Border Patrol's version of a paddy wagon. They had driven over an old cow trail to get to the capture site and although this location was extremely isolated, they had known of this water source from the regular patrols they had made in the area over the years.

The older of the two agents, Oscar Ibanez, engaged in an extensive and animated conversation with the two teenagers in very fluent Spanish and when he was finished he told Buck that his story checked out with what the two young men told him. In simple terms, they had dropped off their load of drugs near a spot just north of Lordsburg on the road to Silver City, heading home they had stolen the horses, and they were on their way to the border and back into Mexico, where they were going to be picked up just over the fence line along Mexican Highway #2, near the Mexican truck stop. Their plan was to take the bridles and the gear in their knapsacks with them so they could sell them in Mexico. They also planned to turn the horses lose on the American side. It was a story that the Border Patrol had heard far too often in recent years.

Once again after Agent Wilson had patted down both youngsters it became clear that they had no cash with them, meaning that they had already passed off the money for the drugs to the designated go-between. The cartel bosses didn't seem to care as much about losing the drugs as they did care about losing their money, and the two mules knew that. Had they shown up back in Mexico without either the drugs or the cash, their lives probably wouldn't have been worth a damn.

After a very brief discussion between Buck and Oscar Ibanez and a full understanding that the entire affair took place on Buck's deeded land, not any of the government lease land. This was a legal matter that Buck had studied and fully understood. It had to do with the legal definition of the use of force and lethal force. Had this capture been made on public land the consequences for both the two young boys and the two cowboys from the Palo Verde would have been quite different.

The two Border Patrol agents put plastic handcuffs on the young thieves and when that was completed Agent Wilson took out his digital camera and took pictures of the two stolen horses and the all the gear that was in the boys' pack. They then put the two youngsters in the paddy wagon and took them away. Buck assumed they were headed for the Lordsburg station where they would be photographed, finger printed, interrogated, and unless they had some criminal record, they would be jailed over night and then, because of their age and because they probably had no previous record, they would be shipped directly back to Mexico. But despite all the procedures and the obvious crime, Buck wasn't sure what would happen to the two youngsters. In his own way he felt sorry for the two boys because he realized that the poverty they must have faced in Mexico made this kind of life a real alternative to what they would have otherwise faced in their village.

What he did know was that these two would be back, sooner or later, again carrying a load of drugs. The fact that these two kids were guilty didn't seem to have much impact on the overall outcome except that they would probably be banned from reentering the United States for five years—a penalty that meant nothing to them because they could make so much money on each trip they made carrying drugs across the border. They would try again. That was a certainty. For these young kids coming from such severe poverty in Mexico, the risk was worth every tough and dangerous mile that they had to travel. They almost had no choice but to try again.

■■■

As he realized what the reality of life on the border was, Buck just shook his head.

When all the details were wrapped up and the two Border Patrol agents headed back to town with their prisoners, the cowboys from the Palo Verde Ranch took their stolen gear which the thieves would have sold for good money in Mexico, probably at a flea market, and ponied their two stolen horses back home.

The Palo Verde cowboys rode in silence. As they moved easily on the trail toward the ranch, Buck for the first time realized that in all the chaos over Phil's early morning phone call, he hadn't even remembered to take his pistol. This whole ordeal had been more upsetting than he wanted to admit.

Suddenly, breaking the silence, Phil, from either frustration or anger, just blurted out, "How they hell are we going to stop this crap? We can't be on the alert twenty four hours a day and these guys just seem to keep coming. It's not only through our place but it's on every ranch here in the valley. You should hear the guys talk about it at the café. Doesn't anyone give a damn? Why doesn't someone do something? They say it's even much worse over on the Arizona border."

At first Buck didn't say a word and then after some thought, he slowly answered his friend.

"Phil, the only way to really stop this is to either dry up the demand for drugs or legalize them. I think the best answer is to legalize the stuff since I doubt if we can stop the demand. But can you really picture some politician in Washington actually proposing that? I guess that we'll just have to keep our eyes and ears open here at the ranch and see what happens. I know that's not the kind of answer you wanted but it's the best I can offer, at least for now. Maybe it's the down side of living in this border country. But you know, those two kids might be lucky. If they had been caught before they delivered their load and the drugs had been seized, they faced the real possibility of being killed when they returned to Mexico. Those drug cartels don't fuck around and they'd want other mules to know that they'd better not make a deal on the side. They would just assume that the two mules sold the drugs for their own gain and stashed the money somewhere. I hope for their sake that they passed on the money to their middle man because their life won't be worth a nickel if the bosses think that they squirreled the money away for themselves. And there won't be much those kids could say to defend themselves. Those kids are messing around with some pretty bad people. A human life doesn't mean a damn thing to them. The cartels don't seem to have much of a conscience."

Phil didn't say a word. He never did drugs and couldn't understand why anyone would want to screw up their body with the all the chemicals. But he knew that Buck was right and that no politician, either in New Mexico, Arizona, or any of the other border states, was going to do a damn thing except rant and rave and posture in public about all the illegal drugs coming across the border and how we had to secure the border, even if their ideas didn't make a bit of sense. What he couldn't get out of his mind was how very young the two smugglers were.

When they finally got back to headquarters they made sure that everything else on the ranch was back to normal. After the dogs were let out, Buck and Phil plopped themselves in a couple of soft leather chairs at Buck's and for the first time since the early morning phone call they both began to relax. They tried to talk about what had happened but there wasn't too much to say except they both kept coming back to the youth of the two drug mules. Neither was hesitant in admitting to their shaky nerves and the anxiety they each felt as they pursued their horses. Buck did ask Phil about Cactus.

"Didn't he bark or give you some warning? He's a helluva watch dog!"

Phil was very serious. "You know Buck, he did start barking and making a real racket. That's what woke me up. I just assumed it was the coyotes, or javelinas, or even some deer. He did his job but I just didn't listen to him."

"That's something to remember for the future. Always trust your dog," Buck said with a smile.

The experience, as most border residents learned, was not filled with all the bravado their imaginations had dreamed up. There were no shootouts or high speed horse chases with the riders breaking through brush and always at a flat out gallop. This was serious and very dangerous business and not in any way related to the kind of chases most Americans had seen in the cowboy movies. In this incident, no shots had been fired, nobody was hurt, and the Palo Verde Ranch got its gear back. Fortunately the two young drug traffickers weren't armed. And that was the best conclusion that there could have been.

■■■

Since it was still early in the day and Buck thought that they had already put in a full day's work, he suggested that they head into Lordsburg to get something to eat and unwind. Actually, he just wanted a chance to get away from the ranch for a short time, away from an environment that at least for the moment, was unsettling. This episode with the horse and the two young drug mules had been far more unnerving that he had ever imagined it would be. He just hoped, against all hope, that it wouldn't be a regular occurrence.

After the short drive to Lordsburg, they parked on a nearly deserted street. They were leisurely heading to a café located between several empty store fronts just across from the railroad tracks when Phil poked Buck and pointed to a young woman walking, on the other side of the street, toward them.

"That's that Selena I told you about that works for the vet. You remember her, that really good looking gal who unfortunately is married and has two kids. The one I told you about who came down to the ranch to ride."

"Jesus Phil, don't get so excited. If she's married with kids why the hell do we care?"

As this conversation was taking place, Selena Maria Bradley crossed the street and came within greeting distance. She was the first one to speak.

"Hi, Phil. It's been a long time. How have you been? I'm surprised to see you in town."

"It's good to see you again Selena. And I'd like to introduce you to my boss, Buck Cooper. He's the one that I told you about. He's finally arrived and he's living here full time now."

Buck tipped his hat and warmly smiled at the young woman that had Phil so tangled up for a while. He didn't say anything but it didn't take very long for Selena to speak:

"You know, Buck, this cowboy of yours speaks very highly of you. He says you're the real deal and that you are going to be a valuable part of this community. I hope he's right. We sure could use some new blood around here." She smiled back at Buck as she spoke.

What Selena didn't say was that she was very impressed in a way that she didn't think she would be. Most of the locals were suspicious of newcomers, particularly one's that seemed to have too much money or even too much education and Selena was no different. But it was something in Buck's manner that seemed to break down whatever barrier she had anticipated. Hidalgo County wasn't an easy place for newcomers to be accepted but Buck and Phil seemed to be making some progress.

"I'm going to do the best I can. I guess Phil told you that this is where I've wanted to live and ranch for a long time. And so far I haven't been the least bit disappointed."

"Well, it was good to finally meet you. I have to run because I have to be back at the clinic. I hope I'll see you again. Maybe you'll invite me down to go riding on that beautiful ranch of yours."

After Selena hurried down the nearly deserted street, the two cowboys went into a little café on the corner. When they were seated—the place was empty except for the two of them—Phil had a sheepish grin and spoke first.

"What do you think? She's pretty good looking isn't she?"

"She's damn good looking, and let's leave it at that. She's also married with two kids. The last thing we want to do right now is get involved with a married, local woman. That would sure start us off in the right direction. And I thought that things were really good between you and Marina. They are aren't they? So stop thinking about your local beauty."

"Gee, Buck, are you getting so old that you can't even appreciate a really good looking woman? I'm surprised."

Buck looked at Phil with a real glare that even he wasn't sure where it came from or why, but said almost defensively, "I said she was good looking."

Before Phil could say another word Buck asked, "Now, what do you wanna eat? I'm buying."

After lunch the two loaded in Buck's truck and they headed back to the ranch. There was no more talk about Selena Maria Bradley.

The ride back was slow and neither Buck nor Phil did much talking. It was one of those almost awkward times when, even between friends, there just wasn't much to be said but their friendship was strong enough so that they didn't have to talk.

■■■

Life on the ranch for the next several weeks fell into a regular routine that turned into a very good time. The rains kept coming nearly every afternoon and the entire range greened up, in many ways far beyond anything that either Buck or Phil anticipated. Even the locals talked about what a good rainy season this was turning into. The two Palo Verde cowboys rode the ranch daily, trying to find the best places for long term grazing, water, and to make improvements where they were seemed to be needed, especially along the fence lines and the dirt tanks. Everything they did was looking ahead to the time when there would be cattle on their range. And as they continued to explore and familiarize themselves with the Palo Verde, the talk was increasingly about getting some cattle. As the grass grew taller each day, Buck was suggesting on a regular basis, "...that since we have the grass, there's no good reason to let it go to waste." Every time Buck uttered those words Phil just smiled.

And then as luck would have it, Buck was at the feed store just passing time with Tater Morrison, a rancher that he knew only casually from over near Hachita, a village east of Animas. Morrison was trying to selling some good Brangus cows, all bred to Brangus bulls for the coming late winter calving season. He and his wife Adeline were retiring, after living at their ranch for more than fifty years and they were eagerly moving over to Las Cruces to be nearer their son, his wife and grandchildren. They had leased their place out to a large neighboring outfit that had their own cattle and their own breeding program so they didn't need or even want what was left of the Morrison cows.

After a particularly lengthy conversation, Buck was just about to purchase a small herd of fifty young bred heifers, sight unseen but based almost solely on the reputation and the word of Tater Morrison. But reason prevailed and the two ranchers decided to drive over to Morrison's spread just north of Hachita to look over the herd. Tater had sold most of his large herd of Herefords but had, for reasons that Buck never did understand, decided to keep back this small herd of Brangus. Once Buck looked them over, he concluded that they were just what Tater Morrison said they were and that was good. The two ranchers shook hands and verbally made all the arrangements that were necessary for the purchase. Buck was a little stunned that all this had happened so fast and that he had spent so much money without giving it his usual lengthy and careful consideration.

"Doc Browning was out and preg tested the whole herd and he says that they're all settled. You can get a copy of the report from him. It should be a good calving season for you."

Morrison was to have the brand inspector do the paperwork and then have them delivered to the Palo Verde in two weeks. Despite the unexpected financial considerations, Buck was just plain excited at the turn of events. Within a few weeks he went from chasing drug mules off his place to getting back into the cattle business, at least a year ahead of his own schedule. There was no indecision about what he had just done. Somewhere down deep it just felt right.

He couldn't wait to get the good news to Phil. He also realized that he'd better head for the bank in Lordsburg, get a short term loan, and have them prepare a certified check to pay for the cattle. This was a much bigger expense than he had planned on for this early in the creation of the Palo Verde but Buck was ultimately convinced that it was a sound financial investment, if there is any such thing in the ranching business. He knew it would strap him financially for a short time but he was willing to take that risk. He knew he would recover enough of the money and pay off the loan to make this a very realistic ranching investment when he shipped the calves next fall and with some luck there would be a profit. This would be just the beginning. He kept reminding himself of all the money he had made when he sold his herd in Montana at almost record high prices. That money, which he had wisely put into very liquid assets, would easily cover this loan if it ever came to that. Cattle money for some new cattle seemed to be a good idea and the cattle he was buying he hoped would prove to be a solid investment. He kept rationalizing to himself that after all, he was a rancher. And no matter how many ways he examined this deal, it seemed to make a whole lot of sense.

The next step was to get to a blacksmith so that he could have some branding irons made. These cattle would all have to have his brand, the B/C, put on their right hip and a V notch on the left ear. Morrison's cattle were all notched on the right ear and fortunately, branded on the left ribs. Buck had applied for the brand while he was still in Montana, almost two months before he had permanently settled in New Mexico and the approval from the state brand inspector had arrived about a week ago. Buck was a little disappointed that his original brand request, the Rafter B/C, his Montana brand, had been denied because someone in New Mexico was already using it. It would have saved him the time and trouble of getting new irons made and it would have allowed for a little continuity. He hadn't said anything to Phil about the brand because he hadn't any expectations that he would be using it so soon. But he couldn't wait to get back to the ranch to tell him now.

Phil was dumfounded when he heard the cattle news. In his wildest imagination he hadn't thought that they would have cattle so quickly and he was a little anxious about what might happen. Without much warning he would be partially responsible for a herd that Buck owned, that grazed on their land and that he would be with full time, including the calving season. It was the first time that he had ever had that kind of responsibility as a cowboy. "Sometimes you'd better be careful what you wish for," was a thought keeping running through his head. But he sure did look forward to the new arrangements and the new planning that would now have to take place on the Palo Verde. How they used the land would now become crucial to their success and Phil had an inkling that Buck was going into some sort of short term debt to get these good Brangus cattle. All of this only made his responsibility seem even greater, because he sure didn't want this venture to fail, for whatever reason. Each day he found himself more and more certain that his life as a cowboy was the life for him.

Buck told Phil to make sure that all the branding chutes at headquarters were in working condition and that the loading ramp was secure. He wanted Phil to grease all the moving parts on the chutes with heavy grease and to double check to make sure that the pipe fencing around the corrals was in good shape. Neither the chutes nor the loading ramp had been used since Buck bought the ranch and he didn't want to find out at the last minute that there were weak spots or that they needed some serious repairs. This branding was to be done the modern way, and in Buck's thinking a more efficient way, running the cows through the squeeze chutes. These pregnant cows were far too big to be roped and dragged to the fire, the way most of the younger cowboys liked to work. For these traditional cowboys, it was their way of trying to keep in touch with the traditions from the past, of the way it had been done for as long as cowboys had been working cattle on the western ranges. But of far more importance to Buck, he didn't want this first branding on his New Mexico ranch to be a sloppy operation.

Several weeks ago, while prowling through the barn, Buck had found the metal fire box that most ranches now used for the brandings. All you had to do was attach a small propane tank, light it and you had enough fire to heat several irons for hours. This was also efficient, it was safe, and you didn't have to worry about having someone to keep the fire going. A wood fire was used on the open range when you didn't have any other option or in the old days when there was no propane, but an open fire just it didn't make much sense when you were working in the corrals.

Buck decided to head to Lordsburg right away. He wanted to stop at the vet clinic to see if they knew anyone who could make the branding irons and check with Dr. Browning about having the reality of having Brangus cattle on his place. And since Dr. Browning had preg tested this herd it just made sense to touch base. It wasn't that Buck was aware of or anticipated any problems. Brangus were a very popular breed in the area and all over the Southwest, but he thought that in a new place under new circumstances it wouldn't do any harm to double check. When Buck looked it all up, he found that Brangus cattle are a cross between Brahman and Angus cattle and were developed in the United States early in the 20th century. The American Brangus Breeders Association was formed in 1949 and the breed had prospered enough so that it is now found all over the world.

Before Buck left for town Phil called him to let him know that Marina was coming down for a couple of days. Buck was glad that their relationship seemed to be flourishing and he was also glad that he liked her, just in case she decided to move in with Phil and become a resident at the Palo Verde. It seemed odd to Buck that he was looking out for Phil the way a father would look out for his own son since Phil didn't need that and Buck didn't want that to happen but that's exactly what was taking place. Or as Buck rationalized, "There can't be any harm since all this seems to be so positive." Things continued to be going very well at the Palo Verde.

Marina had been coming down to the ranch whenever she could get away from the college, where she was finishing her degree. At first she started with Friday to Sunday weekends that had gradually increased to Thursday to Monday weekends. Phil was teaching Marina to ride and even do a little roping, and every so often, when they wanted to get away from the ranch, they spent a quiet and private weekend together up at the Gila Hot Springs, north of Silver City. Buck was sure that it was only a matter of time before Marina would be moving down to the ranch full time. She would have her Masters degree by the end of summer session and then she'd have to find a job. He had no problem with her being at the ranch because the happier Phil was the better cowboy he would become for the Palo Verde and Marina seemed to make him very happy. Their relationship was solid and Buck had come to truly like and admire the young cowboy from the East and this newly emerging cowgirl.

■■■

On the way to town Buck couldn't think of anything but the cattle and how far ahead of his schedule for the ranch that he was. It excited him and even scared him a little because of the financial squeeze it was temporarily putting him in, but he wasn't new to the cattle business and he felt even more confident now because he had come to trust Phil so much. Phil was turning into a real hand.

When he arrived in town he headed directly to the clinic. As he entered into the empty waiting room, the first person he saw was Selena Maria, who greeted him very warmly.

"Buck, how are you? Gosh, I didn't expect to see you again so soon. What's it been? A couple of weeks I guess."

"Well, I don't really get into town very often. I've got too much to do trying to organize things at the ranch and keeping that young cowboy of mine on the straight and narrow."

While all this was taking place Buck couldn't take his eyes off Selena, not because he was being polite but because he just couldn't take his eyes off her.

"What brings you to the clinic? I hope you don't have any vet problems out at the ranch."

"No, no, nothing as serious as that. I just need some information."

After Buck explained that he needed the name of a blacksmith, Selena went to the office directory and got him the name and phone number of the only blacksmith in town and as Buck was about to leave, she looked straight at him and asked, "When are you going to invite me down to the ranch to go riding again?"

Buck was surprised by the request but more surprised by how good it made him feel that she had asked. He hadn't consciously thought about asking her down but he was very pleased that she had done the asking. The fact that she was married didn't seem to enter the picture.

"I hope you're serious about this. If you're not kidding, I'll call your bluff. What's a good day for you to come down?"

"I'm off this Thursday. How would that be? I'll bet it's absolutely beautiful down at the ranch since we've had so much rain this summer. The last time I was there things were still burned out. Green in this country is a true gift. It doesn't last very long but it is beautiful while it lasts."

"Be at the ranch by eight on Thursday morning and we'll give it a shot. I'm looking forward to getting to know you. I'll bet you can teach me a lot about the people and the area down here." He waited a minute to see if she was going to back out. When she didn't he added, very quickly, "Well, I'd better get over to the blacksmith and order those irons. I'll see you Thursday."

"Okay. See you Thursday at eight."

■■■

As Buck left the clinic, Selena followed him with her eyes and a big smile on her face. She wasn't completely sure why.

The blacksmith was on the northeast side of town and as Buck drove over to his shop, he was somewhat taken by how much he was looking forward to seeing Selena and taking her riding and it wasn't because he wanted to learn about the locals. There was something about her that he never found in Jennifer or Rebecca or even his ex wife and he couldn't put his finger on it. He was just hoping that whatever the attraction was it wasn't caused by the fact that Selena was married and that she was unavailable. But that "married" thing kept creeping into anything Buck wanted to think about when he thought that he wanted to see her again. In fact, what he actually kept thinking was, "Not again, Jesus Christ, please not again." The last thing in the world that Buck wanted at this stage of settling into his new ranch was the distraction of another relationship, particularly with a married woman, that would have to end badly. In the last year or so Buck had been through relationships twice and he didn't want to go through it again. Selena seemed to be so different but...

The blacksmith was an older Hispanic man, Tony Gutierrez, and after Buck had some easy conversation with him, Buck drew his brand on a sheet of paper and handed it to him. As he was leaving he gave the old gentleman a small down payment and he also left feeling a great confidence in this newly discovered craftsman.

But this thing with Selena Maria was a turn of events he hadn't anticipated and it was still three days til Thursday. He just wasn't able to get her out of his mind and it was driving him nuts wondering why she had invited herself down to the ranch again since she barely knew Buck. To add to that confusion, he had completely forgotten that he also wanted to speak to Dr. Browning at the clinic about the cattle. But that could wait. Before he left town he picked up a small tank of propane to use for the branding fire. That couldn't wait.

■■■

Buck was sitting on his screened in porch with a glass of iced tea, watching the bright orange and red sunset ease its way down behind the Chiricahua Mountains when Phil called and told Buck that he had some news and that he'd like to come over. Buck told him to head on by. He didn't ask on the phone what this was about because he was sure he'd know in a very short time.

A few minutes later, Phil knocked on the porch door and then walked in, with Cactus trailing behind him. He had a big smile on his face. Buck immediately realized that this was going to be good news. Once Cowboy and Cactus had headed back outside, Phil got right to the point.

"You'll never guess what happened today."

Without waiting for Buck to answer, Phil went on.

"Marina got a job teaching the seventh and eighth grade English classes in Animas, the job she wanted, and she'll be moving in with me in about two weeks. That'll barely give her time to get settled in before school starts, which is really early down here. I know I should have checked with you first but it's something that we both definitely want to do and I guess I just didn't think you'd mind. I sure hope you don't. She loves it down here and I'm pretty sure I love her."

"Hell no, I have no objections. I thought this was eventually going to happen. It was just a matter of time. Just make sure you know what you're doing. Don't do this lightly. But I sure don't want to preach to you. I'll help you any way that I can. You know I think the world of Marina and I've enjoyed the time she's been down here at the ranch. And besides, with your help, she's beginning to make herself into a real cowgirl. Christ, before you know it we'll have another hand here on the ranch and you'll be an old married man."

You could almost hear Phil sigh out loud. He was just starting to appreciate what all this meant for himself and it was good to get that kind of support from Buck. The relationship between Buck and Phil was working out the way they had both hoped it would from the first time they had met at the One-Eyed Cowboy in Missoula months ago, when Buck asked Phil to come and cowboy for him at the Palo Verde Ranch in far off New Mexico.

"I guess this news calls for a beer. And you'd better get that house of yours spick and span. You don't want Marina moving into a pig sty. We should go up to Silver and buy a few pieces of new furniture. We're going to have a lady living at the Palo Verde and you'd better treat her right." Buck paused for a minute and then added every earnestly, "Phil, I really am happy for you."

The two Palo Verde Ranch cowboys talked well into the night and when Phil finally went back to his place the relationship between the two couldn't have been stronger. Buck realized what a good situation this was going to be for Phil and he seemed truly happy. There were really no down sides for Buck, for

Phil, and he was certain not for Marina. Teaching in Animas was teaching in the neighborhood school.

■■■

Buck couldn't stop thinking about his coming "date" with Selena on Thursday. He was surprised by the intensity of his anticipation and it wasn't about sex or lust or any of the other feelings that might have been so natural with such a truly beautiful woman. This was something different and it both excited and worried Buck.

"Jesus," he kept thinking, "she's married and with kids. What the hell am I doing letting her come down here this way? And why am I letting myself get so damned worked up about it?"

He also realized that he had to be careful because despite Phil's relationship with Marina, Buck didn't know how the young cowboy would react to seeing Selena down at the ranch again. But Buck put that out of his head quickly, feeling very comfortable that Phil and Marina now were truly a committed couple and that Phil was well over the earlier little 'disappointment" he had with Selena.

On Thursday Selena arrived at about five minutes to eight and when she got out of her green Jeep she looked just as beautiful as Buck had remembered her from town. She smiled as Buck approached her. She was again dressed in her western clothes and she wore them as naturally as if she was raised and still lived on a ranch. It was something you just couldn't fake. She had a natural style about her...the real thing.

"I wasn't certain that you actually thought I was coming down since I invited myself. But I wanted to come and here I am."

"And welcome you are. I would have been very disappointed if you hadn't showed up. Phil says you ride pretty well and I've got the same horse you rode last time saddled and waiting for you at the barn. Are you ready to ride or do you want to go up to the house and have some coffee first?"

"Thanks for being so welcoming but I'm ready to ride right now. The coffee will have to wait."

The two headed over to the barn where Buck had both horses saddled. Selena commented on how beautiful things looked on the ranch, so much greener than the last time she was down in this part of the valley. Buck told her they were so glad that the rains had come with so much abundance. She grinned because she had been in the Animas Valley long enough to remember when the summer rains, in more years than she could count, never did arrive.

After a quick adjustment of Selena's stirrups, they hopped aboard and headed east toward the mountains. There wasn't much conversation at first. It was as each of them was trying to figure out the other. Selena had never met anyone like Buck. In fact, she had hardly ever met anyone from the East and it was awkward for Buck because he hadn't the slightest idea of who Selena was or what was going on in Selena's head. Maybe she was just here to ride or maybe not. But if not, what was it? For Buck, Selena was as much a mystery as he was to her and he wasn't too optimistic that he would solve the riddle on their ride that day.

They longer they rode the more animated the conversation became although it was still pretty innocuous. Whether it was conscious or not, they each seemed to be trying to stay away from anything that was too personal.

After about nearly two hours of riding on some old, rarely used cow trails, they approached one of the glens on the ranch that was shaded with old oak trees and a smattering of mesquite. The sky was bright with nary a cloud anywhere, just the color blue that dominated warm summer days in the southwest. The resting place was isolated and it was quiet. Buck reined up and the two dismounted. They tied the horses to a couple of trees with their lead ropes, loosened the cinches, and Buck took a blanket that was rolled up and tied behind his saddle and spread it on the ground. When they were both settled on the old Pendleton blanket, Buck took a water bottle from his saddle bags and they each took a drink. Buck, in some ways struggling to make conversation, asked Selena about herself. Without any hesitation she gave just about the same information that she had given to Phil...about her family, her two sons and her marriage. Buck's only observation to himself was that her comments seemed so dispassionate except when she talked about her boys. She barely talked about her husband.

"My oldest son, Jimmy, just began his second year of college. He has a football scholarship at Eastern New Mexico over in Portales. And he's not just a good football player. He's smart, too. He wants to be a writer or a teacher. His brother Cole will be a high school senior this year. Last year he took over as quarterback, filling Jimmy's shoes. He's thinking of following his brother to Portales if he can get a scholarship there which he thinks he can. They are both really bright kids and have all the ambition that their father seems to lack. Cole wants to major in business or finance. I'd sure like to see both of them get out of here and see more of the country before they really settle down. And I don't even know whether they want to settle here or go someplace else." She paused a minute and then added, "They both seem to have a sense of adventure. I guess only time will tell."

Buck didn't want to say anything. He wanted to let her talk so he could get some line on what was going on. It was crystal clear that she had almost no feeling for her husband but Buck didn't know what to make of that or if he was reading something more into her talk than really was there.

"My husband may be offered a transfer by his company, up to Albuquerque. I hope he takes it but I doubt that I'll go with him. I just think that would be best for both of us now that the boys are ready to leave. I'd never pull Cole out of his senior year in high school here. And when he heads off to college, then I'll be alone. You know, I've never been by myself since I was nineteen and there are so many things that I want to see and do."

Buck was stunned. He had no idea of what to say and maybe more to the point, he had no idea why Selena was telling all of this to someone she barely knew, someone she had just met.

Whatever her goals were, or whatever the reason for all this, it completely escaped Buck. A small part of him almost wanted to applaud because there was that tiny opening that maybe Selena Maria was going to be available.

"Have you ever been married Buck?"

Buck gave a quick recap of his marriage and divorce, leaving out most of the details. He wasn't even sure why he said as much as he did.

"I got married when I was far too young." As Selena talked she showed a certain kind of sadness in her dark eyes that upset Buck. "I was a teenager still living at home. I had been out of high school for a year or so and had a pretty good job working in a lady's clothing store. A friend introduced me to this guy who was older and very good looking and I guess at some level I probably just wanted to get out of the house. We dated for a while and I was sure he had some kind of future that we could both share. It just didn't turn out that way. I should have married a cowboy or a rancher. I just love it down here and the kind of life that you and Phil live. I always remembered the good times my cousin and I had when we were kids and we'd go up to my uncle's place near Red Rock. We'd ride and explore all over the country. What I did by marrying so young and having kids right away cost me any chance of getting an education or pursuing a career. It made me so damn dependent that I suppose I've resented it for a long time now. But I guess I'm stuck where I am unless somehow I can find a way out."

Selena stopped for a moment and just looked off into space. Buck wasn't sure when she would continue but she did.

" You know Buck, I've never met anyone like you or Phil and talking to both of you and learning where you've been and what you've done has just got me thinking about so many things again. I'm still young and there is so much that I want to see and do and I want to be around someone who's a doer and would share these things with me. There aren't many like you two in this area, at least not that I come into contact with, especially not in Lordsburg."

Buck remained silent, still not knowing what to say. Finally he decided to ask some questions.

"Selena, where would you go and what would you like to see?"

"You probably won't believe this but I've never been east of Texas and I've only been to California once. Do you know that except for a couple of border towns like Juarez and Palomas, when they were still safe, I've never even been down to into Mexico. I'd like to go to a few first rate museums—I really like art—and see some of the places that I read about. That's why I want my boys to get out of here and do some traveling after college. I don't want them to feel trapped the way I do. They're the first ones in my family to go to college. Me, I'd like to see the ocean again and I'd like to see Montana and Wyoming, and the east coast. That probably sounds foolish to you because those are all places where you've lived but they could be a million miles away or even on the moon for someone like me. I don't want to spend the rest of my life in Hidalgo County and never see what's out in the rest of the world."

Suddenly, out of nowhere, came a clap of thunder and lightning as the clouds, just as suddenly, appeared. Both Buck and Selena knew that those were the signs that meant the early afternoon storms were gathering and Buck could see the clouds building up to the south. They looked ominous. Abruptly he said: "We'd better saddle up and get out of here. We've got a long way to ride back to the house and I don't want anything to happen to you. I really don't like being in the saddle when there's lightning like this crackling all around. I've heard so many stories about ranchers that have had horses and cattle killed by lightning and I don't want that to happen to us."

They both jumped up, Buck grabbed the blanket and quickly rolled it, and they headed over to where the horses were tied. They tightened the cinches and headed back for home at a fast paced trot. Buck kept looking over toward Selena. She seemed very comfortable in the saddle and he couldn't get over how much he liked being with her and how beautiful she was.

Whatever it was about her that made her so special was something that he just couldn't put his finger on. He had already thought that maybe the sudden dark sky and ominous weather was a warning sign of what the future might hold. As they rode through the thundering sky, he tried not to even think about all of that.

Once they arrived at headquarters and tied the horses up in the barn, the sky finally broke open and it poured in a way that only someone from New Mexico or Arizona, who has lived through the summer monsoon storms, can fully understand. The rain didn't last long—this was a teaser for what was probably going to come later that afternoon—but it cooled things off and as Buck always figured on the ranch, "Every drop of rain is just money in the bank."

When the rain slowed down enough for them to head for Selena's Jeep, she walked slowly, obviously not in a hurry. It was as if she didn't want to leave. Buck's impulse was to invite her over the house to have that coffee, but he decided against that for today.

"Buck, I want to do this again and I hope that it won't be too long before I see you. I really like talking to you. It's been a long time since I've had anyone I can actually share things with, someone who would understand. You and Phil are the first people I've met in a long time who have been places and done things and haven't spent their whole lives here."

She paused for a minute then added, very quickly, as if she wanted to hide what she was actually saying, "I can get away this Saturday if you're free."

Buck, maybe foolishly, didn't give this much thought. He just responded.

"I'd like to see you again. Maybe we can drive up to Pinos Altos or the Big Burro Mountains. You tell me where and when do you want to meet?"

"I've got to be at the clinic real early to catch up on some work for Dr. Browning but I should be finished and ready to leave by nine o'clock. Why don't you pick me up there?"

She must have sensed the sudden hesitation in Buck because she quickly added, "Nobody will care. I doubt if anyone will be around. The clinic isn't open for business on Saturdays. I just have to do a few things for Dr. Browning and then I can leave. My husband will be on a day long trip over to Alamagordo and Cole has one of those two-a-day football practice sessions. It'll be okay, I can promise you that."

"Okay. I would like to see you again." He just smiled and he wanted to give her a big hug but decided that was probably a bit premature.

When Selena drove out on the still dusty dirt road on her way back to town, Buck was about as confused as he'd been in a long time. He needed time to figure out what had just happened, what this was all about, but he wasn't confused about wanting to see Selena again. That was going to happen and fortunately it was going to be just the day after tomorrow.

■■■

That night Buck called Tater Morrison to see if there was an exact date for bringing the cattle over to the Palo Verde. Tater said it would be a week from Saturday, a little over a week away, and everything was set. The truck would get to his place by 8:30 and they should be at Buck's by about 11:30. Buck agreed that this all seemed good and as soon as he got off the phone with Tater he called Phil and filled him in on the schedule. Phil said he'd ask Guy Halsey to come over and bring a couple of the cowboys with him that he knew from the café. They wouldn't need too many hands since there wasn't going to be any roping and with only fifty cows and no calves to handle, they would be able to brand them in the chutes in no time at all.

Before he hung up, Buck cautioned Phil, "I want everyone ready as soon as the cattle arrive. We'll have to work fast and finish before the afternoon storms come. There's nothing worse for a branding than rain. We sure as hell don't want to brand wet cows. And even though there are only fifty cows we don't want to stretch this out over a couple of days."

Of course Buck was exaggerating. There was no way that branding fifty cows using the chutes could take more than a few hours. But Buck just wanted to let Phil know that this was to be a pretty precise operation and efficiency was a high priority.

Buck decided that he would do the actual branding, Phil would do the marking, the one who notches the ear, and the other cowboys would make sure that the cows kept coming through the alley to the squeeze chute. They didn't need a gun man, someone who does the vaccinating, since the cows had all received their shots when they were branded as calves. One of the cowboys, Buck figured he'd probably ask Guy Halsey, would control the squeeze mechanism that confined the cow.

Buck hoped the irons would be ready for the branding and after Buck had explained why he needed them on such short notice, Tony Gutierrez had promised that they'd be ready by Monday. Buck had enough trust in the blacksmith's word that he didn't give into his own worries of not having the irons on time.

■■■

The next day, Friday, Buck and Phil rode out to check on the pastures where they had decided they would turn out the cattle .They needed pasture for the rest of the summer and fall and then they'd need pasture closer to headquarters for the winter calving time. They examined pastures with dirt tanks that were now full from the summer rains, and especially checked the fences and the gates that led into these holding areas. The months of checking and fixing whatever needed fixing on the ranch was paying off. Everything was ready for next week's cattle delivery. The very thought of it made Buck a little edgy.

■■■

That afternoon Phil was going to recheck the corral and chutes to make sure that they were all in top working condition, as Buck had requested. He told Buck that when he first looked it all over, some weeks ago, they all looked pretty sound. He wasn't expecting any problems.

As they rode back Buck mentioned to Phil that Selena had been down yesterday. He didn't make a big deal of it but he wanted to get Phil's reaction. The young cowboy already knew she was coming to the ranch when Buck asked him what horse she had ridden the last time. Phil answered that he thought he saw her drive up in her green Jeep and that he thought Buck was a lucky guy to be able to spend some time with her and see her so often. He then added quickly, "Don't forget she's married. Remember what you told me in town about getting involved."

Beyond that there wasn't very much reaction. Buck grimaced at Phil's observation but was pleased. At least Phil was obviously over his earlier crush on Selena Maria Bradley.

■■■

On Saturday morning Buck pulled into the parking lot at the clinic about ten minutes early and he parked as far from the main area as he could get. He still wasn't convinced that meeting at the clinic was a good idea but he didn't really think he had a choice. Besides all that, he was very anxious to see Selena. Selena came outside right on time and was dressed in her cowgirl clothes with a large brown leather bag slung over her shoulder. She had a big smile as she got into the Ford.

"You'll laugh at this but I wasn't sure that you'd show up this time. I know this must be awkward for you but it shouldn't be. We aren't doing anything wrong. All we're doing is talking and we are adults. It's become so important to me to have someone to talk to, someone like you."

Buck showed almost no expression but said, "If you say so."

Selena Maria laughed and gave him a quick poke him in the ribs as they drove off, heading for the Big Burro Mountains in the Gila National Forest, just north of Lordsburg on the road to Silver City. Buck quickly recovered his sense of humor as they headed for their trysting spot.

"Have you ever been up to any of the camp grounds in the Burro Mountains? They are beautiful and they're way off the road. I've only been up there once since I moved down from Montana but I know they're isolated enough so we'll have some privacy."

"I am glad that you showed up," Selena said, getting a little serious," I've never done anything like this before and I'm not even sure what we are doing. All I know is that I like being with you and I wanted to see you again."

"I guess I could echo the exact same sentiments. I don't know what it is about you." This time Buck smiled but this all seemed like it was a helluva lot more than just about having someone to talk to.

"Well, we've really just met so don't think too much about it. Time has a way of taking care of things. It's as if I've been waiting a long time for you to show up in my life."

It was less than a twenty minute drive to the turnoff and then Buck drove in about a quarter of a mile to a beautiful, sandy parking area, with lots of big shade trees and even more privacy. The day was becoming warm and clear and as Buck and Selena got out of the truck, he grabbed a cooler filled with water and iced tea and a sleeping bag that he always kept in the back seat of the truck. Without even thinking about it, he took Selena by the hand. She made no effort to pull away. They both acted as if this wasn't the first time that this had happened but they each squeezed a little as they walked to the place where they would put down the sleeping bag and cooler.

Once they were settled in their little corner of the Big Burro Mountains, Buck couldn't help but blurt out, "Selena, are you sure we should be here together like this? I've never done this with a married woman and I just don't know how I feel about that. But I'll tell you one thing. I think I'm beginning to fall in love with you. I know I haven't stopped thinking about you since you left the ranch on Thursday. I can't even begin to tell you how much I've missed you."

When he finished he just looked at Selena to see what she'd do or say. Buck was surprised at what he had just said but he didn't feel any regrets nor did he have any inclination to take back his own words. For some reason they just seemed to make sense to him and he was sure that they were exactly what he wanted to say. Initially Selena Maria just stared at him with those penetrating dark eyes. Finally, she sat up straight, took his hand and said quietly but with conviction, "As crazy as this seems, I think I'm falling in love with you. It's been so long, maybe never, that I've felt this way about a man. It's very confusing but it does make me feel good. I keep thinking about you, too."

The only thing that Buck could think to say, and he was rarely at a loss for words, was, "Well, what do we do now?"

Buck and Selena just sat there for a moment. Selena didn't say a thing. So there they were. Buck, who was all tanned in his crisply starched blue button down shirt and his silver-belly Resistol set back on his head, and Selena, looking like a model from some high end western magazine, neither knowing what to say next or even what to do. So they did the one natural thing. They embraced and started to kiss each other with a passion and intensity that surprised both of them.

Buck was the first to speak. "This is really crazy. I've never believed in love at first sight but I think that's what's happening here. I just can't explain this any other way. And maybe for the first time in my life I think that this is real." Then he repeated, "What do we do now?"

Selena was still almost trembling but was able to say, "I know I'm falling in love with you and I think I knew that the first time I saw you on the street in Lordsburg. Love at first sight has to be real. This all has to be real. Buck, please hold me. I have no idea what we do next. All I know is that I want to be with you."

After some time, just holding her, Buck spoke again. "Selena, you've got a husband and two boys and we can't ignore the situation that we are in. If we want to be together how do we deal with all of that? This is a small town and we just can't hide and sneak around. You have to tell me what we are going to do. I don't have the slightest idea about how we should handle this."

Selena didn't know what to say. She had actually fantasized about this since she first met Buck in town but she hadn't really dealt with it realistically and she was almost more at a loss for the moment than Buck was. "Give me time. We'll solve this. I know I want to be with you and we'll just have to find a way to do this. My boys will be okay with whatever I chose to do. They don't have much more feeling for their father than I do. I'll have to find a way to get out of my marriage. Buck, you've got to promise that you'll be patient."

Buck didn't say a word. There wasn't much that he could say at that moment and they just continued to hold one another almost hoping for some sort of miracle. After a while Buck asked, "How are we going to see one another?

There are hardly any places we can go in such a small town and you can't keep running down to the ranch. What will we do?"

"We'll figure all this out, I promise."

Although he didn't want to end what had started that morning, after almost two hours at the camp site in the forest, holding one another and trying to talk, Buck thought that it would be best if he took Selena back to town and that he head back down to the ranch. Why he decided to do that he wasn't sure. It really wasn't what he wanted to do. He was sure though that they both needed some time to come to some sort of understanding about what was happening and what they should do about it. For them to try and figure out all of this, while being together, wasn't going to be conducive to solving either of their problems. Selena begrudgingly went along with Buck. They did agree that on Monday morning, since she didn't have to be to work until the afternoon, she would come down to the ranch and they would talk some more.

After he dropped Selena off at the clinic and headed home, he was so absorbed in this new situation that he didn't even remember the drive. Fortunately there wasn't much that he had to do at the ranch on Sunday and since Phil and Marina were all consumed with getting Marina moved down to the ranch, he had lots of time to himself. But it didn't seem to matter. The only good solution he could come up with was for Selena to get divorced and that would be a huge step for her. It was easy to talk about love and all the other things but it was something else to actually take the steps necessary to get Buck and Selena together. Buck wasn't sure that when push came to shove that she would be able to do it. Divorce wasn't ever easy and Buck knew that. And until she was divorced, Buck felt he had to keep some distance because he wasn't about to share Selena with her husband. Buck wasn't cut out to be the extra guy. And, Buck wondered, how he would he react if it ever got to that point that Selena was free and was available. He didn't even know if he was ready to get married again or if this whole thing wasn't mostly motivated by the fact that Selena was married and unavailable. Buck felt his head was going to explode and the only relief he could come up with was to saddle up and ride for a while. That usually helped ease any tension he had.

He was only in the saddle about twenty minutes, riding leisurely across one of the pastures near the road with no particular destination in mind, when off in the distance he spotted three walkers. He reined up and took his binoculars from his saddle bags. He could clearly see that there were two men and a woman and other than one of the men carrying a small pack they didn't appear to have any other baggage. They were nearly three hundred yards away and Buck was sure they hadn't seen him. He followed them for a while, keeping his distance, and decided that they were headed north, and since they weren't carrying big packs he assumed they were just three people who were going to look for work, probably in the chili fields, maybe over by Deming or even Hatch. But that was just a guess. He assumed there was someone waiting to pick them up in Lordsburg itself or they just might try to make it all the way up to I-10, scenarios not uncommon in this area.

Since there was no cell service on most of the ranch he knew he'd have to head back to the house to call this in to the Border Patrol. That's what he did. He cursed the phone company because they could have cell service out this way but since it wasn't going to be financially profitable the phone company wasn't going to put in the extra towers that were needed on the border. It really pissed him off but he knew that there wasn't a damn thing he could do about it. Even on the border, business was business and the dangers of the area played no significant part in corporate business decisions. It just made life a little more difficult for everyone who lived in the area and most of the locals were resigned to that.

After getting home and making his phone call from the land line to the Border Patrol, he unsaddled his horse and headed back to the house to spend more time trying to figure out what he was going to do about his own life. He could hardly contain himself waiting for Selena to show up the next day but he realized that she wasn't coming down with any real answers, if in fact, there really were any answers! One obvious solution that he didn't want to seriously consider was to end the relationship now, before everything was completely out of hand, if it wasn't already to that point. He rejected that as an option even before he had a chance to think it all the way through.

A couple of hours later, while he was sitting outside and trying to think, the phone rang. It was the Border Patrol thanking him for calling in the walkers and to tell him that they had actually picked the three of them up as they were crossing the road just west of Pyramid Peak. The BP confirmed to Buck that these three were in no way drug mules and that they were, in fact, just looking for work that had been promised to them over in the chili fields near Deming.

"Well," thought Buck, "score one for the good guys."

■■■

That whole area south of Lordsburg was nothing but a checkerboard of state and federal land mixed in with some large private ranches. Because it was so close to the border and it was so isolated it was easy to understand why the illegals would come that way, both the walkers looking for work and the drug smugglers. There was no question that they knew what they were doing and had been using that corridor for a long time. Buck was certain that the traffic would continue.

The next morning, Buck was up with the sun and was anxiously waiting for Selena to arrive. He took his coffee out to the porch and as he sat there in the cool morning air, he tried as best as he could to figure out was going on in his life. Buck like being introspective and this was a time when he needed it more than ever.

The first issue was Rebecca. They had stayed in touch on a fairly regular basis but made no specific plans to get together either in New Mexico or Seattle. Buck knew that the ranch wasn't now and was never going to be the life for her. With a law degree there was no future on the ranch, even if she wanted to set up her own practice, and that wasn't very feasible. And the possibility of getting on with the law firm in Lordsburg was so remote that it wasn't really worth thinking about. So where did that leave her? This was a ranch, it was only going to be more so and that just wasn't Rebecca's life. Buck seriously doubted that she'd even consider being part of that life if it wasn't for Buck and that wasn't enough. Most importantly, despite how much he admired her and how he was obviously sexually attracted to her, Buck never felt that he was in love with Rebecca. He was able to make himself feel better by assuming that she felt the same way about him and had gotten on with her life in Seattle. God, he hoped so.

Then he thought about the ranch, Phil, and the future of the Palo Verde in Hidalgo County. The ranch was developing better than he ever imagined. The land was good, the rains finally had come, there weren't any immediate major improvements that had to be made and he really was growing into the desert rat that he thought he was. They had met good people all over the county and were making friends. Both Buck and Phil felt they were planting deep roots becoming real members of the community. Phil couldn't have been a better cowboy and friend and from what Buck could tell, he was prospering in this environment. Marina was sure a plus. Calling him in Montana was one of those chance decisions that you make in your life that just turns out right and with the cattle coming that weekend he was sure things would get even better.

That left Selena. Despite how he felt, Buck couldn't get passed that she was married and had two boys and there was little he could do to resolve that other than wait for her to do what he hoped and supposed she would—get divorced. But he was not optimistic. He knew of other couples who had been in this situation and their relationships, without exception, always turned out badly. Always! The one having the affair, and that's who Selena was, almost never left her marriage and there were a variety of reasons behind that. At the top of the list, Buck thought that Selena wouldn't have the courage to make such a mover after so many years of marriage. Maybe she stayed with her husband because her own self-esteem was low, or because of her two sons, or maybe she was just afraid to actually start a new life. Whatever the reason that might keep her from leaving, at least in the short term, Buck swore to himself that he would wait and wish that he was wrong so that he and Selena would be together. But how long could he wait. He just hoped that the frustration, which was overwhelming, wouldn't get the better of him. The thing that he was sure of was that he was falling deeply in love with her and he was pretty certain that she was feeling the same way. But he wasn't naïve enough to believe the old cliché, 'that love conquers all."

When Buck heard Selena's rig coming down the dirt road, he quickly put his coffee cup away and went out front to greet her as she arrived and parked. When she got out of the car she was wearing sandals, shorts and a T-shirt and her bronzed body just glowed in the morning sunlight. She sure wasn't being very subtle. Buck couldn't get over her style, how she looked and how she carried herself. Since he'd known her he always wondered what would have happened had she gone to New York instead of getting married when she did, and tried to become a model. The way she walked and the way she carried herself seemed to Buck that it would have almost ensured her of some degree of success. But that was then and this was now and she didn't go to New York and he thought that on some level he ought to be thankful for that.

They embraced as if they'd been away from each other for weeks or months and then they kissed passionately. Buck didn't want to let her go and she made no effort to pull away. Finally he said, "Let's go inside and get out of this sun. I'll get us some coffee."

When they got inside and nestled on the soft, tan leather couch, they started to make out like high school kids.

Selena was the first to break the spell. "You know, since I've been married we've always lived in a double wide. Have you any idea how much I've wanted a real house, a house just like this. I want you to give me a full tour. I want to see this whole place, room by room."

Buck told her to go wherever she wanted. He was sort of laughing to himself. He was wondering if she was scouting it out as future home for herself. But he knew that was just wishful thinking.

After the tour they settled in the couch again snuggling in one another's arms.

"Buck, I love it down here, with you. I keep dreaming about the future and thinking about the past. You probably won't believe this, but I can almost count on my fingers the number of times my husband and I have even gone out to dinner at a nice place, not some local café. And as much as I love my two boys, I've even questioned having children. I know you can't undo the past but you can always dream. I just wonder what I would have done or who I would be under some other conditions. Hold me very tight."

"Honey, the future is just waiting for you but you have to do what it takes to make it all come true. There isn't much I can do except be here for you."

"Let's go to the bedroom and I want you to make love to me."

Then Buck made one the toughest decisions he had made in a long time.

"Selena, I think its way too soon for that. We've only known one another a short time and I don't want this to be about sex. And to be really honest, I don't think that I'm secure enough or that my ego would allow me to share you with your husband. I have trouble even now thinking of you in bed with him at night. It's got to be just the two of us. I can't think of us any other way."

Selena hugged him so tight that he was amazed at her strength.

"My husband hasn't touched me in months—maybe even longer. He knows how I feel and he doesn't even try any more. If it wasn't for Cole living at home, I would have my own separate bedroom. You would never have to share me with anyone, I promise you that. I just love you and want you so much."

Buck didn't know what to say. His most immediate thought was that any guy who could sleep next to a woman as sensual as Selena and not try to touch her must be getting his sex somewhere else.

"I just wonder if he has a girl friend in one of those cities he drives to?" was the best he could come up with although he didn't dare say it out loud.

He was still so unsure of the future that he just didn't want this relationship to get too out of hand. He had had great sexual relations with Jennifer and Rebecca and he didn't want this to become another situation like those. What was really confusing Buck was that both Jennifer and Rebecca were beautiful, they were both smart, they were fun to be with and the sex was terrific. Why then, did he feel this way about Selena and not about them?

Looking back now he realized he had never loved them and he was certain that he did love Selena. What was the difference? He knew the difference was real and he knew that how he felt about Selena was absolutely sincere. How this all worked just plain baffled him. Sometimes it kept him up at night and there was nothing he could do about it. It dawned on him that he had only used the word love with one other woman, his ex-wife, and he couldn't imagine that he felt the same then that he now felt about Selena. All he could focus on was how he was going to handle this so it came out right for both of them. He had no answers and Selena still hadn't said that she was going to get a divorce or if that would ever happen. He was afraid to push her. It was far too soon for that, but that didn't ease his frustration.

After more snuggling on the couch, and some talk, hand in hand they walked out to the barn and the small pasture to look at the horses and sort of change the subject. They needed something besides themselves to talk about. The sun was bright, the sky was the deep summer blue, and the puffy white clouds just seemed to be ambling around wherever they wanted to go. When Selena got ready to leave, they again embraced as intimately as they knew how and Buck told her he'd call her or that she should call him if she could figure out some time for them to be together.

After she left Buck tried to focus on the ranch and the work that was ahead of him as he and Phil got ready for the Brangus cattle to arrive. On Tuesday he had to go to town to pick up the branding irons but he knew that there was no chance of seeing Selena at the clinic. He was determined that he wasn't going to make himself and his relationship too obvious to either the people around town or the folks who worked at the clinic. He was certain that they would be the first ones to recognize what was happening and in the back of his mind he never lost sight that what they were doing could be very dangerous in a small town like Lordsburg.

■■■

That evening Phil and Marina came over to Buck's for a barbeque. Since she was in the process of moving onto the ranch, Buck felt he wanted to get to know her as well as he could. At the various get togethers where they had spent any significant amount of time, he was always impressed by how smart she was and the way she acted around Phil. Their relationship seemed so good that it almost made Buck a little jealous but that relationship meant a lot to Buck because of how he felt about Phil. Although she certainly wasn't a cowgirl, or for that matter, even a real westerner yet. Buck didn't count California and

Berkeley as the real West. But he had the feeling that she was going to fit it and if she wanted to she could be a big asset for the ranch. When it came to thinking about Phil and Marina, all Buck could see was the up side.

After dinner, as they were sitting on the screened in porch and enjoying their coffee, Buck casually asked Marina if she'd like to come over for the branding next Saturday. Marina paused before she answered. She wasn't sure how she felt.

"I've never been to a branding but I hear talk from some of the cowboys and cowgirls on campus that it can be pretty rough. But since I've never been to one I'd like to see it for myself, if you don't think I'd be in the way. I want to learn everything I can about ranching and since I'm going to be living down here I'd like to be part of whatever happens."

Phil was visibly relieved. He was afraid for a moment that Marina was going to say no and that would have been a big disappointment for him. He wanted more than anything, for Marina to be involved in every aspect of life at the ranch; he wanted her to be his partner in every way.

■■■

By the middle of the week, with the branding irons in hand, he had three irons made, all Buck had to do was wait for the cattle to arrive. Guy Halsey had agreed to come over along with Hector Salinas and Doc Bowen, two young, local cowboys who did mostly day work all over Hidalgo, Grant, and Luna counties. Those two almost single handedly dispelled the idea that cowboys were a dying breed.

■■■

Buck tried to see Selena whenever he could. Because the clinic closed for a two hour lunch break each day, she was able to meet him in secluded spots just south of town. Sometimes they just made out like two kids and sometimes they just talked and Buck enjoyed that. The more he knew about Selena the more he felt he was in love with her. He was fascinated by her desires to see and experience so much more than was available to her in her marriage and in Hidalgo County. And he loved the way she talked about life and goodness that was there. Buck truly liked her as well as loved her. But consciously or not they both tried not to talk too far into the future although that was something that Buck badly wanted to do. The relationship, despite it being in a good place, was on hold, at least temporarily. Selena still didn't talk in any specific way about leaving her husband.

■■■

By Saturday Buck decided everything was ready for the branding and all they needed was for the cattle to arrive. Guy, Doc and Hector all arrived on time and Buck greeted them warmly, especially Doc and Hector. Buck had never met them before but he had heard so much about them that he was both curious and eager to see them for himself. In their own way they were local legends.

After the preliminary greetings, all five cowboys squatted in a corner of the corral as Buck assigned each of them their job and mapped out where he eventually wanted the cows released and into the specific pasture. It was all easy and very straightforward, particularly for a crew like this one.

As they stood to stretch their legs, Hector asked Buck semi seriously, "Do you drag the calves to the fire in the spring or do you use the chutes again?"

Buck knew he was being tested and answered accordingly. "To get good cowboys like you to work for me I guess we'll have to drag them to the fire. But the next real question is can you rope well enough to not waste all of our time?"

Hector had a smile as big as the corral. "I can rope real good. But you ought to see Doc. He wins all the local roping and if he wasn't such a lazy ass he would be on the PRCA circuit, or at least the Turquoise Circuit and cleaning their clocks. 'Ol Doc, he's a champion."

"Does that mean I can count on both of you next spring? Remember, I'm new here and I want the best. I hear that's you two. We'll be branding all the calves from these cows and maybe we'll have a few more by then. You never know." Buck grinned, as if he wanted to let Hector know that he was willing to play this game.

Doc hadn't said anything. He barely showed any emotion at all. He just leaned against the corral, took another chew and put it in his mouth. It was easy to see that Hector and Doc were true friends who had traveled many miles together and had certainly engaged in this conversation with more than one rancher.

Hector looked straight at Buck. "Amigo, we could do that many calves before you ring the lunch bell. I guess we'll just have to fit you into our very busy schedule."

Off to the side, Guy and Phil hadn't said anything. They just watched the give and take with amusement. Then Guy whispered to Phil, "Hector's testing Buck and Buck's handling it like a champ. I think Hector and Doc really like the boss."

Phil couldn't help but smile. The preliminaries for the branding were going as well as he and Buck had hoped and now all he wanted was for Marina to show up before they got started. As he was thinking about her she came walking over from Phil's and greeted everyone as if she'd been at events like this all her life. She was dressed in jeans with a rose colored button down shirt, boots, and a big straw hat with a stampede string. She looked great and every inch the cowgirl.

Buck was startled. He had never seen Marina dressed like that and didn't even realize she owned those kinds of cloths. But mostly, it made him think about Selena and how much he missed her and how much he wished she was here along with Marina. But that didn't last long because coming down the road and despite all the rain they'd had, creating a dust cloud that reminded Buck of some scene from an Arabian desert film, was the cattle truck with the Palo Verde's first 50 Brangus cows. The real beginnings of the ranch were about to arrive. And right behind the cattle truck was Tater Morrison, in his own rig, stirring up his own cloud of dust.

Once the cattle were unloaded and the cowboys had them all in the branding corral, Tater came over to Buck and introduced him to the cattle hauler, "Tiny" Murietta. Despite his name he was a big man with an unlit cigar in his mouth who was dressed in an old pair of jeans, a T-shirt, sneakers and a Colorado Rockies baseball cap. "Tiny" shook hands, said his hellos to everyone, and then climbed into his rig and was back on the road. He wasn't a great socializer.

"Tater, you didn't have to come all the way over. I'm sure you and Adeline must have better things to do on a beautiful day like today."

"The truth be told, I just wanted to see what kind of an operation you were running over here. I'm mighty impressed so far. Considering this place wasn't used for some time, you've got it looking damn good. It always was a pretty damn good, productive ranch, you know."

"Thank you Tater. I appreciate that and especially coming from someone who's been around these parts a long time and knows this country so well."

"Well, I guess I best get out of your way. I didn't come to help, just to be nosy. I see you've got Hector and Doc on your crew."

"Do you know them?"

"They are almost legends around these parts. And damn, they are good cowboys and ropin' fools. Well, good luck. I think I'd better get back home to my lovin' wife before she comes chasin' after me."

As Tater drove off, Buck headed over to the corral to get the branding started.

The actual branding took less than two hours and went without a hitch. Everyone did their job and did it well. For this crew of cowboys this was easy work. There was hardly a need to break a real sweat. There were n calves to wrestle on the ground, no castrations or dehornings, and not even shots to be given. This really was easy work.

After the cattle had been kicked out of the corral and were back to grazing on their new range, and the propane had been shut off and cooled, Hector said to Buck and Phil, "You guys have the beginning of a good herd here. Them are all good cows. All you need to do is get you a few good bulls...maybe some Brancus, maybe a few straight Angus, or even some big Hereford bulls."

"This place will carry a lot of cows," added Doc, who had said very little all morning.

As the two cowboy friends and Guy were about to leave and all three said that they were sorry but they couldn't stay for lunch, Buck pulled some money from his vest pocket and offered to pay the three. Guy Halsey smiled and said, "That's not necessary. You're my neighbor." He then shook hands with everyone and got in his truck and headed home.

Hector looked semi-serious and said to Buck, "Doc and me don't feel like we really did anything so we can't take any money. Maybe you can buy us some gas if we see you in town. We sort of came here to see what kind of an operation you were running. Sorry we can't stay for your vittles though. But we'll get you when we come back for the branding in spring. If you need us before then you call. This place looks like its goin' to be a good place to saddle up. Pardner, Doc and me enjoyed the morning."

Hector and Doc shook hands with Buck and Phil, tipped their hats to Marina, and as they were getting into their truck, Doc took Phil aside and said, "Keep that guy agoin the way he is. This is goin' to be a good outfit. And he'll need you. This place is big and this won't be no one man operation. Until next time, we'll see you around amigo. Adios."

When everyone was gone, Marina, who watched the entire branding from atop of the corral fence, came over to Buck and Phil and laughed as she gave Phil a kiss on his sweaty, dirty cheek.

"That was more fun than I thought it would be. It seemed cruel at first with the fire, smoke and smell of burning flesh, but when you see those cows just grazing and running a few minutes after they've been branded you just have to wonder how much it can hurt. I'd like to be able to help sometime.

And that Hector and Doc! It was like being in a movie with Gene Autry and his sidekick. They are two funny guys. I sure do hope they come back."

Phil gave Marina a hug and Buck added, "Those two guys are top cowboys and we were lucky to make a good contact with them. I'm counting on getting them back here when we do brand next spring. And just for your information, did you know that the hide of a cow is about eight times thicker than that of a person. And if you ever want to eat another steak or hamburger it's good to understand how that meat gets from the ranch to the supermarket. You know that it doesn't grow in plastic wrapped packages but I'm sad to say that a lot of people don't seem to know that."

Buck smiled as he finished and looked at Marina and Phil and then all three of them laughed out loud.

After a few seconds of quiet thought, he added, "Even though the boys couldn't stay to eat, how about the three of us getting some chow. There's plenty up at the house." All the time he was thinking to himself, "That Marina is sure going to fit in fine around here. Phil is a very lucky guy."

"Food sounds good to me," said Phil as he took Marina by the hand and the three of them headed for Buck's house.

After they washed up and they sat down on the porch with the sun offering a bright but gentle light all ushered in by a light breeze, Buck had a grin as big as the valley.

"I just hope you both realize what we started this morning. There's no turning back now."

■■■

The routine on the Palo Verde Ranch over the next several months adjusted itself so that there were always a solid set of chores for both Buck and Phil. They regularly rode to make sure the herd was healthy and safe from predators. The coyotes were especially thick but Buck was also always on the alert for any sign of a mountain lion. Buck and Phil regularly rode with their rifles, just in case but so far there had been no trouble. With full grown cows this wasn't going to be a big problem but Buck was thinking ahead to when there were calves on the ground. That could be a problem. Every once in a while they did take shots at some of the wild pigs that were multiplying very fast. It was a growing problem all over the Animas Valley and sooner or later every rancher knew that they would have to deal with it in a serious way.

They paid careful attention to the unused pastures to see exactly how they reacted to the good monsoon season and they tried to estimate what the real carrying capacity of the ranch was going to be, both during the rainy season and if they hit a drought, which was a real possibility.

For the first time in some months, Buck and Phil talked about the remuda and tried to determine whether or not they wanted to get into a serious breeding program that would provide surplus horses that they could sell or just have enough horses around to take care of their own needs for the ranch. They decided to put that decision off for a year so they could concentrate on the cattle and the expansion of that herd. They had more than enough good horses to work the ranch and for the time being Buck was sure that he didn't want to incur the costs of buying a top stallion or paying large breeding fees. And Buck was so sure that he didn't want the problems that having a stud around would create. That was his thinking, at least for now.

Guy Halsey had mentioned that he had an old roping dummy in his barn, and that if Buck and Phil wanted to borrow it, it was theirs. They soon had it set up in the corral over at Phil's, and although both knew how to rope, they both started practicing diligently, fully anticipating that the skills they hoped to refine might come in handy during the spring branding when they were going to drag the calves to the fire or if they ever had to doctor a cow or catch a calf out in the open pasture. And when she had time, Marina even gave the roping dummy a bit of a workout.

For Buck there were other projects that were separate from the daily ranch work. He just had an article published in *Cowboy Country Magazine*, and he was already researching an article that he had already sold. It was about Curly Bill Brocius, one of the notorious members of the outlaw gang involved in the famous OK Corral fight over in Tombstone. What intrigued Buck was that Curly Bill also had a hideout in the Animas Valley, on the Gray Ranch, that he had used regularly when the law was after him. The money that Buck got from these articles, although it wasn't very much, was still an added incentive for him to keep writing. For the time being, every extra penny was being plowed back into the ranch.

■■■

As the colder weather approached, and the seasonal changes were a lot more subtle than they were in Montana, Buck tried to gauge how much hay they would need for the winter and he decided that they would also feed cake to the cattle that would be calving in the late desert winter and keep the hay for the horses that would be kept close to headquarters. All he could think about was how different and hopefully easier calving was going to be in New Mexico than winter calving was in the cold and dreary mountains valleys of western Montana.

All in all life at the ranch and the progress the ranch was making couldn't have been more satisfying. Buck knew that he had problems in his personal life—Selena—but he was sure that before winter was over, that too, would somehow be resolved. Buck surprised himself with his new found optimism.

The relationship with Rebecca was fast fading. They communicated more and more by E-mail rather than telephone and as they moved deeper into fall, there was no talk at all of seeing one another for Thanksgiving or even Christmas. Their relationship was dying of inertia and as Buck liked to muse, "Maybe 'out of sight, out of mind' trumps 'absence makes the heart grow fonder.'" That's how it seemed to be working out for these two former lovers. For Buck this was turning out as well as could be expected. Although it had never come up, Buck knew that if they were together, sooner or later the idea of having children with Rebecca would rear its head and it was a conversation he didn't want to have or his position that he didn't want to defend. Because of her age, Buck was sure that Rebecca still had children on her radar. And besides, Selena now seemed to own all of Buck and there wasn't room for anyone else. Buck was very content with that.

Buck continued to see Selena as often as he could. Sometimes they met for their brown bag lunches, and when she could get away for a little more time she either came down to the ranch or they went up to their private spot in the Big Burro Mountains. Nothing in their relationship changed. They always talked of their love and how wonderful it would be if they were together but it always stopped there. They had finally consummated their relationship and neither of them felt the slightest bit guilty. What surprised Buck but made him very happy was that after they made love, Selena, almost breathlessly, whispered, "Buck, with you it really isn't about sex. You actually make love. I didn't know it could be like that." Buck didn't know what to say. It all seemed so natural to him.

But Selena still wasn't talking specifically about getting a divorce from her truck driving husband and Buck continued to feel like he was dangling. He didn't know how or even if he should push the idea of divorce. What he did know was that this couldn't go on like this for much longer.

Occasionally they got away for the whole day. Once they went to the anthropology museum over at New Mexico State University in Las Cruces and one time they went to the new Farm & Ranch Heritage Museum, also in Las Cruces. Buck was always taken with how enthusiastic Selena was, as if she was a little school girl on her first class field trip. He loved the way that made him feel and that Selena really did have an eagerness to learn, to see and experience new things that she so often talked about.

On one of their day trips Buck asked Selena if next time she's like to go to Tucson to see a very important western art show in a gallery just north of the city. He explained to her that the kind of show he was talking about was only presented a couple of times a year in Tucson and involved some of the best artists of the genre. Of course Selena couldn't say yes fast enough.

When Buck met Selena for the trip to Tucson, she was wearing a short skirt, short enough to show off her incredible legs, but not too short, low heals and a form fitting blouse. Once again Buck was taken by the way she presented herself. It almost seemed to him that she had been rehearsing for this type of life for years and now she was finally able to be the woman in public that she always had wanted to be in her dreams.

When they arrived at the gallery on the north side of Tucson, in the foothills of the Catalina Mountains, the parking lot was fairly empty since it was early in the day. They entered the gallery and Buck watched to see what Selena's reaction would be to what was a very major show of western art. Well, if he was thinking that she would be lost he was wrong. Almost from the moment they entered the front gallery, Selena seemed at ease and Buck was completely overwhelmed by her familiarity with many of the artists and the depth and of her observations and her understanding of the finer points of painting and sculpture.

"How do you know so much about western art and all these artists? I had no idea you were a follower of this art or even liked it."

"Buck, this will surprise you but I've almost never been to a gallery like this one. I just read a lot of books and as many magazines as I can get. And I've always been interested in the West and western art. I'd give anything to be able to own some of this work. I used to dream about going to college and taking some classes in art history so I could learn more and more about what good art really is and where it all got started. But these are all my dreams and you'd never understand what it means for me to actually see these paintings and sculpture for real. They are so much better when you can actually see them this way than just reading about them. The color, the design, the scale, the textures... gosh Buck, it's like a whole new world for me."

Buck really didn't know what t say. He was astonished by Selena's reaction and her desire to pursue this even further. He took her hand and they continued to explore the galleries with the works of the leading artists in the western art world hanging on the walls.

■■■

At night Buck often thought about Selena. It bothered him that after all these months that they had been seeing one another Buck had never been with Selena after the sun went down. He had never been able to take a walk with her in the moonlight, or hold her in bed as the sun came up to announce a new day, or see her silhouette in a dimly lit room, or just sit with her in front of a roaring fire with the lights all tamped down low. This was another one of the frustrations that was eating at Buck. Mostly, though, he didn't know what to do about it.

Buck did go to a couple of the Lordsburg high school football games, always by himself or with Phil, never with Selena. He wanted to watch Selena's son Cole play. Buck was surprised at how impressive the younger son was on the field. He couldn't imagine that Eastern New Mexico would pass on a kid that good. Maybe some other school would offer him a scholarship so he wouldn't have to wait for his brother to graduate to get his chance to star, the way he did in high school. Selena had mentioned that Cole had received some interest from Fort Lewis College in Colorado and Northern Colorado in Greeley and after watching him for several games, Buck was sure that there would be quite a few other schools eventually getting into the mix. He actually thought that Cole going to a different college than his brother would be a better situation for both the boy's education and football careers.

When he told Selena what he was thinking about she almost exploded she was so happy.

That Buck cared that much about her sons just made her feel good.

Fortunately, even in such a small setting as the high school football stadium in Lordsburg, Buck never ran into Selena's husband or even Selena at the games. Nor did he want to. In the back of his mind he wondered what would happen if he did run into Selena's husband. He wondered what he knew and if he did know about his relationship with Selena, what would he do about it. Buck wondered if it would be a physical or a verbal confrontation or if there'd even be a confrontation. Buck sort of hoped that he'd never have to find out.

By late November and early December, fall had rapidly phased out the summer. The nights and days were both much cooler and there hadn't been any rain to speak of for a couple of months. But that was to be expected at that time of the year. The range on the Palo Verde stayed rich and the gamma grass continued to provide nutritional forage for all their stock. As a supplement, to make up for the usual lost protein in the winter, Buck was having some cake custom milled over in Willcox, Arizona and he was waiting to have that delivered. Buck and Phil frequently went to the livestock sales in Willcox and Deming, trying as best they could to stay abreast of the cattle prices and the overall livestock market as well as make some new contacts. They probably learned as much in the coffee shops at both sale barns as they did listening to the auctioneers in the ring. Buck knew that if they added more cattle during the year he'd never be lucky enough to find a deal like the one he made with Tater Morrison. Buck also wasn't quite sure that he wanted to have only Brangus cattle so he was trying to learn all he could about what other cattle breeds did well in this desert country. By early December he hadn't made any definite decisions and didn't feel he was very close. But no matter how he looked at things, no matter how much explored all the options, he kept coming back to the idea of staying with the Brangus.

"Why," he thought, "mess with what seems to be working all around this desert country. I'm too new to ranching down here to be instigating new range ideas. These ranchers seem to know what they're doing and who am I to change things."

When Buck talked to Phil about the cattle situation, Phil agreed when Buck told him that he thought that he was probably going to lease the bulls for the next year. Because of the small number of cows they had he was sure that was the best way to go. "Buying bulls," he explained to Phil, "would come later when we are more definite about the direction this place is going and I have developed long range plans for number and kinds of cattle we'll want on the ranch. And I'm not so sure that now we should be creating a bull pasture for when we take the bulls out."

Phil agreed that this seemed to be the most rational plan for the immediate future.

Buck had also been checking to see if there was going to be any government land or any private lease land available to make the project with Steve Anderson plausible. So far he was drawing a blank but it was something that he still wanted to pursue. But it looked like for at least the next year or so there would be no wintering of Montana cattle in the Bootheel of New Mexico. It was a big disappointment for him and he knew it was for Steve Anderson but down deep he had actually expected that to happen. Ranchers didn't give up their graze rights very easily and in the bigger picture, it was probably best for this type of arrangement to wait a year or so until everything at the Palo Verde was in good order. Even though Buck intellectually knew all that he was still a bit disheartened that he had to give his good friends, the Andersons, the bad news.

■■■

By mid December the routine at the ranch was well established and Buck continued to write, even contemplating doing some fiction, an area he had never explored. Although he deeply missed Selena, Thanksgiving had been a glorious time for Buck and with Phil and Marina sharing it with him it only made the ranch feel more a part of all of their lives.

Phil and Marina continued to grow closer and that made Buck very happy. He knew that Phil wasn't going to spend his life working for the Palo Verde Ranch and his relationship with Marina and the experience he was gaining working with Buck and the other cowboys in the valley only made it inevitable that he would eventually head out and get his own spread. Buck didn't know when but he knew it would happen someday. He just didn't want it to happen too soon.

Marina called one morning and invited Buck over for dinner that night. Buck readily accepted because he was getting damn tired of his own limited cooking skills and he was curious about what kind of cook Marina was.

When he arrived at Phil and Marina's he sensed something was a foot. They seemed a little bit edgy and it made him a bit uncomfortable. But that didn't last long. Almost before he had a chance to take off his Resistol and find himself a comfortable chair, the young couple, holding hands, sat down with him and Phil just blurted out,

"Buck, Marina and I are engaged and we plan to get married early next year. You're the first one we've told and we want your blessing more than anything else."

Buck had to take a second to collect himself but it was easy because he just seemed so happy for the two youngsters. The first thing he did was hug and kiss Marina, whom he had truly come to love, and shake hands and even hug Phil.

"I don't know why you think you need my blessing, whatever that is, but you have it and anything else I can do for you. I honestly couldn't be happier for you both. Without getting too sentimental, I want you both to know how much you've both added to this adventure and Marina, you've been a miracle down here."

Phil was grinning from ear to ear. He looked at Buck, the way only two friends can, and asked, "Buck, will you be my best man?"

Buck just sat there for a moment and finally said, "If you hadn't asked I think my feelings would have been hurt. I can't think of anything I'd rather do."

"How about having a toast with us," Marina joined in as she got three wine glasses and a bottle of red wine out of a cupboard and placed it on the table. Even though Buck wasn't a wine drinker, he found that glass of wine completely to his liking.

After a fine dinner and conversation about everything and nothing, Buck realized that it was getting late and as he got up to leave, Phil stopped him.

"Buck, if it's alright with you, Marina and I are planning on going to California sometime around Christmas for a few days to see her family. I've never met them and we'd like to give them the good news in person. They know all about me but we've never met and it would make Marina so happy for me to go."

"Take all the time you need. Have a wonderful time."

Marina's father was a professor of journalism at one of the California universities and her mother was a high school principal. Marina also had a brother a few years older than her who was a Navy SEAL on assignment somewhere in the Middle East. The family didn't know exactly where he was and because of the secrecy of his mission he wasn't able to reveal his exact whereabouts. The irony of all of this, at least to Buck, was that Phil made no mention of his own parents and going back east to see or tell them about his engagement.

A couple of days later Buck raised this question of Phil's parents to the young cowboy.

"Buck, I don't know what to say to them. I'm sure they'll be disappointed that I haven't hooked up with some debutante—do they still have them?—from back east. I'll be telling them in the next day or so, on the phone, but I just don't know that they'll understand or get it at all. We think we want to get married here at the ranch in a civil ceremony and I don't know that they'd even want to come all the way out here. Maybe when they finally meet Marina they'll understand why I love her so much and that she comes from such a wonderful family. But I'm not looking forward to that initial conversation. My parents and I don't communicate very well since I left the East and headed out this way." Then he added with a big smile, "How would you like to be my agent?"

Buck didn't even bother to answer that. He just looked at Phil with an expression that said clearly, "Don't be a coward!" Buck would have liked to help Phil but he just didn't have the slightest idea of what to do. This was one rodeo he was staying out of.

■■■

A couple of days later, around eight in the morning, Buck got a confusing phone call from Selena. She seemed stressed and wanted to see Phil that day at their usual place south of town. She explained that because she was at the clinic and didn't want people there overhearing her, she couldn't tell Buck what this was all about. Although he desperately wanted to know what was so urgent, he didn't push it but he said that he would be there and she'd said that she'd explain everything then.

When he arrived he saw Selena standing next to her green Jeep. As he was driving north to town, Buck had considered every scenario for this meeting, running the gamut from Selena wanting to end their relationship to Selena telling Buck that she had filed for divorce. It turned out to be neither of these.

"Buck, my husband found one of the little notes that you write to me. I don't know how he found it but he did."

"What did he say? Are you alright?"

"The funny thing is he didn't say much of anything. It was as if he was expecting it. He didn't yell or really show any emotion. He just said that he thought I was really stupid if I thought that you would settle for someone like me."

For months Buck had expected some sort of reaction from Selena's husband. He was sure that he had known for some time what was going on and he anticipated a phone call, or some face to face confrontation, or just something. But it never happened. The anticipation made Buck a little edgy but the more he learned about Selena's marriage the less likely he thought that anything would happen. Why Selena's husband didn't want to just knock the crap out of Buck escaped him. He knew what he would have done had he been in her husband's predicament. The marriage between Selena and her truck driving husband continued to confuse Buck. Other than their two sons, what the hell kept them together? Buck even wondered if Selena had left his letter around so that her husband would find it. The more he thought about that the more convinced he was that it was exactly what happened.

Buck held Selena and they talked about this new mess but even after all their talk there still seemed to be no resolution to their dilemma. She still didn't talk specifically about a divorce and Buck was still hesitant to push her too hard. But at least when she had to leave to go back to the clinic, she seemed calmer and was at least for the time being, reassured in her relationship with Buck. Buck was the one who was not reassured.

■■■

A few days after all this news, Selena was down at the ranch for one of their regular trysts. As she was leaving and getting into her Jeep, she paused a minute and looked squarely at Buck.

"Why would someone like you with your education, your money and the careers you've had, be interested in some like me? You're so sophisticated, you've been all over, you've seen so much and I've hardly been out of Hidalgo County. How long would it take for you to get tired of me and want to move on? Then I'd be all alone, I'd be without you and I'd miss you terribly. Buck, I'm so confused and I just don't know what to do. Maybe my husband was right. I can't believe that you'd settle for someone like me."

Buck was stunned, maybe more so than he could remember being in a long time. Her simple comments had struck like a herd of stampeding cattle running over him, but at the same time it answered most of the questions that had been plaguing him since the two had started their romance all those many months ago. Finally he understood her hesitancy about getting a divorce.

Selena was so unsure of herself that she couldn't believe that anyone like Buck could love her and be committed to her and no matter how much she loved him she was afraid to take a risk like getting a divorce. It was that simple!

Buck stood silent for a minute, not sure what to say. Then he put his arms around her as he spoke.

"Selena, I don't know how to convince you about how much I love you and that this isn't a passing fling. The fact that I am the person that you just described and that I swear to you that I have never felt the way I do about you with anyone else, should convince you that you are wrong about it not lasting for us. It will. I just don't know how to really prove that to you. But I honestly think that you know that you are wrong and that you are letting a little insecurity take hold of your reasoning. Love is something that you have to trust and I can't believe that you don't love me. More importantly, you have to trust that I love you and that I will always love you."

Selena Maria was quiet. She didn't know what to say but she did know that she loved Buck in a way that was very real and very deep. Finally, as if a whole new world had opened for her, she gave Buck the biggest hug she could and a kiss so passionate that it almost hurt, and a in a voice close to a whisper said,

"Oh Buck, I know you are right and I guess I just needed to hear you say so. I wanted to hear you say so. I promise you that I will see a lawyer this week and start the divorce proceedings. All I know for sure is that I want to be with you. I doubt that my husband will really care after he gets over the initial shock. I'm sure that Cole already has an idea that something is going to happen. And I'll call my son Jimmy over in Portales and try to explain everything to him. I want to get the divorce over with and then we can get married as soon as you want to. I really do want to spend the rest of my life with you. And if you'll let me, I promise you that I'll be the best cowgirl that you ever thought about. We could even have a western wedding right here at the ranch. Maybe we could do it horseback."

When she finished she smiled, both from happiness and even from relief that maybe all the indecision and months of confusion were coming to an end. All she knew was how happy she finally was and that maybe this was going to turn out the way it was supposed to.

For a moment Buck was so startled that he couldn't gather his thoughts. Marrying again was now a real probability and it took him a few seconds to actually process that idea. His dreams about Selena now had all the possibilities of becoming a reality. When he finally settled down, it just seemed like spending the rest of his life with Selena would be a wonderful way to live and he couldn't wait. For months he had fantasies about her living on the ranch and getting up each morning with Selena by his side. Now it all seemed like it would become real, that it was actually going to happen.

The two lovers went back into the house and spent hours in a state that Buck surely had never experienced. They made love several times and when Selena left, Buck was almost woozy he was so excited. Thoughts of the future rolled through his head at a pace that he could barely control. They were all good thoughts. He had to pinch himself to fully realize that after all these months that had become so trying for him even as they gave him great pleasure, that he and Selena were finally going to be together for the rest of their lives with her living on the ranch and the two of them being together every day and every night.

■■■

So there it was. The last piece of the puzzle that had been hanging over the Palo Verde Ranch and over Buck was finally in place.

The rains had come to the ranch and it was prospering and proving to be the place that he had always envisioned it would be. The New Mexico Palo Verde Ranch was turning out to be the ranch Buck had always hoped that it would be, growing and becoming a productive cattle ranch. This wasn't just a fantasy that he had thought so long and hard about during the many, long, dark, bleak, and cold winters in the Bitterroot Mountains of western Montana. Buck was in the desert that was richer and more fertile than most people ever imagined and it was proving to be the perfect home for him and for Phil. He was sure things would only get better as they worked every day to make the ranch more and more productive.

Phil had found his happiness with a very special woman and Buck was sure that it was going to be wonderful for them both. He had absolutely no doubts about that. What really made him happy was that he was going to enjoy having Phil and Marina at the ranch for as long as they wanted to stay. Their company had become very important to him and an intricate part of his own life. He also was sure that with Selena living at the ranch it would only make for an even more satisfying experience for all four of them. Phil was living out his own dreams and had even found a wonderful woman to share all of them with. Even in his wildest imagination, Buck hadn't envisioned all this working out so well in such a short time. One thing that Buck was absolutely certain about was that Phil was someone to ride the river with.

And Buck found what had been missing for him for so very long—someone to share his life and be intimate with—to fill the emotional emptiness that had persisted since the death of his parents. He was a bit overwhelmed at how elated he was and the pleasure that he felt as he looked forward to his life with Selena Maria Cooper. He had no doubts that he could make her happy and or that she would do the same for him. All the reservations and foolish uncertainties he had had about leaving Montana, all the fears that he had about settling in New Mexico, were now, finally, all resolved.

This was, surely, Buck's country.

READERS GUIDE

1. How do you explain Buck's decision to divorce Holly and her reaction to it? Is his explanation all there is to it?

2. Does Buck's decision to leave the happiness he had in Montana and move to New Mexico seem logical?

3. Would you have left the security of the university to pursue a ranching adventure?

4. Do the descriptions of the landscape in both Montana and New Mexico add to the reader's understanding of the country?

5. Should Buck have "burned his bridges" in Montana when he left?

6. What do you make of the relationship between Buck and Jennifer? Should it have ever happened?

7. Do you fully understand Buck's fears as he headed to New Mexico?

8. Should Buck have pursued his relationship with Rebecca?

9. Should Rebecca have pursued her relationship with Buck?

10. What are your impressions of Phil and his desire to leave the comforts of the East and his family to become a cowboy?

11. Is Buck naïve in thinking he could hold back parts of the new technological world?

12. Would you have moved so close to the Mexican border if you were setting up a new home and ranch?

13. How would you handle the border problems Buck and Phil face at the New Mexico ranch?

14. Would you call the Border Patrol if you saw what you considered "illegals" if you knew they were not drug smugglers?

15. Was Phil being gullible in thinking he could have a relationship with Selena?

16. What do you make of Selena's willingness to leave her marriage and get together with Buck?

17. Do you think that Buck and Selena have a future together?

www.ingramcontent.com/pod-product-compliance
Lightning Source LLC
Chambersburg PA
CBHW031056020726
47495CB00007B/1915